I0741082

CARTEL KINGS AND GANGSTERS

CHITTY, CHITTY, BANG, BANG!!!

Simmeon Anderson

Cartel Kings and Gangsters;

CHITTY, CHITTY, BANG, BANG!!!

By: Simmeon Anderson

Cover Designed By: Jazzy Kitty Publishing

Cover images: novaksights.com

Logo Designs By: Andre M. Saunders

Editor: Anelda L. Attaway

© 2013 Simmeon Anderson

ISBN 978-0-9851453-9-2

Library of Congress Control Number: 2013937213

For Worldwide Distribution available in Paperback and EBook. Printed in the United States of America. Published by Jazzy Kitty Marketing & Publishing, LLC. Utilizing Microsoft Publishing Software. Please be advised this book has strong language and content. Parental Advisory is suggested due to mature content.

ACKNOWLEDGMENTS

First, I have to thank God because if it wasn't for Him giving me life and my gift; none of this would be possible for me. I kept my faith and He never let me down, not once. Actually, I was the one always putting Him down by not putting Him first; but not anymore!

I thank my one and only mother for being strong, and not having an abortion when my sperm donor told her to. She never gave up on me no matter what I put her through; she stuck it out with me. I love you for that mom. Thank you, I will continue to pray for you as you pray for me.

To my one and only sister Susie, thank you for believing in me because without you; I would not of ever made it this far. You are my wife without the sex LOL! Thank you, I will always love you for who you are; don't ever forget that.

To my one and only niece Chanel that tried to edit my book. Thank you baby for trying. I will love you forever.

To all my kids from the oldest to the youngest, it is because of y'all I continue to push hard. Tytianne, you are my first child, stay strong...I love you. Simmeon Jr., now you can be like me, the new me. Not what I use to be, but what I'm about to become. Shanie, I got your back. I love you, I always did and I always will. Ahiyah, daddy loves you baby, you know that. Big hugs and kisses to you. Ashanti, you make me laugh, you little beauteous thing. Shanya, daddy loves you very much. You're my baby girl. All of y'all are a part of my light.

I want to thank the entire staff at Jazzy Kitty Publishing that helped me make my dreams come true. Joe Ashe, who I met in prison and gave me Jazzy Kitty Publishing's contact information; and for pointing me in the right direction. Anelda Attaway, the publisher for making it all happen. Thank you all and God bless you all for helping me make this real.

To all my little homey's that straight cripping with me, keep it rollin'.

All the Bloods that know me and don't L up Nigs. I say that with love and everybody that went out and supported me by getting my book. Thank you all!!! May God bless you, and know that I'm going to keep the pen burning and working for you because without you, my dreams would not become complete.

To all Gang Bangers, transform your light to something right. Don't let the government take your life. If I can do it, all of you can. I must say it isn't easy.

Again, Thank you all.

Claaaat!!! G-rip!!!

I want to continue to bring apparent stories to my readers; one after another. I originally started out with me just trying to write one book, but that didn't happen. I immediately became hooked once I wrote *Cartel King and Gangsters; Chitty, Chitty, Bang, Bang!!!* It became my passion to write, once I saw how my mind creatively worked, and how people responded to my raw materials of my writing. Even though at times I had bad criticism from a small group of people who only made me work harder. The passion of writing grew inside of me making me want to write another book and then another one and so on. This became my only way I could feel free, do, or become who ever I choose to be in my mind through my pen and pad.

When I started I could barely read or write. When I was a child, my mind would always wander off somewhere else.

When I came to prison and knew I was going to get smacked upside my head with an asshole full of time because of the lifestyle I choose to live. I knew I couldn't trust anybody with any work on the streets, so I had to switch my game up. I was on lock up at B, C, D, C, Baltimore, City Detentions Center when it hit me. I had to switch my hustle from a drug dealer to a book writer.

It wasn't an easy road at first because I had no true knowledge on how to write a book or had any help. All I had was a new dream.

Since 2006, when I started I never put down my pen. I got a real kick out of being very creative. I love to break boundaries doing things that others wouldn't do, but it must be beneficial. So now, I'm doing it with my writings.

I remember my mother helping me to activate my brain with a single letter, a single line. She said, "If you would take all of that energy that you use running those streets from gang banging, drug dealing, playing with pistols, and put it into something positive, you will have more than you ever had in your life." So for once in my life I took my mother's advice and give writing a novel a shot. That was back in 2006, and now it is 2013, and I have written eleven books by hand. I wished I would have listened to my mother's advice years ago. Because I wouldn't have waited until I got locked up doing 50 years in prison to get started. However, it is never too late because I'm still breathing, and my mind is still mine.

My dedications go as far back when I first started selling drugs at the young age of nine. I remember the first time as a kid and starting working in a crack house doing a twelve-hour shift for older dudes and eventually of the years moving up the latter in the game becoming my own boss at the age of sixteen, and by the time I was eighteen, and I had a master's degree on the streets.

I worked very hard as a drug dealer. And as my own boss, I worked even harder, so I could play harder. I was always on my block making sure it ran right. I sold weight to dudes that I knew was dedicated to the game, just as I was. And when trouble came from another dealer, or a person of interest in what I had it was never personal just business; that's how I dealt with things on the street. That was all I knew, until now.

I transformed myself from a street hustle, gang banger, to an author. My mind became the product that I use to cook up, or shift in a shifter. My pen became my gun; my pad became my ammunition, and my out of control rage became my strongest weapon to ever transform. My books are my bricks, and the world is going to become my hood. That's how I envision things now. I'm a new gangster slash old gangster in a new game but old to the world books that I should have gotten into years ago and became an author. Nobody couldn't have told me years ago I was going to be a writer. I remember one of my customers that I met, he was writing a book about his life. He looked at me for a few seconds and said, "One day you are going to write a book." I looked at him and started laughing because at the time I wasn't educated enough to write a letter, more less a book; however, look at me now. I just wish I didn't wait until I came to prison to do it.

Everyday I get up and write! No matter what I go through. I'll take the pain and make it pleasure; take emptiness and make it fulfillment; and pressure to a Black Diamond. Writing is all I incorporate and now days my transformation is becoming a success. I work super hard, so one day I can play super hard.

Dedications are everything, without that you have nothing.

TABLE OF CONTENTS

INTRODUCTION i

CHAPTER 1 - Suzie's Surprise 01

CHAPTER 2 - The Robbery 10

CHAPTER 3 - Rock A Bye Baby 21

CHAPTER 4 - Red Rum 49

CHAPTER 5 - Blood in Blood Out Bang Left Til' Death 67

CHAPTER 6 - Pay Back 83

CHAPTER 7 - Back to Town to Headquarters 102

CHAPTER 8 - What Will Make You Laugh Will Make You Cry 119

CHAPTER 9 - The Man Hunt 137

CHAPTER 10 - It Won't be No Smiling on Rikers Island 173

CHAPTER 11 - Hold the Family Down 199

CHAPTER 12 - Rolling Off of Ecstasy Sexy Me Baby 209

CHAPTER 13 - Shake Him Boy 227

CHAPTER 14 - Court Was Now in Session 237

CHAPTER 15 - On Top of the World 250

CHAPTER 16 - Crack them Down 259

CHAPTER 17 - The Rat for Freedom 268

CHAPTER 18 - News Flash Trail Time 283

CHAPTER 19 - Crips & Bloods at War 298

CHAPTER 20 - Pinkey, Suzie & Nadia Go to LA to See Paul 304

CHAPTER 21 - Somebody Wants Their Money Back 324

CHAPTER 22 - It Was Time to Leave the City 340

ABOUT THE AUTHOR 347

INTRODUCTION

NEW YORK CITY is under war with the ongoing gangs, Kingpins, and drug Cartels. Going throughout the five boroughs, F.B.I. Agent Frank Anderson is trying to take his streets back from the Bloods and Crips that are killing each other. The Cartel that are messing up the families behind the drug trade is one hell of a job for Agent Frank, and the rest of the F.B.I. and D.E.A. agents, as well as N.Y.P.D. and their S.W.A.T Team. All of them are working together to stop the madness from all three parties.

James, Mike, and Ty, are the three main leaders for the Crips. They grew up in Brooklyn, New York; and together they were inseparable. Wherever you saw James, you saw Mike and Ty. James was the moneymaker; Ty and Mike were the muscles of the organization. They were all about making money and defending their hood. As for the Bloods, they were the total opposite. They were about sticking high profile drug dealers up and big Cartel drug bosses. It was three of them as well in their circle of bosses; Doggy, 007, and Jimmy. They all came from Jamaica together with nothing, and grew an army of killers and robbers to try to take over the five boroughs in N.Y.C. The only ones that were in their way, were the Crips and the Feds. This is what started the war between the Bloods and the Crips, the power of the five boroughs. WILL THEY ALL MAKE IT TO THE TOP, OR WILL THEY ALL DIE? WILL THE FEDS TAKE THEM BOTH DOWN, OR WILL THE CARTELS BE LEFT TO RUN THE STREETS OF NEW YORK? OR IS TIME RUNNING OUT ON THEM ALL? *The Cartel Kings and Gangsters: Chitty, Chitty, Bang, Bang!!!*

CHAPTER 1

SUZIE'S BIG SURPRISE

It was a cold winter night in Brooklyn. The police were looking everywhere for White Mike and Ty, and the word on the streets was that they had just robbed two banks and killed a teller. Man, these kids were not even eighteen yet, and they were off the hook. White Mike kills you on sight, and Ty loves that knife. You would think the two of them together is a fucked up scene and when you see them, look out, here comes trouble! Somebody is always going to die when they come around, I already know; but they are my homey's and I love them like my brothers.

It all started back in Junior High School when White Mike and Ty were in the 8th grade, and I was in the 7th. We lived on the same block, in the same building, our apartments were even next to each other. They were sick in the head back then. White Mike loved to kill cats, that's all he did when he was 11 years old. He has killed over 75 to 100 cats, he kills at least 5 to seven cats every day. Now as for Ty, he likes to skin them, while White Mike kills them. When Ty skinned them, they made me watch half the time, and I would close my eyes. But White Mike made me watch, and eventually I got used to it.

By the time they were 13, they had killed two people already. By the way, my name is James, and this is my story about three boys growing up in the hood together with nothing to live for.

At the age of 14, they had the respect of the Gangsters already. Every black gangster loved them, and the cops wanted them dead. They started doing hits for the black mafia family, getting paid big money. I'm talking $15,000 a head sometimes, and at least, 4 to 5 heads a week. I'm talking big...money!!! They gave me $50,000, so I started selling drugs. We were a good team, they were the head busters, I was the moneymaker, and kept the money together, and they did all the killing.

Before they turned 15 and I turned 14, we had what the fuck we wanted. No one could stop us, we had girls for every day of the week. We also had seven cars, three motorcycles, and three jet skies. White Mike bought his grand-ma a house in New Jersey and Ty bought his house on Long Island. As for me, I love Brooklyn. We would go to White Mike's house to chill out and have fun.

Fuck bitches, party, and smoke weed; just do the thing. The money was good, and the times were good. Everybody was happy except for the people being killed and skinned alive. One day, I was in Brooklyn doing what I do; picking up money, dropping off drugs, and doing my thing. I was driving my midnight blue CL600 Benz when three Bloods drove up right next to me looking really hard at me as if they wanted to do something to me. So I looked at them really hard with my hand on my gun. I was ready to go all out; like bitch, you don't know who the fuck I am motherfucker. They were in a white 500 Benz, and at the time, it didn't feel good at all. However, nothing happened that day at all. Don't get it fucked up; like I said before, I had my hand on my 16 shot Glock with 2 clips ready for war. I got to one of my crack houses in Bed-Stuy looking for my LT. This motherfucker thought he was God's gift to woman, you could not tell him shit at all. He knew everything about women; I'm not going to lie; he had bitches (yes) he did. His name is Wesley; he called his little click B.L.U. *(Bitches Love Us).* What the fuck kind of name is that? If I was to let him tell it, it was all of that. They were the good times. However, everything so good *never* last forever. When you're out here on the streets' gang banging and making money, time is never on your side. You are always fighting against it. But this is what we do. Everything was working out just fine, until them damn Bloods started popping up everywhere in the city.

I made a stop by my mom's house on my way to White Mike's house to see my sister and how she was doing in school. I love my little sister, she's about the same age as me. I have a little brother too, but he was real young at the time. I was just a few months older than my sister. "What's cracking Suzie, where is mom?" James asked as he was walking into the door. "Upstairs in her room with your daddy bitch!" Suzie said looking at her brother real crazy. "What the fuck is that all about Suzie?" James asked walking over to his sister while she was in the kitchen putting dishes in the dishwasher. "James what the fuck is today's date cuzing? You seem to forget about the small people," said Suzie as she waved her hand back and forth with one hand on her hip. She was waving her hand all in James's face waiting for an answer from him. "Oooh shit! I'm sorry Suzie, there's so much shit to do, damn Happy Birthday," said James while trying to give his sister a hug, but she wouldn't let him. "I don't want to hear that shit bitch! You're always putting me off. What, some bitch got in the way again?" Suzie asked him. She was mad at James for not remembering her birthday. "Yeah asshole, I'll make it up to you tomorrow. I promise you it will be your day," said James trying to reason with his sister. "It better be," said Suzie all up in his face. "Cause I need some time with you by myself, so don't bring no bitch with you," she said as she walked back into the kitchen. "I won't, let me go talk to mom real quick, okay?" James said as he ran upstairs to his mother's bedroom to talk to her. "Mom, mom! Dad are you up?" James yelled while knocking on their bedroom door. "Yes hon, come on in, your dad is still asleep. How are you doing baby?" asked his mom. Then she started hugging him and gave him a kiss. "Okay mom," said James sitting beside her on the bed. "Are White Mike and Ty staying out of trouble?" Mrs. Campbell asked. James's mother was looking at him right in his eyes. "Yes mom they are, we all are. I'm on my way to Mike's house now. Some girls are up there, and they asked me to come hang out," said James while chilling on the bed. "Please baby make sure you use condoms, okay?" Mrs. Campbell said to him. "Yes mom, always," said James as he pulled out a pack of Magnums. "Are you sure them things aren't too big for you boy? They might fall off that little wee, wee," said Mrs. Campbell while laughing at him because she remembers when he was little he found his uncle's condoms before and tried to put it on, and it fell off. "No mom, I'm big enough now. I'm eighteen years old," said James even though he knew what she was laughing at. "So what's up baby, what brings you over here so early?" Mrs. Campbell asked looking at her baby boy. "Mom I've been thinking really hard about what you said about school and all. I think I'm going to go back this year," said James. Then Mrs. Campbell replied, "Good for you baby, good for you. Because money without no brains is no good at all." Just as Mrs. Campbell was about to say something else, Mr. Campbell got up and said, "Well, well, well, that's something good to wake-up to. I'm proud of you son." James's father then gave his wife a kiss and James a hug. "James!!! Come here, I want you to meet my friend Pinkey!" Suzie yelled upstairs to James. As James was leaving out of his parent's bedroom passing his old bedroom to go to his sister's room, as soon as he cracked his sister's bedroom door Suzie yelled upstairs to him, "No dummy we're downstairs!" James closed the bedroom door and went downstairs to see the most beautiful girl; that he had ever saw in his life. His eyes got big, and his heart stopped for a second. "James this is my friend Pinkey, Pinkey this is my brother; the asshole James," said Suzie as she introduced them. Then James was about to say something to his sister, but instead he just smiled at her. Then he said something to her as he was walking over to Pinkey with his hand out to shake her hand. "Fuck you Suzie, and how are you doing Pinkey?" James asked. And he just stood there looking at her waiting for an answer. "Just fine and yourself?" Pinkey said looking at James right in his eyes. Pinkey was light skin (Spanish and Black), and had beautiful gray eyes; she was 5'8", 140lbs, with measurements of 36D-26-42. She also had long black curly hair down to her phat ass, she was a true stallion. As for Suzie, she was a stallion herself; she was brown skin with light brown hazel eyes, 5'7", 142lbs, and her measurements were 36DD-26-44. She had short brown hair; she was an all American beauty. James got himself together to speak after he just stripped her with his eyes. "A lot better now that I meet you. Damn you look good ma! Where the fuck have you been at all this time?" James asked Pinkey as he held her hand as if he didn't want to let it go. Then Suzie got right in between them and said to him, "In school, at home, in her fucking skin nigga! Don't think you're going to be fucking up my friend's life, and her heart nigga! Like the rest of them bitches, you fuck with, it's not cracking motherfucker!!! So think again cuz no, no, no!!!" "It looks like she might hurt his ass, baby come look at your son down here, just look at him," said Mrs. Campbell to James's dad. And then she walked into the living room on her way to the kitchen to get something to drink. "How are you doing this morning Pinkey baby?" Mrs. Campbell asked her on the way to the kitchen. "Hi Mrs. Campbell, how are you doing today?" Pinkey replied to her. "Baby I'm doing fine, I got the day off, so it couldn't be better," said Mrs. Campbell as she was walking from the kitchen going back upstairs to her room. "Suzie why don't you, and Pinkey come with me to Mike's house today, what's up?" James asked. Suzie looked at Pinkey and then looked at James and said, "And who's going to be there? Besides them money-hungry bitches that I always see out there James?" "So what, fuck them bitches. You're my sister, and she's with me, I mean you, you know what the fuck I mean. Don't act like you don't want to see Uncle Mike and Ty. Come on so me and Pinkey can get to know each other," said James. He was hoping his sister agreed with what he just said while waiting for her to say yes. "Tomorrow nigga, we already have plans for the day," said Suzie while looking at Pinkey. "Man fuck them plans, what's cracking? Chill with me for the day," said James to Suzie as he looked at both of them for an answer. "Suzie it is up to you. I don't care...it's up to you. It's your birthday today, I'm with you, whatever you decide to do, it's cool with me," said Pinkey. She was looking at Suzie, but smiling at James. "Alright James, you better not forget about tomorrow too boy," said Suzie seriously while looking at James as if she meant business and was not playing with him. "No, not at all. How can I forget about tomorrow when tonight is looking so, so, good cuz?" James asked while looking at Suzie. Then he looked at Pinkey while licking his lips. James felt like a kid in a toy store because Pinkey was just so beautiful to him. So the three of them jumped into James's whip to go to White Mike's house. James didn't want his sister to feel any way at all, so he got into back of his car and let Suzie drive, while Pinkey sat in the passenger seat. Furthermore, Suzie was a good driver too.

They got to White Mike's house in 45 minutes. When James was five minutes away, he called White Mike to let him know to look out for them. Since they were almost there, Mike was already at the door with his two pitbulls, Sam and Knocker. Sam was the girl, and she didn't play any games at all. She was short and cocky, and always on point. As for Knocker, he always did what Mike told him to do. Both were blue nose pitbulls. Mike was at the door with his Glock 40 in his hand, with Sam and Knocker in the yard right beside him. As soon as James pulled up and jumped out of his car Mike said, "What's cracking gangster? C.L.A.A.A.T!!!" Mike walked over to James, and they peaced each other. "You already know cuz G and C baby, all day...every day. Suzie came to see you and Ty," said James to Mike as he was playing with Knocker and Sam. "Uncle Mike what's up? Please tell me you didn't forget about today?" Suzie asked while looking at Mike waiting for an answer. "What Suzie? Were we suppose to go somewhere today or something?" Mike replied to her and looking at Suzie surprised. All she could do was laugh at him and then she hit him in his chest and said, "Dummy today is my birthday man. Anyway this is my friend Pinkey that I been telling you about." "Damn, what's cracking Pinkey? James did say you were beautiful, but damn girl!!! You're the shit," said Mike. He was smiling at her and shaking her hand. "Wow, thank you Mike," said Pinkey while shaking his hand. "Suzie, why don't you and Pinkey go inside? We'll be in there in a minute; show Pinkey the house," said James as he stopped and turned to Mike with a look in his eyes and pulled out his gun. Mike already had his gun out. James walked over to Mike and both of them smacked their guns together like they were shaking hands. As Pinkey and Suzie was walking in the house, Pinkey was looking at them. She turned to Suzie and asked her, "Suzie, why did they just do that?" "Girl that's something they have been doing since they were kids. That's just how they are girl," said Suzie as they were walking through the door. Ty jumped out of nowhere on her and Pinkey and yelled, "Surprise!!! Happy birthday Suzie!!!" Then Ty gave Suzie a hug and a kiss. All the Loc's that were there gave her a hug as well. Suzie started to cry because she really thought that everybody forgot her birthday, but they didn't. "Uncle Ty thank you, thank all of you for remembering. This is my friend Pinkey, Pinkey this is my Uncle Ty," said Suzie as she wiped the tears from her eyes. "Pinkey how are you doing? I heard a lot about you, and I must say you're very beautiful," said Ty. Pinkey felt a little uncomfortable at first because she didn't know anybody but Suzie. Also, it looked as if all eyes were on her because all the girls who were already there, were looking at her like who the fuck is she and who the fuck is she with? Ty knew that they were watching her, so he walks over to her and says out loud as he was walking pass the group of girls, "What the fuck is y'all bitches looking at, damn? Get the fuck off her dick shit. The party is over there, not over here." Then Ty went over to Pinkey.

Mike and James were walking through the door together. Suzie ran up and hugged them both and gave them a kiss. Then Suzie punched both of them. James walked over to Pinkey and grabbed her hand real gently and then asked her to come with him into the kitchen. She looked at Suzie to see what she was going to say. "Go ahead girl, you're in good hands," said Suzie. As they were walking into the kitchen, James couldn't help but to look into Pinkey's beautiful gray eyes. She had the most beautiful pair of eyes that he had ever seen. Pinkey leaned on the marble kitchen counter top and looked James into in his eyes and asked, "James, do you do this with all the girls you meet?" "No, not at all; you're very different to me. So please don't feel no way at all," said James. He looked at Pinkey sincerely to let her know that it wasn't like that at all.

CHAPTER 2

THE ROBBERY

Meanwhile back in Brooklyn, the white Mercedes Benz belonged to a man named Doggy. Doggy was a Jamaican and a member of the Bloods. He didn't play any games at all. His homey that was with him when they pulled up beside James, was 007 and Jimmy. They had one soldier with them sitting in the back with Jimmy. All these niggas did all day long was try to rob shit or rob nigga. This is what they did for a living all day every day.

A young lady whom James was messing with, put them on to him. The young ladies' name was Tanya. She was sleeping with Doggy, and telling him everything about James and his friends too. Doggy ran the 90s, and James ran the 50s in Brooklyn. They were Bloods from Jamaica, him, 007, and Jimmy had a lot of bodies in Jamaica and in New York as well. And believe me, they had their share of it in Brooklyn, just as much as James and them did. They would rob big drug dealers for keys worth hundreds of thousands of dollars. They would also kidnap niggas, and hold them for ransom for money or drugs. They didn't play any games, and were not to be fucked with. Tanya was one of Doggy's ruby's that was trying to set up James. "I could of had that nigga at the light, but I remembered what you said about them. So I just looked at him really hard, and he looked back at me. And then the light turned green, we still just sat there for a while looking at each other. I knew the boy had his hand on his gun. So I just let it go. I didn't want to fuck it up," said Doggy talking to Tanya while smoking a blunt with her. "Don't worry daddy, ya'll get him, you always do in time boo," said Tanya as she grabbed the blunt from Doggy. "I know ma, what's popping with that nigga uptown? Who you told me about that has fifty keys of cocaine?" Doggy asked. "Yeah he can get it, I'm going up there tonight to fuck and suck the shit out of his fat ass, his little dick ass. After that, he'll go right to sleep. And then I'll call you and let you in Daddy," said Tanya as she turned the TV channel to Tyra. "That's what's popping homey, what's that nigga name again? The Godfather or something like that?" Doggy asked as Tanya passes him back the blunt. "Yeah that's, that fat assholes name, that's him," said Tanya and they started laughing for a moment. This is what they did. Tanya would get them, she was a bad bitch. She was Jamaican and Indian with light brown eyes. She had brown skin, short black curly hair, 5'7", and 136lbs with the sexy measurements of 36DD-26-44 P.H.A.T. in all the right places. She a stallion as well too. They all started to get ready to do what they do best. Get that motherfucking money!

Meanwhile at Mike's house, James, and Pinkey were getting to know each other. James told her a little about himself, and Pinkey told him a little about her. At the same time, Mike and Ty were entertaining Suzie. They loved Suzie like a little sister. The young lady didn't even matter to them, It was all about Suzie today. "So Mike, when are you getting married nigga?" Suzie asked as she was opening up her gifts that all the Loc's gave her. "Please!!! Not ever that, maybe Ty," said Mike . Then Ty just started laughing at Mike for even saying that because Mike knows that will never happen. Play to they die, that is what they lived by. "Cuz, I'm only 18, about to be 19, fuck that shit. I'm too young for that shit Suzie," said Ty as they were chilling, drinking Remy, and smoking purple too. "A young man living like an old one, but you're not the average 18 year-old Ty," said Suzie. Then she gave him a hug for the gifts that he got her. "I like my life just like it is. No one telling me what to do, man fuck that shit Suzie, that is not for me at all," said Ty. He was laughing at her for even saying that to him as the three of them walked to the pool where the rest of the girls were.

Meanwhile back in the kitchen, James and Pinkey were hitting it off real well. She was definitely feeling him, but she wasn't acting too quick with him yet. James was playing it cool as a motherfucker, but it was showing that he was definitely into her. His phone started ringing, it was Wesley calling him. "What's cracking cuzing? Did Suzie like my gift that I got her cuz?" Wesley asked while chilling on the block making sure everything was going like it was suppose to. "Yeah cuz, she did, she loved it. What's cracking with you? You coming up?" James asked. "Whose all there cuzing?" Wesley asked. "Me, Mike, Ty, Suzie, some Loc's, and my Sister's beautiful friend Pinkey who is off limits to you," said James. James just looked at Pinkey and smiled at her as he played with her hand while looking at her the entire time. "I'll be up there in two hours cuz. I'll call you when I'm five minutes away, okay cuzing?" Wesley said. "That's what's cracking cuz. Call me, be safe," said James and then hung up the phone. Then he started back talking to Pinkey about what he wants to do with himself, and if she has plans for her life as well. "Oh yeah, I'm going to acting school for 2 to 4 years to be an actress, and taking up Business Management too," said Pinkey as she sat beside James. "That's real good boo, real good. As for myself, I'm thinking about going back to school as well and stop running these streets, you feel me? I do music too. I'm nice at that shit, you should hear me one day," said James to her. "That sounds good to me. Whenever you're ready, just let me know," said Pinkey.

Meanwhile back in Brooklyn, Doggy and 007 were getting ready to get The Godfather. Tanya picked up the phone and called The Godfather, she told him to get her from her apartment in Brooklyn. He told her to catch a cab, and come to his house in Queens. She told him she would be there in about an hour or two, and she'll see him then. One thing's for sure, don't get it fucked up, Tanya was no joke. She was all about getting that money, and she'll kill a nigga quick. She will cut a niggas throat in a N.Y. second, and she'll fuck you while doing it.

Tanya's cab arrived, so she got her shit together and went downstairs. Tanya jumped into the cab, and told the driver to take her to Queens to where The Godfather lived at. As soon as she was about to pull up in front of the apartment building, she called Doggy and 007 to let them know that she was there. She got out of the cab, and started walking up to the apartment building while she was on the phone with Doggy. "Hey baby what's popping, I'm here, should I fuck him first or kill him?" Tanya asked as she was ringing the bell to The Godfather's apartment. "It's up to you homey, do what you feel," said Doggy. "I'll kill the fat bitch, fuck it," said Tanya as she was waiting for The Godfather to answer his apartments door. "Fuck the man first homey, and give him the drugs I gave you. We need him alive right now, you can kill him later on homey," said Doggy as he and 007 was on their way to meet her to do what they do best. She said, "This is why I asked you first, so whatever you say homey, I'm in." Just as Tanya got off the phone, The Godfather was opening up the door to let her in. "Who were you just talking to baby?" The Godfather asked as he was letting her into the apartment. "Oh just my mom baby, she wanted to know if we were coming over there. She can't wait to meet you. She asked me what we're doing tonight," said Tanya. Tanya already knows they're not going out because all he likes to do is fuck and drink all day. "Oh not tonight baby, I have too much shit in here. Plus, it's just me and you tonight baby, we're all by ourselves. I am going to fuck the shit out of you bitch, all over this fucking place baby," said The Godfather as he grabbed her ass cheek. "No baby, you got it fucked up tonight boo," said Tanya as she sat on his lap playing with his dick. And then she looked at him straight into his eyes and said real softly, "I'm going to fuck the shit out of you, so good." Then Tanya kissed him on his lips. The Godfather's dick got so hard, not knowing that he can die tonight. What an asshole Tanya thought to herself. So she went into the living room and made them two drinks. Hennessey on the rocks before she gave him his, she put the drugs that Doggy gave her in his drink and gave it to him. Now it was just a matter of time before it was over for the young don.

Back at Mike's house everyone is either in the pool or around it having fun. Wesley finally got there, and the music was playing. Everyone was doing them at the party. As the party was going on, one of the girls there got so drunk that she decided to go over to where Pinkey was at. She got up in Pinkey's face acting as if she wanted to fight or something and asked her, "Who the fuck are you, bitch number three, or do you think you're bitch number one?" Then Pinkey turned around ready to fuck her up, but she was too lady like for that shit to be fighting over a nigga. So she just punched her in the mouth, and threw her in the pool. Everybody started laughing at her ass. As she swam to the poolside, her weave got fucked up.

Pinkey knew the girl must of been fucking James or something like that. So she just walked up by the poolside and said to her, "No bitch!!! I'm the bitch you want to be, ho!!!" Then Pinkey just walked back to the table were Suzie and James was and sat back. James walked up to the girl with a bottle of Moet in his hand and poured it all over her. "Bitch stay the fuck out of her face, bitch!!! And take your ass over there with the rest of them four-legged bitches!!!" They saw the look in James's eyes, and she knew it was time to chill out for real. Then James walked back over to Pinkey to make sure everything was okay with her. Suzie got up and smacked the shit out of the girl, right in her face. She also gave her a piece of her mind at the same time. "Bitch!!! Don't you ever get it fucked up bitch, that's my motherfucking home girl over there with my brother, bitch. So show some fucking respect, you wish you can look as beautiful as we do, you fucking ho!!! And you're not even a good looking one at that, bitch!!! So remember that the next time you think about jumping out there and running your fucking mouth bitch!!!" Suzie said ready to give her a beatdown, but her and Pinkey just walked away from her.

White Mike, Ty, and the rest of the Loc's were laughing so hard at her. Also everybody that was outside by the poolside were laughing at what Suzie and Pinkey did to the girl. Suzie and Pinkey called her all kinds of jealous bitches. The girl almost cried for Suzie and Pinkey to stop calling her all bitches those names and she was telling them how sorry she was for doing what she did to Pinkey. "Bitch tell that shit to Pinkey, not me hoe," said Suzie as she walked away from the girl. The girl tried to talk to Pinkey, but Pinkey was not trying to hear that at all. Pinkey just looked at the girl up and down, and kept talking to James as if the girl didn't even exist at all.

Back at The Godfather's house, Tanya started sucking on The Godfather's dick waiting for the drugs to kick in, so she can let Doggy and 007 in. As she was putting his dick down her throat, the drugs finally started to take effect. As he was going out, she just kept sucking him off watching him as he was falling asleep. She had his dick in her hand and jerking him off to sleep. "That was the last time he'll get his dick sucked," she thought to herself. Then she hit Doggy and 007 up on the phone, and told them to come on, she'll let them into the building. Doggy and 007 got out of the car with a bag that had some duck tape and other stuff in it. They told their little homey to stay in the car and look out for them because The Godfather's people can drive up at anytime, and if he sees anybody to call them and let them know what's popping. They told him what car to look out for, if they pull up. One thing's for sure, they weren't worried about the cops. This Motherfucker that they were about to get was a big boy for real. He got N.Y. on lock, people in Florida, and out West in Columbia. He was nothing to fuck with. As Doggy and 007 walked into The Godfather's house to see the fat bitch out cold with his boxers down to his knees. Tanya was sucking on some ice and smiling at them. Doggy turned to her and said, "You're cold bitch, I love you girl." Then he started laughing at her. Him and 007 started to get to work, they duck taped his ass to a chair in the apartment. Then they put some smelling salt to his nose to wake him up. As The Godfather was waking up, Doggy smacked him with his 9mm Smith and Wesson in his face. "Okay pussy, let's get to work," said 007 as The Godfather woke up to see two black men in his apartment with guns. He didn't know what's going on at first, then he yelled, "What the fuck is going on in my house, and where the fuck is Tanya at? You fucking nigga! Y'all better not have hurt her! What the fuck do you want? You fucking monkeys!!!" 007 and Doggy didn't care about the name calling because they already knew where his fat ass was going tonight. When Tanya kicked him in his face that is when The Godfather looked very amazed at what was going on, and to see Tanya with Doggy and 007. All he could say to himself was that bitch is with them two niggas fuck. "Okay you fat fuck, where's the fucking shit at for the last time?" 007 asked him as he was taking a small blowtorch out of the bag and placed it on a table beside him and Doggy getting ready to do what they do best. Then Doggy put his cigar cutter on the table right beside the blowtorch. Doggy started biting The Godfather in his face and at the same time busting up his face with his fist. Then 007 cut the duck tape off of his hands while Tanya stood right there with her gun to his head. 007 taped both of his hands to the side of the chair with his fingers out. 007 then grabbed the cigar cutter, and slid it down his pinky finger, and decided to asked him one time and one time only. "Okay homey, you fat fuck, what's popping where's the shit at?" 007 asked. Doggy turned the blowtorch on up really high, and placed back on the table. The Godfather tried to spit on them, and then he yelled, "Fuck you! Fuck you!!! You fucking niggas!!! This shit is bigger than me and you bitches. You're already fucking dead, you fucking monkeys!!!" As he yelled, The Godfather was looking at them mad as a motherfucker. That's when Tanya took her red flag, and gagged him. Then 007 cut off his pinky finger. A little blood shot out and got on Doggy and 007. The Godfather was trying to yell and scream, but Tanya had his mouth shut. Before he could even get it out, the blood was still coming out. That's when Doggy grabbed the blowtorch, and put it where his pinky used to be. You could smell the flesh burning. He did this to stop the bleeding, and to torture him at the same time. "Now I'm going to ask you one more time. Where is the shit? You fat fuck!!! This is the last time I'm going to ask you bitch!!!" said 007 as he was wiping the sweat up off the The Godfather's face. Tanya and Doggy went to look for what they could find. Tanya came back from out the bedroom with 50 keys, and Doggy found 300,000 dollars in cash, they put it right in front of him. Doggy took the blowtorch to the side of his face, and made a B on it because they already knew there was more money in the house. "Okay, okay, please stop! There's a million dollars in the safe over there, right behind the wall, you can have it," said The Godfather all out of breath. "What is the fucking combination?" 007 asked him while Doggy had the blowtorch by his eye, and Tanya was holding his head. "Okay, okay!!! Please it's 5 right, 17 left, 36 right two times, then 15, and stop!" yelled The Godfather. Then Tanya cracked the safe open to find one million dollars in cash. Doggy came out the kitchen with a larger bag of money, it looked like it was more than a million dollars. It was 5 million dollars, and once The Godfather saw Doggy with the duffle bag, he started to cry because he knew it was all over now. 007 just wiped his tears from his face, and told The Godfather thank you. And that's when The Godfather told them, "I'll see y'all in Hell." Right after that, Tanya walked right up behind him and grabbed him by his neck. She slit his throat with a razor from ear to ear, and left him for dead. The Godfather a.k.a. The Fat Man took his last breath and off they went into the night.

Back at Mike's house everybody was having fun. Ty and Mike were chilling with Suzie, and Wesley was entertaining the ladies as always. And you should already know where James was at and who he was with...Pinkey. James couldn't help but to keep thinking about how beautiful Pinkey looked with her measurements of 36D-26-42. "She's a fucking diamond," he thought to himself. "So here I am telling you all about me, what about you play boy?" Pinkey asked James. She was laughing at him because of what that girl did out by the pool. "He must have some good dick for her to do all of that shit," she thought to herself. "Oh yeah, you're real funny. As for White Mike, Ty and I, we all grew up in Brooklyn. I dropped out of school, but I'm going back soon cuz I want to be a writer one day, I told you that already, didn't I?" James asked her as they were smoking a blunt together. "Yeah, I remember you saying that before, I do pay attention to you," said Pinkey laughing with him. "You are funny as shit Pinkey, but it's more to do than this drug shit. One day I would like to have kids, a wife you know...the whole family thing. I love my Loc's, that's all I got beside my mom, pop, and my sister, and hopefully you now?" James said as he was holding her hand and looking right into her eyes. Then Pinkey reaches over to kiss him, and sticks her tongue down his throat. And then she looked at him into his eyes, and told him in a soft voice while holding the back of his neck, "You got me, just don't fuck it up, because I don't play that shit, okay?" His dick got hard as shit, and he almost came on himself. He grabbed her by her hair, and then he started tonguing her down. He started playing with her breasts, sucking on her neck, and licking on her nipples. Then Pinkey went inside his pants and grabbed his dick and started playing with it. James put his hand between her legs and up her thighs. Then he slid her panties to the side, and started rubbing between her pussy lips to her clit. And when he rubbed her clit real gently, and her pussy was getting really wet. They were sucking on each other's tongue, and both were high as shit. Pinkey started cumming on herself, she was moaning, but had to keep it lady like. As bad as she wanted to fuck the shit out of him, she knew she had to chill for right now. "Hold up James, please stop baby," she said while grabbing his hands, and holding them as she talked to him. "Wait one minute, look, I'm not like them other girls you fuck with that's out there. I like you and all, but let's take it slow please, okay?" Pinkey asked while holding him and giving him a kiss upon his lips. As she looked at James, he knew he probably could have gotten the pussy, but he stopped because he really liked her. So he just chilled, it's better to be safe than sorry, because he didn't want it to seem as if that's all he wanted from her. "Okay baby, whatever you say, the ball is in your hands, because I really want this to work out boo, okay?" James said while holding her tight to him. It put a big smile on her face, she looked at him and said to him, "That's my nigga, and don't you worry it'll be worth it, believe me when I tell you that boy. Now give me a kiss, and let's go back outside by the pool before they come looking for us." "That's what's up, let's go by the beach out here by Mike's house, it's real nice too," said James.

CHAPTER 3

ROCK A BYE BABY

As they started walking out of the kitchen into the backyard where the pool was at, James walked over to where Mike and Ty was and told them where he was going. Pinkey did the same thing; she walked over to Suzie, and told her the same thing. "Now don't let my brother get his way with you, okay girl? I love my brother, but he can be very...you know; just don't let him get his way with you. That's all I'm saying, okay?" Suzie said looking at Pinkey. "Girl, you already know that I'm eighteen and still a virgin. I like him, but I also want him to respect me. So I have to take it easy with him. Plus, that nigga has a big ass dick girl," said Pinkey looking at James while she was talking to Suzie. "I don't need to know all of that, that's too much information. He is my brother Pinkey," said Suzie. Then Suzie and Pinkey both started laughing at each other.

On the other side of the pool, Mike and Ty were trying to get the 411 from James. They wanted to know if he had fucked her or what? "No, I'm taking my time cuz, you feel me? I like her, but I don't know her for real, but it's something about her," said James as he looked over to the other side of the pool at Pinkey and Suzie. Ty looked over to where Pinkey and Suzie was, and he looked dead into Pinkey's eyes. He knew right then that it was something special about her, and his man James. So, he just smiled at her and turned to James and said to him, "Whatever makes you happy cuz, that's all that matters to me. But if she hurts you, you already know what it was cuz." James peaces both of them and Wesley. Then he walked over to Pinkey and Suzie, he took Pinkey by her hand and they started heading for the door. That is when James turned to her and asked her, "Do you know how to drive ma?" Pinkey looked at him as if he was crazy or something and then said, "Are you motherfucking playing or something? Nigga give me the keys, and let me show you better than I can tell you." James threw her the keys to his whip, it was a midnight blue Mercedes-Benz CL600 with 22" viper rims on it. Then he walked around to the other side of the car to the passenger side, and opened up the door for Pinkey. She reached over to let him in. As James was getting into the car, he knew right then and there that he had a good one. Because only a real women will do shit like that for their man.

Back out in Brooklyn, Doggy, 007, and Tanya were splitting up the money, drugs, and guns while laughing at the fat ass Godfather that was dead as a motherfucker. "Man that motherfucker looked funny as shit, yo Tanya, homey how do you do it?" 007 asked as he was counting up the money. "I don't go for looks homey, if I went for looks, that's all we'll have is looks. I go after their money, fuck what the fuck he looks like. You feel me Doggy baby? And I want some dick tonight boo," said Tanya looking at Doggy like she was real horny. "Okay ma tonight, when I come back from the club, I got you. Plus, I got a job to do tonight, that nigga from 93 is selling his own shit. He got the game fucked up big time. We got to go and put a stop to that shit A.S.A.P!!! We must hit that bitch," said Doggy while Tanya was sitting on his lap with her hands down his pants. "You want me to come homey? I'll do it for you homey," said Tanya willing to go do it. "Na, na ma, 007 and the young homey that was with us at Fat Ass's house are coming with us. Plus, I want to see what this little homey is working with too. If he can handle this shit," said Doggy as he was rubbing Tanya's ass. "What the fuck is young homey's name anyway baby?" Tanya asked while she was giving Doggy some head. "Baby Gangster, that's little homey's name ma...shit," said Doggy right before he was about to cum in Tanya's mouth. She had his dick down her throat like a vacuum cleaner. She was good at what she does, not one baby hit the floor. "Just be careful boo, I'll be here playing with my pussy until you get back, okay Daddy?" Tanya said as she was fixing his pants. "Me soon come back, come 007, let we get into they car a Shooter?" Doggy said in Jamaican. "Come in man, Baby Gangster let we go. Tonight killa, you ready to kill that pussy hole Shooter?" 007 asked as they were getting ready to walk out the door. "Yeah, yeah homey, me going to kill a pussy hole tonight, that pussy Fee is a dead man," said Baby Gangster as he grabbed his 50 DE. He put it in his waist, headed out the door, and jumped into a white Benz CL550 with 22" viper rims on it. And off they went to the club playing the CD *"Reasonable Doubt"*, listening to track four *"Dead Presidents"*. They got there in the early morning about one o'clock. Doggy parked the car, and when they got out they walked to the back door in the ally where the back of the club was at. Security let them right in, all that line shit...forget it. We all should know that a real G don't wait for no one. A G do what they do, when they do it. "Okay homey, look don't kill the pussy inside the club...you feel me homey? Wait until we take the pussy outside, and when I say or go to the bathroom then kill the pussy dead!!! Homey you feel me?" 007 said as they were walking in. "Yeah, yeah, homey, I got you," said Baby Gangster. Then Doggy, 007, and Baby Gangster walked in and went straight to the bar, and got three bottles of Moet. They saw the nigga they were looking for, and he was playing it real big in the club. He saw Doggy and 007, so he decides to send them a bottle of Moet. And Doggy and 007 didn't like that. Baby Gangster didn't even drink his bottle of Moet or smoke, he just sat there until it was time to do what he came to do. The man named Chin walked over to Doggy and 007 as if everything was cool, and Doggy and 007 just played along with it. "What's up Blood, what's up homey?" Doggy said as he smiled and peaces him. "Yo, yo big homey, what's popping? Your name is Chin right?" 007 asked as he peaces him. One thing's for sure, they never played about their money. "Yeah, yeah big homey, I do all the running for y'all down the nineties, my little homey's love y'all niggas," said Chin. As he was talking, Baby Gangster had is eyes on him the entire time. "Yeah that's what's popping homey, but we have a new job for you homey, more money. It's in Manhattan," said Doggy. "No-no homey, Brooklyn me for real," said Chin while drinking his bottle of Moet. Doggy and 007 got up from the table and told Chin to follow them, so they can talk to him outside. And Baby Gangster got up right behind them. They went out the same way they came in. Chin was looking at Baby Gangster like who the fuck is he?, and what the fuck is he coming for? "This is a homey right here, his name is Baby Gangster, he's with us. We want him to go with you on this new job, homey," said Doggy to Chin as they were standing with 007 and **B**aby Gangster in the ally. "Okay homey, but I really like Brooklyn, that's where it's popping at for me," said Chin not the whole Manhattan thing. "Look homey, we know you make money on the side. It's okay, because we all do it from time to time, ain't that right Doggy?" 007 asked playing Chin out of position. "Yeah, yeah no bullshit...we all do it at times," said Doggy playing right along. "Look, I'm going to be real with you homey. I needed the money to pay off some doctor bills homey, that's all. You know my kid has a bad heart right? So I just made a little bit...that's all homey," said Chin and he thought they were falling for it, but they really wasn't. As he kept on talking to Doggy, 007 turned to Baby Gangster and looked at him and started to piss. As soon as he did that, Baby Gangster grabbed his 50 DE from out of his dip, and cocked the hammer back. Then he put it right to the back of Chin's head and blew his brains out on the side of the clubs wall. As soon as his body hit the floor, Baby Gangster stood over him taking the rest of his face off. And when he was out of shots, Baby Gangster reloaded and took Chin's arms off, and then reloaded again. By the time it was over, it was over. All Baby Gangster did was look and admire his work and then he smiled at Doggy and 007. "Yes homey, I like how the fuck you get down, homey. Play no games at all...nice," said 007.

As they were walking back in the club, the *"Sean Paul"* CD was playing. "Yes homey, you run with Killer? That pussy can't touch us homey," said 007 peacing Baby Gangster. Doggy did the same too. "Come let's get some pussy tonight, and take them with us," said Doggy as they were partying like rock stars. "Homey, I love y'all niggas, y'all are the don for real," said Baby Gangster as he was drinking his bottle of Moet. Doggy, 007, and Baby Gangster was laughing at Chin, because he never saw it coming. Chin was dead as a motherfucker, a closed casket for real. Blood and brains was left running on the side of the street. And nobody knew what had happened either. Baby Gangster got three bitches just like Doggy said. 007 got two for himself, Doggy got one for him, and Tanya to share for when he gets back to the house after they leave out of the club tonight.

James and Pinkey got to the beach and took a walk down the Boardwalk. And then they went down to the Waterfront. James bought a beach towel with them, and they sat in the sand down by the water, watching the stars and the moon. The moon light was glaring over the ocean seawater. Both the night and the mood was right. James did not know if this was the right time to say what he wanted to say, because he only knew her for a few hours. But he's the type of person that speaks what's on his mind. "Pinkey this might sound crazy as shit, but I'm going to keep it real with you. I don't know what it is about you, but I must say you're very special. I know it sounds real crazy, right now. Just don't think that a nigga is just trying to get in your drawers and that's it, because it's not just all about that either," said James as he held one of her hands while looking into her eyes. The wind was blowing lightly on them as they were sitting back smoking on some purple getting high as shit, all over again. "James it's okay baby, and today is official day number two. And believe it or not, I feel the same way, about you too. All I ask is that you don't play games with me, I'm not for that bullshit James," said Pinkey as they sat on the beach towel kicking it with each other. He started telling her about his plans in life again, and one thing led to another. They were right back at it again. They started kissing, and James put one of his hands between her thick thighs. Pinkey opened up her legs real wide, and James laid her back gently. Then he started to rub her vagina and clit at the same time real softly, making it wet. He was also sucking on her breast, and her pink nipples were standing up firm. She started moaning and sucking on his ear. As they were in the middle of doing them, out of nowhere two thugs walked up on them with hoods on. They pulled out guns demanding James to give them his jewelry, and told him to get up off of Pinkey. Then one of the thugs stood in front of them laughing and telling the other one that they're going to have some fun with her tonight. James didn't like his words,. but he played along with them and he took his hands off of Pinkey's breast. The sight of Pinkey's pretty pink nipples took their eyes off of James. So, James quickly placed one of his hands into the sand, and the other one on his gun. He told Pinkey in her ear to roll and run once he starts shooting. She saw what James was doing with his hand with the sand. She looked at James and did the same thing as well. James started to get up slowly, just like the man told him to. As he was getting up , he quickly threw the sand in one of the men's face. Pinkey did the same to the other one and got out of the way. By this time, James' gun was out and he started shooting the first one in his face. The other one was trying to grab his gun out of his dip, and that's when Pinkey kicked him in his nuts and got out of the way again. James shot him six times in the chest, and they were shot down dead. James quickly grabbed Pinkey by the hand telling her, "Let's get the fuck out of here ma." Pinkey couldn't believe what had just happened right before her eyes. Their lives had flashed right before her, and two men are dead, just like that. As they were running to the car, James asked her if she was okay to drive them back to Mike's house. Pinkey told him, "You motherfucking right, let's get the fuck out of here." They got in the car and sped off, James was sitting in the passenger seat laughing at what just had happened to the two stick up kids dead as a motherfucker, the dummies never saw it coming. James turned to Pinkey on the way to Mike's house, just to let her know he will never ever let nothing ever happen to her. Pinkey turned to him and told him the same. Then she said, "Just don't hurt me James." That's all she asked of him as they were listing to *"21 Questions"* on 50 Cent's CD, while driving back to Mike's house.

As soon as they got to Mike's house James told Mike, TY, and Wesley what had happened to them. James then decided to go home to his mother's house in Brooklyn to chill out for the night. All three of them left James, Pinkey, and Suzie, the next morning James woke up with Pinkey right beside him, and Suzie was right beside her. James couldn't help but watch Pinkey while she was sleeping. His mother was up early and she heard him in his room. "James, baby!!! Is that you?" Mrs. Campbell asked as she walked over to his door. "Yes!!! Mom it's me," he said as he sat up in his bed. "Do you have company with you baby?" Mrs. Campbell asked as she was walking in his room. "Good morning Mrs. Campbell, how are you doing today?" Pinkey asked as she and Suzie were stretching getting ready to get up to make breakfast. "Is that my baby Pinkey? I'm fine dear and yourself?" Mrs. Campbell asked. "Okay," said Pinkey. "What's up nigga? You better keep your word too nigga. I'm going to fix us some breakfast first. Come on Pinkey, let's show him how it's done," said Suzie.

Suzie and Pinkey went downstairs to fix breakfast. So, Mrs. Campbell decided to have a little talk with James about him messing with Pinkey. Because she knew Pinkey, and she knew Pinkey a nice girl. So she asked James to be real good to her. She also told him, she a very sweet person. "Mom you don't have to worry about me and her. I'm not going to treat her like the rest of them. I really like her mom, for real," said James. "Good for you baby now, please take it easy on her, she's a good girl for sure. That's one thing I can say about her, and please don't get her pregnant, okay baby? Not yet, let her at least finish school. And as for you, you go back to school. All that money and no brains is never no good, okay?" Mrs. Campbell said. "I know, I know mom. I love you too, you always keep it real with me. Where is Dad?" James asked.. "At the store working," she said.

Pinkey came back upstairs to let them both know that breakfast is almost ready. She had her hair in a ponytail with one of James' white tees on. James looked so, so good to her. "Baby...Mrs. Campbell breakfast is almost done," said Pinkey as she walked in the room. All three of them started walking downstairs to the kitchen where Suzie was. James said to his mother, "Mom you already know Pinkey can cook, and you had her cooking before." Pinkey started to help Suzie fix breakfast, and made James and Mrs. Campbell plates. "Here baby, here you go, I made it just for you. I hope you like it," said Pinkey. James sat down and started to eat his food. He had a look on his face like damn, this shit is good. He looked at her like he knew he had a winner. He was just imagining how good the pussy was while he ate. And before they went to bed, he was playing with her pussy, her shit was tight as shit. The way he looked at it, it was either one or the other, she was a virgin or she hasn't had sex in a long while.

Back on the other side of Brooklyn, Doggy, 007, Tanya, and Baby Gangster were out shopping, doing them, and having fun spending up Fat Ass' money. They had so much money they didn't even know what to do with it all. Baby Gangster didn't know what to do with himself. He had already bought two motorcycles, two cars, jewelry, and some clothes. You name it and he bought it. As they were in downtown Brooklyn doing their shopping, guess who they saw doing their shopping as well? They saw James, Pinkey, and Suzie. 007 and Doggy couldn't help but to notice how pretty both the girls looked. "Yo Yo homey, see the boys right there...see them? We should of grabbed them bitches the other day," said 007 as they saw James and them walking in a clothing store. "No homey, we did right, too many people was out there that day. Also, it would of been a scene that day, let's just watch the boys today," said Doggy as they stopped doing what they were doing to watch them. It didn't matter that they just got Fat Ass just two days ago. Because this is what they do for a living. They were big time stick up kids, and they only fuck with big time drug dealers. As for James, Suzie, and Pinkey, they continued to go shopping. James didn't know that Doggy, Tanya, 007, and Baby Gangster were there. "Pinkey and Suzie look over here, this would look real nice on both of y'all...you don't think so?" asked James as he was showing them the outfits in the store. "Yes, come on Pinkey, let's go inside and look at it girl," said Suzie as they were walking over to the store. "Damn Suzie, that shit looks good on you girl, I like it," said Pinkey as they walked over to try the Apple Bottom jeans outfit on. "That's what the fuck I'm talking about, that shit looks good girl...let's get it?" Suzie said as they were both looking in the mirror at themselves and showing James. "Alright it's a rap, let's go pay for it," said James. As they were leaving the store walking to the food court to get something to eat, James phone rang and it was Tanya trying to play him out of position. "What's cracking Tanya?" James asked as he answered his phone. Suzie and Pinkey just looked at him. "What's up baby? When am I going to see you again? I miss putting my lips around that phat ass dick of yours boo...what's up with tonight?" Tanya asked as she continued to try to play James out of position. "I can't do that tonight, I'm really busy but I'll call you okay?" James said. Then he got off the phone. Pinkey knew he was on the phone talking to another female, but she played it real cool. She sat back to see what he's going to say first. But as for Suzie, she just couldn't let it go. "James who the fuck were you just talking to on the phone? Telling that bitch bye?!!!" she yelled while looking at him real crazy. "Suzie that was just a blast from the past, that's all damn," said James as they were walking through the mall. "It better be nigga, because Pinkey is no hoe, okay James?" she said. Suzie was making a big deal out of nothing, at least that's how James looked at it. "Suzie it's okay, it's not like he said he was free or anything like that. I got to give him time to let them bitches know, feel me Suzie," said Pinkey trying to calm her down. "Yeah I guess so, fuck that bitch anyway," she said as they were walking outside to the car. Pinkey just kissed James on his lips to try and make him feel better, and to let him know he has a real woman. Suzie just looked at him like fuck up nigga...fuck up and I got you.

Later on that day, White Mike and Ty went out on a hit while James, Suzie, and Pinkey were still shopping. It was a hit out on one of the major players of the Bloods that ran the lower east side of Manhattan. This was something that they did for a living, Mike and Ty did contract killings. They sat out across the street from where the man lived at waiting for him to pull-up. However, at the same time putting their plans together on how they were going to run down on him and take his face off. A red Escalade pulled up with four men in it. Mike looked at his watch and said to Ty, "Just like The Don said, it's 12:30 on the dot...he's on time." The four men got out of the red Escalade and started walking towards the building. Mike and Ty jumped out of their Benz, they were dressed in all red. They started walking towards the four men. One out of the four men is their target. Mike and Ty have a picture of him, so they know who they are looking for. They see him, and he's not even paying any attention. For one, they looked like Bloods to them and acted like Bloods as well. As soon as Mike and Ty got five feet from where they were standing at, they both pulled out 2 Glocks 40 with silencers on them. And started hitting them in front of the building. The men tried to pull out to try to shoot back at Mike and Ty. However, they were not fast enough, not fast as they were. All four of them hit the floor, but the main one that they came for was still breathing. Ty started walking down on him, but shot the other three in the head. Mike walked right up on the one they came for and stood over him. He looked him straight in the eyes, and then he put the gun right between the man forehead. And then he put two shots in his head. The job was done, and now it was time for them to get the rest of their money.

Just right after they were walking away, a little girl was coming out of the building. She walked right into the bodies and started screaming, then ran back inside the building. She started calling for her mother, so Mike and Ty jumped in their Benz and got out of there, because they knew it was a matter of time before people would start coming outside. The only thing that the little girl could describe were two men in all red. When she ran away, she never saw their face because their backs were turned.

Mike and Ty reached The Don's place of business, his real name was Joey a.k.a. The Don. The Don opened the door and said to them, "Yes, yes please come on in, I had already heard the good news. Here goes the rest of your money, 100,000 thousand in cash. Would y'all like to stay for a while, have some drinks, and party with me? I have some of the finest women with me tonight that you ever seen." "Thanks, but no thanks, we got to go, but call us if you need us," said Ty as they were walking out the door. One thing about them two, they never mixed business with pleasure. They got their shit and went partying on their own. They both went on a partying spree for a few weeks in Jamaica. In the middle of them having fun, Ty's phone started ringing, and it was James checking up on them. "What's cracking cuz? I haven't heard from y'all in like two to three weeks, what's hood cuzing?" James asked. "C & G cuz, that's what it is cuzing, your ass is in love. Anyway nigga, where's Pinkey at? She's right beside you, isn't she?" Ty asked while him and Mike was laughing knowing she was right there. "What's up Ty, what's up Mike...all is well?" Pinkey said. She was laying beside James on the bed. White Mike and Ty started laughing real hard, because they knew she was going to be right there beside him. "Cuz, we'll be back tomorrow night, we are going to see you right?" White Mike asked. "Yeah yeah cuz, I'll be there at 12:00 at your house...right?" James asked before they got off the phone. "That's what it is, we'll see you then cuz...One C-safe," said Ty.

Ty and Mike got back in town, and on their way back to Mike's house from the airport they noticed a black Range Rover following them. Therefore, Mike told Ty to pull over at the next gas station coming up, so they can get some gas and see who the fuck was following them at the same time. They pulled over at the gas station and they jumped out with their hands on their guns. It was four bitches that Mike knew from the club. "What's cracking baby...y'all bitches were about to get shot the fuck-up riding behind us like that. Plus, your little sexy ass is not driving the same whip I saw you in before. Life must be real nice, I guess?" Mike said to Vida the girl that was driving. "It got a little bit better hanging with you, but what's up? Can we hang out with y'all tonight Mike or what?" Vida asked while putting her hand in his pants. "Follow me and Ty to my place, were going to do the damn thing," said Mike remembering how good the head was last time he was with her. "That's what I'm talking about my nigga...yo boo, what's up with your man James? Is he going to be there too or what?" asked Vida kissing Mike on his lips. "Yeah, he'll be there, but I don't think he'll be fucking around with you ma...I really don't," said Ty as he jumped back into their whip to go to Mike's house. "Ma, I'll be back, I'm going over Mike's house for a while...love you," said James as he was walking out the door. "Okay baby, I'll be here, I'll probably be in bed by the time you get back," said Pinkey as James was walking out the door to his car. As James was getting ready to pull off he noticed a blue Grand Cherokee with tinted windows that he never saw before. He knew something wasn't right about it. As soon as he but his key in the ignition to start his car, all he heard and seen out of nowhere was the F.B.I., A.T.F., D.E.A., and N.Y.P.D. He heard someone yell, "Put your hands up were we can see them now sir!!!" Blue and red lights were flashing everywhere, one of the agents walked up to James and as he was reading James his rights and said to him, "James my name is Agent Frank Anderson, I'm with the F.B.I., and we would like to ask you some questions downtown at the headquarters sir." "Whatever as long as I can call my lawyer, I don't give a fuck," said James as they were putting him in handcuffs. "You sure can...that's up to you and fine with me. It's just going to take up more time sir," said Agent Frank as he was taking him to the police car. "Can I just call my girl to let her know to call my lawyer for me?" James asked. "You mean the young lady upstairs in your apartment sir? I think she already knows sir," he said while closing the door on him. "Yeah that's who I'm talking about...my girl!!!" James yelled through the window. Frank turned back to the car and opened up the door and said, "I hope your place is clean, I'll have one of my agents tell her as soon as they finish going through your stuff sir." James yelled back at Frank, "Man my house and cars are clean nigga...fuck you, what the fuck you talking about?!!!" Then the Feds took him in to ask him some questions about some homicides that happened uptown in the lower eastside where the Bloods were killed at.

As soon as the police left, Pinkey got right on the phone and called Suzie. Suzie called James' lawyer to let him know what was going on. James' lawyer got down there in 30 minutes. The only thing that James had to say was I want my lawyer and I don't have nothing at all to say. James' lawyer was walking through the door and said to Agent Frank, "Okay, what's the problem sir? Why is my client here? And this better be good sir." "We believe your client was involved with four homicides in the city a few weeks ago. We just want to know where he was on the night of these murders?" Agent Anderson asked while throwing the picture of the four dead men on the table. The picture landed on the table right in front of James, so he could see it. "James, can you please tell them where you were, so we can get out of here," said James' lawyer not even looking at the picture. "I was at my mom's house with my girlfriend all night and then I went home. And that is where I've been since," said James to Frank while throwing the picture back at him. "I'm going to call your family to verify your story, and if you're right, you can go for now," said Frank as he was answering his phone. "Man do what you got to do so I can get the fuck out of here...shit," said James with his feet up on the desk as if he gives a fuck for real.

Back at Mike's house, Mike and Ty have been calling James all night. They knew it's not like James not to answer his phone, because one thing's for sure, they knew James would always be on time. Mike and Ty were starting to get worried about him because they knew he would of at least called them to let them know what's cracking with him. Mike picked up his phone to tried and call James again, right before Mike was dialing James' number, Pinkey was calling Ty's phone to let them know what had happened to James, and that she and Suzie were on their way to get him from the F.B.I. headquarters. Pinkey also told them that she will call back once James is with them. They knew one thing's for sure, it wasn't regular police that they were dealing with, it was the big boys. Mike and Ty started pacing back and forth trying to figure out what the fuck is going on, and what the fuck the Feds would want with James. "Yo cuz, what the fuck could be happening?" Mike said to Ty as the both of them were trying to figure out what the fuck could be going on. "I don't know cuz, but whatever it is we need to call Wesley and make sure he's okay," said Ty said as he grabbed his phone to call him. "Ya cuz do that, check on cuz, that seems like a good idea...call him," said Mike as he lit a blunt of purple. Ty wasn't getting any answer from Wesley at first. Ty had to call him at least six times before he got an answer, then finally he answered his phone. Ty was telling Wesley what had happened tonight with James. Wesley was in bed with a shorty getting head. She was still giving him head, but as soon as he hard it was the Feds his eyes got big as shit, and Wesley pulled the shorty up off of him. "What the fuck did you just say cuz? Did you say the fucking Feds cuz?" Wesley said. He jumped up out the bed and looked out through his window. "Ya nigga, that's what the fuck I just said cuz, the fucking Feds. Pinkey and Suzie went to go get cuz, so they should be on their way back soon. So it must not be that serious, because they let cuz go. I'll let you know more when I know more about cuz...One," said Ty. "That's what's cracking cuz, I'll be here by the phone C-easy cuz," said Wesley to Ty. "C-up Loc," said Ty as he got off the phone with him. As soon as Wesley got off the phone with Ty, he immediately started calling everybody else to make sure they were good, and letting them know what had happened to James. "What the fuck do you think is going on cuz?" Ty asked Mike. "Man I don't know cuzing, we just got to wait and see until cuz gets here, then we'll find out. Until then, just chill and have some fun. I'm going back to fucking some pussy, you feel me cuz?" Mike said. "Ya I feel that for sure, at least until cuz gets here, that's what's cracking," said Ty as they were walking to their rooms. The word around town was that James had got locked up by the Feds that is the word in the street. "Yo, homey, I just got word that the Feds got that Crip nigga James last night homey," said 007 to Doggy while they were chilling at the crib. "Damn yo, Tanya see what's popping with that shit, make sure that shit is for real, ma A.S.A.P., because that motherfucking nigga is worth at least 2 to 5 million flat out," Doggy said as they were sitting at the table eating. "Okay baby, I got it...I'm on it. Gangster come with me homey, I'll drive you...play shot gun," said Tanya as she was getting up from the table with Doggy and 007. "That's what's popping homey," said Baby Gangster as they were walking out the door. And just before Baby Gangster walked through the door, he turned to Doggy and grabbed two clips from him. Both of them had the same gun a Glock 40, so Doggy just gave him two of his. "Take care of Tanya homey, don't let nothing happen to her," said Doggy to Baby Gangster as he got the clips from Doggy. "Homey stop that bullshit, you should already know what it is homey, she's like a sister to me," he said. Then they continued to walk out to the car to drive to Brooklyn to see if what they had heard was true about James getting locked up by the Feds. Because they really wanted James, and they will stop at nothing to get him.

On the way to Brooklyn, Tanya was driving. They were just driving across the Brooklyn Bridge and went straight to Flatbush were the Crips be at. As soon as they got there, the first person she noticed on the block was Wesley out there chilling with his Loc's. Tanya parked and they just sat there for a minute watching them for a while. "Baby Gangster, that's James right hand man, right over there homey, you see him? We should grab his ass, he's worth about 500 thousand or more," said Tanya to Baby Gangster as they were sitting there watching him. "Let me get his ass, right here...right now homey?" Baby Gangster asked. "No homey, we didn't come out here for that nigga. That's who we're looking for right there, that is my little spy and he don't even know it," said Tanya. She called him to the car and the young Loc walked over to her thinking she really wants him. But instead she was really using him for information about what had happen to James. "What's cracking baby? I haven't seen you in a while Tanya, who's that with you?" the young Loc said looking at Baby Gangster. Tanya took his mind straight off of that. "That's my cuzing nigga, you need to be worrying about this pussy right here boy? I heard your boy James got locked up last night? Did he get out yet?" Tanya asked him. She acted like she was really concerned about him. "Yeah he should be out by now, his girl and sister went to go get him," said the young Loc as she was kissing him, baiting him in for the kill. "That's what's up, that's good news. So what's up with you? When are you going to take me out and take me shopping boo?" she asked while rubbing him on his head. "Aye, I'll call you later on around four o' clock, and let you know something then baby, alright?" he said while kissing her. "Okay baby, I'll call you later on, I know you're real busy right now, okay baby?" Tanya said as she gave him a kiss and pulled off heading back uptown. She got straight on the phone and called Doggy to let him know what was going on with James' situation, and that her and Baby Gangster was on their way back to the crib.

Meanwhile back at Mike's house, Mike and Ty where sitting by the phone waiting to hear from James, Pinkey, or Suzie to call to let them know what's going on with their man. "Cuz I should call Suzie to see what's cracking with cuz? It's taking them a long time to call us," said Ty as he walked back and forth. "Cuz take it easy, everything is going to be fine, give them a chance to call us back. They're going to call us cuz, just chill, play your three c," said Mike because Ty kept walking back and forth. Then right after Mike had said that, the phone rang. It was Pinkey calling to let them know what was going on with James; that the police wanted to lock him up. But James' lawyer wasn't going for it, because they didn't have shit on James. She also let them know that it was about a homicide that they had him for. But the good thing is that James was on his way downstairs as they speak. "That's hood, that's what's cracking, tell him to call us as soon as he get out, and y'all drive off from there," he said to Pinkey. "I sure will, he'll call you back as soon as he gets his ass in the car. Let me go wait for my baby," said Pinkey and then got off the phone. She went back into the building, and sat by Suzie. Both of them were waiting for James to come out with his lawyer. They sat there for about 20 more minutes, Pinkey was just about to see what was taking so long. And then from out of a side door comes James with his lawyer. Pinkey and Suzie was so happy to see him, they both ran up to him at the same time. Agent Anderson was walking with them and he said to James, "This is your last time if you want my help?" "Look, I told you then and I'm telling you now, I don't know nothing about no murder. So stop wasting my time, because time is money," said James. "Look James, we know what's going on with you and your boys. It's just a matter of time before we get you cuz!! We already know they do the hits and you make the money. It's just a matter of time cuz!! So keep on playing hard ball, we have a place for guys like you," said Agent Frank as James was leaving out the door. Then James' lawyer turned to Frank and said to him, "Now if your done Agent Anderson me, my client and his family would like to leave now? We all have things to do, so are you done now?" "Yeah for now, we will be in touch, know that and know it well, and it will be real soon," said Frank to James as he was walking out the door with Suzie,

Pinkey, and his lawyer. James started to wonder who put them on to them. As soon as they got outside his lawyer turned to him and said, "You better keep your nose clean." James turned to him and said, "Don't worry, I have everything under control, fuck them pigs." Then James' lawyer told him that it's not a game, and they're trying to take him down for real. So stop doing whatever he's doing for now, until things cool down. James told him yeah, but he knew that James didn't take him or the police seriously. James, Pinkey, and Suzie walked over to their car and got in, and the lawyer. Mr. White did the same as well.

As they were driving from the F.B.I. headquarters, Pinkey and Suzie were so happy to get him. They didn't know what was going on at first with James. "I'm so-so happy to see my baby, I thought they were never going to let you go boo boo. Me and Suzie was coming up that motherfucker for real baby. I love you so much James, give me a kiss baby," said Pinkey sliding her tongue down his throat and giving him a hug too. "Pinkey is definitely keeping it real with you, we were on are way up there to get you," said Suzie as she hugged and kissed him. "Damn all this love, that's what I'm talking about, just keep driving the fuck away from here. Baby let me see your phone please?" James asked Pinkey. Pinkey handed James her phone so he could call Mike and Ty. He didn't want to use his phone, because there is no telling what they did with it, he would rather be safe than sorry. Mike answered his phone thinking it's Pinkey calling him, "Yo what's cracking Pinkey with cuz?" "C.LA.A.A.T!!! Nigga, it's me you talking to, but check this shit out cuz, someone is talking to the pigs. I'll tell y'all more about it when I get there cuz," said James to Mike as they were on the phone. "Okay cuz, that's what's cracking, it's good to hear from you," said Mike. "What's cracking cuz?, I miss your crazy ass," said Ty to James while Mike was still on the phone. "Tell that nigga Ty, I hear his ugly ass in the background," said James to Mike. And then Ty laughing at them. "Man, tell James fuck him cuz, fuck you harder cuz, I still love you," said Ty to Mike to tell James. "No homo cuz, you heard him James?" asked Mike as he was laughing at Ty. "Yeah I heard him cuz, love is love," said James. "You know what it was cuz," said Ty to Mike to tell James. "I'll be there first thing in the morning, just to be on the safe side c easy cuzing," said Mike as he was getting ready to get off the phone. "That's what's good in the hood, I'll see you in the morning cuz C Love," said Mike as they were hanging up the phone.

As they were driving home, James notices a car following them, he already knew who it was. That's one of the reason why he just went straight home instead of going to Mike's house. He knew that they were going to follow him, and that would not be good. He also told Pinkey and Suzie what was going on with the car behind them. "See them bitches right there behind us? It's the Feds, what the fuck they think I'm an asshole or something?" James said as he was watching them watching him. "What the fuck is wrong with them, why don't they just leave us the fuck alone," said Suzie as she was looking at them in the rear view mirror as she was driving. "Man fuck them, let's go get something to eat, I'm hungry as shit," said James to Suzie and Pinkey. "Were do you want to go eat at baby? It's 3:40 in the morning," said Pinkey while looking at James waiting for an answer from him. "I know a spot in Brooklyn, a diner on Utica Avenue, they stay open all night," said Suzie as she was driving to the Brooklyn Bridge. "That's what's cracking, let's go," he said to them. "Okay that's what's up, I want some pancakes and eggs," said Pinkey as she lit a blunt up.

It was around 4:30 in the morning when they reached the diner in Brooklyn. As soon as they parked, the car that was following them also parked around the corner. James knew the Feds were following them the entire time that is why he went out to eat instead of going straight home. James, Pinkey, and Suzie walked into the diner and took a seat. And while they were sitting there, out of all people guess who shows up to grab something to eat? It was Doggy, 007 and Baby Gangster, they were just coming from a club that was a few blocks away from the diner. James couldn't take his eyes off of them. As soon as they walked into the diner, he just kept saying to himself, "I know that I know them from somewhere, but I just can't remember from where right now."So he just left it alone for now, but he kept his eyes on them at all times, because where James was sitting at he was right across from them watching them. Pinkey and Suzie didn't like the vibe that they got from them either. "Them niggas that just came in over there give me the creeps baby," said Pinkey to James as she was eating her food. "Shit, you just took the words right out of my mouth Pinkey," said Suzie.. "I feel the same way, but fuck them niggas, don't fuck your morning up behind them," said James as they were eating. "Yo homey, we should take that nigga right here, right now homey? And them two bitches that's with him too?" 007 said to Doggy as they sat down getting ready to order their food. "Yeah homey, that sounds real good right now, Doggy what's popping homey?" Baby Gangster asked waiting for Doggy to answer him. "Ni homey, that nigga just got out, and believe me when I tell you this shit the Feds are not far away from him right now, or they're watching him We'll get him, watch me, we always do," said Doggy as their order came to the table. "Man all we have to do is make one phone call and a van of homey's are here just like that homey. You already know what it is homey, and we got this bitch ass nigga," said Baby Gangster to Doggy, hoping Doggy would do it. "Chill out homey, he's not going nowhere, we will get his ass at the right time and the right place homey," said Doggy as they ate. "Whatever you say big homey, whatever you say, you're the big homey," said Baby Gangster to them both while looking at , James, Pinkey, and Suzie. And while James, Pinkey, and Suzie were sitting at the table, he never took his eyes off of them. But guess who walks through the door, Wesley with two of his bitches looking something like a pimp. He was so happy to see that James was alright and free. "Yo cuz, what's cracking cuz!!! You could of called me? Mike told me what it was cuz. What's up Pinkey and Suzie, what y'all been up to? Pinkey I know your ass is happy cuz is home," said Wesley trying to be funny at the same time. "Cuz I just got the fuck out like two hours ago. I was hungry so I came here, what's cracking?" James said to Wesley and piecing him. "You know me, chilling with bitches and getting paid, so how's the married life cuz?" Wesley said laughing at James like it was real funny. "I'm not married cuz, but if you're trying to say how's life with Pinkey, good my nigga," said James to Wesley's crazy ass. "Good for you cuz, more women for me cuz," said Wesley laughing at James like it was really funny. "Wesley, them ladies you have with you look hungry over there cuz?" Pinkey said as he sat his ass down at their table. "Man them bitches can wait, fuck them hoes, they'll be alright," said Wesley as he looked at them both.

James, Pinkey, Suzie, Wesley, and the two ladies that he had sitting there at the next table ordered their food and they sat there for a while. James and them were finished first, James paid for everybody's food. Pinkey and Suzie got up to leave and the two ladies that was with Wesley walked with them outside while James and Wesley were behind them talking to each other. James, Pinkey, and Suzie got into their car, Wesley and the two ladies got into his car and they drove off.

Doggy, 007, and Baby Gangster just sat there for a while, because Doggy knew the Feds weren't that far away. He knew it would be another time that he can get him. Plus, all Tanya had to do is get him to go out with her just one time, and the rest was ball game.

On the way home, Pinkey was driving, James was in the passenger seat, and Suzie was lying down in the back seat asleep. James was horny as a motherfucker, and Pinkey was a little bit herself. She was looking so good to James too. She had on a blue Gucci jean jacket with the matching short mini skirt, along with a white beater with a black Louis Vuitton bikini suit on underneath with Gucci shoes on. Her hair was in a ponytail looking good as a motherfucker. They were sitting at a red light and James reached over and kissed Pinkey on her lips. And at the same time, he put his head between Pinkey thighs and pulled Pinkey bikini bottoms over to the side. Then he started rubbing her clit and playing with her pussy. He noticed Pinkey's pussy was real wet. The light had turned green so the car behind them started blowing at them, so James just stopped and waited until they got home, because he definitely needed a shower. They pulled up in front of the apartment building and went into the parking lot. Pinkey woke Suzie up, and all three of them went upstairs. Suzie went into the guess bedroom and as soon as she got into the bed, she fell asleep. Pinkey went into the master bedroom to the bathroom and turned on the shower. Then she went back into the bedroom and took off all her clothes. She turned around and looked at James and then she walked back into the bathroom and got into the shower. James' dick got hard immediately when he saw Pinkey's fine phat ass with measurements 36D-26-42 looking dead at him. Her breast sat up firm with nice light pink nipples, and her hair was in a ponytail down to her phat ass. James got out of his clothes faster than he got in them, and went behind her and got right in. Pinkey grabbed a washrag and began to wash his back. James grabbed a washrag as well and began to wash her back too. James' dick was hard as a motherfucker. While Pinkey was washing his back, she grabbed James' dick and started playing with it while kissing him at the same time. She started rubbing his balls with the rag in one hand, and jerking the head of his dick with the other hand. James started sucking on her breast, and then he started biting on her hard nipples real softly. Then he pushed her against the shower wall and he cocked one of her legs up. And then he put his middle finger inside her pussy while his thumb was rubbing her on her clit. James pulled her by her ponytail with his other hand, she started to moan real hard from his two fingers that he had now up inside her and his thumb rubbing on her clitoris at the same time. She started biting her lip and pussy juice was running all down her inner thighs. Pinkey could not stay still, she told James, "Just don't hurt me Daddy, please take your time with me, I never did this before, James please baby." James picked Pinkey up and carried her into the bedroom, and laid her on the edge of the bed. And then he got down on his knees and started sucking and licking between her thighs while playing with her clit with his two fingers. Then he put his mouth over her pussy and started sucking and licking it. He stuck his tongue inside her pussy while rubbing her clit with his finger real, real gentle at the same time. Pinkey started to have multiply orgasms, moaning real loud. Pushing his face into her pussy and going crazy, she was also playing with her breast and rubbing her nipples. James stopped to put her in the middle of the bed, and they started doing the 69. Pinkey had one hand on his dick putting it down her throat, and with the other hand, she was playing with his balls. James went deep down between Pinkey's thighs to her ass crack, licking her asshole. Pinkey got James' dick, on the side of her face moaning, because James is tossing her salad real good. She's trying to suck his balls and jerk his dick at the same time, but she is having a hard time concentrating because what he is doing to her feels so good.

James gets up and pulls Pinkey to the edge of the bed and then he started rubbing the head of his dick on her clit. Pinkey is telling him to please take it easy with her, James takes his hand and sticks the head of his dick inside of Pinkey's mouth and she opens up her legs real wide when she felt the head of his dick go inside of her. James grabbed her by the shoulders and pushes his dick all the way in her vagina. Pinkey started moaning at the top of her lungs while grabbing James tight around his waist. He felt her legs shaking, so he knew she was about to have multiple orgasms. That's when James started to fuck her really hard. It felt really good to Pinkey, so she started to try to fuck him back. She was grabbing his ass and pushing it inside of her, she loved it. James was too, he never had pussy like this before. He turned her over on her side, cocked one of her legs up to her chess while making her hold it with her hand. At the same time, he was holding her hip and pulling her by her ponytail. And all you heard was his balls smacking Pinkey's wet pussy, and her phat ass. And then he put her on all fours, you know it as back shot. And then he wrapped his hand around her ponytail and at the same time pulling on her shoulders, banging her back out. She put her face into the pillow because she didn't want to wake Suzie up, but all it did was arch her back up more. So James got all pussy, and he was killing it. He felt his ass about to cum, so he pulled his dick out and put it right between her ass crack and let off all over her back. She was still coming, and he just laid there beside her kissing her telling her how much he loves her. Now, Pinkey was ready to go to asleep.

CHAPTER 4

RED RUM

The next morning James got up early and jumped in the shower. It was nine o'clock in the morning, when he got out the shower and got dressed. He walked over to the side of the bed where Pinkey was sleeping, and gave her a kiss right before he walked out the bedroom door. Then he stops by Suzie's room to look in on her, just to make sure she was okay. He grabbed another phone that was in the house on his way out the door. He called Wesley to let him know that he was on his way to get him so they can go to Mike's house to talk. Wesley told him he'll be waiting for him; just blow the horn when he pulls up in front.

Wesley had some time to get himself together because James was coming from downtown Brooklyn. Wesley lived in Crown Heights on Utica Avenue and Eastern Parkway. Wesley still had the two girls with him from last night. They were still knocked out cold; Wesley just got dress and left them there asleep. James pulled up out front blowing his horn; Wesley started walking out the door to the car. He got in and off they went to Mike's house so they could get down to the bottom of things. James took Eastern Parkway, going the back way. He came to downtown Brooklyn to take the Brooklyn Bridge to get to Manhattan; and then took the Holland Tunnel to get to New Jersey were Mike's house was at. James pulled up in Mike's driveway, and Mike had his two big ass pitbulls out front. James and Wesley jumped out the car walking into Mike's house. They went downstairs in Mike's basement to talk about what was going on with the Feds shit. "What's cracking cuz?" James asked. "All is well," said Mike as he peaces James. "Yeah cuz I'm okay, but we're not okay. We got a rat around us cuz, because they knew too much too fast cuz. They knew about the bodies uptown, they knew I handled all the money, and y'all body shit cuz. The only thing they didn't know is where y'all three lived. They knew where I live, because they got me at my house," he said as he lit up a blunt. "Who the fuck could be talking to them pigs?" Ty asked trying to think about it. "I'll try to find out; I have a Loccet that's a cop. She's cool, calm, and you know collective cuz. I'll have her look into it for us A.S.A.P.," said Wesley. "Yeah cuz do that for real, get on that and who ever that is, is as good as dead cuz," said Mike. "That's goes without saying Loc, but for now stay on point, you feel me? Because cuz we fucking with the big boys, I'm talking about the Feds, A.T.F., D.E.A., and N.Y.P.D., you name it I seen it cuz," said James to all of them as they were smoking weed. "I'm going to get on it right away cuz, Mike let me use one of your bike's cuz?" Wesley asked Mike so he can go see what he can find out. "Go ahead cuz, take the Ducatti and don't fuck it up either," said Mike.

Wesley walks outside, grabbed a helmet and the keys on the way out the door. He got on the bike and rode off to check on his friend to see what she can tell him. As for Mike, Ty, and James they were still in the basement trying to figure out what the fuck could be going on. "Yo cuz how the fuck do they know all our moves? We need to find out what the fuck is going on?" Mike said to them as they were in the basement chilling. "I feel you, if anyone feels you it's me, Loc flat out cuz. Let's just hope Wesley can find out something cuz," said James because he just went through the bullshit with them. "I know cuz, I know," said Mike as they were still getting high as a motherfucker. "So what the fuck we are going to do until then cuz?" Ty asked them. "We're going to do what the fuck we been doing. Get that motherfucking money Loc, a rat can't hide forever cuz," said James not listening to what his lawyer said to him.

Meanwhile back in Brooklyn, Doggy, 007, and Baby Gangster was chilling at one of their spots, doing what they do; smoking, drinking, and playing the playstation. Doggy's phone started ringing and Baby Gangster threw it to him. It was one of their little homey's outside on the block letting them know Wesley was out there in their hood seeing some bitches that live on the block. "That's what's popping homey, I'm sending someone out there right now," said Doggy to the young homey. "Homey what's popping? That's the boy James?" 007 asked ready to go get his ass. "Yeah homey, it's that nigga Wesley and his brother; grab that nigga Wesley and eat his brother," said Doggy to 007 and Baby Gangster. "Say no more homey, I'm on it Blaaaat!!!" Baby Gangster yelled as they were leaving out. "If you can't grab him, then kill him. Let them motherfucking Crabs know to stay the fuck out of our hood. Don't do it on the block unless you have to," said Doggy. "Okay homey, that's what's popping; I'll follow his ass if I have to," said Baby Gangster. "I'm coming homey; fuck that; just to make sure everything is popping off right!" 007 said as they were walking out the door. "Yo homey where's my fifty DE at?" Baby Gangster asked. "Tanya still got it; remember you told her she can use it? Take my forty homey, you good," said Doggy giving Baby Gangster his Glock 40. "Fuck it, it's just as good homey, it is what it is...let's go homey," said Baby Gangster as him and 007 were walking out the door.

They both were strapped, they weren't that far from their hood. Tanya was already on the block waiting for 007 and Baby Gangster to pull up. Wesley was out there doing what he does best, talking to some bitches; knowing he's dead wrong for being in their hood. Simeon got off the bike to go to the store and 007 and Baby Gangster were pulling up. Wesley didn't even see them coming; he had his back turned to the street. They pulled up right beside him; Baby Gangster jumped out and started running down on him trying to make Wesley get into the car. Wesley started to fight with him for the gun. Wesley grabbed it with his hand and at the same time trying to pull out his gun to shoot Baby Gangster. But Baby Gangster already let off into Wesley's chest two times. Wesley hit the floor, trying to pull his gun out only to shoot off in the air. Simeon was in the store when he heard the gunshots go off. He dropped everything he had in his hands, and came out running with his guns in both of his hands. People were running up and down the street trying to get out of the way of the gunshots. Simeon was looking to see where Wesley was, he saw Wesley on the floor with Baby Gangster about to put some more shots in him. Simeon quickly started running down on Baby Gangster busting his gun and hitting Baby Gangster in his arms and legs. Baby Gangster turned around started shooting back at Simeon while running back to the car with 007. 007 jumped out of the car real quick letting some shots off at Simeon. Simeon ran behind a car and started letting off into their car. 007 and Baby Gangster got out of there. Simeon started running down on the car as it was pulling off shooting out the back window, and then he ran to his brother's side while pulling out his phone to call for some help. Wesley's eyes started rolling in the back of his head, he started spitting up blood, and it didn't look to good for cuz.

As soon as Simeon heard the sirens coming, he grabbed his brother's gun and his gun and gave it to one of the girls that were out there with them to put up before the police came. Simeon was just sitting there holding his brother. The first one on the scene was the ambulance, and then the police came shortly after trying to find out what had happened to Wesley asking Simeon questions. Simeon told them that he was in the store and he heard gunshots, so he ran out to find his brother bleeding on the ground and that's when he called 911 for help. He made sure they understood that was all that he saw, The police already had a idea of what had happened because Simeon had a blue bandana wrapped around his left hand, and one around his neck too. Wesley had one around his risk, on the left side, and one in his left pocket. The police already knew what was going on, that they were in the wrong hood at the wrong time.

The ambulance took Wesley to the hospital, straight to the Emergency Room. The doctor's started working on Wesley immediately, but they were losing him fast. The police took Simeon into custody for questioning, because no one around the area was telling them anything. That's how it is most of the time anyway. Simeon kept telling them the same story over, and over, and over again. He got so mad at what they were doing, because he did not know what was going on with his brother. They wouldn't tell him anything, then finally they let him go so he could go and see his brother Wesley.

On the other side of Brooklyn not too far from where the shooting took place, 007 and Baby Gangster pulled up in front of the house were Doggy was at. 007 had to help Baby Gangster up to the house, because he got shot in his legs and arms. Doggy heard them out front and opened up the door to help them get inside. He knew something was wrong because Baby Gangster was shot. He had a bandana wrapped around his legs and arms to stop the bleeding. 007 and Doggy put Baby Gangster down on the couch; Baby Gangster yelled to Doggy to give him some weed so the pain can go away. Doggy told one of the little homey's in there to roll up something for him. 007 asked Baby Gangster if he was alright? Baby Gangster told him, "Yeah, yeah homey, I'm alright. It just went in and out, that's all. Give me some purple, I'll be fine homey, where's little homey with that purple?" Then Doggy asked what had happened and then 007 started telling him what happened out there on the block. Doggy wasn't really that mad at them for what they had to do. He was just fucked up about Baby Gangster getting hit more than anything else.

Back in Jersey at Mike's house, James, Ty, and Mike were just chilling out. Mike and Ty were entertaining some shorty's that Ty knew. James was just sitting back chilling and smoking some purple, high as a motherfucker. James phone started ringing; it was Pinkey calling checking up on him. James told her he was just chilling and smoking, waiting for Wesley to call to see what was going on that's all, and he'll be home as soon as he hears from him. Pinkey told him she loves him and to call her when he's on his way home. James told her he loved her back and got off the phone. As soon as he was about to put the phone down, it rang again. This time it was Simeon calling him to tell him what had happened to Wesley, and that he's at the hospital. James couldn't believe what he was hearing over the phone. James told Simeon not to worry, and they were on their way right now. James got off the phone and called Mike and Ty; they told him what was going on with Simeon and Wesley. All three of them jumped into Ty's truck and started to drive to the Holland Tunnel to get to Manhattan to get to the Brooklyn Bridge to the hospital were Wesley and Simeon were at. James, Mike, and Ty were so upset, and that was all they kept talking about on the way there. James was saying to Mike and Ty, whoever did this is going to pay with their lives. Ty and Mike were already on the phone calling up every one letting them know what had happened to Wesley. Mike and Ty already knew how James felt about Wesley. He loves them as if they were his little brothers.

As they reached the hospital, they quickly parked, jumped out and went straight into the hospital. On the way in, they called Simeon to tell him to meet them downstairs. Simeon was right there waiting for them, he took them to the Shock and Trauma Unit were Wesley was in surgery. They sat down and that's when James started asking him what had happened to him and Wesley? "He's not doing too well cuz, the nurse came out about twenty minutes ago and told me he died three times already," said Simeon with tears coming down his eyes. Ty didn't like the sound of that at all, so he stopped a nurse in the hallway. "Man fuck this shit, nurse, nurse can you tell us, what going on please with our brother?" Ty asked trying to see what going on with Wesley. "What is his name sir?" the nurse asked. "His name is Wesley Night; can you please let us know something on him please?" Mike said to the nurse. "Give me a few minutes; I'll be back, okay? I'll be able to tell you something...give me a minute," the nurse said to them as she walked off. "Simeon what the fuck happened out there tonight?" James asked Simeon as they were in the waiting room. "Cuz all I know is that I left Wesley for 2 minutes, just to go to the store cuz. Then I heard gunshots outside, so I came out the store to see a fucking Mutt standing over Wesley about to finish him off. I started going crazy cuz; gunning at them motherfucking slobs. I hit one of them, but not as bad as the Mutt got cuz," said Simeon as they were sitting in the room. "Don't feel bad, it could be a lot worst cuz, good thing you was there on point, you saved cuz life. "Hello, you asked me about your brother, Wesley Night earlier right? He's still in surgery," the nurse said to all four of them. "Nurse, how bad is he looking for real?" James asked the nurse. "Well the only thing I can say is that he is fighting for his life right now as we speak. He died 6 times, they're doing the best they can for him. Just pray for him, that's all you can do right now for him. I will let you know if I hear anything else," the nurse said and then she walked off.

James, Ty, Mike, and Simeon was just trying to figure out what Blood set did this to Wesley. Simeon told them about the white Benz that he shot up, and that's when it hit James, and he remembered the white Benz that pulled up beside him that day at the light. And he remembers seeing it again at the diner in Brooklyn, the night he came home. "Yo cuz!! I know who the fuck it is cuz," said James as he jumped up like he won something. "Who cuz? Who the fuck is it?" Ty said looking at James. "Man it's them same niggas that run that hood, them fucking Mutts that be over there, I'm sure of it cuz, I'm sure of it," he said walking back and forth. "Say no more...it's on and cracking Loc, those niggas are going to pay for that shit," said Mike as he got on the phone.

Back at the house were Doggy and 007 were at, Doggy didn't like what had happened to Baby Gangster. Plus, he didn't get to kill Wesley, because Wesley started fighting back reaching for his gun. That's when

Baby Gangster had to give it to him. Then 007 started telling Doggy, about Simeon coming out of nowhere coming to Wesley's aide. Then Baby Gangster started telling Doggy, the only thing that he was mad about was that he didn't get to take off his face. Because to Baby Gangster a murder, is not a murder until his face is off.

Doggy asked 007, "Is Tanya still out there?" "I think so, hold on I'll call her to find out for you," said 007. He called Tanya and she answered her phone, "Hey Tanya, it's 007, are you still out there on the block? And is that nigga Wesley dead?" "Yeah, I'm still out here, and the word on the street is that he is dead," said Tanya. "Okay, keep me updated if you hear anything else about him. I'll call you later on," said 007, Then Tanya asked, "Is Baby Gangster alright?" "He's fine, I'll call you back," said 007 Then they got off the phone.

Doggy and 007 started looking at Baby Gangster's gunshot wounds, they knew it wasn't that bad. All of them went in and out, but they still sent one of their little homey's to the store to get some stuff to clean out his wounds. Baby Gangster wanted to go himself, but they both told him to chill out inside the crib until the little homey got back from the store. So he just sat back and smoked some weed. While Baby Gangster was chilling, Doggy told him that it was some bitches in the back and to go do him.

As the little homey ran to the store for Baby Gangster, Doggy, and 007 went to go check on something that Doggy already had lined up to take somebody off for some money, drugs, and guns. That's what all them niggas did for a living, was rob and kidnap people. They hustles for blood money; and it started back in Jamaica, when they were kids living on the streets. Doggy's father came to American looking for a new life for him and his mother, but he got killed in a drug deal gone bad. And as for his mother, she went to jail for life for the murder of the two men that killed her husband. The only one that was left to take care of him was his godmother that he was staying with in Jamaica until she died. As for 007 parents, they died in Jamaica in front of their house, right in front of him. The gunmen were trying to get inside the house to rob and kill them all. His father and mother weren't having that, because they knew, if they got inside, they would kill them all. So his father and mother tried to jump them in front of the house, but it didn't work. 007 was only nine years old at the time, and he watched it from his front window. He had to run for his life, and take his little sister with him. They almost didn't make it out of there alive. Doggy and 007 ran into each other, about a few months after that. They never left each other's side from that day on. They came to American on their own when they were fourteen years old.

Meanwhile back at the hospital, James, Ty, Mike, and Simeon was trying to figure out what was going on with Wesley's condition. Five minutes after they were there, the nurse walked into the room where the four men were sitting at. "Hello, Wesley Night is out of surgery; you can go see him, but he is still in bad shape," the nurse told them. Then the nurse took them to where Wesley's room was. As soon as they got there, James, Mike, Ty, or Simeon didn't want to go any further. They couldn't believe it was their man inside of the room. They had so many different type of machines hooked up to him. He didn't look like the same Wesley that they knew. They just stood there for a while looking at him through the glass window. James had to be strong for Simeon, so he walked into the room. And then Simeon, Mike, and Ty went right behind him; it was enough to make a man cry. Simeon sat by James in the room. James was like a big brother to both of them. "Damn cuz!! Cuz look the fuck up right now. Look at this shit they got running in and out of cuz!!!" Simeon said with tears running down his eyes for the love of his brother. "Just chill cuz, I know it's hard, but we got to be strong, for cuz right now. Wesley I know you can hear me right now, so we are all here telling you to fight and be strong cuz. We know you're going to make it through this. Ty, Mike, and Simeon are all here with me, we love you cuz," said James as tears ran down his face. "What's cracking cuz? We got your back and don't you ever forget that too cuz," said Mike to Wesley hoping he would wake up. "Cuz just hang in there keep fighting don't give up, we love you, we're out here for you cuz. Keep your head up high to the blue sky Loc," said Ty as he was talking to Wesley. All Wesley could do is look and move his eyes. He couldn't talk or move at all. This shit would make the biggest gangster cry to see your man fucked up like that. James, Mike, Ty, and Simeon sat there and called everybody to see if any one heard anything about them niggas whereabouts. James and Simeon sat right at Wesley's side talking to him, just telling him don't worry about nothing. Just for him to get better, that's all. Pinkey and Suzie came in shortly after and it was the worst thing that they had ever seen. Suzie ran straight over to Wesley holding his hand and crying. Pinkey was on the other side, sitting by James also crying. The nurse came in the room to give Wesley some pain medication though his IV to stop the pain. Suzie and Pinkey were trying to be strong, but they couldn't help but cry. James told Pinkey and Suzie to stay and be strong for Wesley because they were about to hit the streets. So they can try and find out where the Bloods was and who did this to Wesley. James also told Pinkey to call him if anything goes wrong with Wesley. Pinkey and Suzie let them know that they had their backs, so they can go on and do what they got to do. All they ask them to do is to call them time to time to let them know that they are okay.

The four of them left out the hospital to handle their business. They jumped back into Ty's truck and got out of there on a warpath. It was time for somebody to pay. The main one that James wanted was the one who gave the order to hit Wesley. As they were on their way to their hood, Mike's phone started ringing. "Yo what's cracking cuz, talk to me? Tell me something hood cuz?" Mike said as they were driving off from the hospital. "Yo cuz, word on the street is them Jamaica Bloods niggas did it cuz!! Them niggas from the 90s. One of them niggas name is Doggy, he's the OG of that set for the Mutts. He's the one that gave the word to that Mutt nigga, Baby Gangster to hit up cuz," said Jay to Mike as he was sitting on the block chilling. "Good looking...keep your ears to the street for me cuz, we'll get at you in a minute, one," said Mike to Jay. "Yo James!!! Jay just put me onto the nigga in the white Benz; his name is Doggy, he ran the Mutts in the 90s cuz. We got to get at them Mutts," said Mike to James as they were driving to the hood. "I'm going to kill them slob!!! All of them Mutts. Whet! He fuel; they tin', we are some bitches cuz? Call up everybody now; and tell them to meet us around the way. We're going to motherfucking war with them Mutts!!!" James said mad as a motherfucker ready to kill shit. "They tried to kill my little Loc!!! I want them slob heads cuz!!! Them bitches going to die, all of them!!!" James said. James was so upset that he almost crashed into incoming traffic on the way to the hood. Ty told James to take it easy and that they are going to get them. James was so full of fire; you can see it in his eyes. Then Ty said, "Yo cuz, say no more you already know what it is was cuz, were going to get them motherfuckers!!!"

As soon as they reached the hood, James pulled over and parked. All four of them jumped out and Simeon told James he's going to pick up some of his Loc's, and he'll be right back. He said to give him fifteen minutes, and for them not to go without him. So James let Simeon know that they would be right there waiting for him and for him to just hurry up because them niggas is going to pay for this shit.

On the other side of Brooklyn, 007, and Doggy, took Baby Gangster home. He took two ruby's with him so he could freak them out at his place. He told Doggy and 007 he'll be back later. Doggy and 007 left him, and went back to their house to chill. Baby Gangster was supposed to meet them back at the house in a few hours. Some time had gone pass and Doggy said to 007 as they were sitting in the house, "Yo homey what's up with Baby Gangster? He should've called us by now?" "Yeah, yeah, homey I'm going to give him a call and see what is taking him so long homey," said 007 as he picked up his phone to call Baby Gangster. As soon as Baby Gangster got the phone, 007 knew what it was; he was still fucking the two ruby's he had with him, so 007 asked him how long is he going to be. Baby Gangster told him not that long; he was almost done and give him two more hours. 007 told him alright and that they were just checking up on him. Just for him to call when he's on his way. Baby Gangster told him it would soon, and he'll call as soon as he was done and he'll be on his way. He also asked 007 what was popping with Tanya? 007

let him know she had just walked in though the door and asked did he want to talk to her? Baby Gangster told him he'll see her when he gets there. Baby Gangster got off the phone, and went right back to doing what he was doing. He had one ruby sitting on his dick riding him, and the other one sitting on his face. The one sitting on his face was facing the one that was riding his dick. They were kissing each other and playing with each other's breast. He was doing him, and the pain was not on his mind at all.

Back on the other side of Brooklyn, James, Ty, Mike, Simeon, and the rest of the Loc's was all there. James was letting them know how he felt, and what he wanted done. Jay and Trigger was there, they both were under James and as for Mike, you can see the fire in his eyes. It was not a game tonight, somebody got to die. They closed down all their shops that they had. Everyone was out looking for Doggy, 007, and Baby Gangster. It's not about money right now; it's about C Love for cuz. Everyone was out looking for them; it was like one hundred Loc's out there ready to kill for the love of Crip, their way of life. Left til death Chitty, Chitty, Bang, Bang nothing but a Crip thing.

Meanwhile back at the hospital, Pinkey and Suzie are right by Wesley's side while he's fighting for his life. He still is in bad shape, and he lost a lot of blood. One of his lungs had collapsed while he was in surgery. Pinkey and Suzie just prayed for him hoping he'll get better.

The nurse came back into the room to let them know the rest is up to him rather he lives or dies, they did all they could do for him. All they can do now is sit back and wait.

Now the doctor came in to talk to them. "Hello ladies, right now as I see it, it looks like he's a very lucky young man. He died six times, you know that right? I never seen that happened before in my life. Someone who dies six times and lives. He's a very strong young man, so he should be fine. Just let him get his rest, because he needs it," the doctor said to them as he was looking at Wesley "Thank God he's going to be fine Suzie, I'm going to call your brother to see what's going on," said Pinkey as she grabbed her phone to call James. "Wesley is not out of hot water yet girl, let just hope he'll be okay, and if I know my brother like I do, he's out looking for them niggas that did this to Wesley girl, right now as we speak. So if I was you, I would just wait a while and give him some time to call you, he'll call," said Suzie to Pinkey just as she was getting ready to call James. "You know what, I'm going to take your advice, you know him better than me, but right now I'm hungry girl. You want something to eat?" Pinkey asked Suzie, putting her phone back down. "Yeah I'm hungry than a motherfucker, get me a burger or something, whatever you get will be fine," said Suzie as she left out the room walking to the elevator. As soon as the elevator door opened up, there were two detectives getting off while she was getting on. She just knew they were going to Wesley's room, she could just feel it. She got downstairs to the hospital lobby and started walking to the front to go outside to a pizza spot across the street.

Back upstairs, the detectives walked in Wesley's room trying to wake him up. Suzie came from out of the bathroom flipping out on them as if they were crazy or something. The nurse and doctor's came from all over, telling the two detectives they needed to leave now and come back another day. So they waited outside of Wesley's room, trying to talk to the doctor's for about 20 minutes. By this time, Pinkey was coming back with the pizza walking right into Suzie, still flipping on the two detectives. They told Pinkey to get her friend before they lock her up for disorderly conduct. Suzie told them, "Disorderly conduct my ass!!!" The two detectives left and told the doctor they will be back another day.

Meanwhile James, Mike, Ty, Simeon, and the rest of the Crips, was looking for the Bloods in the hood. No one was outside at first, so they pulled up by the store on the corner. One of 007 little homey's was walking out to the store. He didn't even see it coming. Spade and Jay was in a van, they pulled upright beside the little homey. Spade and Jay jumped out the van, grabbed his ass and threw him into the van with them and drove off. Ty didn't even ask him anything yet; Ty took out a hunting knife, and grabbed his right hand. He made him give him his pinky finger, and Ty cut it straight off. The young homey started yelling like a bitch, and what made it worse, Ty threw salt on the nub of his pinky. The little homey already knew what they had came for. So he started telling them everything he knew. The only thing he knew was where Baby Gangster lived at. He told them Baby Gangster lived in Crown Heights in Brooklyn on Carroll Street between Albany and Kingston, the corner building on the left hand side. He didn't know what apartment he lived in because he never went upstairs. But he knew what kind of car he drives, it is a red BMW; he just got it.

They pulled over in a alley on the way to Baby Gangster's house. Ty took the young homey out and slit his throat, and then watched him bleed to death. Ty jumped back in the car with James and Mike; they drove off continuing to Baby Gangster's house. As soon as they hit Baby Gangster's block Carroll Street, they saw the red BMW on the corner of Albany and

Carroll. James, Mike, and Ty, pulled up in front of the building and parked. James called Spade on the phone telling Spade to hit that nigga when he comes out of the building. Simeon got out of the truck to hit up Baby Gangster himself. Simeon goes into the building across the street. They just sat there and waited until they saw him come out of his building. Spade jumped out the van looking like a bum, drinking on some 20/20 Mad Dog, but the bottle had juice in it instead of liquor.

Thirty minutes went by, Simeon is across the street; he can see somebody coming out of the building with two girls with him, he knew it was Baby Gangster, because he had on red rags, his flag color, all over him. The two girls that were with him was Bloods too. Simeon just waited until he was out the building and close to his car. Baby Gangster eyes was on the bum in front of his car, but it really was Spade playing like a bum. Baby Gangster put his hand on his gun, looking at Spade telling him to move from his car. Spade was acting like he was drunk as shit. One of the girls walked up to him and started telling him to move and started to kick him. Simeon saw the window of opportunity and started running across the street. By the time Baby Gangster knew what was going on, it was too late. He turned right around into Simeon's bullet. Baby Gangster brains hit the girl that was walking with him, right in her mouth and face. The other girl that was with Baby Gangster was trying to pull out, but Spade pushed her brains out on the sidewalk and she hit the ground like a brick. The first girl started screaming and Simeon put the gun in her mouth and told her to shut the fuck up. Then Simeon took her ass to the van.

Ty jumped out of the truck with James, and Mike. He ran across the street to the van, jumped in with the rest of them, and pulled off. The girl was so fucked up in the head from what she had just seen. Her homey had just died right in front of her; she couldn't even get herself together. Ty started to ask her where the fuck, do Doggy and 007 live at. She started telling them everything she knew and they took her for collateral.

CHAPTER 5

BLOOD IN BLOOD OUT BANG LEFT TIL' DEATH

Back up in the Bronx, Doggy, 007, and Tanya was wondering what was taking Baby Gangster so long. Doggy tried to call him like five times already, but he got no answer. So he told Tanya to go check on him to see if he's okay, but Doggy thinking more like he probably fell asleep from the pain from the gunshots. Plus, he was fucking too, because he had two ruby's with him when he left out. Doggy told her to take Sam with her, so she did. Then they left out to go to Baby Gangster's house. Tanya told Doggy she'll call as soon as she knew something. As soon as Tanya pulled upon the block, she saw police everywhere. As she was driving up closer, and closer to Baby Gangster's building, she could now see what was going on. She saw the police by Baby Gangster's car with tape all over it and in front of his building too. So she stopped the car to get a closer look, and to see who it was on the ground in front of the building. She couldn't believe her eyes, at what she saw. Baby Gangster was dead on the ground, and one of the young ruby's was dead on the corner. Tanya got on the phone, and called up Doggy immediately to let him know what she just saw with her own eyes. As soon as Doggy heard her say, "Baby Gangster is dead homey, he's dead!!!" Doggy threw the phone across the room. 007 jumped up and asked him what was wrong. Doggy told 007 what was going on. 007 started going mad and breaking up everything in his path. They couldn't believe what was going on. Tanya left from Baby Gangster's house to go get her girl Shitty. When them two get together watch out, somebody is going to die tonight.

James, Mike, Ty, Simeon, and the rest of the Loc's, pulled up in front of the house where Doggy and the rest of the Bloods are suppose to be at. The first thing James saw is the white Benz 500, so now he knew that he was at the right house. It was four more cars there, five all together. As they were sitting there, two more cars pulled up in the driveway. As they were sitting there getting ready to run up in the house. Guess who pulls up in front? Tanya with Sam and Shitty. James eyes got big as shit, because all this time this bitch was a Blood, and trying to get him set up the whole time. "That was a hit on me it was me all this time, they wanted not Wesley," he thought to himself. Then James' eyes turned to fire, and they immediately got out their cars, van, and trucks. Some of the Loc's ran around back, and some went on the side of the house by the window. James and Simeon were out front, and Mike and Ty was around back. Doggy was in there walking back and forth, mad as a motherfucker, and 007 was too. Mike was at the power box out back getting ready to turn the lights off. Mike was about to cut the wires, but he had to wait until James and Simeon take out the men in the two cars out front. James and Simeon both had silencers on their guns, they had H&K MP5 with drums on them.

James ran down on one car, they didn't even see him coming. All you saw was blood and brains hit the window. Simeon ran down on the other car at the same time, and the only thing that went wrong was that the driver's head hit the horn. So Doggy looked out the window to see what was going on. As soon as he looked out the window the lights went out in the house, and everybody immediately grabbed for their guns. The Loc's took the house by surprise, James and Simeon was kicking down the front door. Mike and Ty were around back gunning out the back door and windows. X-Man and Trigger was on the side with Spade and Jay and they were shooting all the Bloods in the living room. Some of Bloods shot back and X-Man was the first one to get hit. He got hit in the chest and arm, but he had a vest on and that's what saved him. Trigger pulled X-Man to the side of the house and took his gun from him. Doggy told some of his homey's to run outside to see what the fuck is popping. Some of them ran for the back door and some of them ran to the side windows. The ones that ran for the back door walked right into Top Gun, he was on the roof with a street sweeper giving it to them and shooting them in their necks as if they were tree branches cracking in half. One of them tried to bus a shot off at Top Gun, but as soon as he turned around he turned into a 12-gage slug right in his chest. Blowing his back out, killing him and dropping him dead to the ground. White Mike came running from the back with an AK 47, and some more Bloods was trying to run out the back door of the house. White Mike was letting off at them as soon as they were coming out the house splitting them in half like twig. Ty tried to run up inside the house with two soldiers with him. They ran though the back door, running down the long hallway. Tanya and Shitty was in the kitchen hiding by the wall by the door that goes out to the long hallway right where Ty and the two Loc's were at. Shitty gets down low, Tanya hit's them up high, and they came out banging on them. Tanya and Shitty hit the two Loc's in the head and landing body shots. Tanya and Shitty both tried to hit up Ty, but he gets out of there. Tanya was yelling at Ty as he was running out the door, "Pussy hole Fee dead!!! Come on Crab bring it nigga!!!" And Shitty right beside her banging side by side. Mike sees Ty running out with a hell storm of bullets behind him. Ty got hit in the legs and falls on the back porch. Mike runs up to help Ty with one hand pulling him off the back porch to the side of the house and with the other hand busting at Tanya and Shitty. Back around front James, Simeon, and some of the Loc's are trying to get in through the door. James and Simeon both have a H&K MP5, and the rest of the Loc's have handguns. Doggy picked up his M16 and started shooting through the wall, and some of the Loc's got hit. Simeon and James are trying to get out of the way of Doggy's gunshots. James ran over to Simeon and throws him to the ground, but at the same time he gets hit by 007 with two Glock 9mm. James got hit in the back of his head once, and in his back. He hits the ground, and as he's falling he lets off, but does not hit anyone. 007 sees that James is down and runs out on him to finish him off. Top Gun is on the roof and also sees James down on the ground, but he is out of shots. So he throws the street sweeper down to the ground. However, 007 is right up on James, so Top Gun grabs his two Glock 40 and runs to the edge of the roof and jumps off banging at 007 at the same time. Top Gun hits 007 in the head two times and half of his skull looked like it came off. 007 hits the ground like a brick. Doggy sees his man down, and starts shooting at Top Gun all in his legs.

By this time, Simeon is up and gunning like a mad man trying to run down on Doggy. Simeon grazed Doggy in the head, and hit him in his shoulder. Kevin comes out of nowhere running from the side of the house giving them cover to get James out of there. Simeon grabs James, and Kevin grabs Top Gun. Then one of the other Loc's pulled up with the van and Simeon and Kevin got both of them in.

Ty and Mike were still around back with these two crazy bitches trying to gun them down. The van pulled up around back and a man opened up the vans side door gunning into the back of the house. Simeon jumped out and helped Mike with Ty into the van. At this time, you could hear the police sirens, so they get out of there.

Mad Max runs outside behind the van shooting at it, and someone in the passenger side started shooting back. Mad Max runs around front to see that 007 is dead on the ground. But one of the Loc's was still alive crawling. Shitty and Tanya were coming out front with Doggy holding him. Shitty saw the Loc crawling on the floor. She turned to him and put her foot on his back and put two shots in the back of his head, and he dropped dead.

Mad Max runs to the car where some of his dead homey's are. He pushes the driver out of the driver's seat and then started the car up. Tanya and Shitty helped Doggy to the car. Doggy didn't want to leave 007, but he knew he was dead. They jumped in the car with Mad Max and drove off. Bodies were everywhere, two more homey's got away with them. They jumped into the car that was next to them and got out of there. Police was everywhere they tried to hit the highway, but it was backed up for miles. Simeon got on the phone immediately and called up a doctor they all know. Kevin was putting pressure on the back of James' head with his rag to stop the bleeding. They got on the highway just in time before the highway got jammed up. The doctor told Kevin to come on through. They got to the doctor's house in ten minutes once they got off the highway. Simeon carried James inside and Mike carried Ty. Kevin and the rest of the Loc's also came inside. The doctor immediately told Simeon and Mike to take them downstairs to the basement. The doctor had his basement set up like a shock trauma unit. It's a spot where gangster's go when they can't go to the hospital because they would go to jail. The doctor would fix them up for some money. The doctor started telling his nurse what to get ready, and then he started telling Simeon, it looked like he might not make it. That is when Mike put his gun to the doctor's head and told him, "If he don't make it, you don't make it either, you fucking hear me?" The doctor looked at Mike with that big ass gun at his head and told him, "Don't worry he'll be fine." The doctor and one of his nurses started working on James, and the other nurse was working on Ty's legs. All Simeon could think about was, "What the fuck am I going to tell Pinkey and Suzie?" The doctor was doing all he could for James, one because he knew if he died, he would die too. And that was not what he had in mind.

Tanya, Shitty and the rest of the homey's kept driving. Tanya was driving and she got on the highway to go to Doggy's house in Long Island. At first they didn't really know how bad that Doggy was hit, until Shitty cleaned off the blood from his head. That's when she realized that the bullet had just grazed him in the head. And just to be on the safe side, Tanya still called a doctor they knew to meet them at Doggy's house in Long Island to check him out. The doctor told her he'll be there in 30 minutes or less. Tanya picked up the phone one more time to call Pit to let him know what was going on. While she was talking to Pit telling him what had happened at the house in the Bronx, he started zapping out as soon as she told him what happened to 007. Then he was ready to kill all Crips in the city. Tanya told him to meet her at Doggy's house in Long Island and to call Jimmy to see if he knew what is going on. Pit told her he is going to call him now, and he's going to pick him up right now as they speak, and he'll meet her out there A.S.A.P. Shitty just kept saying how she's going to kill them over, and over, and over again. That was all she had on her mind, was getting even with the Crips for what they had done. Shitty was a gangster, a badass one at that. She was Jamaican and American and she had honey brown skin. She was 5'9", 140lbs with measurements of 36DD-26-44 phat to death with long black curly hair that was always put into two ponytails. She was a true stallion that would kill you quick.

Tanya finally reach their exits, so she turned to get off of the highway. As soon as they hit the main street to Doggy's house, she called the doctor to see how far he was. The doctor told her that he was about 5 minutes away from the house. And that she should see him pulling up any minute now. Tanya got off the phone and continued to drive to the house, they're only about 3 blocks away. She's in the back seat with Doggy still putting pressure on his head to stop the bleeding. Tanya reached the block, and just as she goes to pull up in the driveway to park, she noticed the doctor's car pulling up behind her. So she immediately parked the car. Then Tanya told Shitty and Sam to help Doggy get out the car while she runs to open the door, so they can hurry up and get him inside the house. Sam and some of the little homey's were carrying Doggy into the house, and Shitty and the doctor was right behind them. They put Doggy on the couch in the living room and the doctor immediately started to get to work on him. The doctor told them it was a good thing they put pressure to his head to stop the bleeding. Then he took a look at Doggy's arm, he noticed that it wasn't too bad. Then he looked at the one in his shoulder too and it was okay. So the doctor started to stitch him up. "He'll be fine, but he's going to need to rest for a few days," said the doctor. Then doctor gave Tanya a prescription of medication for Doggy for the pain. Tanya grabbed the prescription and her and Shitty headed out the house to go to the drugstore to get the medication for Doggy. On their way to the drugstore, Tanya and Shitty just sat there for a while, they couldn't believe what had just happened to them. They had fire in their eyes, it was not a game. "I can't believe Baby Gangster, 007, and my two ruby's are all dead homey. The Crabs are going to pay for that shit!!! We're going to lay low for a while and then we're going to come out and go full blast at them bitches!!!" Tanya said to Shitty as they were driving to the pharmacy. "Homey all you got to do is say the word, and it's done. I only met that nigga Baby Gangster one time, but he was my homey and that's all that matters to me. There's the drugstore, it's coming up on your right side," Shitty told Tanya as they were driving with tears running down their eyes.

Tanya made a right turn into the supermarket, the pharmacy was inside so they parked in the parking lot. They both got out, and started walking to the supermarket doors. While they were walking in, some nigga was trying to holla at them. Tanya and Shitty didn't even look at the motherfucker, they just went into the back of the supermarket straight to the pharmacy part to get the prescription filled. Usually they would take the niggas number just to see what they' re working with and get their ass set the fuck up to get robbed, and more likely killed too. It looks like it's those niggas lucky night tonight. One thing's for sure Tanya and Shitty were some badass bitches. They could be in the Smooth Magazine easily. Tanya was Jamaican and Indian, brown skin with light brown eyes, She was 5'7" with the measurements 36D-27-44, and short black curly hair.

As for Shitty she has a Jamaican background, but as born in American, She had honey brown skin with honey brown eyes, 5'9" inches tall with measurements 36DD-26-44, long black curly hair that she always kept in two ponytails. Both of them were definitely stallions from head to toe.

They got the prescription and off they were back to Doggy's house. They got to the house in 10 minutes. Tanya went into the kitchen to get Doggy a glass of water so he can take his medication and rest. Shitty went into the living room and sat down on the couch beside Doggy. She grabbed the TV remote control and turned on the TV to the six o'clock news. And guess who faces were all over the TV? 007, Doggy, Baby Gangster, and the rest of the homey's that died out there.

Back at the hospital, Pinkey and Suzie were still chilling with Wesley. Pinkey started to get worried about James, because she knows he would of called by now. So she decided to call his phone to see what was going on with him. She got no answer the first time she called. Suzie was trying to tell her not to worry because everything is going to be fine. Then Suzie told her to try again, but this time leave a message for him to call back. Just as soon as she was about to call back her phone started ringing, she answered it. "Hello!! Baby, why you didn't answer your fucking phone? You had me worried like shit!!" Pinkey said thinking she was talking to James. "Pinkey, this is Simeon not James, I don't even know, how to tell you this," said Simeon to Pinkey trying to get his words out. "Tell me Simeon, what the fuck is going on, with James?" Pinkey said trying to get herself together for what Simeon had to tell her. "James got shot up badly tonight, he's okay...cuz is strong. We're at a doctor's house that we know. He just got out of surgery, he's sleeping right now. I didn't want to call you yet, until I knew what was going on with him first," said Simeon. As he was talking, she was crying over the phone. "Simeon!! What do you mean he just got out of surgery? Simeon, what the fuck is going on? Where are y'all at Simeon? I'm on my way now," said Pinkey. Pinkey felt her heart hit her stomach. "Trigger on his way as we speak, he should be there any minute now. I'm so sorry Pinkey, I'm sorry I tried everything," said Simeon while crying to her over the phone. Pinkey knew she had to say something to calm him down. "Simeon please calm down, it's not your fault. I know you did everything you could. How bad is he Simeon?" Pinkey asked him. "Cuz got hit in the back of his head," said Simeon. By this time Pinkey had the phone on speaker so Suzie can hear what was going on. "What the fuck, no this can't be happening, fuck no!!!" Suzie said falling to her knees. Pinkey was trying to be strong for them, she ran to Suzie to help her up. Then she said, "I'll see you when I get there Simeon bye." Pinkey got off the phone and turned to Suzie and they both just started crying. It was so much going on they just couldn't take anymore. As they were sitting there crying, Trigger came walking through Wesley's room door with six Loc's. Three of them stayed with Suzie because she decided to stay with Wesley. She told Pinkey just to go, and let her know what was going on with her brother. And to tell him she loves him very much. Pinkey grabbed her jacket and went over to Wesley and gives him a kiss on his cheek. Then she walked over to Suzie and gives her a hug and told her she'll call her as soon as she gets there. Pinkey, Trigger, and three of the Loc's walked out of the room to go to the elevator and went to the lobby to go to the parking lot to Trigger's car. Trigger was driving a midnight blue Benz CL600, he pressed the remote control to open up the car door to let her in his car. She got into the passenger side, then Trigger got into the car and they drove off to the doctor's house where James was. On the way to the doctor's house Pinkey started to ask Trigger what had happened. Trigger told her, "All I can say right now is that it was an all out war. And don't worry because James will be fine." Then Pinkey started talking to him like a mother, more than his cuz girlfriend. "Trigger, you all need to be careful out on the streets, because I don't want to see nothing happened to y'all," said Pinkey. Trigger definitely liked what she was saying because it showed that she didn't just care about James, she cared about all of them, and this was the first time he had met Pinkey. He heard a lot about her, and he liked both what he saw and heard. It was no doubt in his mind that she was not the one for James as his wife. He said to himself, "James got a good one." He was definitely happy because it was no fake ass bitch that he usually sees James with.

As soon as they got there Pinkey jumped out of the car and ran to the door of the house. Simeon was at the door to let her in. The second person she saw was Ty wrapped up on the couch. He was popping pills to stop the pain. Pinkey stopped to talk to him for about 2 minutes and then she asked where was her baby at. Simeon took her downstairs to the basement. The first thing she saw was the nurse fixing the IV bag, so the fluid could flow through James' arm and through his body. All Pinkey could do was put her hand over her mouth and walk over to him. He looked just as bad as Wesley, if not worse. She started shaking her head. Pinkey took a seat beside him and then she got on the phone to call Suzie to let her know that she had got there. Pinkey started telling Suzie James' condition, that it was just as bad as Wesley's. Suzie told her she'll be there in a few hours that she's going to hang out with Wesley for a little bit longer. Pinkey told her okay, and got off the phone. As soon as she got off the phone, James woke up trying to talk to her. "Baby!!! Are you okay boo? Suzie said to tell you she loves you baby," said Pinkey to James with tears running down her eyes. "I---m O----k I l-o--v--e y-o--u," said James. He was struggling to talk to her so Pinkey stopped him in his words and said, "Okay boo, you don't have to talk, get your rest, we know you love us, and Wesley's okay and doing fine too, he's going to make it." All Pinkey could do was rub James' hand and sit by his side while trying to be strong for him. She definitely let him know she was not going anywhere. She's going to be right there. X-Man came over to her side and told her not to cry, everything will be okay, and that they have one of the best doctor's in N.Y. City. Pinkey turned to the nurse and asked her, "How long is he going to be like this?" "He lost a lot of blood, and being that it's a head shot it will be at least two months of bed rest, and then in two weeks he should be coming around," said the nurse.

Mike was on his way downstairs to where Pinkey was at with James. The first thing Pinkey asked Mike was what happened yesterday night? That is when Mike started telling her about the war going on between them and the Bloods. How it started back in the day, the beef was dead, but out of nowhere they tried to kill Wesley so they went to war with the Bloods, and James got shot by one of them. Trigger jumped right into the conversation telling her don't worry that the fucking Mutts is going to pay for what they've done to him and Wesley for sure or his name is not Trigger. One thing she knew for sure, they loved James and she loves them for that.

Meanwhile back at the Bronx the same night that the shooting took place, the police rolled up securing the scene. Homicide was the second ones on the scene, Det. John and Stg. Green. As soon as they got there they called the Feds and Agent Anderson was the next one on the scene. They had a helicopter over the crime scene. They all knew it was one of Doggy's houses. They couldn't believe all the dead bodies. They were everywhere as they were walking through, they knew it was a Crip and Blood war. They were also checking to see if anyone was still alive as well. However, they expected everyone that was there to be dead, but one of the police yelled out, "I have one alive!!! Over here!!!" Agent Anderson and Det. John ran over to see who he was talking about, it was 007. The police officer said he got a pulse from him. Agent Anderson immediately called for an ambulance to take 007 to the hospital. The ambulance got there in about 10 minutes and they took him to a school football field where a helicopter was waiting to take him to the hospital because he wouldn't of made it if he had went in the ambulance.

As soon as they got him to the hospital, they quickly got him out of the helicopter and rushed him straight to shock trauma. The doctor's immediately started doing surgery on him. 007 condition was critical, he was truly fighting for his life. Agent Anderson told one of the agents to go with him to the hospital for security reasons.

While they were locking down the crime scene looking for evidence. CSI and crime lab were out there taking all blood samples on the scene. They were trying to hurry up because it was about to rain really bad, and the rain would damage any fingerprints or blood that's at the crime scene.

So they had to work fast. The first thing Agent Anderson did was put out a APB, on the Bloods and the Crips. He knew which two sets were beefing, the J.B.G. for the Bloods, which means Jamaican, Blood, and Gangsters. Not all of them were Jamaican, but the ones that ran it was Jamaican. As for the Crips B.J.C.C., which means Black Jack Cartel Crips, both of these gangs were dangerous and he wanted them off the street for good before some more innocent people get killed. One thing's for sure, Agent Anderson wasn't going to get any sleep until they were all off the streets of N.Y.C. They had so many bodies to deal with, at least 20 body bags. It was like a little war in the Bronx, all Agent Anderson could say is thank God that no one got hurt besides these gang bangers. He felt if this is the life they chose...so be it. Then this is what they'll get out of life. He just didn't like seeing the young ones dying because they didn't know any better.

People were starting to come around trying to see what was going on, so the police had to put up yellow tape to keep the people back from the crime scene. One young lady ran through the tape crying because she knew it was her brother dead on the ground. One of the police tried to grab her up off of her brother. "Get the fuck off of me, it's my brother!" the lady yelled at the officer. That's when Agent Thomas stepped in and told the police officer to just leave her alone. She sat there for about ten minutes holding her brother crying. Then Agent Thomas grabbed her hand, and gently pulled her up, so homicide could do their job. He sat her down in a police car and asked her what was her name. She told him her name was Christy and that was her brother that is dead over there on the ground. One thing he noticed about the young lady was that she was dressed in all red. One was she a gang banger, or two, was she just representing for her brother. It was one or the other, so he sat down with her and talked to her trying to see what she knew, but she was not telling him anything at all. "I heard gunshots, that's it. And I was not running to see who was doing the shooting. The first time I saw anything was when the police came. I just know what my brother had on when he left out the house this morning, so when I saw him laying on the ground I knew it was him," said Christy. "I am so sorry for the loss of your brother," said Agent Thomas "and if there's anything else I can do for you, feel free to call me at this number." Then he gave her one of his business cards. "Call me anytime if you need to talk or if you hear anything else," said Agent Thomas. She took the card, so he walked away and left her with officers to help her out.

Agent Anderson made sure to keep it quiet about 007 being still alive. Just to be on the safe side, he got him out of there just before the news reporters got there. Channel 2 got there first, and then came Fox 5 News, and last be not least Channel 11. He also made sure he told all the police that was out there to kept it quiet. One thing's for sure, Doggy, James, Mike, Tanya, Shitty, and Ty's faces were number one on the F.B.I.'s top ten list. Most of the dead bodies had no faces at all. They would have to be finger printed at the morgue.

Agent Anderson sat out there for one more hour, and then he made his way back to headquarters to find out what was going on with the bodies that they brought back, and the blood samples that the CSI lab took. Homicide stayed out there knocking on everybody's door. Every last door they knocked on, no one saw anything. Well at least that is what they were telling the police. As soon as Agent Anderson got back the first thing he did was call A.T.F., because he found some 223-assault rifle shells on the ground.

One thing Agent Anderson felt in his bones for sure was that it was going to be a lot more bodies in the city. Therefore, they would have to pay very close attention to all the places where the Crips and Bloods be at. Agent Anderson got a cup of coffee, he likes it black, no sugar no cream. He sat in his office taking out all of the Crips pictures starting with James making a pyramid with their picture from OG down to forcer. He had all of them just about starting from James, White Mike, Ty, Wesley, Kevin, Simeon, Top Gun, Spade, Jay, X-man, and Trigger. He did the same for the Bloods starting from Doggy on down. The same way like he did the Crips. Doggy, 007, Jimmy, Baby Gangster, Chin, Sam, Mad Max, Pit, Tommy Gun, Tanya, and Shitty. All he did was look at them over and over again. He was now looking at two pyramids of two different organizations that was out to kill each other so he had to put a stop to their madness. He was not going to let it keep happening in his city.

He called homicide to see how everything was going on out there. They were just getting ready to leave from out there, and go all around the Crips and Bloods hoods to see what they can find out because they knew somebody knew something. They just wasn't saying anything that's all. Anderson told them he was at headquarters putting together the puzzle. He'll call them if he comes up with anything.

CHAPTER 6

PAY BACK

Back at Doggy's house in Long Island, Tanya, Shitty, and the rest of the Bloods are starting to get tired of sitting in the house. Some weeks passed by and they were starting to get restless by just sitting in the house all day and night. So they started to put a plan together to get even with the Crips for what they done to 007, Baby Gangster, and the rest of them. "Look fuck this shit, tomorrow were getting out of here and killing some of them bitches. I'm tired of just sitting around waiting! Fuck them pigs!!!" Tanya said mad as hell talking to everybody. "Look, I definitely feel you homey, but you and I know that them pigs is still looking for us on the street," said Pit to Tanya trying to calm her down. "Yo homey, all of us been on the news, on nearly every damn news channel there is. They had Doggy's picture on TV all week long, not to mention some of our face's as well too homey. They're out to do a full investigation, and we're not just talking about N.Y.P.D., we're also talking about the F.B.I., D.E.A., and the A.T.F., homey some big boy shit," Jimmy said to all of them in the room at the table. That's when Tommy Gun jumped up and said to everybody, "Homey!!! I don't give a flying fuck, Bloods in Bloods out homey. It's whatever with me homey!!!" Shitty jumped up right behind Tommy Gun and said, "Bitch just say the word homey, you already know what it is. A bitch keep it popping for her homey." Shitty was mad as a motherfucker, and that is when Tanya jumped up and said to everybody, "As far as we know, the police is looking for all of us and the Crips as well, so be it. I'm ready to get it on and popping homey." That's when Shitty jumped up and said to all of them, "Man fuck them pigs!!! And the Crabs!! They can all get it homey!!! Baby I'm with you, what's popping homey." Then Shitty was looking at Tanya waiting for a answer from her. "Man you can't have all the fun homey, I'm coming fuck that shit. What it is homey, I'm with you," Tommy Gun said to Shitty and Tanya. Tanya turned to him and said, "That's what's popping homey go on your own. Me and Shitty riding together, let's get it on and popping. Blaaat!! Blaaaaat!!!" Tanya said throwing up their set high. "I love you homey, let's get these Crabs tonight for Baby Gangster, 007, and Doggy homey," said Shitty to Tanya peacing her. And that's when Tanya held out to one of the little homey's and yelled, "Call the hood and see what we can find out about that Crab ass nigga James. I want to know who the bitch was with him and Suzie. Find out where the fuck his family is at too. All of them Fee dead pussy!!!

It was time for them to go out and get even and they were out for blood, and nothing less. Shitty got on the phone made a few phone calls to try and find out all she can find out on them. She got on the phone with ones of their homey's. Her name was Meka, she said that she had something for them. Meka was about her work, she was dark skinned with brown eyes. She was 5'8", 140lbs. with measurements of 36DD-25-44, and she had long black curly hair, she was an all American Stallion.

Back in the Bronx where the big shoot out took place Homicide was back out there. This time Agent Cox was with them, he's one of the best of the F.B.I. He was under Frank Anderson. Cox didn't get to look over the crime scene because he was away on vacation. Cox even cut his vacation short to get back to work. Cox was about his job almost more than anything. Cox had been through two marriages, and is working on his third one as we speak. The only thing he has time for was golf, because he can play and think about a case at the same time. Cox is the type of cop, whatever they miss in the investigation he finds by going over the same spots that they haven't. "Det. John!! Call Baltimore and make them put out an APB on Doggy. He likes to play out there a lot, we're two minutes away from solving the case, I can feel it. The answer is right in front of my face. Sgt. Green what's up with them blood samples? Did the lab come back with them yet or what?" Cox said to Stg. Green as he was going over the crime scene. "I'm on it right now sir, give me two minutes," said Stg. Green to Cox. "I see you're up early this morning Cox," said Agent Thomas. He had just got on the scene, he likes to go over things himself. Once he heard Cox was back in town and on the crime scene, he had to come out there just to see what Cox would find next. They were work buddies. "No need Stg. Green, I already made the phone call on my way over here. One thing's for sure, it looks like our boys been out here, James and Ty definitely have been out here on the night of the shooting. The blood samples came back positive on both of them," said Thomas to Cox and Stg. Green. He had just got off the phone with the lab. "Good, good! I see you're right on time as usual Thomas. Now all we have to do is get them to close this fucking case and go play some golf," said Cox as he got on the phone with Frank to fill him in on what was going on. Frank was at home still in bed after three days of working non-stop. Frank told Cox to put out an APB out on James and Ty. Cox told him he already did it. Frank got off the phone and jumped in the shower. It was time for him to get back to work.

Back at Kings County Hospital in Brooklyn, Suzie was still there with Wesley. She's been there so long that they gave her a twin size bed to sleep on. The sun was starting to come up. Suzie was dead tired, but she manages to call Pinkey to see what was going on with James and the rest of the Loc's. "Pinkey what's up girl? And how is my brother doing? And be real with me girl?" Suzie said to Pinkey waiting for a answer from her. "Girl he doing fine, he been getting a lot of bed rest. You know he got hit in the back of his head, but he's going to be fine," said Pinkey while she was sitting beside James. "Pinkey hold on for a minute, my mom is on the other line calling me," said Suzie. And then she answers the other line, "Mom what's up? I was just on the other line with Pinkey, she was just telling me about James, and she said he's going to be fine. He just needed to rest for a while, that's all," said Suzie as she was looking at Wesley while he was asleep. "God bless her heart for being there for that boy. God knew he needed her more than ever, and how is my boy Wesley doing? I've been praying day and night for all of them. Please give Mike and Ty my love too baby for me," said Mrs. Campbell. She was on the phone with Suzie while she was in the kitchen making breakfast for her and Mr. Campbell. "I sure will Mom, I still have Pinkey on the other line, and I'11 see you soon. I'll be by the house today to take a bath, okay?" Suzie said to her mother. Then Mrs. Campbell said to Suzie, "Listen baby do yourself a favor, don't come by here right now. It's not a good time, if you know what I mean okay? They are everywhere baby," said Mrs. Campbell to Suzie hoping she don't come by the house because she knows the Feds have been all over the area. "Okay mom, I understand you, I get the picture. I love you. I'll tell everybody you said hi, bye Mom I'll talk to you later on love you bye," said Suzie and then she clicked over to the other line. Pinkey almost fell asleep waiting for Suzie to come back on the phone. Suzie had to yell in the phone to her. Pinkey finally got up, "Pinkey that was my mom on the other line that had called," said Suzie. Pinkey thought she was still on the phone with her mother, so she was ready to hang up the phone. "But she's gone now, she gave everybody her love especially, you for being there for her son. She also told me to stay away from the house because the police has been by there looking for James," said Suzie. "I feel like it's no reason for the police to be around your mother's house and for them to be following us around," said Pinkey. Then Suzie explained to her, "Pinkey, they're not looking for the two of us, but if they see us they will follow us to where James and the rest of Loc's are at. So we can't go by the house at all." So Pinkey now knows she can't go by her and James' place that they have together either. But Pinkey still has her apartment that she had before she started fucking with James. Pinkey and Suzie were feeling the same way about the whole situation. They needed to get into the tub to wash their ass, so they decided to meet each other over by Pinkey's house. Both of them got off the phone and got their minds right to get ready to meet each other over by Pinkey's place to get some rest, and get into the tub too. They haven't got in the tub for at least two weeks. But little did they know that Tanya and Shitty was on the streets looking for them. They wanted to send a message to the Crips. Pay back for 007 and Baby Gangster even though police was out looking for all of them.

These two bitches did not give a fuck. They called up their girl Meka again to see what she knows about Pinkey and Suzie. One thing they knew for sure, Wesley was shot the fuck up in the hospital somewhere in Brooklyn, and that James might be at the same hospital too. If they find Wesley, then they should find James too, at least that is what they thought. Shitty got Meka on the phone, Meka told her Wesley's is at King County Hospital. They knew exactly were that was, they asked her if James were there too? She told them no, he's at some doctor's house, she didn't know were at right now. She'll try to get it for them, and for them to call back later on, and then she should have it for them. Knowing where Wesley was good enough for them to start with. Plus, Meka told them Suzie was at the hospital with him. And that's who they want for real. Suzie they will try to catch, and catch up with that bitch Pinkey later on.

Meka was fucking one of James' boys, she never told him she was a Blood. They started heading to the hospital, they were ten minutes away from there. They knew what type of car Suzie was driving. Suzie drove a midnight blue Lexus LS 430 with tinted windows and twenty on it the heir rims, so they know exactly what to look for. They got there and drove around the whole block until they saw her car. She was parked right on Albany Avenue and Rutland Street, and they drove right pass it and parked a few cars from her car. Tanya and Shitty was sitting in a candy apple red Audi S8 with tinted windows and twenty-two five rims. They just sat there and a hour went pass and no Suzie yet. They had to sit and wait patiently for her to come out. Shitty got out and walked down the block pass Suzie's car, she had a fitted hat and a hood on, and so no one could recognize her.

Pinkey was still getting ready to leave to meet Suzie. She kissed James and walked to her car. Top Gun ran out behind her to go with her for her safety just to make sure nothing happened to her. She told him she was okay, but he insisted on going with her. He jumped in the passenger seat of Pinkey's Mercedes Benz truck. It was black with beige leather interior with 22" heir rims with tints. Pinkey apartment was downtown Brooklyn on 4th Avenue, she had a condo down there.

Suzie was getting ready to leave out of Wesley's room. She gives him a kiss on his lips right before she left out. He was sleeping still and in bad shape. Then she turned around and walked out the door to the elevator and the elevator so happened to be right there. Suzie took it to the lobby and got off, she had to walk down a block to get to her car. One of the Loc's left out with her just to make sure she get to her car safely. As she got closer to her car she unlocked the door by pressing her remote control button on her key ring. The Loc asked her if she wanted him to come along for her safety. She told him no, she'll be find. And that someone is already with Pinkey. He watched her get into her car and drove off.

Shitty was sitting two porches away from Suzie's car. Shitty got up and walked right behind the Loc. She pulled out a Glock 40 right out of her dip with a silencer on it. She hit the Loc up two times in the back of his head, and three times in the back. And then she ran up to Tanya's car and jumped right in. Suzie already drove off the block pass Tanya. Suzie was at the end of the block, getting ready to make a left turn onto Troy Avenue. They let her make the left turn, so she wouldn't notice them. Tanya asked Shitty, "What happened to the Loc that was with Suzie?" "Bitch you already know what it is, that nigga is out of here homey," said Shitty. Tanya turned to her and said, "Damn bitch he was kind of cute." Then they both started laughing at each other. They were now on Troy

Avenue with Suzie a few cars right behind her. Suzie knew Tanya from her fucking with James. She also knew that Tanya's a Blood now from the shoot out in the Bronx a few weeks ago. Because when James, and the rest of the Loc's, was ready to run up in Doggy's house they saw her and Shitty pull up on the scene. Therefore, Tanya can't get to close up on her, so they play a few distance from her. Suzie drove straight up Troy Avenue to Eastern Parkway and made a left turn to go downtown. She got on the phone with Pinkey on the way there, because she was so tired she needed someone to talk to, to help her stay up. "Shit girl, I'm doing that now as we speak, so by the time you get here the tub is all yours girl, and Top Gun is outside too, I told him he could come upstairs. But he said he'll, rather wait downstairs for me. Plus, he knows you're on your way too," said Pinkey to Suzie as she was soaking in the tub. "I told my bother little Loc, I don't need him. I'm cool so he stayed at the hospital with Wesley. Girl I'll call you back when, I get 5 minutes away from you, okay?" Suzie said. "Okay, see you soon," said Pinkey. They got off the phone with each other. Suzie turned on her CD player, she was listening to Mary J. Bilge *"Growing Pains"* flying in and out of traffic. Tanya and Shitty was right behind her, but still at a distance.

Pinkey was still in the tub, she haven't been at her apartment in a few months, and she damn sure haven't been in the tub for a few weeks. She only had shower at the doctor's house, that's all. So she was enjoying, every minute of it. But she also knew that Suzie wasn't that far away from her either. So she got out and washed out the tub, so when Suzie gets there she can take a bath too. As soon as she finished washing out the tub her phone started ringing. It was Suzie letting her know she was just a few blocks away from her and that she will be there in about five minutes or so.

Pinkey got off the phone, and started to get dressed. She took out a outfit for Suzie to wear too. She put her hair in a ponytail, and then she put on her pink bra with her matching pink panties on. Then a white beater over her bra and panties. Then she put on her blue Yankee fitted hat with her blue jeans Louis Vuitton outfit with some Manolo white sneaker to match her outfit. Pinkey and Suzie almost wore the same size in jeans, they also wore the same shoe size. She pulled out a dark blue Gucci jean suit, for Suzie to wear with some Gucci sneakers that matched the outfit. Pinkey had a lot of new underwear, so she pulled out a lace, black Victoria Secrets bra and panties set for her to wear with it, and a black Gucci shirt to go with it. Suzie was just pulling on the block, she called Top Gun to let him know she was pulling up. Top Gun picked up the phone and Suzie pulled up right beside him. Top Gun answered his phone, "What's cracking Suzie? What you trying to do, creep up on a nigga or something girl?" "Nigga you better be watching your back. What the fuck is wrong with you? You don't even see me beside you nigga!!" Suzie said as she sat there beside him. That is when Top Gun looked at her and said, "Okay Suzie, you don't have to go there with me, I feel you cuz." Suzie always fucked with Top Gun like that because he was like a brother to her. Suzie drove up a few cars and parked. She got out and still fucked with Top Gun all in his face playing with him while Tanya and Shitty drove by nice and slow. They drove up the block and made a left turn, Shitty got out and started walking towards the building, Suzie was already going into the building. Shitty was walking to the building, someone was on their way out of the building, so Shitty walked right in. Suzie was already on the elevator. Shitty was in the lobby watching to see what floor Suzie gets off on. Suzie got off on the 5th floor. The elevator came back downstairs, Shitty got on it and pressed the 5th floor. As soon as she got on the 5th floor, she got off the elevator. Shitty started walking down the long hallway trying to figure out what apartment she went into. Being that it was mostly white people that lived in the building, it shouldn't be too hard to find. Shitty went by the stairs just in case one of them happened to come out. A little girl was coming out of her apartment and Shitty stopped her to ask her if she knows a girl by the name of Pinkey. The little girl not knowing what was going on told Shitty were Pinkey lived at. Shitty told the little girl thank you and called Tanya on the phone to let her know that she got the apartment number and for her to come on in. That is when Tanya told her that she forgot that Top Gun knows her. So Shitty would have to take care of him for her. Shitty got right back on the elevator and went to the lobby to the front door. She walked right up beside Pinkey's truck where Top Gun was at. She let off three shots through the passengers window into his head. His brain hit the windshield and the driver's window. Tanya was already walking up the block, Shitty had put something in the door to hold it open so they can get back in the building. Tanya and Shitty both got on the elevator to the 5th floor. They didn't take out there guns yet just in case someone in the hallway, the less bodies the better it is for them. Inside Pinkey's apartment, Pinkey was already dress, Suzie was in the tub enjoying every minute of it. Pinkey was about to go take out the trash. She goes in the kitchen to grab the trash bag and turns around to walk out the front door. She grabbed the doorknob and unlocked one of the locks on the door. She was getting ready to unlock the next one, not knowing Shitty and Tanya was on the other side of the door waiting for whoever it is that's about to open up the door. They didn't know it would be this easy, it like taking candy from a baby. Just as Pinkey was to unlock the second lock. Suzie started calling her and her cell phone started ringing. So she didn't unlock the second lock, Shitty and Tanya didn't know what the fuck was going on inside the house. So they just both stood on the side of the door with their guns out because they knew someone was going to come back. Tanya turned to Shitty and said to her, "Maybe the bitch forgot something?" Back inside the apartment, Pinkey walked into the bathroom with Suzie. On the way to the bathroom Pinkey grabbed her cell phone. It was Trigger asking her if everything was okay, she told him yeah and asked him why? That is when Trigger told her he's been calling Top Gun for about twenty minutes now and got no answer. And asked her if he's in the apartment with them sleeping or something? Pinkey told him no. He should be in her truck. Suzie was over hearing the conversation and got up out the tub. She grabbed her phone and hit Top Gun on her Nextel, she got no answer. She knew that's not like him. Pinkey's window was right in front. Although he was parked right in front, they really couldn't see if something was wrong or not. Something told Suzie to walk to the door and look out through the peephole, that's when she saw two shadows by the door. Suzie quickly ran into Pinkey's bedroom and got dress while telling Pinkey something is not right and for them to get the fuck out of there. They're going to have to go down the fire escape. Shitty and Tanya is still on the other side of the door. Tanya tell Shitty to go downstairs just in case they are onto them. Shitty took the stairs down to the lobby. Pinkey and Suzie making their way down the fire escape they get to the first floor and made it down the rest of the fire escape and jumped to the ground. As they ran to Pinkey's truck, and opened up the passenger door to see what going on with Top Gun. Top Gun's lifeless body fell right out, dead as a motherfucker. Pinkey started screaming, Shitty heard the screaming from inside the lobby, and made her way to the front door. Suzie was right behind Pinkey and she sees Top Gun's gun on the floor and grabbed it. Suzie grabbed Pinkey, and they made a run for it to Suzie's car. Suzie threw the car keys to Pinkey for her to drive. Just as they were taking off Shitty was coming out the building banging at them. Suzie got hit in the right arm, as she was getting in the car. Suzie started shooting back with her left hand, and by this time, Tanya was outside. They both ran to their car, and that's when the chase began. Tanya and Shitty was in a faster car, but don't get it fucked up that Lexus was out of there. Pinkey was driving through Brooklyn like a mad woman. She was running red lights while driving straight downtown to the Brooklyn Bridge to the F.D.R. Tanya and Shitty were right behind them, but not shooting at them yet while they were downtown. But as soon as they got on the Brooklyn Bridge, they started shooting at them. Driving in and out of traffic, Shitty shot out the back windshield as they got on the F.D.R. drive. As they were about to get on the highway, Suzie turned around and started shooting right through the back window into Tanya and Shitty's front windshield, hitting Shitty in the shoulder. Tanya started driving with one hand, busing with her free hand at them. Shitty got her arm out the window, banging at them. hitting the back of the trunk. Tanya hit the dashboard up. Suzie let off back hitting the whole front of Tanya's car.

Pinkey is driving in and out of traffic flying, doing like 120 mph, and Tanya's right behind them. They flew right pass a state trooper, he was clocking them doing 130 mph and saw them shooting back and forth at each other. He got right on his radio and then got right behind them. Tanya yells to Shitty, "Fuck them, get these pig off of us now!!" Shitty sticks half of her body out the window and takes a good aim right through the windshield, she hits him right in his head. The next shot hits him in his chest, and then she shot out the tire. The police car goes out of control. It hits a car and flips on its back, slides on the other side of the road into the incoming traffic and hits a Mack truck.

While all of that was going on, Suzie takes aim at Tanya's front wheel and shoots the tire out. The car goes out of control. Tanya crashes into another car. All traffic behind them is stopped now. Pinkey and Suzie got out of there. They jumped off the highway, and take the street. Tanya and Shitty jumped out of their car. You can hear the sirens coming. They just can't get through the traffic to the scene. Tanya runs up on a man, and his wife. Tanya was on the driver's side pulling his wife out the car. Shitty on the passenger side telling the man to get the fuck out of the car. Shitty had her 45 cocked in his face. That is when he got out immediately. They got out of there A.S.A.P.

On the way to where James was at Suzie and Pinkey were trying to figure out how Tanya and Shitty knows where Pinkey lived at. Suzie was thinking to herself and turned to Pinkey and said, "The only way they could have found out where you lived was if they followed you from the hospital." Then Suzie started looking for her cell phone. She couldn't find it at first, but then it started ringing. Therefore, she found it and it was Mike calling her letting her know what was going on. He got word that one of their little Loc's was found dead outside around the corner from the hospital. Mike also asked her if she and Pinkey was okay? That is when Suzie started to tell Mike what had happened to them. She asked him how to get to where they're at. That is when Mike told her he thinks it will be best if they just go straight to his house in New Jersey. He also told her where she can find, his extra set of keys for his house. So Suzie and Pinkey can get into his house. He also told her to call him when she gets there. Mike turned to Ty, Simeon and the rest of the Loc's, and told them Top Gun is dead. They all just sat back mad as a motherfucker, they wanted to get even.

Tanya and Shitty drove to one of their hoods in Brooklyn, and got rid of the couple car's that they took. And took one of their little homey's cars to get back to Doggy's house in Long Island. Police was everywhere, but they did not notice them because they were looking for a stolen car, a gray Volvo s40. They jumped on the highway to get to Doggy's house. As soon as they got there, Tanya called Sam as they were pulling up in the driveway. Sam was already at the door looking out for them. Tanya parked and her and Shitty jumped out and ran inside the house. Doggy was looking a little better than before. Tanya started telling them what had happened. They were mad as shit because they wanted to send a message to the Crips by killing Pinkey and Suzie. Even though they got Top Gun, to them that wasn't good enough, but by them getting Suzie and Pinkey it would have been a statement to them. Now they were on their guard, and they might not get another chance like that again. Shitty cleaned out her wound and patched it up, they were both mad as a motherfucker.

Shitty and Tanya just sat back rolling up some purple, and started kicking it. They just couldn't believe what them two bitches did out there on the street. Shitty started talking to Tanya first about it. "Homey, them fucking bitches is lucky as shit homey. I was trying to kill them fucking bitches. One thing I can say, that bitch can drive her ass off," said Shitty to everybody that was there in the house. "Who's that? That bitch Suzie or Pinkey's homey?" Tommy Gun asked as he was smoking weed with them. Nah that bitch Pinkey's homey, I give it to her, that bitch is kind of nice, but not as nice as my bitch. My bitch was on them bitches ass, isn't that right baby?" Shitty said jumping in Tanya's lap. "You already know what's popping homey," said Tanya sticking her tongue down Shitty's throat. "You love me baby?" Shitty asked Tanya and rubbing on her breast. "You already fucking know what it is homey," said Tanya to Shitty. "I love you homey," said Shitty back to her as they sat there smoking some purple.

Pit started asking them what had happened, he wanted to know detail by detail. He also asked them, "I am going to see y'all on the news tonight or what?" They said, "Hell yeah!!" And they started laughing at Pit. Then Tanya took a pull off of the weed and passed it to Shitty and said, "That bitch Suzie can shoot a little something, something." That's when Shitty turned to Tanya and said, "What you're trying to say homey? I killed two motherfuckers today. It might not be the two we wanted to pop off at, but they're Crips, it's better than nothing."Everyone stopped and started laughing for a minute at Shitty and Tanya, this is something they always go through. While everyone was laughing Sam got on the phone and made a call to Baltimore to see what was going on with their homey out there. They told them that the police were trying to crack down on them down there in Baltimore, so it would be best for them to stay up top for right now. Or for them to get out of NY all together. Tanya told Sam to tell them niggas we're good.

Shitty passed her the weed, and cracked open a bottle of Rummy. She started to take it to the head for herself at first. That's when Tanya walked over to her and took the bottle out of her hand. She gave Shitty the blunt and sat her ass beside her. Doggy walked in and grabbed the blunt from Shitty and sat in between them chilling.

Meanwhile Pinkey and Shitty is just getting to Mike's house in New Jersey pulling up in the driveway. They both jumped out at the same time. Suzie went straight for the keys, while Pinkey went to the front door. Suzie grabbed the keys and threw them to Pinkey so she could open up the door. Pinkey and Suzie both couldn't believe all that was going on. They never been through anything like that in their life before. Suzie started telling Pinkey, "Don't worry they didn't die in vain." As soon as they got in they locked the door and turned on the lights. Suzie got her phone out to call Mike to let him know they reached there safely. Suzie also asked Mike where was his girlfriend at because she needs to talk to her A.S.A.P., Mike knew what she was talking about. "Go upstairs to my bedroom to my fireplace because there is a special alarm box on the wall. When you find it, press 252, and then when the light turns green, press 787. Then you'll see what you're looking for," said Mike to Suzie. Suzie told him okay, and got off the phone.

Suzie and Pinkey ran upstairs to Mike's room. They went straight for the fireplace, Suzie started looking for the alarm box, it was not too far away from the fireplace. Suzie pressed the 252 code first, and the light turned green, and then she pressed 787, and out of nowhere the fireplace opened up. Suzie and Pinkey could not believe their eyes. It was as if they were in a clothing store. Suzie knew Mike had guns, but she did not know he had guns like this. He had everything from 22 all the way up to M50, he had over 50 head guns, and over 20 different assault rifles. He had knives that they never seen before, he was ready for whatever. He also had two pictures of Scarface on the wall, and one of him too. He had all types of shit, she thought she seen it all when she saw some hand grenades. Pinkey ran over to them as if they were toys. Suzie stopped her and told her, "You don't know if that shit will go off girl, are you fucking crazy or something?" That is when Pinkey put it down and turned to Suzie and said, "I was just thinking of blowing them up too. Suzie got a few hand guns from off the wall, two 45 Colt with four clips a piece, two Glocks 9mm's with four clips, also she loaded them up with hollow tips. In addition, they grabbed two bulletproof vests. This time they were going to make sure that the next time they run into them two, they would be ready for them.

Suzie's arm was still bleeding, so Pinkey got a warm rag and started to clean out Suzie's wound. Pinkey jumped in the shower, and then Suzie's phone rang and it was Mike calling to tell her to grab some girl for him, and get some rest. Also to meet him out by the doctor's house. She told him okay, and got off the phone. Suzie grabbed everything for Mike and they put everything into two duffle bags. Then she just laid back until Pinkey got out of the shower. And then she jumped in right behind her.

Pinkey washed out her bra and panties by hand and put them in Mike's dryer to dry. Then Pinkey yelled upstairs to Suzie and asked, "Suzie is James okay?" "Call Mike back and find out when you get out the shower, because I did not ask Mike," said Suzie to Pinkey. Pinkey got right on the phone and called him back. Mike answered the phone and told her, "He's doing fine, he's okay, don't worry." And then from upstairs Pinkey told Mike, "Mike tell James that I love him and I'll see him soon. We're going to rest for the night." "Okay Pinkey, keep it cracking," said Mike. Pinkey got off the phone and ran back upstairs to Suzie. Suzie just got out of the shower, and was washing out her bra and panties. She also put them in the dryer to dry. Pinkey laid back on the bed and started rolling up some purple waiting for Suzie to come back upstairs before she lights it up.

Meanwhile back at the F.B.I. Building, Frank, Cox, Thomas, and the rest of the police were putting together the rest of the puzzle. Frank got on the phone with A.T.F. to see what was taking them so long to come. As they were talking the door opened up. It was one of the prettiest police bitches that they ever seen. Thomas could not take his eyes up off her. Her name was Agent Paris, and she was so sexy. She was a red bone, 5'6", 140lbs, with light brown eyes. Her measurements were 34DD-25-42 phat in all the right places with long brown hair to her back. She's an all American Stallion with small feet too. Everyone had to get a hold of themselves, Frank was the first one to stick his hand out to her. Agent Paris shook his hand and Frank asked what was going on. Frank started filling her in on what was going on with the case. "It's a lot of big guns involve and a lot of bodies in the last two months. It's a manhunt out on the men that are involved in these cases," said Frank. And then he showed her the two-pyramid pictures that he had put together of the Crips and Bloods that he had on the wall. Then he started breaking it down to her from head to toe, from boss to pupp, to OG to soldier. The in and outs of what they knew about both organizations, their hoods that they play in, what the Crips are about, and what the bloods are about. Paris could tell it was somewhat personal with Frank, she could tell by the tone in his voice. In addition, by how much time he puts into his cases.

They started going over all the murders that happened in the city that were gang related from the first one until now. It was one murder that he did not like talking about, it was the first homicide that he was called to do on the Crips and Bloods. He left that one out, and started telling her the about the hit on Wesley that took place, the hit on Baby Gangster, the one by the hospital, Chin found by the club, and Top Gun found dead in front of Pinkey's house. Not to mention, the big ass shoot out in the Bronx, that's where they had the most body counts. One murder they did not tie them to yet is The Godfather's.

CHAPTER 7

BACK TO TOWN TO HEADQUARTERS

Agent Paris was looking at all of the pictures of the dead bodies. It was one picture that she just couldn't take her eyes off of. It was the one Frank does not like to talk about. That one kept him on the case to make sure he would put them away for good. He worked day and night on it non-stop, he was going to make sure they go away for a long time.

They started going over the shooting that just had happened recently on the highway. The only thing that made them look at it was the extreme shoot out on the highway. In addition, a state trooper was shot, and got in an accident and died on the highway while chasing four suspects. The only thing, it was four women, not men. It was two cars he was chasing, two of the suspects crashed their car, and took a couple's car and drove off. The couple's car was found not too far away from the Bloods hood that is another reason why Frank is looking into it. He had an idea, it was Tanya and Shitty. However, he did not know who was the other two girls in the chase. But he knew it had something to do with the Bloods and Crips for sure.

Cox jumped in the middle of the conversation saying, "It's safe to say, It was an all out drug war, and they will not stop until all of them is either dead or locked up for life. It was an ongoing senseless war for real, but this is what they do. Kill each other for nothing, that's why Frank gives them the name Cartel, Kings and Gangsters those who fight for power." They know it's going to be a lot more killing going on. Just as they were trying to put the puzzle together, Cox phone rang and it was Det. John from homicide, he was at the hospital with 007. "It looks like 007 is going to make it. It's good news if he talked now, but bad news if he doesn't, because it would be a waste of time for them to save his ass," said Detective John. Once Cox got off the phone, he immediately left out to go to the hospital to be there just in case 007 woke up so he can interview him. He got on the elevator and went straight to the parking lot to his car. He got to the hospital and parked, and then walked into the front of the hospital took the elevator to the 7th floor. As soon as he got off the elevator, he knew exactly where to go. All he had to do was look for the police officers that were in the room with him. They were going to make sure no one gets in or out. Cox asked one of the officers, "Did he get up yet?" One of the cops told him, "No, he just got out of surgery ten minutes ago, and he has not said a word yet." "As soon as he gets up call me, and do not let him make a phone call. No one is to know that he's alive. Do you understand?" Cox said.

She rather liked him herself, she's telling him a little bit about herself. Thomas asked her, "Paris, how long have you been working as A.T.F.?" "Six years," said Paris. "How long have you been a D.E.A. Agent?" Paris asked Thomas. "Seven years," said Thomas.

As they were driving through were the Bloods be at, Thomas had seen something by the alley from the corner of his eye, so he turned to Paris and told her to back up fast. As soon as they backed up they saw that it was a women laying on the ground. So, Thomas jumped out the car and ran to her aid to see how she was doing. Thomas grabbed his radio and called for an ambulance immediately. They were uptown in Manhattan,

Paris backed up in the alleyway, and she got out the car to help Thomas out. Thomas started doing CPR on her trying to keep her alive until the ambulance got there, it took them 10 minutes to arrive. When the got there they had to immediately inject a needle into her heart to bring her back. Cox was calling Thomas's phone to see if he and Paris can meet him at Pinkey's house were Top Gun was gunned down at. Thomas told Cox that they would be there in twenty minutes. They jumped in Paris's car and headed for the Brooklyn Bridge. Pinkey lived downtown Brooklyn, Paris turned on the siren to get through traffic. Cox was already there, Top Gun's body was already gone. However, Cox knew Top Gun was out there seeing someone, he just had to figure out what apartment it was that he was visiting. Therefore, he decided to knock door to door to find out.

Paris and Thomas were just pulling up on the scene. Cox was getting ready to walk in the building. Paris parked and they got out of the car and walked over to Cox. Paris asked, "Cox, how do you know that this is the building?" "Our victim was sitting right there, and gun shells were found in front of the building," said Cox. Cox had just got off the phone with Frank at headquarters asking Frank to contact someone downstairs in property and to check the car in the parking lot to see if they can get an address out of the Benz truck that Top Gun was sitting in when he was killed. Cox had an idea that the Benz truck would point him in the right direction. However, he could not he sure until they go door to door starting from the bottom to the top. Every time someone came to their door they would ask them if they ever seen the Benz truck before. Every door that they knocked on told them yes. However, nobody knew what apartment the young lady lived in. As they were getting ready to go to the third floor, Cox's phone rang and it was Frank with the address and apartment number to Pinkey's. "Someone downstairs in property ran the tags through the DMV, and this is what they came back with, the truck belonged to a young lady by the name of Pinkey Simmons and she lives on the 5th floor in apartment 14C. Also, she has no prior arrest record," Frank told Cox. Frank made sure of that. "Thanks Frank, I'm going now," said Cox to Frank.

Cox told Thomas and Paris what was going on. "I'm going to go downstairs to the supers apartment to get the keys, so we can get in the apartment," said Paris. Because to them, this could be a homicide already or a kidnapping case. They were hoping it wasn't a double homicide. Cox and Thomas were already by the door waiting for Paris to come back with the keys, and for Frank to call back with any information about the young lady. Paris got off the elevator with the supers wife, she had the keys to let them in. As she opened the door, Cox, Thomas, and Paris's guns were drawn out immediately just in case the perpetrator(s) might still be in the apartment. The supers wife quickly moved out of the way, and got out of there. The first thing they noticed was that all the lights were on and also the TV. The next thing was that the tub was still full of water. That's when Paris looked at the bedroom window and saw that it was wide opened, and it was a fire escape exit. She turned to Thomas and said to him, "This is where they left from." Meanwhile, Cox was looking at the pictures throughout the apartment. When he saw Pinkey's picture, he knew right then who she was, James' girl. That's when Cox turned to Thomas and Paris and said to them, "We need to put out an APB out on her to see if anyone has put out a missing person report out on her." He started thinking to himself, "If she's not dead already." Then Cox said, "And what is a girl like her, doing with a guy like that?" Paris turned to him and said, "Good girls love bad guys, that's all it is Cox, let's just hope she didn't get caught up in all this bullshit. I hope she is somewhere alive." Just as Paris said that Cox's phone rung, it was Frank with some information about Pinkey. He told them that her mother lives in Upstate New York in Buffalo, and Pinkey goes to L.I.U. (Long Island University) in downtown Brooklyn that is not too far from here. That's when Paris said, "I'm going to check the school to see if she's there on campus." Then Paris walked out the door to go to the elevator, and as she was leaving more police was coming on the crime scene. The crime lab truck, Stg. Green, and Det. John were pulling up too. Frank was on the phone with Pinkey's mother asking her, "When was the last time you heard from your daughter?" Pinkey's mother told Frank, "I haven't heard from her in over three days. But it's not unusually for her not to call." "Do you have a number to Pinkey's so I can call her?" Frank asked. She told him to hold on, and she called the number on the three way.

Back at Pinkey's apartment, Thomas hears a cell phone ringing and he answers it. It was Frank and Pinkey's mother on the phone. Pinkey's mother started to worry. Frank told her, "Just calm down, we don't know yet exactly what's going on, but if you hear from her please tell her to call me at this number 212-555-5520. And if you hear something, please let me know, and I'll do the same for you." Pinkey's mother told him okay, and hung up the phone.

Back at Mike's house in New Jersey, Pinkey and Suzie was laying back on Mike's King size bed watching CNN news, when a newsflash came across the TV of a missing person that they believe was kidnapped from out of Brooklyn. As soon as they heard the name *"Pinkey"* they jumped up to call her mother to let her know that she was okay. She didn't want to call her on Mike's house phone just in case her mother's phone was tapped. So she called her cousin Lisa to let her know what was going on and asked her to call her mother to let her know that Pinkey's okay.

After that Pinkey went downstairs to cook some breakfast for them. It was already around 12:30 in the afternoon. It was time for them to roll out and get to the doctors. Pinkey couldn't wait to see James, which he was all she had on her mind.

Suzie was on the phone with one of the Loc's from the hospital checking up on Wesley to see how he was doing. He was still in bad shape, but he was doing a lot better. They sat down at the table to eat the breakfast that Pinkey made. She made pancakes and eggs with turkey sausages with some orange juice. After they were done eating, Suzie ran upstairs to get them two duffle bags while Pinkey got one of Mike's car keys. Suzie's car was shot the fuck up, so it would be foolish to drive that car. Pinkey grabbed the car keys to Mike's midnight blue Benz 600 with tint and regular rums on it, because they were trying not to have too much attention drawn to them, and because it's a nice little ride. Pinkey walked out the door to start up the car. Suzie's upstairs getting everything they needed together, and then she started making her way downstairs to the car. They jumped in and off they went to the doctor's house to check on James. Pinkey was making sure she's doing the speed limit, because they have two duffle bags full of guns in the back seat. They damn sure wasn't trying to get caught up at all. They were sitting back listening to

"American Gangster Jay-Z", but not too loud because they really don't want to draw any attention to them as they were driving through the turnpike.

Suzie got on the phone and called the hospital to Wesley's room to check on him. Simeon answered the phone and Suzie was happy to hear from him. "Simeon, whats up with my baby boy, how is he doing?" Suzie asked. "He doing a lot better, hold on someone wants to talk to you," said Simeon to Suzie. Suzie did not know who was about to get on the phone, but when she heard his voice she was so happy it was Wesley, but he couldn't really talk, because he was still fucked up from the gunshots. Suzie was telling Wesley as soon as she done seeing James, she'll be right up there to see him. Simeon got back on the phone and Wesley couldn't even talk, his words came out slowly, and by the time he got a word out two minutes had almost went pass, so Simeon told her come through once she's done with seeing James.

They were almost there, the doctor lived in uptown Manhattan. As they were pulling up, Suzie was on the phone calling Mike to let him know to open up the door. Then two young Loc's came out the doctor's house to help them with the two duffle bags. They were both getting ready for war, both sides were out for blood. Pinkey and Suzie walked right in and went straight downstairs to the basement where James was at. Pinkey grabbed his hand and kissed him on his forehead. Then James opened his eyes, but he really couldn't talk, he just started to cry. He didn't like Pinkey and Suzie seeing him that way. Suzie went over and kissed and hugged him, and then she sat on the other side of him.

Mike came downstairs with them, and the two Loc's that grabbed the duffle bags that were upstairs with the rest of the Loc's getting ready to hit the streets. It was going to be a lot of bloodshed. Mike went back upstairs with the rest of the Loc's to make sure Suzie got everything he told her to get. They had Glock's, H&K's, Smith and Wesson's, and Thompson submachine guns. They also had magazine drums for every machine gun , and silencers for the up close and personal situations.

New York City was about to get really real on the streets. Homicide and the F.B.I. had a lot of work ahead, and a lot of bodies were about to drop. Pinkey and Suzie stayed downstairs with James. Suzie got back on the phone with Simeon to let him know she was on her way over to the hospital. "Pinkey will you be okay?" Suzie asked. "Go ahead, I'll be fine. Just call me when you get there to let me know what's going on," said Pinkey. Suzie got up to hug and kiss her brother, and then started to go upstairs to head out the door. She yelled upstairs for Mike, Mike was standing at the top of the stairs. Suzie went upstairs and told Mike where she was going. "Do you need someone to come with you?" Mike asked her. "No, I got all I need right here with me," said Suzie. Then she showed him the two guns she got from his house and kept walking out the door to his car.

Suzie started driving to the Brooklyn Bridge to get to the hospital in Brooklyn where Wesley was at. Suzie was talking to Pinkey the entire time on her way to the hospital. Traffic wasn't bad and as soon as Suzie got five minutes away from the hospital that's when she called Simeon to have someone meet her by the Emergency Room entrance just in case the Bloods are somewhere around watching them. Simeon and Kevin were out front waiting for Suzie to pull up. She pulled right in front of the

Emergency Room entrance and Kevin jumped in the car and parked it for her while she and Simeon walked inside to the elevator to go see Wesley. They got on the elevator, and this time Wesley was on the third floor. He was doing a lot better from the last time Suzie was there. He was still weak, but he didn't have all them machines hooked up to him. As soon as they got off the elevator they ran into Det. John and Stg. Green from Homicide, they were on their way to Wesley's room to see if they could get him to tell them anything. Suzie started going off as soon as she saw them. They had came before, but this time they had a picture of Pinkey and James with them asking Wesley, Simeon, and Suzie, what do they know about her. They knew that they knew something, because Suzie is James' sister, and Pinkey was with Suzie the other day. They really wanted to take them in, but they also knew it wouldn't get them anywhere, because none of them are going to talk to them. Plus it's more of a Feds case than the States. And the Feds wants to catch them in the act. Frank gave them six months on the streets after that game was over. The Feds was out to get all of them on racketeering, murder, drugs, and King Pin charges. Frank was out to give all of them a life sentence behind bars, so they don't want to fuck up the Feds case. Therefore, after they were done harassing them, they left.

Suzie called up Pinkey to let her know, what was going on. Pinkey was a little bit upset about them having her picture. So Pinkey already knew she had to get ready for them for when she runs into them. A nurse came with a wheelchair to help Suzie and Simeon take Wesley downstairs because the hospital was releasing him today, Kevin was still downstairs. As soon as they went downstairs, Frank was there with Stg. Green, and

Det. John in the lobby waiting for them. They already had Kevin in custody.

Frank walked up to Wesley and just looked at him. Then he told Stg. Green, and Det. John to take him away. That's when two other cops took Suzie and Simeon to the Federal Building for questioning. This was going to be a long day for all of them.

Back uptown, Pinkey is sitting beside the love of her life while his boys were upstairs debating which hood to start with first. They're getting ready to go on a killing spree all throughout the city, even with everything that is going on at the doctor's house. Pinkey is still trying to call Suzie, but she was not getting any answer. She was just talking to her fifteen minutes ago. So, the first thing that came to her mind was something with the police. She didn't want to start panicking, so she went upstairs and called Mike to the side to let him know what she thinks is going on without stressing out James or alert him to what was going on. "Mike, I just got off the phone with Suzie fifteen minutes ago, and I tried to call her back, but I got no answer. Right before I got off the phone with her, she was telling me about the police coming to the hospital harassing them, but they were fine leaving out with Wesley," said Pinkey to Mike.. Mike turned to her and said, "Look try not to worry about them right now. James need you right now Pinkey. I'm more than sure they're okay. Give her some time, she'll call you and we both know that. Just give them some time." Pinkey looked at Mike and told him he was right and gave him a hug. Then she went back downstairs to James. Mike went back into the living room to get everything organized. They have been at the doctor's house for more than three weeks.

Back at the Federal Building they were questioning Wesley about what happened to him and about the rest of the murders in the City. Wesley had nothing to say throughout the entire investigation. Frank knew he wasn't getting nowhere with him, or the rest of them for that matter. So after a few hours went pass, Frank decided to let them go. But he kept a close watch on them. He knew even if he kept them for 72 hours there would still be a lot of killing going on. He really didn't want to do it, but he had too. This was the only way he could get them on the type of charges on them. So he can put them away forever. First he let Suzie, Simeon, and Kevin go and tell them that they're going to keep Wesley a little bit longer. So, Suzie called Pinkey to come get her. Pinkey was there in about 30 minutes. Then Frank decided to question Wesley for one more time. Wesley still wasn't telling him shit. The first thing Suzie did when she got to the car was call James' lawyer so he can come and get Wesley because she knew they had no real reason for keeping him. Suzie kept telling Pinkey that Wesley is more the victim, if anything. James' lawyer told her he'll be down there as soon as he is done at the courthouse. Suzie took the long way to go back to the doctor's house to make sure no one is following them.

Wesley is still at the Federal Building telling Frank to suck his dick. "I didn't do shit, you don't have shit on me!" Wesley said to Frank, mad as a motherfucker. Then Frank told him, "Look you're right, you didn't do shit. You're more the victim for now, but I do know how shit works on the streets. They get one of y'all, y'all get one of them. Now frankly, I don't give a fuck if y'all kill each other. But when it come to them innocent kids on the street that's playing, and running up and down just trying to have fun, and then comes y'all pieces of shit, shooting everything and everyone in your way! I'm going to damn sure do my fucking job! When is the bullshit going to stop Wesley?!! Please feel free to tell me!" Wesley just looked at him and didn't say a word. Then Frank said to him, "I thought so." And with nothing to say, Frank just walked out the room. He left him to think about all the shit they done on the streets.

Meanwhile back at the doctor's house, Pinkey and Suzie were downstairs with James. Suzie started to cry, so Pinkey sat beside her to see what was wrong. "Suzie, what's up girl, why are you over here crying?" Pinkey asked her. "Pinkey, believe it or not, I care about Wesley a lot girl, I really wanted to take him home and take care of him, maybe he'll see that I really fuck with him. Then out of nowhere these fucking pigs took my baby from me!! Without me being able to tell him how I felt yet," said Suzie. "Suzie look, you will get your chance baby, it's not over yet. Wesley didn't do shit, they're going to have to let him go. Just chill out and give it some time, he'll call you. And as for him, knowing how you feel, he should already know. Who was the only one at the hospital with him? You right? Not none of them so call bitches he be fucking with. So, if he don't see that, he's a fool girl, and I know he sees it. So just chill out, the nigga is yours okay?" Pinkey said to Suzie while rubbing her hand. "Yeah I guess you're right Pinkey, I'll just want him to call me as soon as he gets out," said Suzie. "No!! Go there, and be there for him Suzie. Be right there when he comes outside, go ahead, I'm good and tell him I love him for me," said Pinkey to Suzie. "I sure will Pinkey I love you girl, tell my brother I love him," said Suzie to Pinkey giving her a hug.

On the way back to the Federal Building, Suzie called James' lawyer to see where he was. "Hello White, how far are you? I'm on my way back down there. They let me and his brother go, I just dropped them off. I'm about ten minutes away," said Suzie while she was driving to the Federal Building. "I'll be there soon I just got out of court, it's going to take me a while to get there. But I'll be there, I'll call you as soon as I get in the building," said James' lawyer coming for Wesley talking to Suzie.

Suzie got off the phone and put in Alicia Keys CD *"As I am"* on song number 11, while she was driving to go get Wesley, she was almost there. She had the window cracked and smoking some purple with her Chanel frames on. She pulled on the side of the building being that she had just smoked some of that good shit. She sat in the car and just watched the exits because this is where more than likely they would let him go at.

James' Lawyer called Mrs. White telling Suzie he had just got there and he's walking in now. Suzie told him okay, got off the phone, and went back to listening to Alicia Keys. By this time, she's listening to the whole CD. Then look at who she sees walking out the door with Mrs. White, Wesley. She sees Wesley was about to make a call, and Mrs. White shakes his hand and walks off. She sat there to see if it was her that he was calling. So she drives up to him real slow, at the same time her phone started to ring. And when she looks down at her phone its Wesley calling her, and a big ass smile came across her face. Suzie pulled up beside him and she rolled down the passenger window and yelled to him, "Wesley!! I'm right beside you...get in nigga." "Damn, what you been here all this time waiting for me girl?" Wesley asked Suzie while jumping in the car with her. "You can say something like that, you okay boy?" Suzie asked him. "Yeah, I'm good, what's cracking with your brother?" Wesley asked her. "He's doing okay, we can go up there for a while. Then I'm going to take you home and get you all better nigga," said Suzie. "That's what's cracking, I'm all for it," said Wesley. "Was I the first one you called?" Suzie asked him looking at him. "Yeah why? I wasn't calling none of them other bitches. None of them even came to see me, or call for that matter, why you ask?" Wesley asked her looking at her. "I just asked that's all, let's get out of here," said Suzie as they drove off. It put a smile on Suzie's face. Something had happened really special at the hospital, because she never thought she would be trying to fuck with Wesley at all. And he never knew it was about to go down like this either. They were almost to the doctor's house to check on everybody, and then she was going to take him home.

Meanwhile, Tanya and Shitty was out and about, and this time they had Sam with them. They drove to one of their hoods in Brooklyn to check one of their homey's named Meka to see what's popping with her. Tanya called her as soon as they hit the block. "Yo Meka, homey what's popping, where are you at?" Tanya asked Meka as she was parking. "I'm in the building homey, what's up?" Meka said to Tanya. "Come outside, I'm in front," said Tanya jumping out of her whip. "I'll be right there homey," said Meka walking to the front door. Tanya jumped back in, Shitty was in the passenger sit, and Sam was in the back of the truck. Meka got some purple lit up, and she passed it to Sam. And then she started talking to Tanya, "What's popping homey's?" Meka said to all of them. "That's what we want to know, what's the word on the street Meka?" Tanya asked her as she was smoking the weed. "Well it's like this homey, that nigga James got hit bad, he's at some doctor's house in the city somewhere homey. That nigga Wesley was getting out the hospital and the Feds ran down on him, Simeon, Kevin, and that bitch Suzie. They let all of them go, except for Wesley. But now he's out with that bitch Suzie, she went to go get him. And I heard they're looking for y'all motherfuckers too, that's what's popping for right now homey," said Meka smoking as she was talking to them. "That's what's popping, call us if you hear anything else about them niggas or them fucking pigs. Homey keep your ears to the streets, homey...one, homey we're out of here," said Tanya as she peaces Meka. Then Meka peaces Shitty and Sam, and then grabbed her blunt of purple and went back into the building. Then Tanya, Shitty, and Sam drove off to see what else was going on.

Suzie and Wesley got to the doctor's house and were downstairs with Pinkey and James. James was happy to see that Wesley was alright, but Wesley didn't like how James was looking. And when he found out Top Gun was dead, and some of his little Loc's, it really fucked him up, because all of this happened while he was in the hospital. He wanted to go with the rest of the Loc's tonight, but he knows he wasn't ready yet. Plus, Suzie wasn't letting him out of her sight not for a few days. And he kind of liked it for real, because he knew she really cared about him. More than he can say about them other bitches. However, they started to call his phone once the word got out on the street that he was out. But Wesley didn't even bother to answer his phone for them. He just looked at it like this, everyone that he needs is right here with him. So he just laid down on the couch beside Suzie and took a nap with his head on her lap and her hand in his hair.

Meanwhile, back at the hospital were 007 was at, he was starting to come around after he had to go through seven surgeries. The police that were at the hospital immediately called Det. John and Stg. Green to let them know what was going on with 007. As soon as they got off the phone, John called Cox to let him know that his boy was up and well. Cox told John and Green to meet him at the hospital. Cox was hoping it can be the break that he needed in the case. So, he jumped into his car, and flew down to the hospital. As soon as he pulled up to the hospital, John and Green were already there. The three of them walked in through the front door, went straight to the elevator, got off on the sixth floor, and walked directly over to him. Cox just looked at him for a minute and then he started to ask him questions. "So 007 before you say anything, let me inform you that you're looking at a lot of time. We have gunpowder residue from your hands. So we know you were out there shooting a gun that night. We didn't get a gun off of you, but we know you are one of the shooters, and it's a lot of dead bodies. So do you want to help yourself, or go to prison?" Cox asked 007 waiting for an answer from him. "Look here homey fuck you, do what you got to. I just want to call my lawyer," said 007 to Cox. "Okay asshole, have it your way, and I'm not your fucking homey, take his ass to jail!!" Cox said to him and to the police in the room. So, Stg. Green read 007 his rights and Det. John put the handcuffs on him. They got all his stuff together and took him to jail.

Cox called Frank to let him know what just had happened. Frank wasn't really that mad, because at least one of them was off the streets for a while. As soon as they got 007 downtown, there was a bus waiting for him to take him to Rikers Island. That is where he was going to stay until his trial was over. They put him on the hospital tier, because he was still fucked up from the gunshots. The first thing they did was search him, and gave him a bed. It was too late for him to get on the phone, plus, he needed to rest. He wasn't fully strong yet, so he decided to just go to sleep until morning. Then he got on the phone and called his girl, so she could call his lawyer, and also let everybody know what is going on with him.

CHAPTER 8

WHAT WILL MAKE YOU LAUGH WILL MAKE YOU CRY

As soon as Wesley got up, he woke Suzie up. So they could leave to go to his aunt's house in Brooklyn. He told his Aunt May that he was going to stay with her for a while. Also, he wanted to spend some time with his two little cousins. Pinkey was still sleeping, she was right beside James. Suzie woke her up to let her know that she was leaving, and that she and Wesley were leaving to go to his aunt's house. Mike, Simeon, Kevin, and the rest of the Loc's were upstairs getting ready to go out.

On their way to Brooklyn, Wesley called his aunt to let her know he was on his way with Suzie. His aunt didn't mind Suzie coming at all. His aunt liked Suzie, she just didn't like some of the other women Wesley was fucking with. She called them no good gold diggers, every last one of them. She lived by Kings' Plaza in Brooklyn.

They pulled up in his aunt's driveway, and his two little cousins came running out. Their names were Simone and Troy and they were only ten and nine years old. His aunt was standing at the door talking to him, "Boy you better keep your ass out of trouble, are you going to stay here for a few days Wesley?" "Yes Aunt May I am, I'm not going nowhere at all," said Wesley to his Aunt May. "I know you're not, because me and Suzie is not having all that running back and forth going on in here," said his Aunt May. That's when Suzie said something to him, "Tell him again Aunt May were not playing at all." Wesley just had to laugh at them.

Aunt May was inside cooking. Suzie and Wesley sat at the table with his cousins, and Aunt May was just taking the turkey out of the oven. Everything else was on the table, so she brought the turkey over to the table. And then his cousin Troy said a prayer for the table, "Dear Lord, thank you for this food we are about to eat. Lord, thank you for bringing my big cousin home to us too Lord. I prayed that You would bring him home, and You did. Please don't let nothing happened to my family and my family friends amen! One more thing Lord, let him stay with this beautiful girl, I like her amen!" Troy said as he looked over at Suzie and smiled at her. Aunt May said to him, "Boy what's wrong with you? Sit down and let's eat." But Wesley looked at Suzie and said, "It's okay Aunt May, I think he's right." Suzie started blushing real hard and the kids started laughing. "It feels good to be home with my family. And to have a real women with me and around them," Wesley thought to himself. After they ate, Suzie helped Aunt May with the dishes. Wesley went upstairs to his old room to lay back for a while and chill. After Suzie was done with helping Aunt May with the dishes she went upstairs to Wesley's room. He was laying in his bed listening to Mary J. Bilge's CD. Suzie asked Wesley for a towel and a washrag, so she could get in the shower. Wesley got up and gave Suzie what she needed, along with some boxers, and a white beater. So when she gets out of the shower, she can put it on. She grabbed everything she needed, and made her way to the shower. Wesley laid back on the bed, and then he got up to go use the bathroom. "Suzie baby, I got to use the bathroom, is it okay that I come in ma?" Wesley asked her as he stood at the bathroom door. "Yeah baby come on in, you can get in the shower with me if you like to?" Suzie said. "Are you sure of that ma?" Wesley asked her though the door. "Yes! Get your ass in here," said Suzie.

Wesley wasted no time at all. He used the bathroom and then got into the shower with her. He had staple stitches in his stomach, so he really couldn't stay in the water for long. But damn if Suzie wasn't looking good as a motherfucker to him. Suzie was 5'9", and had short brown hair, brown skin with pretty brown eyes. Her measurements were 36DD-26-44, she was not F.A.T but P.H.A.T.!! A straight stallion!

Wesley knew it was about to go down, but he was in no condition to do it in the shower. Suzie started taking her time and washing him up. She started kissing him passionately, and rubbing his dick playing with his balls. She was also sucking on his neck all the way down to his chest, and sucking his nipple. Wesley started rubbing the soap all over her breast, her ass, and her thighs. Wesley started sticking his tongue down her throat while holding her by the back of her head with one hand and the other hand playing with her body. He knew he couldn't beat it up like he wanted to. "Wesley baby," said Suzie looking at him. "Yes Suzie what's up ma?" Wesley said to her. "Where do we go from here?" Suzie asked while looking at him waiting for an answer. "The sky is the limit baby," said Wesley while kissing her on her lips one more time. Suzie turned to him and said, "Damn nigga that shit was good, and I didn't have no dick in about eight months." "Girl that pussy is mine, I love it damn!!" Wesley said looking at her. Suzie sat up some looking at him real crazy too and said to him, "So Wesley, what's up with all the other bitches? You know!!! I'm not having that shit nigga, at all!!" "I got you baby, fuck them bitches, it's about us, fuck the world and I mean that baby!!" Wesley said looking at her real serious. Suzie said to Wesley looking at him while laying on top of him, "I feel that's okay, but let's take it one day at a time, but know this right here nigga, this is my feelings that your fucking with, my feelings. Fuck what my brother is going to do to you. I'm going to get your ass myself nigga, I'll ride with you to the end, just don't hurt me, okay?" "I got you blue rags, til death. I love you Suzie, for real!!" Wesley said to her while kissing her and rubbing her on her back.

Back at the doctor's house, Kevin and some of his little homey's were getting ready to make some moves on the street. They were heading out the door to go to Brooklyn to pick up some money and drop off some drugs at one of their spots in their hood. They're doing their best to keep a low profile on the streets. Police were everywhere on the lookout for both parties.

Out by Doggy's house, Tanya and Sam was getting ready to hit the street. Meka called Tanya to let her know that some Loc's was out early on the block. Meka's aunt lived in a Crips hood, no one knew that she was a Blood. She kept a low profile about her being a Blood. She was more like Tanya's and Shitty's eyes and ears to the street. "Yo Tanya, what's popping homey?" Meka said to Tanya. "You already know what it is homey, five popping bitch!!! What's popping?" Tanya said to Meka. . "This damn nigga just told me that Kevin, and some other Loc's are on their way over here homey," said Meka. "Oh yeah? We'll be there, we're on our way homey. Let me know as soon as them Crabs get there, we're not that far from the Brooklyn Bridge homey, we'll see you soon," said Tanya. Then Tanya got off the phone and continued driving while talking to Shitty and Sam. "Yo Shitty, what's up bitch...what's popping? The Crab ass nigga is coming around me, a hood. Sam you hear me homey?" Tanya said. "Yeah, homey that's me, all day homey, this Glock 40 going up in a nigga today!!" Sam said as he was smoking a blunt of purple. "That's what's popping homey...pass that motherfucking purple to me homey," said Shitty as he grabbed the blunt from him. "Shitty, that's all you think about bitch!!!" Tanya said. "What's up homey? You know that my shit bitch!!!" Shitty said back to Tanya.

Kevin and his two Loc's were just reaching the block. They pulled up in front of their spot, Kevin jumped out and ran up in the building to get the money, and drop off some more shit. The other two Loc's sat in the car waiting for him. They got the music up, but not too loud. But loud enough where they can't hear someone running down on them. Kevin was upstairs making sure his money right and talking with his little homey. Tanya, Shitty, and Sam were five minutes away from the block. Meka was already on the phone with them letting them know everything that's going on. So they already knew what to look for and Sam already knew what to do as soon as they get there. They're about three blocks away from the block. Sam got his Glock 40 out, ready to do what he do.

Kevin was getting ready to come out the building, and he ran into a shorty he was fucking with on his way out. Tanya, Shitty, and Sam was just turning the corner, the two Loc's was just sitting in the car chilling. Not even paying attention to what was about to go down. As Kevin was coming out through the front door, his full attention was on the girl he was walking with and not watching his surroundings at all. Sam was hanging out the passenger window getting ready to gun Kevin down, the first shot hit him in the arm, and the second one grazed his neck. That's when Kevin hit the floor and pulled out his gun and started busing back. Tanya and Shitty took out the two Loc's in the car. Kevin hit Sam in the shoulder, and shot out the back windshield. Tanya and them took off, and Kevin ran to the car to see both of his Loc's dead, they were hit in the head. He pulled them out the car so he can get out of there, because he could hear the sirens, which means the police were coming. So Kevin was about to get out of there, but he stopped for one second and turned around to see Nicole still on the floor balled up. Kevin ran to her yelling out her name, "Nicole, Nicole get up ma!! They're gone!!!" Kevin did not see her moving at all. So he turned her on her back to see that blood was coming out of her mouth and her eyes was rolling in the back of her head, she was choking on her blood. She got shot in the chest one time, and all Kevin could do was cry and close her eyes. He laid Nicole down to rest and got out of there. As he was making a right turn off the block the police was just coming on the block. The three bodies were dead on the ground and one of them had nothing to do with none of the shit that was going on in the city. And that's what Frank didn't like. He was the first one to get the call about the girl getting hit. Frank didn't like what he heard, because it's not the first innocent victim to get killed by the Crips and the Bloods hands. Frank knew it was not going to be the last one either. The young lady was no older than 20 years old. All Frank could do is what he does best, try to get them off the streets.

The first one on the scene was Homicide, Stg. Green and Det. John. They were the ones that gave Frank the call. Nicole's mother was outside crying because she lost her only child to the streets. Stg. Green was trying to calm her down. It was just too much for her to handle, so he took her over to a police car. He had her take a seat in the car so she could get herself together. It was going to be a long day in Brooklyn.

Kevin pulled up in front of the doctor's house bleeding like a motherfucker. Kevin called Simeon on his phone to come outside and help him out saying, "Yo, yo cuz!!! I need your help, I got hit...I'm out front cuz." Kevin was breathing real hard and sweating hard too. Then Simeon said to him, "Me and Mike are coming out right now cuz!!!" They ran to the car helping Kevin out into the house. Now Mike felt like it was time for them to get out of the doctor's house because they have already been there for almost two months. They both took Kevin downstairs to the basement so the doctor can fix him up. Ty got on the phone with Pinkey, she was over Wesley's house with Suzie, Ty told her to come and get James and take him to Mike's house out in Jersey because it was too much traffic going on at the doctor's house. It was time for them to leave. Pinkey told him okay, and she'll be there with Suzie in about 45 minutes. The nurse was looking at Kevin's arm while the doctor was looking at his neck. The doctor said he was very lucky that the bullet just grazed him.

So Kevin started telling them what had happen to him when he was on the block, "Yo cuz I got to the block about to pick up the money and drop off the work right!!! I'm coming out the building with this shorty that I fuck with on the block and out of nowhere them fucking Mutts roll up and started shooting at me and my two Loc's. Both of them got hit in the head, I got hit the fuck up, so I clap back right and hit one of them, so they drove off right. I ran to the car to check on cuz, both of them was dead as a motherfucker. So I turned around to see what's up with shorty right!!!" He had to stop to catch his breath. Mike turned to him and said to him, "I feel you cuz, what happened next cuz?" Mike said to Kevin with tears running down his face, "My little shorty that was with me got hit cuz, and died.

Nicole cuz is gone. They hit shorty in the fucking chest cuz!!!" Mike said to him, "Damn cuz shorty was cool as shit too...damn!!" Then Kevin said to Mike, "I know Mike, I feel like it's my fault cuz. If she wasn't walking with me, she would still be here cuz!!!" Thinking it was his fault that she was dead. Mike was trying to make him feel better and said, "Cuz don't kill yourself about it, it's done and over with now. Now we got to get even with them fucking Mutts cuz!! And for our two Loc's and for shorty too. Them slobs got a pool hall downtown that is where they be at. We can catch some of them down there. First let's get James out of here." Just as Mike said that Pinkey and Suzie was coming through the door. Wesley was in the car waiting for them to come back out. Mike was telling them quickly what was going on. They grabbed everything they were suppose to and got out of there.

Tanya, Shitty, and Sam got back to Doggy's house in Long Island. Tanya started telling Doggy the story first. "Yo homey what's popping?" Tanya said to Doggy. "You already fucking know what's it is, 5 popping 6 dropped, all day every day. What happened on the streets out there Tanya? And what the fuck happened to Sam, homey?" Doggy said to Tanya. "Yo homey for real, we did our thing out there today!! We got two of them Crab ass niggas, and we hit that bitch Kevin the fuck up too homey!! We wasn't out there playing with them fucking Crabs!! We were eating them bitches flat out!! Blaaaat!!!! All day homey!!" Tanya said to Doggy as they were looking at Sam bullet holes. "That's what it is homey, we let them motherfucker Crabs know it was on and popping nigga, we was giving it to them niggas, homey. Sam did his thing, you already know!! Shitty did her thing homey," said Tanya to Doggy. Then Shitty said to him, "Tell him again baby and you know I did mine...them bitches didn't even see it coming." Then Shitty started demonstrating what they did out there on the block. Then Doggy said to Shitty, "Good, good that's what I'm talking about, let them bitches know flu ass niggas!!" Then Doggy asked Jimmy, "Yo Jimmy, I need you to go pick up some money and drop off some work to homey at the pool hall for me in Brooklyn A.S.A.P. homey. Can you handle that homey?" "I got it homey," Jimmy said to Doggy. Then Doggy said, "Take Sam and Pit with you and call me when you're on your way back." "So Tanya baby, it went down like that?" Doggy asked Tanya. Then Tanya said to him, "You already fucking know it Daddy, I'm ready to go out again." Tanya walked up to Doggy and gave him a kiss. "Nah ma chill here with me, you, and Shitty," said Doggy to her. Doggy pulled out some purple and easy roll's, and started rolling up some of that good shit. He threw on some Frayser Boy and Tanya and Shitty started bouncing up and down. Then Jimmy, Sam, and Pit walked out the door to go to Brooklyn. Tanya and Shitty kept telling Doggy over and over what had happened. Doggy just sat there laughing at their ass, because they kept making funny faces trying to react to the look on the Loc's face before they killed them. This was funny to them, but always remember what will make you laugh will make you cry later.

Doggy got on the phone and called some homey's in Baltimore to see what was popping down there. "It's was real hot down here. Police are kicking in every door down here looking for you as if you're down here or something," he said to Doggy. So Doggy asked his man, "When are you coming up top to see me?" "Next week sometime, as long as these pigs stop fucking with me," said his homey.

Pinkey, Suzie, James, and Wesley were just going through the Holland Tunnel, they were half way there to Mike's place. James was starting to come around a little bit. Soon him and Wesley would be able to hit the streets again. Pinkey pulled up in Mike's driveway, they already had the keys to Mike's house. So, Suzie opened up the door, while Pinkey and Wesley helped James get out the car. Pinkey and Suzie told James and Wesley that they'll be back, they're going to get some Chinese food. Suzie and Pinkey just wanted to gossip for real. "So Suzie, tell me girl…what happened girl? Y'all two in the car all lovey-dovey and shit," asked Pinkey. "I'm not even going to lie, that dick was good. That nigga knows how to work that shit…shot the fuck up and all," Suzie said to Pinkey bragging to her. "Word!!" Pinkey said back to her. Then Suzie kept telling her about what had happened. "Yeah that nigga like that for real. Girl we started in the shower, I got in first you know! Then you know he got in right behind me and shit. I started washing up his sexy ass body, and one thing went to another, you feel me!!" Suzie said as they were pulling up in front of the Chinese restaurant. Pinkey said to her, "Yeah I definitely feel you, that's what I'm talking about. So you're saying, he handled his money right? Go Wesley, dick it…dick it good." "Girl, I was loving it, we did it for like two hours almost," said Suzie as they walked in the Chinese spot. Then Pinkey said to her, "Did you let that nigga know don't fuck with your feelings like them others he fucks with." Then Suzie said to her, "You know I put that in check!! That shit is dead girl!! That nigga knows not to fuck with me, but guess what Pinkey?" Suzie said facing her as they were ordering their food. "What girl, what?" Pinkey asked. "That nigga bus all up in me girl, I'm not going to lie that shit felt good ummm!" Suzie said to Pinkey smiling at her. Pinkey said to her, "Suzie, your ass is crazy as shit. When me and your brother did it...girl!! He bus in me too! I'll know for sure this month if I miss my Period." They started wondering what was taking the Chinese people so long. Suzie started looking behind the counter and said, "Girl are you crazy or something, man what taking these Chinese people so long with our food?" Then Pinkey said to Suzie, "I know right...I'm ready to go, shit." A young girl came from the back and said, "Okay sorry, here's your order, $52.45 please, have a good day." "Let's get out of here," said Suzie as they were walking out the door.

Pinkey and Suzie jumped in their car and drove back up the street to Mike's house. They were going to sit back and chill out for the day. As soon as they walked in, James was on the phone with Ty and Mike. They went to Brooklyn to handle something. It was time for them to show the Bloods they are not playing.

Back on Rickers Island, 007 is on the phone with his wife Tee. She though he was dead, they all did. "Babygirl, make sure you call Doggy for me," said 007 to Tee. Then Tee said to him, "I could call him now if you want me to boo?" "Yeah, yeah, do that baby," said 007. "Hold on baby," said Tee as she clicked over to call Doggy's phone on the three way. "Hello Tee, what's popping?" Doggy said to her. "Hold on Doggy, baby talk," said Tee to 007. "Yo Doggy, what's popping homey?" 007 said. "007, that's you homey...homey what's popping!?" Doggy said happy to hear from 007. "Pussy ass pig locked me up homey, I'm on Rikers Island homey," said 007. "For what? What did they charge you with homey?" Doggy asked. "For right now murder homey," said 007. Doggy said to him, "I'm going to call the lawyer right now for you. And it's good to know that you're still with us homey." "They can't take me out just like that, just stay out of shit homey," said 007. "I got you homey, B-up C-down, you already know homey...One," said Doggy.

Doggy got off the phone with 007 and told everybody that was at his house that 007 was still alive, and that he just got off the phone with him. Jimmy, Pit, and Shitty was on their way out the door to go to Brooklyn to pick up some money and drop off some shit. Everyone was happy about the news. Tanya was trying to tell Shitty don't go, but she went anyway. She told Tanya that she knew what she was doing and she would be fine.

Doggy sat back with Tanya, smoking on some weed on the couch in the living room. Tanya started playing with Doggy's dick, she stuck the head of his dick down her throat. Doggy just sat back loving it, smoking and laying back on the couch. Tanya was in her zone, sucking his dick like a popsicle listening to some Frayser Boy music. Making her tongue spin around his dick's head, grabbing it like a suction cup. Doggy started busing off in her mouth, she didn't let nothing out not one drop. His toe started curling up, Tanya jammed his dick down her throat, grabbing his balls together. Doggy loves when Tanya gives him head. She's the best that ever did it to him. Jimmy, Shitty, and Pit were almost there, they were about 10 minutes away from the pool hall. Jimmy was driving and Shitty was in the passenger seat. Pit was in the backseat chilling.

Meanwhile Mike, Ty, and X-Man was out in Brooklyn by Doggy's pool hall. Ty was out front playing like a bum chilling. Mike and X-man ran up in the pool hall. It was three workers in there working and they made all of them get down on their knees. Then Mike and X-man killed two of them immediately as soon as they were down on their knees. The last one Mike just pistol-whipped him. Pushing his gun down so far down his throat that he started throwing up. Mike kept beating him with his gun until his brains and blood was everywhere in the pool hall.

Jimmy, Shitty, and Pit had just hit the corner. Shitty already had her eyes on Ty because she knew that no bums didn't play at the pool hall like that. Ty was on Jimmy's side of the car. Jimmy was about to get out of the car, but Shitty knew something wasn't right at all. And that is when it hit her so she yelled, "Drive, drive homey!! Go!! It's a set up!!!" As soon as Shitty said that Ty jumped up with two twin 45's, banging at their asses. Then Shitty stuck her gun out over the top of the car banging back. Jimmy started to mash on the gas pedal trying to get out of there. Ty ran in the street right behind them banging. Ty shot out the back windshield, Pit started to shoot back with Shitty. Jimmy got hit in the back of his head and his brain hit the front of the windshield, the car went out of control and crashed into a park car. That is when Mike and X-man came running out, busing at them with Ty. Shitty and Pit jumped out the car, and started running on foot trying to get out of there.

You could hear the police sirens coming, so Ty, Mike, and X-man ran to their whip and got out of there. Shitty and Pit was still running on foot, Shitty flagged down a cab, Shitty had brains and blood all over her face. The police was there within five minutes from when they left the block. Shitty and Pit took the cab to one of their hoods in Brooklyn, not too far from the pool hall, right by Meka's house.

On their way there Shitty called Tanya to let her know what was popping. "Yo homey, what's popping Shitty?!! What's wrong homey?" Tanya asked. "Them fucking Crabs hit Jimmy up!! And they got the worker too. As soon as we hit the block they were there waiting for us homey!!" Shitty said. Tanya was mad as shit at what she just heard from Shitty. Then Tanya asked Shitty, "So what's up with Pit, is he hood homey?" "Yeah, yeah homey! Pit is right here with me, we had to leave the whip. Jimmy was driving and he crashed into a parked car, police is everywhere homey. When I get to the hood, I'll call you back homey," said Shitty. Then Shitty got off the phone and told the cab where to go.

Back in New Jersey by Mike's house, Wesley started talking to James about Suzie and him fucking with each other, "Yo cuz I need to talk to you." "What's cracking cuzing?" James asked Wesley. "It's about me and Suzie cuz, you know we're fucking with each other. Please cuz hear me out first, I know you probably don't approve of it cuz, because of how I am, but it's different," said Wesley. "Stop for one second Wesley, look my sister is old enough to make her own decisions. So whatever y'all two do is between y'all two. That something your crazy ass got to deal with, not me cuz, you," James explained to Wesley. "So I guess it's all good with you?" Wesley asked again for a complete blessing. "You can say that because, she'll kill your ass," said James. "I feel you cuz, that's what's cracking," said Wesley. And then they both peaces each other.

Suzie and Pinkey was in the kitchen fixing the Chinese food talking. Pinkey said to Suzie, "Girl we got to get our asses together. We both start back to school in a few months Pinkey." "I know this shit it crazy girl. I got to get it together. All this cow girl shit, got to come to a stop," said Suzie. "Who the fuck are you telling? I love my baby, but school comes first," said Pinkey. "Girl if we don't have that we don't got shit. I love my brother and my baby, but you are right Pinkey," said Suzie. Then Pinkey said to Suzie, "Yeah but we also got these crazy ass bitches, running around the city looking for us too. What are we going to do about that Suzie?" "If it comes down to it, we're going to handle our business. Fuck them bitches that's what the guns are for," said Suzie. "I feel that cuz," said Wesley playing with them. "Wesley boy what you want?" Suzie asked. "Food baby! Food!!" he said. "We'll be out there in 2 minutes, now go back out there with my brother's baby," said Suzie. "Hurry up! A nigga is hungry!!" Wesley said.

Suzie and Pinkey finished putting the food in the plates, and made their way to the living room. "Come on you hungry ass nigga come and get it," said Suzie as her and Pinkey walking into the living room with the food. "Shit you say it like, you got something else for me to eat boo?" Wesley said to Suzie laughing. Then Suzie said to him, "I might do have something for you to eat. Hurry up and eat your food first nigga. Then I'll be your desert." "Now that's what the fuck I'm talking about," said Wesley to Suzie. Pinkey sat by James and Suzie sat by Wesley. All of them seem to have sex on their mind at the table while they were at the table eating. James' phone started ringing, so Pinkey answered it for him. "Hello, what's up Ty? Hold on, James is right here, hold on," said Pinkey as she passed James the phone so he could talk to Ty. "What's cracking cuz?" James said. "We got them niggas, that's what's cracking cuz, that Mutt Jimmy is out of here cuz, straight to the blue skies," said Ty. "Did you look at his face cuz?" James asked. That's when Ty said to him, "Yeah cuz, but he's out of here, that's for sure. And some of their little solders are gone too." "So when I'm going to see y'all?" James asked. "We're in the city right now. We'll probably be there tomorrow night have fun cuzing. I'll call you C-easy Loc," said Ty to James. "C-easy cuzing," said James as he got off the phone with Ty.

James started telling Wesley, Pinkey, and Suzie what had happen. "Yo cuz, I just got off the phone with Ty. The nigga got that Mutt nigga Jimmy last night. His bitch ass is to the blue skies cuz," said James to Wesley. James jumped up with a big smile on his face and said, "That's what's cracking nigga Claaaat!! Claaaat!!! C-up B down blue sky nigga!" "Baby calm down its going to be okay, eat boo," said Suzie trying to feed him. Then Wesley turned to her and said, "Baby, you just don't know how bad I hate them bitches." Pinkey said, "Wesley you think me and Suzie don't hate them just as bad as you, and my baby do, they were shooting at us too...you know. Suzie didn't you get shot too girl?" "I sure did," said Suzie. "Okay, I feel you Pinkey, but them fucking Mutts think they can start shit and get away with it," said Wesley to them as they were eating. "I feel you baby, I'm right here. I just don't want you to get all worked up baby...that's all. Come here boo...boo give mama a kiss," said Suzie. Wesley reached over and gave Suzie a kiss on her lips. Then Pinkey came over to James and kissed him. James and Wesley felt good, because they got one of their OG to their set. After they finished eating James and Pinkey went into the living room to chill out. Pinkey had some purple rolled up for them to smoke. Pinkey sat on James' lap, and lit up the blunt.

Wesley and Suzie went upstairs to one of the guess bedrooms to chill. They were upstairs listening to some music laying back. Suzie was laying on top of Wesley and they lit up a blunt too. Wesley started playing with Suzie's breast while she was smoking sitting on top of him. Then she passed the blunt to Wesley and started unbuttoning his pants. She pulled his dick out through his boxers, she started sucking and licking his dick, going up and down while taking her tongue and wiggling it around the head of his dick. She put the head of his dick in her mouth and then slide it down to the back of her throat. Suzie was also trying to put his balls in her mouth as well.. She was trying so hard that her nose started running. Wesley was loving it, she kept on going up and down and side to side, shoving his ten inches down her throat.

Back downstairs James and Pinkey was getting it on. Pinkey was on her knees giving James head too. He was holding the side of Pinkey's head, rubbing it while pushing his dick down her throat fucking Pinkey in her mouth. Pinkey was taking all that dick down her throat like a champing. James started to wrap Pinkey's ponytail around his hand pulling her head back and forth. James took his other hand and started playing with her breast. Pinkey's nipple was hard as shit. James started rubbing his dick on the inside of her mouth. James pulled Pinkey up off the floor and off of her knees, and then he bent her over on the edge of the couch. Her pink pussy was sitting out like a football. Pinkey grabbed her left butt cheek and spread'em and told him, "Stick that motherfucker in me baby please!!" James grabbed his hard ass dick pushed it between Pinkey's phat ass and pink pussy lips. He started ramming his dick real hard up in her. Pinkey was loving it, she started moaning real hard, calling his name over, over, and over again. James started pulling Pinkey by her ponytail, hitting it from the back banging her motherfucking back out. Pussy juicy was running all down between her inner thighs. James eased his thumb in her asshole and Pinkey started moaning louder, and louder, by this time he had his thumb all the way in her asshole.

Back upstairs, Suzie was riding Wesley like a cowgirl, going back and forth, and then up and down. Wesley was playing with her breast rubbing her nipples. He started sucking them one by one and then he put her breast together. Then took his tongue and started licking both of Suzie's nipples. Suzie started going crazy. She grabbed his balls from behind and started squeezing them together trying to push them up all the way up in her. Suzie was feeling it up in her stomach, hitting her G-spot. Suzie had her hand on his chest, pushing down on his dick. She was moaning out of control, and Wesley stuck his middle finger in Suzie's asshole, pushing it against her pussy and asshole wall. So his dick can hit his finger. He started finger-fucking Suzie in her ass while she was riding his dick. Suzie started talking to Wesley, "Oooh...ooh o shit hit it!! Hit it baby, yes, yes...right there right...fucking there...shit!!! That how I like it baby, right there, yes!!! Yes!! I'm coming!! Shit! Shit!! I love you baby...yes!! Shit!!"

Back downstairs, James was gunning Pinkey out of control and sweating bullets. James was about to cum, he pulled his dick out, and pushed it in her asshole. Pinkey started trying to run, he grabbed her by her shoulders, and held her down. Pinkey started saying, "Oh shit!! James what the fuck!! Oh shit baby oooh...oooh! Shit! Yes!!!"

CHAPTER 9

THE MAN HUNT

Back at the pool hall in Brooklyn. The police and the Feds were everywhere. Trying to put together the pieces. Homicide was there first, then they called the Feds. As soon as Frank walked on the scene, he went straight to Stg. Green and said, "Stg. Green." "Yes sir," he answered. "What is going on down here?" Frank asked. "It's like this Frank, that body over there in the car, he's one of the Bloods. His name is Jimmy, we have his license over here, and the two in the pool hall were Bloods. Also they were found execution style inside the pool hall, two to the head," Stg. Green said. "Did anyone see anything?" Frank asked. "We have one at the hospital that's now in custody. He's getting medical treatment right now as we speak," Stg. Green said. "Did he say anything to you?" Frank asked. "No, he didn't say nothing at all Frank," said Stg. Green. Then Frank said to Cox, "Cox, get your ass down there and see what he has to say now!!" "I'm on it Frank, like yesterday," said Cox. Cox jumped straight in his car and headed straight for the hospital. Frank is out there pissed off as a motherfucker, he's tired of all the bullshit. The back and forth, some Bloods get killed and then some Crips get killed. And every now and then an innocent bystander gets killed. That is what Frank didn't like.

Cox got to the hospital and not one word from the Bloods. So Cox called Frank to let him know what was going on, "Frank, I'm leaving the hospital now, not one word from the Bloods at all." "Fuck these little street punks!! Love to play hardball don't they!" Frank said. He was furious and he was tired of the bullshit. "Sir, I did all I can, we still have him in custody. Some of the cops that were there told me, he had some drugs on him. So they're going to take him in for that sir," said Cox. "Okay, okay, Cox, I'll see you back at headquarters," said Frank. "Yes sir, I'll be there in 30 minutes or so sir," said Cox. Frank got off the phone with Cox and started pacing back and forth. Then he started talking to Stg. Green from Homicide, "I can't believe that we don't have no one at all to come forward to help us put these punks away." "People are scared to come fourth Frank," Stg. Green said. "People just don't believe in us no more Green. No matter what we got to take back these streets from these punks!! They're out here killing each other over a color, it's more to life than that, isn't it Green?" Frank asked. "Yes Frank, well at least I believe so Frank, I feel you. Maybe we need to be more interactive with the people," Stg. Green said.

Back on the other side of Brooklyn, Mike, Ty, and Kevin are chilling with the rest of the Loc's. They were partying hard and had music playing at their C-walking celebration. They got some of their Loccet's there with them stacking and throwing up their sets, smoking and having a good time. Simeon just got there, Kevin was filling him in on what was going on. "What's cracking Kevin?" Simeon asked. "That's 6 niggas, it's a lot of blue tear drops in the sky tonight," Kevin said. Then Simeon said, "Yeah muddy water crying cuz?" "Yeah you know it," Kevin said to Simeon. Then Mike walked up on them and said, "What's cracking cuz, you missed all the fun cuz?" "Damn let me guess, the pool hall downtown right?" Kevin asked. "Claaat, Claaaaat!!! You know it man," said Ty walking over to Mike, Simeon, and Kevin. "Were not playing with them fucking Mutts at all!" Ty said again. "I feel you cuz! That's what's cracking cuz," said Simeon to all of them. Simeon grabbed a beer and sat back on one of the couches beside one of the Loccet's and started smoking the blunt she had. They were sitting back doing them watching American Gangster, and an all-time favorite Scarface. It was definitely their time to shine, but for how long only time can tell. Simeon definitely felt good about what went down. Because he knew, if nobody loved him, he knew his brother did. "Yo cuz that motherfucker slob head was everywhere," said Mike telling the story. "Yeah cuz, the one we left behind started pissing, and shitting on himself cuz, like a little bitch," Kevin said making everybody laugh. "That bitch Shitty and Pit got out of there too. I think they get the picture now," said Ty to everybody. Simeon turned to Kevin and said, "The one you left alive, that sounds like a *shitty* situation cuz." They all started laughing at each other and telling the story over and over again. It was just one big happy family. Ty loves the fact of how he played it off so cool. He knew Shitty saw him, because she never took her eyes up off of him, not for one second. He loves it when he runs into a real soldier. Too bad she was just on the other side.

Back on Rikers Island, 007 was making his way through, he finally got off the hospital unit into population. The jail was on lock down, for right now at this moment. As soon as 007 walked on the tier, he noticed he was on the wrong side of the jail, because he was Blood. They had put him on a Crip tier. 007 knew he had know win at all. He was still recovering from the gunshot wound to the head. He wasn't even in the cell for five minutes when a CO came to his cell that knew him from uptown. "What's popping homey, I heard you just got here," said the CO to 007. "Yeah homey, I just came off of the hospital tier. Yo homey, what's up with the jail putting me on this side?" 007 asked. "I don't know, but I got you homey, that's why I'm here homey, so I can take you to were you belong at," said the CO to 007 as he called control to open up 007's door. His door popped right open, and 007 didn't waste no time getting out of there. The Crip thought they had something to drink. The CO turned to 007 and said to him, "Homey, it's a good thing Doggy called me. We had one homey last week that something happened to over here. Homey still in the hospital, and your wife called me too this morning just to make sure everything is okay. I got some shit for you too, once you get settled in. I'll be around to give it to you first thing." "That's what's popping homey, good looking too," said 007. As soon as 007 got where he was supposed to be, 007 felt at ease, because he knew he was around his homey's. The first one to walk up to him and help him was Blood Face, he was from Brooklyn. "What's popping homey, you just getting here right?" Blood Face asked 007. "Yeah young blood, I was on the hospital tier for two weeks. Then they put me on the Crip tier for 10 minutes. That's when homey came and got me," said 007. "Good thing homey came and got you, we had a homey over there last week. He's still in the hospital fighting for his life. By the way homey, my name is Blood Face homey," he introduced himself to 007. "What's popping, I'm 007 out of J.B.G homey," said 007 as soon as 007 said that Blood Face knew off top that 007 was a big boy for real. He heard about their set. e knew they were about putting in work. "That's what's popping big homey, well it's all love here homey for sure," said Blood Face to 007. Blood Face knew they were one of the biggest set in NY, and he also knew they go the hardest when it comes to warring with the Crips.

Blood Face started introducing 007 to the rest of the homey's. "Homey!!! Come here for one minute, meet the new homey 007 from J.B.G," said Blood Face. Then all their homey's one by one started walking up to 007. One by one, peacing him, throwing up their set, showing him nothing but love. Blood Face told him, "These are my three homey's Mack, Tech, and Gunner, their under me," "What's popping, what's popping 007?" Tech said to 007. "That five is what's popping Tech, what's popping Mack, and Gunner," said 007. They all introduced themselves and helped 007 get his shit together. They all can see that 007 wasn't fully well yet, he was still in recovery. "Let us help you out homey," Tech said to him, 007 could feel the love in the air.

The cops that got 007 over there called him up front. They walked over to the side, he gave 007 a cell phone, some weed, Newports, and three real ice pick's. It was time to set up shop. 007 went back to his cell where the rest of the homey's were at. As soon as he got inside the cell, he throws the stuff on his bed. Blood Face was happy to see that we're about to flood the place. 007 told him to roll up a few blunts, shit was about to definitely pop off. 007 gave Tech an ice pick and he gave Blood Face one too. The phone was already charged up and the first person 007 called was Doggy to let him know he got everything that he sent him. "Yo Blood, what's popping homey? I'm good," said 007. "So I see everything got to you, that's what's popping," said Doggy, "I got some bad news to tell you homey." "What's that homey?" 007 asked. "Jimmy's, dead homey, he's dead, they got him at the pool hall in Brooklyn," Doggy said. "What the fuck who James? Them boys...them?" 007 asked. "Yes homey, them pussy's hold...them," said Doggy then he yelled, "yo Blood!!! Fee killed them boys...them you know. Long time him Fee dead man. Them take out!! Them pussy hole Fee dead man!!!" 007 was so upset he just sat there for 2 minutes without saying a word to Doggy. All three of them knew each other from Jamaica. Jimmy came to America right after Doggy and 007 did.

Back in Brooklyn Cox, Thomas, and Paris went back to the crime scene at the pool hall. They all had a feeling it was more pieces to the puzzle. Paris was just getting started doing what she do best. "Look over here, the shooter had to be right here Cox, what do you think?" Paris asked. "I think your absolutely right Paris, please keep going," said Cox. Paris kept looking, and then she came across something. "Sir!!! Over here, look…one of the shooters had to be sitting right here, while the other was inside killing the other two. The tire marks from the car start right here. And we also know they shot back from the car, because there are bullet casings in the car. And over here, there are bullet fragments in the wall," said Paris. "And don't forget, there are some bullet holes in that toy store over there too Paris," said Thomas as he pointed it out to her. "Oh I didn't forget Thomas, I was about to get to that next. Now as I was saying, okay shooter number one was over here, shooter number two and three was inside. So who was in the car with our dead guy? They never made it into the pool hall," said Paris. Then Cox interrupted her and said, "Very good Paris, I'm very impressed with your work." Paris quickly said, "Thank you...now let me go back to my work, as I was saying Cox." "Sorry go on please," said Cox. "Okay, that's when shooter two and three came out the pool hall most likely running and shooting at the car. And as it was trying to get away, the driver got hit right in the back of his head," said Paris. "So it would be safe to say, it was shooter one right Paris?" Cox asked. "Right Cox...you're absolutely right about that, one 45 caliber is what killed the driver. He was out here and he never went inside the pool hall at all," said Paris. Then Thomas asked, "What would we do without her Cox?" "I don't know Thomas," answered Cox. Then Paris said to them, "Why thank you guys, but we still have a lot of work to do." One thing's for sure, Paris was about her work, and so were Thomas and Cox.

They started going door to door to see if anyone saw anything. It was just like any other crime scene that the Bloods and Crips did, no eyewitnesses at all. People were just too scared to come forward. Ever since that DVD tape *"Stop Snitching"* came out, no one would say anything. They went knocking door to door, but it was just like always, nobody saw nothing. As they were getting ready to leave a man approached them, he was a junkie, he tried to grab Paris by her arm. Then Cox and Thomas jumped in her defense, as if the man was trying to bring her a move or something. Paris just looked at him and asked him, "Can I help you Sir?" Then the junkie said to her, "Can you please give me ten dollars Ms.?" "No, I don't support drug habits sir," Paris answered while snatching back her arm from the man and started to walk away. Then the man yelled out to her, "I was out here the night all this had happened!!!" He stopped Paris, Thomas, and Cox in their tracks. Paris looked at him for one second. Thomas and Cox was about to run the man away. But Paris turned to them and said, "Hold on, let's hear him out first!" That when the junkie started talking and telling Paris detail by detail what had happened out there. She knew he was telling the truth about what had happened that night. So she pulled out ten dollars to give to him. "What is your name Sir? And where do you live?" Paris asked him. He pointed over to the building that they just came out of. So Paris asked him, "Will you be able to come to court Sir, if I need you for this case?" He quickly said, "I sure will, just come and get me." Paris gave him one of her business cards, and he walked away from them. Then Cox turned to her and said, "Do you really believe he is going to come to court Paris?" "I don't know, but it is worth a try Cox," said Paris.

After that, all three of them got into their cars and went back to headquarters. Frank was in there waiting for them, while Paris was telling Frank about her eyewitness. Frank knew it wasn't the best eyewitness ever, but it might just work. That's when Frank told Paris, "I used a junkie before in a case." Frank explained to Paris, "the only thing with them type of people is that you're just going to have to stay on top of him that's all." That's when Frank started filling them in on what was going on with the DA's office, that they're about to do a big sweep in the City. They're about to go hood to hood, and lock up as many Blood and Crips as possible and send them away for whatever they can get them for. They were now looking at the Bloods and the Crips as terrorist. They felt it was time to take a lot of them off the streets so they can try to break their organizations down. At least for a while, and hopefully some of them that they are looking for will get caught up too when they start raiding their hoods.

It started to rain like cats and dogs as Pit and Shitty were on their way back uptown. Not one word from either one of them at all. All they can do was think about Jimmy and getting even. The rain was coming down so hard that Pit could only do a 25 mph speed limit. It was bumper-to-bumper traffic out there, Shitty just couldn't take anymore so she said, "Yo dog, I can't take this shit no more homey. First Baby Gangster, then 007, then Doggy, and now Jimmy's dead. Them motherfucker Crabs are going to pay for what they did Pit. I'm not going to stop until all of them are dead homey." Shitty grabbed an easy roll while Pit was driving, and rolled up some weed to ease her pain. Then Pit turned to her and told her, "Don't worry little sis, I got you. I love you like my sister homey. I will not let nothing happen to you." "Pit it's not even that homey. I just want to get even for them homey's, that's all dog. I know one thing's for sure homey, right now Doggy and 007 are going through it right now as we speak. Because him and 007 came from Jamaica first, and then Jimmy came. That's when I met them, and I didn't have shit. My mom was smoking crack, and the bitch tried to sell me homey!! If it wasn't for Doggy, 007, and Jimmy, I would probably be dead or worse...a prostitute!! Selling my ass to get high. I love them niggas dog. You know what that bitch of a mother was trying to do to me homey? That bitch was trying to sell me homey to Jimmy for some drugs. That's when Jimmy took me in from that day on homey. Doggy and 007 loves me like a daughter too homey. I was only 12 years old at the time Pit...that fucking bitch of a mother," said Shitty as tears started running down her face and her eyes were red. Pit grabbed her hand to let her know it was okay. Shitty passed him the blunt to smoke. Then Pit turned to her and said, "Damn homey, I'm sorry about your moms, I didn't know all of that homey. It's okay homey, fuck that bitch, she isn't shit...you feel me homey?" "Yeah I feel you, I feel everything you just said to me. I wish this rain would stop dog, at this rate we won't get there until five in the morning. Pit pull over so I can use the bathroom. I have to piss homey," said Shitty.

So Pit pulled over on the side of the highway, so Shitty got out and ran into the grass to piss. While she was taking a piss, she stopped for a minute to think back about the times her and Jimmy use to share together. The rain started to come down harder and all the blood from Jimmy was washing off of her face. Shitty got herself together and got back in the van. Pit turned to Shitty and said, "Are you okay homey?" "I'm okay, let's get uptown, see if someone will let you in," said Shitty. "No don't!" Pit said as he put his blinker on to get over. Someone let them in. " Get off at the next exit and cut through Chinatown. It would be a lot faster that way, because it was bumper to bumper traffic on the highway," said Shitty

They finally got to their exit, and got off and started driving through Chinatown. Pit had to make a stop in Chinatown to the store, he parked and got out while Shitty sat in the van. He had to get cigarettes, gum, and something to drink. He got everything he needed, paid for it, and then got back in the van. Shitty already had rolled up another blunt. Pit handed Shitty the bag with the stuff in it and said, "Homey, I hope this can help out a little bit?" "Good looking homey, I needed something to drink. I got cottonmouth homey, you're alright Pit's. You might make a bitch give you some pussy dog," said Shitty. After Shitty said that she started laughing. "Oh yeah that's what's popping homey. I would dick your little phat ass down shorty...flat out homey," said Pit. "Damn Pit this is good as shit," said Shitty. Then she started choking off of the purple that she was smoking. She passed it to Pit and he took two pulls and started choking off of it too. Shitty started laughing at Pit, she thinks he's funny, so she might give him some pussy. But for real, Shitty really fuck with bitches, more than niggas. Once in a blue moon she'll fuck a nigga.

They're almost out of Chinatown and the rain was still coming down hard as shit. They got a while before they reach Long Island. So until they reach Doggy's house, they're just getting high as shit talking to each other. Shitty asked Pit, "What made you become a bad boy?" "Homey that's all I know from day one from when I was a kid, money, drugs, and murder. That was my life homey you feel me? I did good in school and shit. But a nigga needed money. I met 007 when I was eleven and he showed me everything I know about the game, and I never looked back," said Pit. "I remember Pit when you were small, I didn't see too much of you. But I do remember you, you thought you was big shit too homey," said Shitty and then they both sat back and started laughing at each other.

Back on the other side of town, Ty, Mike, Kevin, and the rest of the Loc's made their way to New Jersey to Mike's house where James, Wesley, Suzie, and Pinkey was chilling at. As soon as they got there Pinkey opened up the door for them and said, "What's up Ty and Mike, all is well?" "Yes Pinkey, all is well sis," said Ty back to her. "Yo cuz, what's cracking gangster?" Kevin said to Wesley as he walks over to him to peace him. "6z, 2z, 3z, and that 7 we play cuz Claaat!!!" Wesley said back to Kevin as they peaces each other, and locked their C and broke the five.

The house was packed, it was at least twenty of them in the house. Ty and them was telling James and Wesley what had happened. Ty was laughing so hard he almost pissed in his paints. Simeon had just rolled up, and he went straight over to Wesley and James and peaces them both.

Suzie, Pinkey and the rest of the Loccet's went out back to get their smoke and eat on. Suzie and Pinkey started barbecuing just before they came. It was a good day for them so far. They were really one big family.

Mike, Ty, and James went out back by the pool to sit down. James had to talk to them to let them know what he had to do, "Look cuz I got to go out to LA to holla at Paul cuz. He's talking some real good shit right now, he talking about taking me to Columbia with him to meet the Cartel family." "That sound like a good move," said Mike. Paul was the one hitting them off with all that work that they had been getting, he was the man out in LA...the one to see. "Man all I know is...if I go out there it's on and cracking when I get back cuz. We'll be running more than NY, we'll be able to flood the whole east coast cuz," said James to Mike and Ty. "So we'll be able to lock shit down for real cuz, that's what the fuck I'm talking about Loc's," said Ty to James and Mike. It seems like a good plan that James have, the only thing that can stop them now is to make a fuck up on the streets. They have to play this shit like chess. Every move that they make, has to be done right. They have to find away to get rid of the Bloods real quick, because all this war is bad for business. It was too much heat coming down on them from the law. So for James to get out the country and back, was damn near impossible to do. Well at least that's how he looked at it. But everybody was all for it, the come up. They would be unstoppable, nothing would stand in their way at all...nothing.

So James made a phone call to Paul in LA, telling Paul to come get his money, he's ready for him. Paul is Mexican, he runs everything out in LA for the Columbian Cartel in Columbia. Paul makes a lot of money with James, he been fucking with James for a while now. James went with Paul one time to Columbia, but he never met the Cartel bosses before. This would be his first time meeting them. James knew whenever the bosses asked to see you, you knew it was one or the other. Either to kill you, or bring you in their circle as one of them. In either case, James was ready to go, but how was he going to get there without getting caught up by the Feds? "James!!! My man what's good my friend. I hear you're having some problems with some Jamaicans?" Paul asked. "I hope y'all have everything under control soon my friend?" "Not done yet Paul, I'm working on it right now as we speak cuzing, but I'm ready to see you Paul," said James. "Okay, okay my friend someone will be there soon. But James, I want you to get everything under control okay, because it's bad for business my friend. Plus, I would like for you to come with me to Columbia too. But this time, I'm going to take you to meet the bosses of the family okay?" Paul said. "Yeah, yeah Paul that sound real good to me cuz, but I have one problem. How I'm I going to get through airport security with all of this shit going on? It's making me real hot right now," said James. "Don't you worry about that, I will take care of that for you James," Paul said. Then James got off the phone with Paul.

Paul went into his backyard to use his satellite phone to call one of the bosses in Columbia. It was always safer to call overseas that way. "Jesus, what's up man?" Paul asked. "Not too much Paul, just chilling with the family," said Jesus. "When are you coming back over to our part of town?" Paul asked. "I'll be back in N.Y. real soon, the family would like to know when you and James are getting here?" Jesus asked. "Very, very soon my friend, James is just taking care of something on his end. After that we are on our way. I hope that's okay for them?" Paul said. "Yeah,

yeah that's okay, I'll see you soon," said Jesus. Then they hung up.

Jesus was just down there visiting, he ran N.Y. James usually would bring Jesus, Paul's money. But Jesus had been out of town for a while. So when he's gone, Paul sends someone else to get it from James. Everybody's out back by the pool at Mike's house. James took Trigger to the side to talk to him. James needs Trigger to go pick up some money for him, and drop off some work in Crown Heights in Brooklyn from one of his crack spots. James was starting to tell him to take X-man with him, but Trigger insist on going by himself. He had other plans to go do first. Trigger met a young lady like three weeks ago. He was trying to fuck her for a while now and this was his chance, at least he thought it was. Not knowing the little bitch fucks with Tanya and Shitty real, real heavy. "Yo cuz, I'm good...I'm going to go by myself. I'll be back in a few hours. It's no need for cuz to come with me. I'm hood cuz, believe me when I tell you that cuz. I got to stop and get some pussy cuz," said Trigger. "Look cuz, I don't give a flying fuck what you want to do! You should take cuz with you!," said James to Trigger. Trigger quickly said, "Cuz I keep on telling you, I'm hood let me call this bitch real quick cuz." Trigger makes his call, "Yo Meka what's up ma? I'm trying to come through, and get you, what's cracking ma?" "Baby where are you at, mama's trying to come see you, I'll come to you if you want me to boo?" Meka said. "Yeah, yeah I'll come to you, where you want me to meet you at ma?" Trigger asked. "Okay Daddy, I'm in Brooklyn," said Meka to Trigger knowing he going to come and get her. "Good can you meet me in Crown Heights Ma?" Trigger asked her. "Yes baby, where would you like to meet me at?" Meka asked him. "Meet me on Carroll and Troy by the game room okay?"

Trigger said. "Okay Daddy, I'll be there, give me one hour...is that okay with you baby?" Meka asked. "Good for me ma, I'll call you when I get there," said Trigger thinking he was going to get some pussy.

Meka got off the phone with Trigger and then she immediately called Tanya and Shitty to let them know what's popping. Meka said, "Yo homey I got that nigga coming to meet me right now in Brooklyn homey." "That's what's popping homey, when and where homey?" Tanya asked. "In one hour in Crown Heights by the game room on Carroll and Troy," said Meka. "Good we'll be there too, that's what it is homey," said Tanya smiling ear to ear.

Tanya got off the phone with Meka turned to Pit and Shitty to let them know too what's popping. "Yo homey, me and Pit got to go do this for Jimmy homey flat out," said Shitty jumping up and down, happy as shit that she can feel it. "Be my guess homey. Handle your business, do what you do," said Tanya to Shitty and Pit. "Come on let's go homey...Blaaat!!!!" Pit said as they ran out the door.

Pit and Shitty made their way out of the house back on the highway flying back to Brooklyn. Traffic is real bad on the Brooklyn Bridge. They're half way there, in about another 30 minutes or so. Trigger just rolled up on Meka right as she was going in the pool hall. All he had on his mind was sex, but if you was to see Meka you would too. Meka was dark skinned with brown eyes, 5'8", 137lbs with measurements of 36DD-25-44, and long black curly hair, an all-American stallion. Trigger stops her as she was going inside the pool hall. Meka told Trigger to come inside and have a drink with her first. All she really was trying to do was kill some time until her homey's got there. Trigger sat at a table with her, they ordered some drinks. Meka just played along with the plan, so she started playing with his dick. Then she started kissing him, acting like she wants him, and then he started playing with her pussy. Nobody could really see what was going on because of where they were sitting at. "Damn baby you got a big ass dick, you're trying to put all of this up in me baby? Shit I don't know about all of that shit, damn!!! You're trying to kill a bitch," said Meka as she was rubbing Trigger's dick playing with him. "Nope ma I'm going to eat it first, get it real wet, then I'm going to go real easy with you ma, so what hood?" Trigger said to Meka as he was rubbing between her inner thighs, and rubbing her pussy lips too. "Let me get one more drink first and then we'll go have some fun okay baby?" Meka said. "That's what's cracking ma," said Trigger not even knowing what was really going on for real.

Pit and Shitty was only ten minutes away from the game room. Shitty can't wait to get even. All she had on her mind was Baby Gangster and Jimmy. Pit was running red lights just to get there, they were only two blocks away. Shitty called Meka to make sure everything was set up. "Yo homey, what's popping, we're right outside...whenever you're ready," said Shitty to Meka. Meka started acting like she was talking to her mother. "Okay mom, I'll pick you up some cigarettes on my way home. I'm going out with my friend right now as we speak, I love you bye," said Meka. Meka just gave Shitty the code that she was on her way out the door. "You ready baby?" Meka asked. "Whenever you are ma," said Trigger. Trigger didn't even know what was about to go down. He took one more drink while still playing with her pussy and Meka acting like it's all-good. "Come on baby let's go, let's get out of here, my pussy is wet damn!"

Meka said.

They started heading for the door while Trigger got his hand all up her ass. Meka left her purse inside the game room by the bar so she can have an excuse to get out of his car long enough for Shitty and Pit to run down on him. Shitty and Pit sees them coming out. The both of them cracked their doors getting ready to run down on him. They're just waiting for Meka to get out of the way. They were dressed in all black from head to toe. They were both watching Meka and Trigger get into the car and once they were in the car Trigger started playing with Meka's breast by sucking on her nipples. He stuck two of his fingers in her pussy, and Meka started playing with his dick trying to kill time. Trigger stopped and started the car to pull off, it was now time for Meka to put her plan into action. "Baby oh shit!!! Hold up, I forgot my fucking purse inside by the bar, shit. Give me one minute Daddy. I'll be right back okay boo," said Meka as she gave him a kiss and jumped out and ran over to the pool hall door. While she was going in, Shitty and Pit was getting out of their whip making their way over to Trigger sitting in his car chilling. You can see the fire in Shitty and Pit eyes. Trigger was still sitting back in the car. He took his gun out and put it under his seat. The only thing he had on his mind was fucking Meka. Shitty was on the driver side closing in on him, running down real slow. Pit was coming down on him on the passenger side. Both of them was creeping down on Trigger with their guns out and ready. Trigger didn't even see it coming, because one, he got the radio up to loud to hear them coming, and plus, he lit up a blunt that he had in his car from last night. So he's damn sure not looking for anyone. Shitty is down right beside the rear passenger driver side door getting ready to pull on

Trigger's door handle to open up his door. Shitty is trying to put it into Trigger's mouth. Shitty grabs Trigger's door handle and quickly pulls on it, but it was locked. Trigger jumped up as he sees Shitty and grabs for his gun. But Pit is already in on the passenger side, pushing Trigger's shit back his brain smack up against the driver's window and the driver's side of the windshield. Trigger busted off into the floor one time while his brain was running down the window and windshield. Shitty shot through the driver's side window five times into Trigger's seat. "Yeah bitch!!! That's for my motherfucking homey's!!! You Crab ass nigga...fuck you. Blaaaat!!! Blaaaaat!!!" Shitty said as she was crying. Then her and Pit just walked away and jumped into their whip and got out of there.

By the time anyone heard the shots or knew what was going on they were out of there. Meka was playing her part to the end, she was acting as if she just lost the love of her life. So Meka yells, "Oh, God!! Somebody call some help!! Please!! My man has been shot, please help him!!!" Then she stands there for a minute. As soon as she knew nobody was watching her. She got out of there A.S.A.P. She started walking to the corner as if she was going for help, but instead dips off into her whip and got out of there. And just as she was leaving the police was coming up the street. You should already know the first ones on the scene. It was Det. John and Stg. Green from Homicide, Cox wasn't with them this time, well at least not yet. John walked up to the officer who first got there and asked, "Officer what do we have here?" "Well sir one dead body, his brains all over the driver's side window and windshield. What was left of it at least; he was also shot in his chest as well," the officer answered. "Do we have any eyewitnesses at all?" John asked the officer. "Yes over here sir, an elderly women said she saw it all. She also said it was a young lady also with him too, but she took off right before they pulled up," said the officer. "Officer bring the lady over here please," said John. "Yes sir, ma'am please follow me over here," the officer said. The first real eyewitnesses in the case, John knew it was the Bloods and Crips warring. He walked back over to her, she was a small black women looking like she was in her early sixties. "Hello ma'am my name is Det. John, this is my partner Sgt. Green," said John. "Hello ma'am, can you please tell us what you saw here today, and take your time please?" Stg. Green said taking out his pen and pad getting ready to write down everything she said to them. "Yes I sure will, I was in the bar by the pool tables until people walked in. The man over there in the car and a young lady, I noticed them because they were well dressed. But I think the young lady was in there waiting for him first because she was there first, by herself. Then he came in when she went back outside. That's when I saw her with the young gentleman that's dead over there, being real nasty with him in the bar," said Mrs. Candy. Then Mrs. Candy started smiling thinking back when she was young. "Okay ma'am, what is your name please?" Det. John asked. "Mrs. Candy sir, that is it Det. John," said Mrs. Candy. Then Stg. Green started asking her some questions, "So this is the guy you saw was with the young lady with earlier right?" Green showed Mrs. Candy a picture of Trigger. "Yes sir, that's him," said Mrs. Candy. "Okay please continue Mrs. Candy," Stg. Green said. "The lady was on the phone first with someone else beside him, I don't know who," she said. "Ma'am how do you know she was on the phone with someone else?" Stg. Green asked. "I was right next to her, at first she was telling someone on the phone he's coming and that is when she got off the phone and started walking outside. That is when she came back in with him," said Mrs. Candy. "Okay ma'am please continue," Stg. Green said. Then Mrs. Candy continued saying, "That is when she came back inside with the young gentleman that is dead over there in the car." "So what else did you see them do while they were inside ma'am?" Stg. Green asked. "They had some drinks by the table over there and started fooling around, you know that nasty stuff. Then her phone rang again, they got up and went outside into his car, because I could see them from where I was sitting at. They were in there for like 10 minutes. Then she got out of the car and came back in to get her purse. But she stopped and watched for a minute like she was looking for something to happen," said Mrs. Candy. "Okay ma'am can you please come down to the station with us please?" Detective John asked. "Yes I sure can sir, because to me it seems like she knew what was going on for real. She didn't care about him at all, because she left him here. She started off like she was crying. Then she ran off, she didn't care," said Mrs. Candy.

Shitty and Pit was feeling real good right now. They got some pay back. Trigger is dead and they are on their way back to Doggy's house in LI smoking some weed and just kicking it. "Damn homey, we got that Crab ass motherfucker, we got that bitch!!! That's what's popping homey...Blaaaat!!! Fuck that nigga," said Pit to Shitty throwing their set up high. "No doubt homey, you did that. I can't take that away from you, just take me to my bitch Tanya so we can go out tonight homey," said Shitty jumping up and down in the passenger sit. "Man what's up with me homey? I'm trying to ride," said Pit to Shitty. "Homey you can go, go out with Doggy and them, it's bitches night tonight," said Shitty to Pit. "Man that's the bullshit I be talking about right there Shitty," said Pit. "Look homey, it's girls' night tonight okay. First, we're going to the Bronx to a comedy club, and then out to eat homey," said Shitty looking at Pit real crazy like what nigga. "Fuck it, it's your world...I'm just living in it," said Pit. "So let me guess, so now you're going to act like a little bitch because I won't let you go with me and Tanya?!!" Shitty said to Pit looking at him laughing at him. However, Pit didn't find it funny at all. Shitty reached over and gave Pit a kiss on his lips. "Never a bitch, bitch I'm good homey have fun," said Pit to Shitty she started smiling at him.

They pulled up in front of Doggy's house and when they got out of the van, Tanya met them at the door. "So what's popping homey? What happened Pit and Shitty?" Tanya asked them. Before Pit could say anything, Shitty stopped him and said, "I'm not even going to front homey, Pit did his thing, homey put in work today, he got down for his crown homey. That Crab ass nigga Trigger is knocking on Heaven's door right now as we speak homey." Then she peaces Tanya. "That's what the fuck I'm talking about homey Blaaaaat!! Blaaaaat!!! Blaaaaat!! We're going out tonight bitch," said Tanya to Shitty. Doggy came walking right behind Tanya saying, "Yes homey, that's what I'm talking about, pussy Fee is dead that's what's popping Pit." "Yo Doggy, let's do something tonight homey, go out or something homey?" Pit suggested to Doggy. "Yeah, yeah homey, that sounds good to me," said Doggy to Pit. "Let's go to the club and fuck with some hoes...you feel me homey?" Pit said to Doggy. "Yeah that's what's popping, let's make it happen," said Doggy. "That's what's popping homey, I haven't been out in month homey," said Sam to both of them. "Let me call Meka and make sure she's okay, plus, we can take her with us Tanya?" Shitty said as she was dialing Meka's number. "Call her up homey," said Tanya. "Yo Meka what's popping?" Shitty asked her. Meka was just getting in the shower. "Yeah, I'm good, I'm back at my place bumming around, smoking some purple, and shit...what's popping?" Meka said. "Look homey where going out tonight, me, you, and Tanya okay?" Shitty told Meka. "That's what's popping homey, call me when you're ready," said Meka to Shitty and then Shitty got off the phone with Meka. She told Tanya what's popping and started rolling up a easy roller. Tanya was just sitting back bumming around asking Shitty and Pit over and over again, what they did to Trigger. And to Tanya shit like that makes her pussy wet.

Back in New Jersey at Mike's house everybody is chilling doing them. James' phone started ringing, it was one of his Loc's calling to see if someone was on their way to see him. James looked at his watch and knew something isn't right, because Trigger should of been there already, and should be on his way back. James got off the phone with the Loc. He tried to call Trigger's phone, and it went straight to the answer machine. James didn't like that, because he knew it wasn't like Trigger not to answer his phone. So he tried again, this time he got an answer, and it was Det. John. So James quickly hung up the phone and threw it across the room. James already knew it wasn't good whatever happened to Trigger. Pinkey and Suzie knew something was wrong too. "Damn cuz, I think something happened to Trigger cuz!" James said. "Like what cuz?" Mike said to James. "I called cuz phone, and fucking Homicide answered his shit!" James said. Then Ty said, "That don't sound good at all Loc." "Damn cuz what the fuck!!! You asked that nigger to take someone with him. Cuz is always chasing after pussy!!! I bet you cuz, that's what the fuck happened to cuz, I bet you," said Simeon and he was mad as a motherfucker. "Baby please don't tell me something had happened to Trigger! Please baby, this is too much shit for me James," said Pinkey to James with a look in her eyes as if she was about to cry. "Pinkey don't worry baby, it's going to be okay," James was trying to tell her. "No its not James!!! What's next? I'll got a phone call about you!! Mike!!! Or Ty!!! Fuck this shit, I can't take this shit," said Pinkey and then ran out of the living room into the bedroom. She was crying about all that been going on with her, Suzie and everybody getting killed and now Trigger. James was going after her Suzie stopped him. "Let me go talk to her, let me go James. You just go do what you got to do, I got her okay?" Suzie said to James then she walked over to the room. As she was walking over to the room door, James was upset and he said to her, "Alright sis, whatever you say." "Mike, Ty, and Simeon y'all already know what it was cuz. Put the word out on the street. See what the fuck happened to Trigger. Let everybody know what going on now!!!" James said to them."Cuz these slobs is going to pay for what they did cuz for real," said Mike to James like he already knew what had happen to Trigger.

Suzie went into the bedroom after Pinkey and sat beside her and said to her, "Pinkey baby you got to get it together. It's fucked up, what happened today and what's going on? One minute it's all good, and the next it's all Hell. That's just how the game is girl." "Suzie I feel you, my father sold drugs. He died from selling drugs. I don't want the same thing to happen to my Baby. My father was a big time drug dealer out in Buffalo, you know that already and look where it got him at, dead!"

Pinkey said as she started crying harder. "I feel your pain Pinkey, believe me when I tell you this. My brother is going to be okay, trust me when I tell you that okay?" Suzie said to Pinkey holding her. "I guess so Suzie, I guess so," said Pinkey to her. "Now let me and you go out tonight, we need to get out girl," said Suzie to Pinkey jumping up off the bed. "And if we do, let's not hang out in Brooklyn tonight," said Suzie. "Okay that's what's up, I would really like for my brother to stop doing what he's doing and get his life together one day," said Pinkey. "Pinkey, all I can tell you is don't worry, he'll be fine and one day and all of this will come to an end. But you have to give him time to. But tonight is ladies' night. Just me and you, and we're going to the Bronx tonight to the club to have some drinks, get fucked up, and then come home get some dick and go the fuck to sleep...feel me?" Suzie said to Pinkey. Then both of them started laughing at each other. "That sounds real good to me Suzie, let's make it happen girl," said Pinkey. Then the both of them got up and started getting ready to go to the club. But little did they know Shitty, Tanya, and Meka were getting ready to go out to the same club. It was going to be a night that no one will ever forget. Tanya and Shitty was on their way to get Meka in Brooklyn. Tanya called Meka to make sure she was almost ready to go. "Yo bitch your almost ready or what?" Tanya asked Meka over the phone. "Yeah hoe, where the fuck are y'all at?" Meka said to Tanya as she walks into her bedroom from out the shower. "I'll be on your block in ten minutes bitch," said Tanya as she was smoking on a blunt. "Call me when you pull up in front of my house bitch," said Meka as she was getting dress. "Bitch, just make sure you have your hoe ass ready hoe," said Tanya. "Yeah, yeah bitch, let me finish getting ready bitch, east side bitch," said Meka then they got off the phone. Tanya got off the phone with Meka when they were half way there. They were just coming across the Brooklyn Bridge entering downtown Brooklyn.

Back in Jersey by Mike's house, James was knocking on the bedroom door to talk to Pinkey just to make sure everything was alright with her and Suzie, both of them told him to come on in. So James entered the bedroom. "What's cracking? Is everything okay with y'all?" James asked as he walked in. "Yes everything is fine James, let me get out of here so y'all two can talk for a few. I'll be out here if y'all need me," said Suzie as she was leaving out the room. "What's cracking ma you okay boo?" James asked Pinkey as he sat beside her. "James it like this boo, you are my first and my last love. I don't want to lose you, baby," said Pinkey as she jumped into his arm's crying to him. James held her kissing her on her forehead. "Baby you're not going to lose me," said James rubbing her back. "James please just listen to me baby for one minute, please okay?" Pinkey said to James holding his head looking him right into his eyes. "Go ahead baby, I'm listening to you," said James. "Baby it's like this, I love you...you're my first love. I just don't want to lose you James. I lost my father from this same shit in Buffalo baby. Because of this drug shit, he died when I was only seven years old. My brother's doing life because of the man that killed my father. What I'm trying to say is, I just don't want to lose you baby!!! You make my life complete! Please be careful out there...please baby!!! Don't let nothing happen to you please!!!" Pinkey said crying hard into James arms. James grabbed her and put her head into his chest. He started rubbing her hair and her back telling her it's going to be okay. Pinkey just kept on crying holding James as if it was her last time. Then James turned to Pinkey and said, "Baby please stop crying, it's going to be okay. I'm not going nowhere trust me...okay? Please, I love you girl. This will all be over soon, just give me some time baby, okay?" James said as he was holding her hand, kissing her, and wiping her tears. Then Pinkey turned to him and said, "Please just be careful, I can't take a phone call like that. I seen what it did to my mother, and I don't want the same thing to happen to me, Baby?" Pinkey started crying really hard. James just hugged and kiss her. He told her he loved her. Then Pinkey told him, "Me and Suzie are going out tonight. Not in Brooklyn, but to the Bronx." Then James told her, "Okay, go on and get ready and be careful." James went back out into the living room to see what the word on Doggy and his crew. James got everybody looking out for them. They got the word back that Trigger got shot up and is dead. They already knew what had happened. It was just to confirm what they already knew.

Doggy and his homey's were getting ready to go to the club in Manhattan. The club that they were going to was called Jack. All of them were iced out from head to toe. Doggy had on a red Yankee fitting hit with a brown Gucci jeans suit on with a red Polo shirt on with a red Gucci shoes. He also had two 3-carat diamond earrings in each ear. Plus, a 10-carat platinum chain with an iced out cross on it. And a big face iced out watch and 2 pinky rings with red diamonds in them. As for Pit he was keeping it hood, but iced out in an all red Gucci sweat suit with red pride on. As for Sam, Mad Max, Tommy Gun, and the rest of the little homey's were ready to go. It was 15 of them all together, all of them were dress from head to toe. They had 5 rides all together. Doggy was in his white Benz and Pit was driving shotgun. Sam was in his red Lexus LS430 with

20's on it. Mad Max was driving his motorcycle a GSR 1,000. It was all red with black lines in it with chrome rims. Tommy Gun was driving a black Dodge Caliber with 20's on it with a system in it. Tonight was their night or at least a night none of them will ever forget. Tanya and Shitty was already at Meka's house in Brooklyn picking her up. All three of them were looking good as a motherfucker. Tanya had on a red Seven jeans suit with some Prada shoes, 3 carat diamond earrings with a rose gold chain with 10 carat in it, an iced out cross, and an iced out women's Gucci watch. She had platinum rings on all her fingers and 6 platinum fronts in her mouth, four up top and two down the bottom, iced out looking good. Shitty was killing them, she had on a red Apple Bottom jeans suit with some Louis Vuitton shoes. Rose gold earrings with 3 carat and six fronts just like Tanya. Also, two platinum chains on that were iced out and platinum and rose gold rings on with a Gucci fitting on with her hair in two ponytails. As for Meka that phat ass was the ass for the night. A apple bottom red mini shirt with the jacket to match. A see-through black Gucci shorts with some black Gucci open toe shoes on with a ankle bracelet on iced out. Platinum and iced out from head to toe and her hair was in two ponytails like Shitty. All three of them was in Tanya candy apple red Range Rover Hse 07 model sitting on twenty's.

Tanya, Shitty, and Meka was just pulling up in front of the club. They pulled up into the parking lot and parked. As soon as they got out all eyes was on them. They were at the Gentlemen Ten Club in the Bronx. Just about all the big wigs in New York went there.

Pinkey and Suzie were on their way to the club. Suzie was driving her black Benz truck that James bought for her birthday. Both of them was looking like movie stars. Suzie had on a blue Gucci jeans suit with a black see-through shirt, and a black Victoria Secret bra on. Some Gucci open toe shoes on, 3 carat in her ears, a platinum chain ice out. Platinum rings on every finger and her nails done. She also had on a platinum ankle bracelet on her left leg. As for Pinkey, she was looking sexy too. Pinkey had on a black Louis Vuitton matching bra and panties set with a white Seven shirt with a blue Seven jeans suit on, and Chanel open toe shoes. Platinum from head to toe, they were ready to party tonight. But Pinkey just kept on getting a bad feeling about tonight. "I hope everything is going to be fine tonight, for some reason it just don't feel right Suzie," said Pinkey. Pinkey really didn't want to go. Then Suzie said to her, "Girl chill out, don't worry it's going to be okay Pinkey." Suzie grabbed her hand trying to calm her down. "I just can't help it Suzie, I'm going to try to have some fun tonight," said Pinkey to Suzie trying to get herself together. "That's what the fuck I'm talking about, we're going to be alright out here. I doubt we will see any of them out here tonight Pinkey. We will be there in about thirty minutes," said Suzie as they got off the highway.

Meanwhile Tanya, Shitty, and Meka was already there upstairs in the V.I.P. part popping bottles, Jay-Z's new album was playing American Gangster. Suzie and Pinkey just pulled up in the parking lot. Something just didn't feel right at all to Pinkey. She was trying not to think about it, but she couldn't help it. Suzie knew the nigga working at the door, so they walked right in with no problems. They got a table downstairs right under Tanya and them. Jay-Z's album was still playing as they ordered some drinks and bottles of Moet. But Pinkey mind wasn't there at all. She just didn't feel right.

Back in New Jersey everybody getting their guns ready. No one can sit still at all. James, Mike, Ty, and the rest of the Loc's are just waiting for the phone call that someone has seen Doggy and his crew. "What's cracking cuz?" Ty said to Mike because Mike was mad as a motherfucker. "I'm ready to kill this motherfucking slob ass bitches cuz!!" Mike said mad as a Motherfucker. "Yo Mike, take it easy...we're going to get them fucking Mutts," said Ty walking up to Mike. "Man fuck this shit cuz, I'm ready to go look for these fucking Mutts now," said Simeon to Ty ready to go. "Chill cuz, play your three C Loc, we're going to get them Mutts...just chill," said James to Simeon. Just as James said that the phone started ringing, it was a nigga that he knew that worked at the club Jack letting him knew Doggy and his boys just got there. He told James it was at least 15 of them together. James quickly told everybody what was cracking. They all ran out the door to their cars. They were in New Jersey so they were not wasting any time because it was a nice ride to club Jacks.

Back at Gentleman Ten in the Bronx, Tanya and Shitty are doing their thing with Meka. They got Meka in a sandwich freaking her out. Shitty was in the back of her, and Tanya was in the front grabbing her ass, while Shitty was grabbing her breast. It looks like they're going to turn her out tonight. One thing's for sure, niggas love to see bitches dancing together. Tanya started tonguing Meka down. Shitty started feeling all over on Meka, and then Shitty stopped for one minute to go to the bathroom. Back downstairs, Pinkey and Suzie was on the dance floor. Pinkey had to use the bathroom, so Suzie went with her. On their way to the bathroom, Suzie and Pinkey was talking about James and Wesley, Shitty was already in the bathroom in one of the stalls. While in the stall Shitty hears someone talking and they sound real familiar. So she peaked out to see Suzie and Pinkey. Shitty couldn't believe her eyes that Suzie and Pinkey was at the same club that they were at, and she was getting ready to make a move on them. But she didn't have her gun on her, she left it by Tanya and Meka. So she just sat there and listening to them talk shit to each other. "Damn Pinkey, I really fuck with Wesley girl, that dick is out of this world, Damn!! That nigga makes me feel good girl!!" Suzie said to Pinkey as her nipples started to get hard just thinking about him. Pinkey was feeling the same way about James. "I know that's right girl and as for your brother, if he keeps busting in me girl!! I'm going to get pregnant, but that dick feel so good girl damn!!" Pinkey said. Shitty just couldn't take it anymore. Plus, the bottles of Moet was getting to her. Shitty ran out of the stall like a mad women, punching Pinkey in the face and jump kicked at Suzie. But Suzie jumped back and grabbed Shitty's leg and kicked Shitty straight between her legs. Then Pinkey pushed Shitty down off her feet and started punching her in her face. Shitty was trying her best to fight them back. But she couldn't handle the both of them. While Shitty was down on the floor Suzie was kicking her all in her stomach. Shitty was still trying to fight back, but she had no wind at all. Plus, in the back of Suzie and Pinkey's mind they're thinking, "All of Shitty homey's are out there in the club somewhere." So they knocked Shitty out cold, and made their way to the door, Then they made a run for it to the nearest exit. Some young lady walked in and saw Shitty on the floor bleeding, and ran back out to get some help. One of the bouncers came back in the bathroom with her to see what was going on. Tanya started looking for Shitty when she saw the crowd of people by the bathroom door. Tanya knew one thing Shitty had went to the bathroom, so she and Meka went downstairs to see what was going on. As soon as they got there they saw Shitty still on the ground. People were standing all around her. Tanya and Meka pushed their way through the crowd of people and helped Shitty up to her feet. "Yo Shitty! What the fuck happened to you homey?" Tanya asked her while her and Meka was helping her up to her feet. "Them fucking bitches was here, them Crab ass bitches homey! That's what the fuck happened," said Shitty as she was bleeding from her nose and mouth. "What the fuck is you talking about homey?" Tanya asked Shitty again. "Man Pinkey and Suzie them Crab ass bitches," said Shitty and right then Tanya knew what Shitty was talking about. Tanya and Meka started making their way through the crowd of people with Shitty in between them and started making their way to Tanya's truck outside. Suzie and Pinkey were already long gone from there. But one of Tanya and Shitty homey's that was there at the club followed Suzie and Pinkey onto the highway. Tanya, Shitty, and Meka just got into the truck, Tanya didn't know which way to go at first until her phone rang. It was her homey letting her know what highway she was on and she was right behind Suzie and Pinkey. Tanya jumped on the same highway to catch up to them. She was driving in and out of traffic, driving top speed. "There them bitches go right there in the black Benz truck homey," said Meka as they were racing on the highway. "Shitty, get your shit together homey, I'm coming up on your side, hit them bitches homey!!" Tanya was racing up beside them in her candy apple red Range rover. That's when Suzie saw them coming up on Pinkey's side and she knew it was them because Shitty was hanging out the back passengers window ready to shoot. Then Suzie yelled at Pinkey, "Start shooting!!

Start shooting!!" Pinkey saw them racing up so she jumped in the back behind Suzie and pulled out her two twin 45 Colt and start banging at them through the back passenger window on her side shooting at Shitty. Shitty started shooting back and shot out the back passengers window trying to hit Pinkey. Pinkey jumped down on the floor getting out of the way of the bullets. Suzie started busting out of the same window that Pinkey was busting out of with her right hand, while still driving with her left hand. As they both was flying in and out of traffic. Tanya was in the far left lane. Suzie was in the far right flooring it. Tanya fell two cars back behind Suzie. Shitty was reloading her guns, and while Shitty was doing that, Meka was putting in work. She started shooting at them from the back passengers side window. Suzie was down low, still whipping in and out of traffic. Bullets were flying from the back windshield straight through the front windshield of Suzie's truck. Suzie was blowing her horn for cars to get out of her way. Tanya started pulling up on the side of them again, this time Shitty and Meka was ready for them. Suzie saw them coming and Pinkey was reloading the two 45 Colt trying to get ready. As soon as they pulled up beside them, Suzie hit them right into the side, and Pinkey lets off at them. Suzie sends Tanya and them into incoming traffic and that is when Suzie and Pinkey got out of there. Tanya still driving through the incoming traffic at full speed. Tanya managed to get back on the other side, but by this time it was too late, Suzie and Pinkey was long gone.

Suzie's truck had more bullet holes than Swiss Cheese. Tanya's truck looked the same way too. Suzie and Pinkey knew that their trucks wasn't driving too far, so Pinkey got on the phone and called James. "Baby!!

Some shit had happen with me and Suzie," said Pinkey to James. He was on his way to deal with Doggy and them. "What ma what!!?" James said to Pinkey in a loud tone. "Them bitches tried to kill us tonight, Tanya and Shitty. But don't worry, we're okay," said Pinkey trying to get herself together as her and Suzie was driving. "What!!! Where the fuck are those bitches at now?" James asked Pinkey worried. "We lost them on the highway Baby, Baby this shit is fucking crazy, we're on our way back to Mike's house. We're going to try to make it there at least," said Pinkey to James. "Okay baby, I'll see you there when I'm done. I love you baby," said James. "I love you too," said Pinkey back to James. As soon as Pinkey got off the phone with James the helicopters were out there and really heavy too. It was time to get out of there and off the streets fast.

Back in Brooklyn James and the rest of the Loc's was just pulling up in front of club Jack. James was in his midnight blue Aston Martin. In a blue Gucci sweat suit with his hoody on. Two platinum chains on that was iced out and some platinum earring with 6 carat in it. James had two guns on him a 44-bull dog and a Glock 40. All eyes were on him as soon as he stepped out of that Aston Martin. Ty and Mike were right behind him with their system playing real loud as shit. Playing Snoop Blue Carpet Treatment, song 8. They jumped out of an Audi R8 specs and started Crip walking, throwing up their set. The rest of the Loc's pulled right behind them from H2 Hammers to big boys Benz. About 7 big boy whips Loc out. James sees Doggy's car, his white Benz and like 5 more cars and bikes. Some Bloods were chilling over there by the cars. They started looking over at James and them real hard. "Yo cuz that the Mutt right over there by them cars. I remember that white Benz tag number," said James looking back at them real hard. "So what's cracking cuz?" Ty said to James with his hand in his dip. "Man send three Loc's over there to take them Mutts out cuz. Simeon, Wesley come with me homey," said James to them. Ty, Mike, Kevin, and X-man on the outside of the club. Then Ty sent three Loc's over there by the cars to put in some work. James and them got in through the back door. The nigga that called James let them in. The music was playing loud as shit. Buck the World was playing, and James and them was making their way to one of the bars to the left. They ordered some drinks, but didn't drink at all. They were just casing out the place looking for Doggy. James took his drink and went straight upstairs to the V.I.P. part of the club. The first person James sees is Mad Max, so he knew Doggy isn't that far away. James stopped for one second to pull out his 44-bull dog and his Glock 40 looking around for Doggy. James sees Doggy way in the back of the V.I.P. room. He's on the phone, but out of the corner of his eye Doggy sees James coming up on them real slow. James sees Doggy jump up, so he knows something is wrong and start telling Mad Max that something is not right. James sees Mad Max about to run his way and Mad Max is pulling out at the same time. James lets off at Doggy and Mad Max running toward them. Mad Max threw Doggy to the floor and pulls his guns out from behind his back and starts busting back at James. People started screaming and running so James couldn't get a clear shot at Doggy. Doggy lets off through the crowd of people and shot a girl in the back of her head while trying to shoot at James. James jumped down and rolled to the side and started busting back. Simeon and Wesley were making their way upstairs running through the crowd of people. Simeon hit Ty on the Nextel on his 2-way telling him to crack off on the

Mutts outside. James is on his back busting at Doggy and Mad Max. Doggy trying to make a run for it to the side exit. He gets hit in the leg and Mad Max tries to cover him. Ty and Mike sends some Loc's to crack off on the Bloods outside. As soon as they did that, a crowd of people was coming out of the side exit of the club running. Doggy was running in the crowd of people. Sam was right behind him. Mike started looking in the crowd to see if he saw James and them. But instead he saw Doggy hoping on one leg. Mike started running through the crowd of people. Running down on Doggy. Mike ran right in front of him pointing his guns in his chest. Doggy eyes got big as shit. Then Mike hit him up, Doggy's gun dropped right out of his hand and he hit the floor. Sam sees Doggy is down with Mike standing over him about to finish him off. So Sam Ran down on Mike, hitting him up and taking Mike up off his feet. It a good thing Mike had his bulletproof vest on. Sam ran down on Mike to finish him off. Then out of the crowd of people, here comes Kevin. "C-up motherfucker!!" Kevin said as he gunned down Sam. Doggy is bleeding, and trying to move. By this time, the police is outside telling Kevin to drop his weapon on the ground. Then Kevin dropped his gun and put his hands behind his head and then got down on his knees. Everybody got down to the ground and the police outside started locking them up.

Back inside the club the shoot out was still going on. James, Wesley, and Simeon was still shooting out with Pit, Mad Max, and some of the Bloods soldiers. By now, the police are making their way in the club. A cop runs down on James telling him to put down his gun. Pit still was shooting trying to shoot his way out and shot a cop in the back of his head. Cox and Paris were just coming in through the door upstairs. They both opened fire on Pit taking him off his feet. James got his gun up off of him and threw it in a crowd of people. By this time, Paris was on him telling him to get down, and James got down on the ground. By this time, the police were everywhere. Thomas from the D.E.A. was trying to call help for the officer that was down on the ground. But it was too late, he was already dead. The one thing they felt good about was that they got the shooter, and that Pit was down too. Everybody was leaving in handcuffs, Bloods and Crips. It looks like the manhunt was over. You would hope the streets would be safe or at least quiet now at least for the night, because everybody was going to jail tonight.

Doggy died two times on his way to the hospital. Some of the Loc's got away and some of the Bloods did too, but not all of them. James was one of them that did not get away. Cox told the cop to take James to F.B.I. headquarters so he can be questioned by him. Cox got on the phone to call Frank to let him know the good news.

CHAPTER 10

IT WON'T BE NO SMILING ON RIKERS ISLAND

As soon as James got there, guess who was waiting for him? Frank Anderson himself, from the F.B.I. Gang Intel. "Hi James, I told you it would be a matter of time before we get you, didn't I? Now do you have anything you would like to tell me?" Frank asked James with a smile on his face, and with a look like, I got you now. James started laughing and then he said to Frank, "Yeah!!! Get the fuck out of my face pig!! You already know what it was pig! Call my fucking lawyer asshole, isn't shit changed from back then to now." "Okay James, just like Burger King have it your way, no problem. Let me give you heads up asshole. We got your sister and your girlfriend in custody. Their truck was all shot the fuck up. They are at the hospital as we speak. They were involved in a police chase tonight and crashed. Your sister was fucked up real bad. We don't even know if they're going to make it or not. So you have fun, just think about that asshole," said Frank to James. James just looked at Frank as he left out the room, looking at James smiling at him. When Frank left James, he left him with something to think about. All James could do was pray for them, hoping everything is going to be alright. One thing's for sure, we all know that when it rain it pours, and tonight it is pouring cats and dogs hard outside. You can hear the rain coming down smacking the building window really hard. James' lawyer White finally gets there. He's in the room with James looking at his charges that they have him for. "James, I told you to chill out didn't I!" White said mad at James. "Look White!

Fuck all of that shit right now. Find out what's up with my sister and my girl for me?" James said to White. "Don't worry, they are doing fine for now. The hospital called your family, and then your family called me. It seems like they were in a shoot out with some other females. And it doesn't look to good at all James. They're going to jail too James, as soon as they come out the hospital," White told James, James didn't like that at all. "Look White! Get my people out of this bullshit!" James said to him. "I'm already on it, don't say know more. I got you James," said White as he was walking out.

Paris, Thomas, John, and Green are all at the hospital with Doggy, Pit, Sam, Shitty, Tanya, Meka, Pinkey, and Suzie. Doggy, Pit, and Sam are fighting for their lives right now. It's so much police in the hospital that you would think they were protecting the President of the United States. No one was getting in or out without a clearance. It was just too many of them on one floor. It looked like a police headquarters. Thomas started talking to Paris and John about the night. "I'm glad we got these motherfucker off of the street," said Thomas to them both. "We didn't get all of them Thomas, but we did do a good job tonight," said Paris to them both. "Me and Green missed out on everything. By the time we got into the club, y'all had the situation under control man," said John to all of them. "It was fucking crazy yo, no bullshit, this Blood and Crip shit is crazy. That fucking Blood didn't die, lucky motherfucker," said Thomas to Paris knowing he's going to be the one to inform the dead cop family. "Two innocent people dead inside the club plus a cop. I hope the Judge throws the book at their ass. Fucking animals! I tell you, just animals," said Paris to them as they were sitting in the hospital. Then one of the doctor's walked out into the hallway where Paris, Thomas, John, and Green were sitting to let them know that Doggy and Pit was going to pull through. All of them felt good about the fact that they are going to pull through because they really would like them to stand trial for their crimes. This was one of the largest cases in New York City. It wasn't looking to good for the Bloods or the Crips right now . They were NY's number one enemy. Frank came to the hospital to check on Paris and them. "Good, good work to all of y'all for getting these animals off the street," said Frank clapping as he walked in. "All in a day's work sir," said Paris to Frank. "I wish you were there to see it sir," said Thomas to Frank. "As long as it got done, that's all that matters, and believe me this is going to be a long trial. We got those motherfuckers," said Frank with a smile. The local news station had their TV cameras were all was outside of the hospital trying to get information on all of them. Paris and Thomas gave a little bit as they were leaving the hospital.

007 was at Rikers Island smoking with some of his homey's when he heard Doggy's name on TV. He came out of his cell, and went by the TV. Doggy's face was all over it, along with everybody else's pictures too. 007 knew it's not looking good for the Bloods and Crips, they got them on murder charges, conspiracy, racketeer, and king pin charges. "Damn homey, shit don't look good, fuck!!" 007 said to all the homey's that was there in the unit. Then Blood Face walked to him and said, "Damn homey, it looks like they will soon all be here with us soon. What the fuck is really good homey?" "Damn homey, that's all your homey's on TV?" Mack asked 007. "Not all of them homey, some of them were Crabs, homey. Like that Crab ass nigga James. His bitch ass Fee died homey," said 007 to

all of them mad as shit. 007 got up and walked to his cell to get on his phone to call his girl Tee to see what she knows. "All I know is that Doggy in the hospital fighting for his life right now as we speak. And Tanya, Shitty, and Pit are there too. They all got shot up real bad," said Tee. "Tee, what is my lawyer saying about my case baby?" 007 asked her. "He's telling me he should get you a bail Wednesday when you go to court," said Tee to him. "Okay that's what's popping, I can work with that. Is he sure of that?" 007 asked her. "He not really sure, but more than likely you should get one baby," said Tee to 007. 007 got off his phone and went back out of his cell into Blood Face's cell to roll up some purple. Then started smoking with the rest of them and letting them know what was going on for real. "What's popping big homey, you okay?" Blood Face asked 007. "Na homey, shit don't sound to good right now. But fuck it; it is what it is homey," said 007 to them. "I feel you homey, I feel you. We're all here for you big homey...we're here from the top to the bottom big homey," said Blood Face to 007 as he peaces him. "Yo Blood Face you think my little ruby is coming in today homey?" 007 asked Blood Face about his CO girlfriend. "I think so homey. As a matter of fact, that bitch is here today homey," said Blood Face to 007. "A nigga need to see her A.S.A.P homey. Flat out, I need some pussy homey," said 007 to Blood Face.

007 got on his phone and left her a message on his ruby Kenya's cell phone letting her know he needs to see her. And he has two hundred dollars for her, and that he needs some pussy A.S.A.P. Meanwhile he just sat back and continued smoking with the rest of the homey's waiting for her to call back or come through.

Blood Face and them are still watching the news on TV. None of them knew that 007 and Doggy was that big uptown. "Damn homey, y'all was really getting it uptown. That's what the fuck is popping homey," said Blood Face to 007. "No bullshit big homey, that's what's popping. The nigga was getting cream uptown. I can't wait to get uptown homey and hook up with them homey," said Mack. Just as Tech was about to say something. Kenya walked up on Blood Face asking for 007. "I think he is in his cell babygirl, go look ma," said Blood Face to Kenya pointing his finger to 007's cell. "Just tell him I'll be back after I make my rounds; my LT on my ass today," said Kenya to Blood Face as she left back out. "You got that homey, I got you, I'm going to tell him now," said Blood Face to her as she was leaving back out to do her rounds. Blood Face got up to go to 007's cell to let him know he just spoke to his little ruby Kenya. "Kenya said that she'll be back as soon as she makes her rounds, because her LT is on her ass right now," said Blood Face. "That's what's popping homey, I'm just chilling now, getting my mind together. I'll holler at y'all homey later," said 007 to Blood Face. Blood Face went back to his cell with the rest of the homey's. And they just kept on doing their thing.

Kenya finally was finished doing her rounds; now her LT was off of her back. So she was on her way back to 007's cell. Plus, they just called yard for them to go outside. 007 stayed back because he already knew that Kenya was on her way back. Blood Face stayed back to watch out for them. As soon as Kenya got in there, 007 already had his dick out laying back on the bed. Kenya started giving him some head. She jammed 007's dick all the way down her throat; and was rubbing his balls together. 007 started pushing down on her head. She started shaking his dick in her mouth just like a pitbull would do. Slobbing all over his dick and her mouth. Kenya dropped her pants down to her knees, and then sticks her head out the cell. 007 got up and grabbed her, and stuck his dick up in her, ramming it all the way up in her pussy. Kenya was holding on to the cell door and the wall, pushing her ass back on him. She was biting on her bottom lip with her eyes close loving it. 007 like a wild bulldog gunning her out of control. Holding her by her hip with one hand, and rubbing her clit with the other one. Her pussy was wet as a motherfucker. "This is what's popping girl! I needed this ma, yes damn!!" 007 said as he slapped Kenya on her phat ass. Then started pulling her by her shoulders, and got her in the Doggy style fucking the shit out of her. She was loving it and said, "Ummm! Yes Daddy, yes ummmm! Right there right fucking there! Hit it Daddy! Hit it! Okay yes!! Mummy shit! Damn yes! Yes!! Stick it all the way in yes!! I'm your bitch! Daddy umm oooh yes' oooh, oooh yes!! I'm coming Daddy!!!! Ummmmm!!!! shit!!" Kenya started coming really hard; 007 didn't even pull out. He busted all up in her and she's loving it. As soon as he was done, he sat back on the bed. Kenya started sucking his dick again. She was trying to stick his dick and balls in her mouth at once. Kenya was a nasty ass bitch. She loves to fuck and suck dick. She started rubbing his dick all across her face. 007 was about to cum again, all on her face and in her mouth. She loves to drink his babies. She started rubbing his nuts all on her face sucking it all down her throat. By this time, he was good. She wiped her face and pussy off and got the fuck out of there fast. "Good looking homey, I needed that," said 007 lighting up a blunt. "Anytime baby for you, keep it popping boo," said Kenya to 007 as she was going. "You already know ma," said 007 and got up and washed his dick off. Then he called Blood Face to hit the blunt that he had rolled up.

The very next morning around 4 am, 007 and the rest of the Bloods were getting up for breakfast. It was about five homey's all together that goes and eat breakfast. As they were walking in the dining hall, Blood Face and a Loc by the name Sean locked eyes. They knew each other from uptown. Sean shot a few of Blood Face pops uptown. Sean was already sitting down at a table with some of his Loc's. Blood Face and a few of his homey's were just walking in. Blood Face or Sean would not take their eyes off each other. You can feel the tension in the air. As Blood Face was walking pass the Loc's table. Him and Sean was both mugging each other. "Yo big homey, you see that Crab that I was mugging over there?" Blood Face said to 007 as they were in the line getting their food. "Yeah homey, what's up with that, it's about to go down or what homey?" 007 asked looking at Sean himself. "That bitch ass nigga shot up some of my little homey's, homey," said Blood Face to 007. "So what's popping nigga! What are you trying to do homey! You trying to ride on them Crabs or what homey?" 007 asked to Blood Face. "Man fuck that shit we going to catch them niggas on the walk homey," said Blood Face to 007.

As they sat there still eating Sean called one of his Loc's over to his table named Yellow. "What's cracking cuz?" Yellow asked Sean as he sat at the table with Sean. "See them Mutts over there cuz?" Sean asked Yellow. "Yeah cuz what's cracking? We going to ride on them Mutts or what?" Yellow asked Sean looking at Blood Face and them. "You already know cuz on the way coming back. In the hallway cuz," said Sean to Yellow. "That's what's cracking cuzing, C-up B-down," said Yellow throwing up BK. Then Yellow passed the word down to the rest of the

Loc's. Everybody was on point. All together it was seven Loc's ready to put in work. A lot of them were real thirsty, the CO started calling the table one by one to leave out. The Loc's was leaving out first. The Bloods were three tables behind them.

It was about to go down, Blood Face and 007 walked together side by side. One of their homey's were up front, two of them were behind them as they were leaving out.

As they were walking out the Chow Hall; 007 had his hand in his dip and holding on to his knife ready to go. Blood Face was doing the same thing too. The Crips was already in the long hallway waiting for the Blood to come down the hallway. They were just sitting in the cut on the low, out of sight but not out of mind. You can feel the tension rising in the air. The Loc's was ready in the cut. There are several blind spots that they had to walk through to get back to their housing unit. They had CO's in front and in back, but they were way in the back and way in the front. They really couldn't see anything at all.

Blood Face and 007 was in the middle of their homey and as soon as they were in the middle of the long hallway, two Crips were moving in on their two soldiers from behind. They started hitting them up, it was cracking off. Then 007 and Blood Face turned around to help their little homey out. Then Sean, Yellow, and the rest of the Loc's jumped out on the one Blood that was up front. Sean and Yellow ran down on Blood Face and they started hitting Blood Face up about three or more times. One Loc's ran up on 007 swinging his knife at him. 007 blocked it with his left arm and then he grabbed the young Loc's arm. Then 007 started stepping on the young Loc neck and head. Then he hit him in his ribs cage one time, and the young Loc went down. 007 turned around and tried to help out Blood Face by hitting Sean in the back. But Blood Face was already going down. He took one hit too many. 007 were going to hit Sean again, but he moved out of the way just in time the CO's were running down the hall and calling for back up at the same time. Blood Face was down and 007 were standing right beside him fighting off Yellow and Sean. The other Bloods were down and two Loc's was down as well. Yellow and Sean got out of there. By this time, the CO's were all over the place locking shit down real fast.

Back at the hospital, days had passed by and everybody were recovering. Doggy, Pit, and Sam are now breathing on their own. As for Tanya, Shitty, Meka, Suzie, and Pinkey they are doing fine, but are on their way to jail. The F.B.I. are getting ready to take them to headquarters for questioning. None of the girls never got shot on both sides, but they both were in a car chase with the police and crashed. As for James Kevin, Mike, Ty, and Simeon they were already locked up. They had them in separate holding cells. As for Wesley, he was one of the lucky ones that got away that night. Thomas and Paris was the ones to take the girls into headquarters. Then Frank decided to question the girl himself first. Pinkey was the first one Frank decided to try and crack. "Hello young lady, my name is Agent Anderson. I would like to ask you a few questions. Okay your name is Pinkey right?" Frank asked her looking at her. Then Pinkey said to him, "Last time I checked it was." "Look Pinkey, you're not a bad girl at all. You or your friend Suzie. Y'all was just around some bad people. If I was you, I would be helping myself. Pinkey you know you could be going away for a very long time. Right now, you and Suzie are facing attempted murder, weapons charges all in one, and running from the police. But all of this can go away, if you just help yourself," said Frank to Pinkey trying to bait her in for the bite. Pinkey was now about to give him a piece of her mind, but as soon as she was about to say something. A lawyer from James' lawyer firm walked in stopping her. "Pinkey! Don't say a word!! Agent Anderson, are you trying to interview my client without me being present in this room?" Ms. Lowe asked him. "No, I just told her the time she was facing, that's all Ms. Lowes," said Frank . "Well I would like for you to stop because, my client is innocent Agent Anderson," said Ms. Lowes. "Well that is for the courts to find out and decide Ms. Lowes," said Frank. "Can you please let me know what's up with Suzie?" Pinkey asked Ms. Lowes. "She is doing fine Pinkey, you will see her soon. Don't talk to no one about your case at all, okay?" Ms. Lowes said to Pinkey as she walked out of the room.

Frank walked over to one of the holding cells where Simeon was at just to see if he can get anything out of him. "Look here young man, I'm not going to waste your time; so please don't waste mine either," said Frank to Simeon. Simeon looked at him as if he was crazy or something. "Motherfucking pig! I don't have shit to say to you. Get the fuck out my face," said Simeon to Frank. "Look, do you what to help yourself...yes or no? Because you're looking at life, asshole. So what do you want to do?" Frank asked Simeon hoping he'll get him to talk to him. "Okay fuck it, this is what I would like to do first. I would like to fuck your mother first. And then fuck your wife right in her asshole, damn yeah! I can feel that. Fuck you pig, where is my lawyer bitch!!" Simeon said to him laughing at him. Frank just looked at him and shook his head. And before he walked out, he told Simeon, "Your lawyer is out fucking your mother right now. And when he's done, I'll be fucking her next asshole!" Frank said to Simeon making Simeon laugh at him. By this time, Cox, Thomas, and Paris were in the building. "Is transportation on their way to take away this asshole yet?" Frank asked Cox mad as a motherfucker. "Yes sir, they're on their way, they should be here any minute now," said Cox to them. "If it's anyone of them that I don't like being here is James' girl friend Pinkey and his sister. They're not hard asses at all. They are just good girls gone bad, and I got nothing out of them," said Frank to Paris, Thomas, and Cox. "Damn not one word Frank?" Cox asked him. "Not one word at all. Then her big time lawyer showed up, walking in telling her don't say nothing at all. This isn't going to be no walk in the park people," said Frank to them all. "Well, by the look of things some of them will go down. We do have some evidence on some of them. We have Ms. Candy and the junky at Doggy's pool hall. So, not all of them are going to walk away," Frank was telling all of them. "That's exactly what I'm talking about Cox. Some of them will be back on the streets. We have no drugs from none of their crack houses," said Frank to them. "Well one thing's for sure, we got them on gun charges, murder, and racketeering. So some of them will go down for a very long time Frank," said Cox to them. "Let me call the DA office and see what she got for us first. I already heard that their lawyer was already trying to negotiate a fucking deal," said Frank to all of them. Then Frank got on the phone with the DA's office. The DA that was on the case, her name was Ms. Jones and she sent a lot of big time people away in the past. "Hello Frank, how can I help you today? Frank please tell me you got one of them to talk to you?" Ms. Jones asked. "No my dear, not one. None of them would crack Ms. Jones," said Frank. "Well, try not to worry yourself about it Frank. But for right now some of the bigger players that we already have, their lawyer is trying to negotiate with me Frank. But don't worry yourself about that right now. And as for the girls, they're not looking at that much time. Maybe five years, no more than that. Most likely they would get probation. All of the girls records are clean. But, as for James and Doggy and their boys, they are the main players in this case. They are the ones on top. They are the Cartel King and Gangster! I can tell you this. They will go down for something Frank," said Ms. Jones to Frank over the phone. "Okay Ms. Jones, I'll call you if I hear something else…take care," said Frank. Then as he was about to get off the phone she said to him, "You to tell the family I said hi…bye Frank." Frank turned to Paris and Cox and told them they could go home and rest if they like. Thomas and Paris decided to go home for a few hours. Cox decided to stay with Frank, and by this time John and Green was there.

Meanwhile, Frank was trying to get something on Wesley, but he had nothing on him at all. Nobody was coming forth being an eyewitness, nobody seen him at the club that night. "It look like he's going to get away free Frank!!" Cox said to him mad as a motherfucker. "Shit! We will find something on him, but for right now Thomas and Paris y'all can leave. Cox you're staying here with me right?" Frank asked. "Yeah Frank, I'm chilling with you," said Cox.

Thomas and Paris took the night off. Paris is from D.C., so Thomas asked her would she like to stay the night over at his place? Thomas been had his eyes on Paris. Paris kind of liked him too, so she took him up on his offer. But first they stopped at a local bar that Thomas goes to, to have some drinks and play pool. Thomas was a regular there. They walked in and both of them sat by the bar by the pool table. By then, a waitress named Jan walked over to them (one of the waitresses that Thomas knew) to take their order. Then Thomas said to Jan, "Let us have two Heineken's please." "Okay Thomas, two Heineken's coming up. I'll be right back," said Jan . Thomas turned to Paris and said to her, "What do you know about pool Paris? Try to play me?" Thomas said to her. "Come on, what do I got to lose, unless you're trying to put some money on it?" Paris said to him smiling at him. As she grabbed a pool stick, and told Thomas to order her a strong Long Island Iced Tea. Jan just got back with the Heineken. Thomas told Jan to bring back a double shot of Remy for him, and the strong Long Island Iced Tea for Paris, and some Buffalo wings with blue cheese. Jan just took the order and left. Meanwhile, Paris was getting ready to break the balls on the pool table. Thomas was just standing there drinking his Heineken looking at Paris's ass while she was bending over getting ready to make the shot. She knew it too, so she cocked it out even more at him, and then took the shot. "Not bad, not bad at all. Which one are you taking, the high ball or low ball?" Thomas asked her. "I'm taking high ball," said Paris while smiling at him. Jan came back with their drinks, and told them their order will be up soon. Thomas couldn't help but to keep his eyes on her because Paris was phat as a motherfucker. She is a red bone, 5'6", 140lbs, light brown eyes, 34DD-25-42 with long brown hair to her back. An all-American stallion with small feet, small full lips with pretty white teeth. They played about six games, sat down and ate, and had about three more drinks. By this time, they were ready to leave. They were both ready to leave because they were both feeling it.

They got to Thomas's place; Thomas asked her, " Would you like to get in the shower first Paris?" "No, go ahead. I'll get in behind you," said Paris. Thomas set out a towel and washcloth for her and a big white tee shirt and a pair of boxers for her. Paris turned on his CD player, she put on Alicia Keys. As soon as he came out the shower she jumped right in. Thomas just knew he was going to get some pussy tonight. He was acting like a kid in a candy store. He was just laying back on the bed. As he was laying back just chilling, he noticed Paris didn't take the boxers or the white tee with her into the bathroom. He was going to say something to her, but instead he didn't. He was starting to doze off a little bit and just as he was about to Paris came out of the shower. She was standing at the foot of his bed and all she had on was her gun holster with her gun in it. Thomas got up to see the prettiest brown nipples that he had ever seen. Her breast was firm as shit and her stomach was flat with a belly ring in it. Her ass was just so phat, you can sit a cup on it. Thomas was just laying back with his boxers on and his is dick was hard as a motherfucker. Paris walked right over him and pulled his boxers off real aggressively. Then she started sucking his dick and jerking him off at the same time while licking his balls, sucking and sticking them in her mouth. She was also sticking her tongue out and wrapping it around the head of his dick. She was jerking the head of his dick and putting his nuts in her mouth at the same time. Then she got up and sat on his face and started fucking Thomas' face. Thomas started pushing her ass into his face and sticking his finger in her asshole. Paris yelled, "Yes! Baby...ummmm ohhh yes!

Sss shit! Ummm! Uuummmm! Shit Thomas that shit feel good baby! Yes! Right there...lick that shit boy! Ummm! Yes! Fuck!" Paris started coming on Thomas' face. Her legs started shaking, so Thomas laid Paris on her back. She cocked her legs up high to her chest and opened them up real wide. Thomas got on top of her and held her head with one hand, while holding her breast with the other hand. He started sucking the shit out of her nipples, and then he started fucking the shit out of her. She was throwing that pussy back as hard as she could. All you heard was his balls slapping on that phat ass of hers. Then Thomas started sucking on her neck, pulling her by her hair. She was pulling him closer to her yelling, "Mummy ooohhh ye---s! Hit it baby yes! I'm loving it ye--s! Right fucking there yes! 0000h! 0000h! I'm about to cum! I'm about to cum! Shit Thomas yes!!" Paris started cumming all over the place. She was curving so hard her pussy started blowing out air. Paris was holding him tight, Thomas pulled out and started busting all over her nipples, breast and stomach. Then Paris started rubbing it all over her nipple's and in her mouth. Then she started rubbing her clit again, and then Thomas sat up on her face and tea bagged her. Paris started sticking his balls all in her mouth and started jerking his dick off while she was making herself cum again.

The following morning Frank came in early to work. Cox is already there. Doggy was in one of the holding cells. He just got there from the hospital. Shitty, Tanya, and Meka were in a holding cell too. So Frank turned to Cox and asked him, "Do you think it is possible to get one of them to talk for their freedom?" "I don't know Frank if that's possible at all. These type of people that we are talking about Frank have ties all over the country; California, Washington, Chicago, Oklahoma, and Texas,"

Cox replied. Frank thought about what Cox was saying because they did have everything they needed except one thing their freedom. So to Frank he though he can work with that, a testimony for their freedom. If they were to testify he would let them go. Frank continued to walk down the hall to Doggy's holding cell. Cox was doing the same with Tanya, Shitty and Meka. Doggy's lawyer was already there waiting for Frank. Frank met Doggy's lawyer right in front of Doggy's holding cell. "Good morning Agent Anderson how can I help you?" Frank asked. "I'm here on the behave of my client. My name is Ms. Diamond," said Doggy's lawyer to Frank. Frank shook her hand and said to her, "How are you doing? I believe I knew your father. He is the Judge downtown right?" Frank asked her. "Yes, yes he is sir," said Ms. Diamond. "Okay Ms. Diamond, this is what it is. I'm ready to give them back their freedom for his testimony on James?" Frank said to Ms. Diamond. "My client already told me no deals Frank. So I guess I'll be seeing you in court, have a nice day," said Ms. Diamond to Frank As she walked away, all Frank could do was shake his head. So Frank decided to catch up with Cox in the hallway. Cox got the same thing; not one of them would talk at all. So Frank decided to call transportation to tell them to come get them and that they were done with them.

All of them were on their way to Rikers Island. All of them were at headquarters for at least 72 hours. They made the front page in the paper in the Daily News. This is what the paper had to say, "Both Bloods and Crips organization establishment has been taking down by the F.B.I. It was a seven-year investigation, a successful bust. Over fifty people all together, one of New York's largest gangs the Cartel Kings and Gangsters will be facing heavy charges in the Supreme Court on murder, guns, and racketeering charges. The police say they still have a lot of cleaning up to do with in the city." Frank was happy when he read the front page of the Daily Newspaper.

On the way to Rikers Island, all of the girls was on a bus together. As they were coming out of the F.B.I. building reporters were everywhere trying to take their picture. They were doing the same thing with James and Doggy, and the rest of their crew. Every last one of them was putting down their heads as they were walking out the door on the way to Rikers Island. They also stopped at the hospital to pick up the rest of the girls. They had so much police out there with them that you would think they were protecting the President of The United States. The bus with the females had Pinkey and Suzie up front. Tanya, Shitty, and Meka were in the back of the bus, and two CO's in between them to make sure nothing go on. On the other bus, they were doing the same thing, they were going to make sure nothing goes on at all. In the back of Pinkey's mind, she just couldn't believe all of this was going on with her and Suzie. She thought it was a dream, but she knew it was so real. "Good girls gone bad," she was thinking and started laughing to herself. Suzie turned to her and said, "Pinkey! What's up, you okay girl?" Pinkey turned to her and said, "Yeah, I was just thinking about everything that's all." "Like what?" Suzie said to Pinkey. "Were like good girls gone bad," Pinkey replied and then they both started laughing at each other. "Well Suzie it looks like we're going to be famous after all," said Pinkey and they both started laughing again. "I know they told me at the hospital. We made front page shit!" Suzie said to Pinkey. "We'll be alright, we just got to stay together that's all," said

Pinkey to Suzie.

At the back of the bus Tanya, Shitty, and Meka was chilling and all of them were mad as a motherfucker. They both started cursing at the CO, doing what they do best. "What the fuck y'all looking at fucking hoes!" Shitty said to the CO and the rest of the girls on the bus. "Look at that motherfucker over there looking like a pencil dick," said Tanya to Shitty. All three of them started laughing at the CO. Then it started to rain, it was raining cats and dogs outside, so hard that they had to drive really slow.

They finally got to Rikers Island, and they were heavily guarded by a combination of law enforcement; the Us Marshall, D.E.A., A.T.F., and the N.Y.P.D.. They all were there to make sure nothing goes wrong. As soon as they got there both busses was in silence. Reporters were everywhere trying to take pictures of them but the windows were tinted. They started letting off the girls first. They started with Pinkey and Suzie because they were in front. They went in with the first group of ladies, and got them processed in. Then did the same with Tanya, Meka, and Shitty. After they were done with all the ladies, they started on the second bus that had James, Mike, Ty, Kevin, Simeon, and the rest of the Loc's. They took them off and processed them first, because reporters were still trying to take their pictures. After they were done with them, they started taking Doggy, Mad Max, Pit, Sam, and the rest of the Bloods off the bus. Reporters were trying to take their pictures too. They processed them in, and then started on the rest of the buses. It was going to be a long night for all of them now. They all had to be stripped one by one from head to toe, and then they were given a shower. Then they took them to the part of the jail, where they had to go. All James could think about at the time was that he was so happy that Wesley got away. "Cuz it's a good thing Wesley got away?" James said to them as they were going to where they belong. "No bullshit Cuz. Where going to be sitting for a while too. At least until this shit is over Cuz," said Mike to them all. "I know Cuz, like a year or two or more. You feel me Cuz?" Ty said to them. "Fuck it, as long as one of us got away, shit can still get done," said Kevin. "Suzie and Pinkey should get a bail right?" Ty asked James. "Yeah, yeah! They don't have shit on them at all," said James to Ty. James felt good that Pinkey kept her head up, and Suzie did too. He knew they will be home soon. As for James and them, they were on their way to C-74 mid 7. It was all Loc's there. As they were walking down the hall, both sides started beefing with each other, the Bloods and Crips. "Ha you fucking Mutts see y'all in the fucking yard!" Ty yelled at the Bloods as they were walking. "Fuck you, you fucking Crab flu ass nigga," said Pit back as they were walking to their housing unit. "Bitch ass slob ass nigga. You better keep it G up nigga!" James said to them back. Doggy turned to James and said to him, "You fucking Crab, this shit isn't over yet Blaaat!! Blaaaat!!!" James looked at Doggy with fire in his eyes and said, "Claaat!! Claaaat!!! You fucking Mutts!" Ty was right behind him, and everybody started throwing up gang signs. Mad Max started yelling to them, "Man B-up C-down Crabs!!" Then Kevin yelled, "Blaaat! Blaaaat!! Killa nigga it's on and cracking cuz. You fucking busters, mark ass slob niggas!" Throwing up BK at Doggy and them.

By this time, the CO's broke it up and took Doggy and them to where they were going. In addition, some CO's took James and them to where they were going too. The CO's knew this was just the beginning because they Knew as soon as they hit the yard together it was going to be an all out war. And a lot of the CO's knew that it was going to be a lot of money flowing around the jail too.

As for Cox, John, Green, and Frank they felt a job well done. The streets were a little bit safer with them behind bars. Thomas and Paris was just getting themselves together, they had just reached headquarters. Frank and the rest of the police were on their way back from Rikers Island. It looked like they're going to celebrate tonight. Then Frank turned to Cox and said to him, "That was a long seven years man." Cox just shook his hand and said to him, "I know but it's over now, at least on the streets. No more James or Doggy." But one thing Frank knew for sure was when you take some of them off the streets, double always come back in their place and that a new leader will be born on both sides the Bloods and the Crips, so he knew the celebration will not last for too long. Maybe a few mouths, if that. But it still felt good to him to at least get them two sets off the streets for now. Cox called headquarters to let everybody know it was all over.

Back at Rikers Island, James and the rest if the Loc's are going to C-74 mid-7. It's mostly all Crips on that side of the building. As soon as they got there, some of the Loc's started showing them mad love. Some started C-walking. All of the Loc's knew who James and them were because their set was well known. Both of their faces had been on the TV all week long. Plus, their set was the largest set in N.Y.C., also they were well known for getting money.

Yellow knew James from the streets, he use to buy weight from him. "What's cracking cuz?" Yellow said to James. "You already know cuz! G and C all day every day," They both peaces each other and brook the five. All of the Loc's started piecing each other. "Yo cuz, y'all niggas are the shit. I love y'all niggas yo," said one of the younger Loc's. "Yo cuz y'all beefing with that Mutt nigga name 007 right?" The little homey asked. "Yeah cuz what's cracking?" James asked him. "Man cuz we hit that Mutt ass nigga up. Him and that nigga Blood Face real good cuz. Me and cuz did that. Cuz was beefing with Blood Face uptown; Yeah we did that," said Yellow to James. "That's what's cracking cuzing. Did you get him real good cuz?" James asked Yellow. "Man them Mutts had to go to the hospital uptown cuz," Sean said. James definitely felt good about hearing that shit. James started C-walking up and down the tier. The first thing Ty wanted to know is where is the weed at. So Sean took Ty to his cell so they can smoke. Kevin went into his cell to put his bed together so he could go back to sleep. The rest of the Loc's was either drinking or smoking and getting to know one another. Their face's still was on the news. James and Yellow was just chilling and kicking it. Smoking and drinking catching up with each other because James haven't seen Yellow in years.

It was now lock down time, everybody was getting ready to lock in except for James and Yellow, Yellow was the worker man on the tier. Doggy and the rest of his homey's were just getting on the tier. 007 had his mirror sticking out looking at them as they were coming on the tier. Some of the homey's started sounding off at them. "What's popping homey?! Blaaat! Blaaaat!!" said some young Bloods. They were happy to see some of their comrades come through. They have been on TV all week long, plus 007 were there already. A lot of young pups were out to prove themselves too. "Homey, what's popping man?" 007 asked to him as he walked up to Doggy. They both were happy to see each other. They peaces each other, and put down the Cz and made the Crab. Doggy didn't like the scared look on 007's face. "Yo homey! What the fuck is popping?" Doggy asked as he looked at his comrade's face. "Them fucking Craps ass niggas homey. Nothing real heavy at all homey," said 007 to Doggy. "Man fuck that, the bitch ass nigga going to pay for that," said Doggy to him. He was mad as a motherfucker about what had happen to his comrades face. "So Doggy what you think is going to happen now homey with this case?" 007 asked him. "I really don't know homey. Did you hear what had happen to Jimmy? About his death?" Doggy asked 007. Both of them were feeling sad. "Yeah homey, that's fucked up...what's up with that?" 007 asked. "Shitty and Pit got that nigga Trigger for homey," said Doggy to him. "It's not over, it's just the beginning homey," said 007 to him. Then Doggy started to let 007 know that James and some of his Loc's was locked up too. Both of them had on their minds were just getting even. 007 sent Doggy some weed so he can do him. "What's up with Tanya and them homey?" 007 asked him. "Homey there here too, but they should be good homey," said Doggy to 007. "Well, tomorrow we should see them at breakfast homey. That is if they let us go," said 007 to him. "Homey, I'm going to get at you. Let me get my shit together," said Doggy to him back as he started making up his bed so he can smoke and lay back.

As Doggy was in his cell getting himself together, he really felt like rolling up some weed. So he turned to his cell buddy and asked him, "Yo homey, what is your name?" "They call me Bloody Pimp homey," he said.

The reason they called him Bloody Pimp was because he was known for pimping bitches uptown. His father was a pimp, his grandfather was a pimp, and his great-grandfather was one too. He came from a family of pimps; it was a family tradition to be a pimp. "Yo homey you feel like rolling up some purple?" Doggy asked him. "Fuck yeah homey, give it here," Bloody Pimp said to him. So Doggy passed him the weed to roll up. "So little homey, what are you locked up for?" Doggy asked him. "For attempted murder, some nigga uptown was trying to fuck up one of my niggas. So I hit his bitch ass up. He lived and got me locked up for it. My lawyer said the niggas not coming to court, so I should be going home soon," Bloody Pimp said to Doggy while he was rolling up the weed. "That's what's popping homey, get the fuck out of here. So what you're going to do when you get uptown homey?" Doggy asked him. "Back to pimping and 007 said he's going to hook me up too homey," said Bloody Pimp to Doggy. "You knew me and 007 came from Jamaica together, and Jimmy too. Did he tell you that?" Doggy asked him. "Homey, the name you just said, that's the one them Crab ass nigga killed right?" Bloody Pimp asked him. "Yeah homey, that was my brother. I miss him...you feel me?" Doggy said thinking about Jimmy.

By this time, Doggy finished putting his bed together. Bloody Pimp had the blunt rolled up ready to smoke. He tried to pass it to Doggy to light it up. Bloody Pimp wasted no time getting it lit either. They were just sitting back in the cell and getting to know one another. Doggy took a liking to Bloody Pimp. Plus, his pimp story was funny as shit. He had picture books of his great-grandfather, his grandfather and him with all his hoes in it. Some of the pictures was old as dirt. Every picture had a story to tell behind it, and he knew all of them. As for Pinkey, Suzie, Tanya, Shitty, and Meka they all was on the hospital unit in the jail. Suzie was doing a little bit better than Pinkey, so she was on the other side of the hospital unit. Tanya was on the same side that Suzie was on. They were hurt the most out of all five of them. None of them will be together for a while, except for Shitty and Meka. Tanya and Shitty needed medical care for a few days. As for Shitty and Meka they were in the same cell, right beside Pinkey. They were waiting to get a bed, all three of them. "Yo bitch! You fucking Crab, you're lucky as shit. That they put your pussy ass over there bitch!" Shitty said to Pinkey "Homey, this is some bullshit! What's popping with Tanya? Do you think she's going to be okay homey?" Meka asked. "Ya she'll be fine man, Tanya is a strong bitch homey," said Shitty.

Pinkey was sitting in the cell and then she got up to ask the CO a question. "Ms. Cop what time do we use the phone around here?" Pinkey asked the CO. "In the morning from 8am to 12pm. Then you lock in, and then you come back out at 3:00. Then later, you lock back in at 10:00 pm for the night, every day," the CO said to Pinkey. "Will I be able to see my boyfriend or my sister?" Pinkey asked her. The CO started laughing at her first and then said to her, "No baby, but you will see your sister in time, that's it. And as far as your boyfriend go, you will see him every time you go to court okay?" "When will that be Ms.?" Pinkey asked. "In about three days or so, but usually you would of gone to court within twenty-four hours. But it seems to me your lawyer is a big shot. They asked the DA to put your case in front of a friend of theirs. So I guess y'all girls will probably go home when you go to court," said the CO. As Pinkey was sitting there they were bringing in another girl, and they decided to put her in the cell with Pinkey. "Yo aren't you that girl that was all on TV this week?" Nideay asked as she walked in the cell with Pinkey. "Yeah that's me," said Pinkey. "My name is Nideay, what's yours?" Nideay asked. "Pinkey, and what are you locked up for?" Pinkey asked her. "Fucking with my boyfriend trafficking drugs. His damn ass got me in here. I already know your story. I seen it all on the news," said Nideay, "So how long have you been here at this jail?" Pinkey asked. "Three weeks, going on four," said Nideay to her. "Damn do you got a bail?" Pinkey asked her. "I got a bail already more like a ransom. Three hundred and fifty thousand dollar. My family not fucking with me right now, for fucking up," said Nideay to Pinkey. "Why are you up here on this floor for?" Pinkey asked her. "Police was chasing us, and I crashed the car. They said I died, and they had to bring me back," said Nideay to Pinkey. "Damn girl, your story is something like mine. So where you from?" Pinkey asked. "Well, I live in Manhattan, but I'm from Chicago. I go to school in downtown Brooklyn at L.I.U," said Nideay to Pinkey. "Oh shit, I go to L.I.U. too girl. What the fuck...damn that's what's up," said Pinkey. "I met my boyfriend in Manhattan, his name is David. My family didn't like him at all. But I still fuck with him and now I'm here," said Nideay to Pinkey. "Yo I feel your pain. What time do we eat Nideay?" Pinkey said to her. "5:30 in the morning, 11:00 am for lunch, and 6:30 for dinner," said Nideay. "Damn! So fucking early, shit! I don't know if I can do that one there," said Pinkey. "The good thing about that is we don't go nowhere, they bring it to us because we're in the medical unit," said Nideay to Pinkey. "Okay, I can work with that. I'm about to lay my ass back and go to sleep," said

Pinkey. And just as Pinkey said that they had two beds ready for them. And two beds ready for Shitty and Meka too, but not in the same unit. They were all happy to get in a nice bed. The hospital holding cell had beds in it, but not like the unit ones.

Pinkey was happy to meet Nideay and their beds was right beside each other. Nideay was a beautiful black and Japanese girl. Everything a woman should have, beautiful honey brown skin with light brown chinkey eyes, 5'11", 140lbs, measurements of 34CC-24-40 and PHAT in all the right places. Her hair was black long and curly all the way down to her ass. She had real small feet and she kept her hair in a ponytail. She also had beautiful white teeth and small full lips. She was definitely a stallion. Her family was going to get her out. They just wanted her to stop fucking up, that's all. But she loved her man ride or die.

CHAPTER 11

HOLD THE FAMILY DOWN

Back uptown in Brooklyn. Wesley starting to make a move for his Crip family. He was trying to keep shit moving, but police keep hitting their spots back to back. Plus, Wesley is taking too many losses. He already took two hundred thousand in losses' already. Something got to give, it don't look good at all. But no matter what, all he had on his mind was getting his comrade free and who the hell is giving the police all this information about them. So Wesley decided to change up his program. It looked like it was starting to work. As he was taking care of business, Wesley decided to call up two of his comrades Spade and Jay. Both of them niggas was about playing no games at all. They had that jailhouse look like it was about them. Tattoo's everywhere, cocky as a motherfucker, and played with them hammers real heavy. Both of them were dark skinned with their hair in cornrows, and a mouth full of gold teeth with diamonds in them. They were fly as a motherfucker, you really wouldn't see one without the other. These niggas look like they work out all damn day. Pull-ups and push-ups, and some back arms too. "Yo cuz we have a problem, we got a rat somewhere around us," said Wesley to both of them. "Ya! Who the fuck you think it is cuz. I'll break their fucking neck?" Spade said to Wesley mad as a motherfucker. "I don't know yet," said Wesley to them both. "Do you thing it in the family cuz?" Jay asked him. "Na, na, na cuz, it's definitely an outsider," said Wesley to both of them. "Cuz it sounds like to me like someone is trying to play the fifty cuz," said Jay to both of them. "I'm on it cuz, I got a Loccet that work downtown at the police headquarters. I haven't talk to her in a while so I'm going to give her a call today and see what's cracking with her," said Wesley to them. "You already know cuz, C-safe Claaaat! Claaaat! Let us know something as soon as you hear something," said Spade to Wesley, As soon as Wesley said that Jay and Spade pulled off. Then Wesley got on the phone trying to call Tasha. That is the Loccet that he was talking about. He got no answer, so he just left a massage on her phone for her to call him back as soon as she gets his massage. He knows she'll call back because she was a Loc. Last time he spoke to her she told him she was going on a vacation for three months. He's been trying to get a hold of her for a while now. He was just hoping she was back in town by now.

Ten minutes went pass and then his phone started ringing, it was Tasha. "Yo who is this?" Wesley asked. "Nigga I told your ass I was going away for a while. And I also told you I wasn't taking my phone with me either. So what's cracking in the hood cuzing?" Tasha asked Wesley. "Man all type of shit been happening since you been gone girl," said Wesley to Tasha. "Like what nigga?" she asked. "Man! James and everybody is locked the fuck up. I'm out here trying to hold shit down. Somebody out here is rating on us. You already know why I'm calling you. Get on it like yesterday for me cuz!" Wesley told her. "Damn cuz, I didn't know it was like that. I'm getting on it first thing cracking. Call me tomorrow in the afternoon. I'll be back at work then, C-safe cuz," said Tasha. And she damn sure was going to get on it first thing in the morning. Wesley knew if it was one person he can count on, it was Tasha. They knew each other from the fourth grade, they grow up together. Plus, she was Loc out too. Now all he had to do was make it through the night. His phone started ringing again. "Wesley, what's up man? I've been watching the news. Your people was all over it. What's up with that shit? Plus, I need to see you man. I need some coke my nigga, what's up?" Joey asked Wesley. "First of all nigga, I don't do shit. And don't you ever asked me about that shit again," said Wesley mad as a motherfucker. "Yeah yeah! Just come see me today big money okay?" Joey asked him. "Nigga I'll call you to let you know I'm coming. Don't call me back. I'll call you," said Wesley to him. Wesley didn't like the way Joey sounded on the phone either. Plus, he was talking real reckless over the phone. And it's not the first time either. Plus, this nigga had coke. Why would he be asking Wesley for some. Wesley tried not to worry about it because he already had shit to do today. Plus, Joey probably just wanted somebody killed. One thing's for sure, Wesley knew something wasn't right about the whole situation. He wasn't trying to fuck with him anyway today. He had other shit to do that was more important than seeing him. But Wesley knew something wasn't right. Plus, he really didn't want to see nobody until he spoke to Tasha.

Meanwhile, Wesley was out doing his runs until he hears from Tasha. By the time he was finish doing his runs, it was now eight o'clock at night. Spade and Jay was with him, they were at one of Wesley's new stash houses in Brooklyn. He had to change up spots, because shit just wasn't looking right' too many of their spots have been hit in the last month. So he wasn't taking any chances at all because they were at the stash houses counting money and getting the drugs together so they can hit the streets. But Wesley couldn't stop but think about Joey all night long, because it's not like him to call and ask for shit. Wesley was just hoping that Tasha called him with some information by tomorrow because they were losing too much money and a lot of little soldiers too. "Yo cuz, all of a sudden today, out of the blue, that fat fuck Joey calls me, and asks me for some shit cuz," said Wesley to Spade and Jay. "Man we suppose to be asking him for some shit. What the fuck is really hood in the hood my nig!" Spade said to Wesley and Jay," I don't know right now about him. So I'm not fucking with it; it just don't feel right at all," said Wesley to them both. "You want us to handle it cuz?" Spade asked him. "Na cuz, if I'm not going myself, what makes you think I'm going to send y'all two cuz," said Wesley to both of them as he was getting ready to cook some coke up on the stove. "Ya I feel you cuz, when was the last time you heard from him?" Jay asked. "Man like three or four month ago, but this time he was talking real, real reckless over the phone. And he was also talking about drugs too. The funny part about that, is that motherfucker have more drugs than a little bit," said Wesley to both of them as they were getting their shit together. "You think his bitch ass is trying to take us out the game or something cuz?" Spade asked him. "I really can't say right now for sure, but if he calls again, I might go with him. I don't know for sure," Jay looked at Wesley like he was crazy for second guessing himself. "Yo cuz, if you feel that way, don't second guess yourself at all. Fuck that shit, all money is not good money cuz…flat out, you feel me big homey," said Jay to Wesley. "Yeah, I guess so homey, that is the realist shit I ever heard your dumb ass say cuz," said Wesley. And then they all started laughing.

Spade started rolling up some purple. Spade was counting the money in the money machine. Jay turns on the CD player and puts in *"American*

Gangster" Jay-Z's CD and grabbed a bottle of Hennessey, three glasses with some ice, and a bottle of Pepsi. Big whilley style is how they lived by and play by. They love and will die for. Spade finished counting up the money, it was 350,000 dollars. They all sat at the table for a while, and started smoking and drinking. Once the smoke was gone, Wesley went back into the kitchen to continue cooking up some coke. He grabbed a scale, weighed out an eight of a key, and got a box of baking soda. He weighed out forty four grams of baking soda with the eight of key. Put it in a coffee pot, put some water in it, and put it on the fire on a low flame. The coke was so good that he had to break it up with a hammer before he could mix it with the baking soda. He was turning the coke into crack, getting it ready for the streets. When it was done cooking, he threw some ice in the coffee pot, so it can harden it up into crack. Then he poured the water out, and put the crack on some paper towels to help it dry off faster along with a fan right on it as well.

As soon as Wesley was done, his phone started ringing. He looked on his caller ID first to see who it was. And speaking of the devil, it was that motherfucker Joey. Wesley just decided to answer his phone to see what he wanted. "Look who's calling me now cuz. It's that nigga Joey," said Wesley to both of them, "You going to answer it cuz?" Spade asked him. "Fuck it, I'm just going to tell him I'll see him tomorrow cuz. What's cracking Joey?" Wesley asked him. "I'm just calling to see what's going on my friend?" Joey said to him. "I'll see you tomorrow Joey, I'm in for the night," said Wesley to him. "Damn man, I got five bitches man! Three for you and two for me. What's up man?" Joey asked him. "I'm at the dinner table right now Joey," said Wesley as he was in the kitchen. "What are you doing cooking crack man!" Joey said out of order. Wesley didn't like all that reckless talking over the phone. "Look, I'll just holla at you tomorrow okay?" Wesley said mad as a motherfucker at Joey. "Make sure you do homeboy," Joey said to him. Wesley didn't like the fact that Joey was acting real crazy. Wesley could of left Jay and Spade at the table and gone, but he didn't like how he sounded at all. Plus, he knew that the family was depending on him, so he just stayed with Jay and Spade, and just finished up what he started to doing. "What's up cuz, what's on your mind?" Jay asked because he seen a look on Wesley's face. "Man that nigga had bitches over his crib. But I told him I ain't fucking with it tonight because I know the family needs me right now," said Wesley to both of them. "Man cuz if you want to go, cuz go?" Spade said to Wesley. Letting him know that he and Jay got this. "I feel you cuz, but family comes first, you feel me Loc?" Wesley said as he was cooking some more shit up. "That is so true cuz, I feel you," said Jay.

Wesley went back into the kitchen, and turned on the fire real low. He put the glass coffee pot back on the stove and started cooking up some more coke. He had weighed out another eight of a key out. He did the same with the baking soda forty-four gram. Broke the eight with a hammer until it was like sand. He started mixing it up while the water was getting hot on the stove. While Wesley was cooking on the stove, he started thinking back to when James use to show him how to cook up coke. It took Wesley three times watching James doing it. Then he finally got it down packed. James showed him a lot of tricks in the kitchen. And just like how James showed him, he did the same with Jay and Spade. "Damn cuz, you do this shit like its nothing cuz," said Spade as he was watching Wesley cook up the coke. "I remember doing my first key cuz. That was four years ago, now I'm good at what I do," said Wesley to Spade and Jay as they we're watching Wesley in the kitchen doing his thing. "So when you first did it what had happened homey?" Spade Jay asked was just watching him. Doing what he do best. "Yo cuz no bull shit. The first time I did it, I fucked up big time. The fucking pot broke on me, and all that shit was gone. I had the fire on to high, that is what fucked it up cuz," said Wesley as he was cooking still. "I know you was like Damn! I fucked up what the fuck! Damn that's a lot of shit to fuck up cuz," said Spade to him as he jumped up and down as he was talking to Wesley. "Back then it was a lot, now days that shit isn't nothing. It's like fucking up an eight of a key today now," said Wesley as he was about to take the coffee pot off the stove. He was showing them how to cook too at the same time. "Cuz that shit is like a car, a bike! Fuck some jewelry cuz! Feel me!" Spade said jumping up and down again. Spade started shaking his head side to side. "Shit that's why I always come to you to cook for me cuz. Fuck that, me myself…I couldn't do it, not a key lost right now," said Jay to Wesley as he was watching Wesley do his thing. "Cuz I'm going to tell you just like James told me. You have to learn how to cook your shit. Because the day will come when I'm not around you, you feel me cuz?" Wesley said to Spade and Jay as he was putting the ice in it to shock the crack to make it harden up. "I feel you cuz, that shit you just said is some real shit cuz," said Jay and Spade as they watched Wesley do what he do best.

The three of them was sitting at the table, and started bagging up some work. They bagged up almost a key of crack. It took them throughout the night to finish. It was now going on four o'clock in the morning. When they were finish bagging up all of the work, none of them even wanted to go home, so they all stayed the night at the stash house. As soon as they doze off, Wesley phone started ringing. He looked at it first, and then he looked at his watch. It was now going on twelve in the afternoon. They had fallen asleep for a few hours. The phone is what woke him up. Jay and Spade was still asleep. Wesley just went on and answered his phone. It was a jail phone call. It was his baby Suzie, he heard her voice on the recording. He immediately woke up out of his sleep. He was very happy to except the call. "Yo what's up baby?" Wesley said to Suzie. "What's up boo! What are you doing? You better not be fucking nobody nigga! What bitches you got around you?" Suzie asked him waiting to hear what Wesley got to say. "Man girl! If you don't cut that shit out. I was eating all last night with Jay and Spade, girl chill out," said Wesley waiting for Suzie to reply to what he said. By this time, Jay and Spade was getting up. "Who the fuck is that on the phone?" Spade asked as he wiped the cold out of his eyes. "Suzie cuz," said Wesley to Spade and Jay. Jay was just getting up himself. "What's cracking sis, you okay ma?" both of them asked at the same time. Wesley put Suzie on the speaker phone so everybody could hear her. "I'm okay Spade and Jay! Y'all two just let me know if Wesley tries to stick his dick in something out there," said Suzie to both of them. Both of them started laughing at Wesley. "Damn cuz, she out to get you boy! You better not fuck up cuz," said Spade while laughing again at Wesley. "Wesley boy you better know what's good in the hood nigga," said Suzie to him making all three of them laugh. "Look ma, do you think with all this shit going on. I have time to fuck around!

Ha Girl?" Wesley asked her waiting for Suzie to answer him back. "I'm just fucking with you baby. I know you're doing what you got to do; I love you baby. Did my bother call you yet?" Suzie asked him. "Nah not yet, you're the first one to call me baby. You should be going for your bail hearing soon too," said Wesley to her. Then he asked her what's up with Pinkey? "I'm on the medical unit and Pinkey is too. But she wasn't fucked- up as bad as me," said Suzie to him. "Damn ma, I wish I can hold you right now," said Wesley to her. As soon as he said that the phone told them they have one minute left to talk. "Baby I love you, I got to go now. I love you," said Suzie to him starting to cry a little bit. "I love you too. I'll see you soon, keep your head up," said Wesley to her as both of them got off the phone.

Wesley just went and laid back thinking about his baby Suzie. Spade got on his bike, and went to Harlem to pick up the money for the brick of coke, and drop off a brick of coke at the same time. Jay went by the spot in Brooklyn to drop off the work, and pick up the money. He met Spade on the way back to the stash house. On the way back, Jay's phone started ringing. It was some shorty's that him and Spade met at the club two weeks ago, asking him what is he and Spade doing tonight. And if they would like to meet them at the club. Jay told them for sure, and set up a time, and that was that. They got back to the spot. Wesley was knocked out cold. So they just put the money in the safe, and left back out. Spade left his bike and got in the whip with Jay. They were going to do them tonight. They had six females and it was just them two.

Before they went to the club they stopped at the weed spot. That was on Rutland and Rockaway the Dread's store. He had the best Jamaican chocolate and purple you can every smoke. "Dread what's cracking cuz?" Jay said to him as he jumped out of his midnight blue Range Rover HSE. He had the Asanti Grille package sitting on some AF 153 2 tone 24" rims with midnight blue ostrich leather seats looking like whoa!! "Rude Boy!! What's cracking man?" The Dread said back as Jay walked in the store with him. "I need some of that chocolate and that purple too cuz. One ounce each cuz," said Jay as he grabbed a six pack of Heineken. "You went some frontal leaf shotter?" The Dread said as he signals his worker that was behind the counter to go get the weed for Jay. The Dread knew Jay and Spade for years, he watched them grow up in Brooklyn. Jay and Spade respects the Dread too. They had seen the Dread in action before. Some stick-up kids tried to rob him before, and the Dread pushes their shit back. Every since then, nobody fucks with him at all. "Yes Dread, good looking cuz, I'll probably see you tomorrow homey. Me and Spade got 6 shorty's to deal with tonight," said Jay to him as he was paying for the weed. "Rude Boy!! You better get some stone for your wood, you hear me?" The Dread said as he reached over the counter and gave him two of them. *(Stone is used to keep your dick hard)* Jay got the weed, some easy rolls, two frontal leafs, and the six pack of Heineken. The two stones Dread gave him for free. *(Frontal leaf is used to smoke weed in)*.

CHAPTER 12

ROLLING OFF OF ECSTASY SEXY ME BABY

Jay got back in the truck with Spade. The Dread walked over to the truck and gave Spade a pound, then they drove off to start their night. *(A pound is a handshake)* On the way to the club in Manhattan, they stopped at the Jamaican Soul Food spot in Brooklyn on Kingston Avenue and Bergen Street to grab something to eat; they made some of the best soul food in Brooklyn. As they we're waiting for their order, they started smoking in the truck getting their self ready for the food. It was still real early and nobody in NY goes to club until at least twelve at night. That's just how it is in The Big Apple. The city that never sleeps. Jay was smoking on some chocolate, and Spade was smoking some purple. Then they started passing the weed back and forth to each other.

All the little kids around the hood was loving the truck. They were all bopping their heads to the music, Buck the World was playing. Jay jumped back out the truck to go get their food, as soon as he opened up the door. A big ass cloud of weed smoke came out right behind him. Jay had on some Gucci frames, a Levis Jeans suit, and a blue and white Yankee fitted hat. He was iced out from head to toe, ready to do his thing tonight.

A few young Loc's came up to Spade while Jay was walking out with the food. Spade knew some of them from Rikers Island when he was there last year. "What's cracking cuz, I haven't seen you in a while, What's hood?" Tank said *(He was a Loc)*. Tank was locked up with Spade and was suppose to hook up with him when he came home from jail. "What's cracking cuz!!" Spade said as he peaces him. "I lost your number cuz. I just got out cuz! You feel me?" Tank said as he started telling the other two Loc's about Spade that was walking with him.

Jay just jumped in the truck with the food and gave Spade his food; then they sat there and ate their food. Spade was kicking it with his man Tank and then he introduces him to Jay. Before they left, Spade gave Tank some weed, and a few dollars to put in his pocket. He also gave him his number again, and told him don't lose it, use it. "No doubt cuz, I got it cuz. The only reason I lost it in the first place was because I went on lock up for fucking up a CO. Them bitches threw away all my shit," said Tank to Spade as he was rolling up some of the weed that Spade gave him. "Just call me cuz and I got you for sure alright?" Spade said to him as he started eating his food. "I got you one cuz," said Tank as he threw the C-up high and walk off with the other two Loc's.

After they finish eating, they pulled off and was on their way uptown. As they were driving, Jay cell phone started ringing. It was one of the shorty's about their date tonight. "Holla Jay," said Robin as she heard his voice. "What's cracking ma, what's up?" Jay asked her as he was turning down the radio to hear Robin better. "I'm on my way to the city now. I just got to pick up two more of my girl friends first. They live in the city, Valeria, Raquel, and Lauren are with me so far. I just got to get Eve and Dream, and we'll be there okay boo?" Robin said to Jay as she was blowing her horn because they were stuck in traffic. "Okay ma, call me when you get them. I'll be by the phone waiting for your call," said Jay as he looked at Spade and smiled at him. "What's up cuz...what's the smile on your face about?" Spade asked. "Its own and cracking cuz! We got six bitches!! Yo cuz fuck please tell me you got the E's?" Spade asked. Spade went right into his pocket, and pulled them out smiling. All together Spade had twenty five of them. They were out to do the damn thing tonight. Plus, they had the stone that the Dread gave them. It was going to be a long good night tonight. "Cuz you should already know! What it was player!" Spade said to Jay as both of them started laughing. They got the hotel room on the way to the city in downtown Brooklyn by the Brooklyn Bridge at the Marriot.

They got them a suite with two King size beds and a big ass Jacuzzi in it that was in the middle of the floor in the room, and a big ass walk-in shower; they were going to do them tonight. They were almost in the city, it was around nine at night. Jay's phone started ringing again; it was Robin calling Jay back. Spade turn down the music for Jay. "What's up ma, you got everybody with you?" Jay said as he was driving. "Yeah baby everybody is with me now," said Robin. "Okay ma, meet me by the Greyhound bus station boo," said Jay to Robin.

"I'll be there in 20 minutes, is that good boo?" Robin asked Jay as she started back driving her black Hummer. "Yeah! Good for me ma. I'll see you in about 30 minutes," said Jay as he got off the phone. And Jay turned to Spade and said, "Yo cuz! It's going to be on and cracking tonight you feel me! Nigga?" Jay peaces him and laughed.

They are about ten minutes away from them. They are going out tonight to Jay-Z's club *(The 40/40 Club)*; but first they were going to stop by the strip club called Score. They were just pulling up by the bus terminal on 42nd Street. Robin was already there waiting with her hazard lights on. Jay and Spade pulled up right beside them, and told them to follow them. They started driving to the strip club Score first. Robin decided to call Jay on her cell phone. "What's up nigga! I know you got some smoke right?" Robin asked Jay. "Yeah ma, you already know. What's up you need some?" Jay asked as he was driving. "Yeah my nigga, that'd what's good!" Robin said as she pulled over behind Jay to get some weed. As soon as she jumped out to get the weed, ma was looking good as shit. All eyes were on her, she was a straight stallion. She was Puerto Rican and Dominican, mama was from Staten Island. Four of them were from Staten Island and two of them were from the Bronx *(Eve and Dream)*. As soon as Robin hopped out and started walking over to the truck. People started blowing their horns at her sexy ass. Robin had on a Louis Vuitton two piece short mini skirt with the jacket to match. Along with some open toe shoes on. Her hands and feet were done. Long black curly hair down to her phat ass. She was 5'7", 140lbs, her measurements were 34CC-25-40, thick in all the right places. "What's up poppa?" Robin said to Jay and waved to Spade as she walked over to Jay's window. "Get in real quick ma," said Jay to her as he unlocked the door, so she could jump in the back. Then Spade handed her some weed, eazy roll and some E pills *(Ez pills is Ecstasy)*. "What the fuck is these poppa?" Robin asked as she looks at the Ez pills real crazy," They're Ez ma, Ez ma! Don't worry you're with us. Y'all will be okay, we got you," Jay and Spade both said to her. "Man I hope these shit don't have us bugging the fuck out Nigga!" Robin said as she looked at Jay and Spade waiting for their respond to her. And to be real about it, Robin and her girl always wanted to try it, but they didn't know where to get it from. "Nah, nah ma you are good, y'all with us tonight. Y'all in good hands," said Jay to Robin trying to ensure her that they were good and that nothing will happen to them. "Because I heard this shit make you want to fuck all night long. And Jay nobody's leaving with anybody else. We are leaving with y'all tonight right nigga?" Robin asked as she put the shit in her bra. "Girl you already fucking know this ma, y'all isn't leaving with nobody else. We're going to do them when we get to the 40/40 Club. So just smoke the weed now and save the pills for later on," said Jay as Robin was getting out. "That's what's up," said Robin as Jay and Spade started smiling at each other. And off they go to the strip club Score.

As Robin jumped back in her Hummer, and passed the weed and pills to Valeria. Valeria eyes opened up real wide, when she saw the pills. "What the fuck is this shit?" Valeria said as she looked at the bag of pills real hard. "Ez bitch, you know you always wanted to try them!" Robin said to Valeria looking at her and started smiling at her. "Oh shit, I'm popping one of this shit right now!" Valeria said to Robin. "We might as well," said Eve while laughing and holding her orange juice. "Fuck it everybody can take one, it's only twenty of them," said Valeria to all of them. "Jay told me to wait until we get to the 40/40 Club first," said Robin as she was driving behind Jay and Spade. She grabbed one of the Ez's, and threw it back and drunk her water right behind it. "I hear this shit feels so good when you're having sex. You just want to fuck all night long," said Dream as she popped her pill. The pills were double stack dolphin, the light blue one's.

They were just pulling up in Score's parking lot. It was value parking; all eight of them walked in Score together. Jay, Spade, Robin, Valeria, Raquel, Lauren, Eve, and Dream. All the ladies we're looking sexy as a motherfucker from head to toe. Valeria was an Italian stallion; her body was like a hour glass, you can sit a cup on her phat ass and that motherfucker would not fall off at all. Raquel was a American black stallion; she was born in Brooklyn, and raised in Staten Island. Lauren was a Jamaican straight from Kingston five the ghetto. She was a dark skinned a beautiful sexy young lady, and she was thick in all the right places. Eve was Columbian and black with short black curly hair, 5'5" and 137lbs and she was built like a brickhouse. As for Dream, she was exactly like her name, a man's dream comes true. Jay paid for a V.I.P. spot for all of them and ordered some champagne for them. He gave the bartender two grand and told her to take three hundred out for herself. By this time, the girls was starting to feel the Ecstasy. "Yo poppa, this shit is good!! Damn baby," said Robin to Jay all fucked up as she sat on Jay's lap and started playing with his cornrows. "Damn ma, y'all took them already, didn't you?" Jay said to Robin looking at her eyes. "Yes baby, please don't be mad at me baby!!" Robin said looking at Jay. Jay knew if he said the wrong thing, he could fuck up the whole night. "Nah ma, I'm not mad at you at all. Shit, give me and Spade one," said Jay to her as he looked at all of them throwing his E back himself. Spade did the same thing too. "After this popped, let's just go to the hotel okay?" Robin asked Jay high as shit. "That's what's cracking boo," said Jay.

A few hours had went pass, by now the girls were ready to go get fucked. They were having so much fun in the strip club Score. But it was now time for them to leave. They all jumped in their trucks and was on their way back to Brooklyn. Nobody really felt like going to the 40/40 Club anymore, so instead they whet straight to the hotel. On their way back to Brooklyn, they stopped by a liquor store for some Remy, candy, water, and orange juice. Spade made sure he got some Halls cough drops. He had something on his mind that he wanted to do with them. "Yo! Spade what the fuck you got Halls for cuz?" Jay asked him thinking Spade had a cold or something. "Damn cuz, I got to show you everything. Don't I nigga?" Spade said to Jay as he look at Jay, high as shit. Jay's phone started ringing it was Robin's high ass; she was high as a motherfucker. "What's up cuz yo! Boo what's cracking ma?" Jay asked her. "Boo...I'm high as shit you hear me boy!! Damn baby this E shit is good, we are all high as shit in this bitch!!" Robin said as she went in her Fendi bag and got her Cartier frames, and some gum to bite on. Then she put in Frasier Boy Gone Off the Bey CD.

They were almost at Brooklyn Bridge when Spade started telling Jay about the Halls games. Spade and Jay both had their Gucci frames on while high as a motherfucker. "Look cuz, I'm going to tell you for free. This time, one time only nigga. You listening to me cuz?" Spade asked as he turned down the music to let him know what was hood. "Okay cuz it like this, you take the Halls and you put it in your mouth. Just like this, and then you gently lick the clit with it," said Spade as he was showing Jay what to do with it. "What the fuck are you talking about nigga?" Jay asked and started laughing at Spade. "Motherfucker! Just shut the fuck up and listen nigga. Okay look, you put it in and then in her pussy. Let it sit in her pussy, until it is gone...you feel me man! Them bitches is going to go crazy cuz! When you lick their pussy with this shit trust me," said Spade as he started laughing again. "So what your telling me is to lick them bitches pussy with this shit right here and they're going to go crazy?" Jay asked him. "Yes! Yes! Yes!! My nig trust me on that. I put my flag on that shit," said Spade as he put his flag in his left hand as he said that.

They were in Brooklyn pulling up in the Marriott about to park. All of them had their frames on; shaded as a motherfucker. Their suite was on the 14th floor; as they were in the elevator some of the girl's started rubbing on each other. As soon as they got to their floor to their room and opened up the door. The first thing they saw was the Jacuzzi, it was in the middle of the floor. They had a sauna in the room as well where they put down all their bags. Jay and Spade had a book of CD's for the CD player that was in the room, and Robin got right on the phone and ordered a fuck movie to get everybody in the mood. Raquel went straight to the CD player and she got Boosie's CD out *"Bad Ass"* and put it in the CD player. Valeria went straight to the bathroom, and Eve went straight behind her. Jay went and turned on the sauna. Spade started filling up the Jacuzzi with warm water. Robin was on the bed smoking and watching the movie. She started playing with her pussy. Dream and Valeria was on the bed with Robin, as for Eve, Raquel, and Lauren, they were on the other bed. Spade and Jay was the first ones to get out of their clothes. They were just in their boxers. Both of them got in the sauna and told the girls to come on in with them and bring the weed. All of the girls got undress, all of them had on Victoria's Secret on. Robin had a black and pink out lining see-through top and bottom on with booty cutters on with half of her ass out. Valeria had on a blue top and bottom see-through booty cutters on. Raquel had on a black and white matching see-through with a thong on. Lauren had an all white see-through top and bottom thong on with her ass hanging out and you can't even see the thong line in her ass crack. Eve had on a all black bra and panties on the booty cutters as well. Dream had on a light blue bra and booty cutter on see-through ones too. Every last one of their pussy's looked like footballs. They all had belly rings too. They walked into the sauna one by one. They all sat together and started smoking some weed. Jay and Spade knew they were fucked up. And by them being in the sauna, it was making them feel better and more higher. As they sat there their hair started to sweat out. It didn't matter because their hair was all theirs. They all started coming out of their bra and panties. Some of the girl's started rubbing each other. Robin sat down between Jay legs. She pulled his dick out through his boxers and started sucking it.

As for Lauren, she went right between Spade legs and started doing the same thing. Eve sat right beside Spade to his left, and Raquel sat on his right side. They started passing the blunt back and forth to each other. Spade started playing with Eve's pussy and at the same time sucking on Raquel nipples.

As for Jay, he was in the middle of Dream and Valeria, and he was doing the same thing to both of them while Robin was sucking his dick. It was starting to get real hot in there, so they all went to the Jacuzzi to get it cracking off.

As Jay and Spade was coming out of the sauna. All the girls was in the Jacuzzi. Then Spade went and got the Halls. "Yo cuz here nigga," said Spade while handing Jay a pack of Halls. "Man cuz this shit better work," said Jay as he opened up the pack of Halls and put two of them in his mouth. The Jacuzzi was built into the floor. Spade and Jay both jumped in. Spade was on one side with Raquel, Lauren, and Eve. Jay was on the other side with Robin, Dream, and Valeria. Robin asked Jay to come on the bed with all three of them. So all four of them got up and went on the bed. All the girls were naked by this time. Jay told Robin to lie back on the bed, and for Dream and Valeria to lay beside her. Then Jay got between Robin's legs, and started licking her on her inner thighs. Then he went straight to her clit. Licking it gently with the Halls in his mouth. He put one of them inside of her vagina. Jay started rubbing Robin's breast while he was eating her pussy out. The Ecstasy pills been took effect on all of them. Now as for the Halls, it was having its own effect as well. "Oh shit! Poppy! What t---he fuck your...doing...ummmm ummmmm!! Yes daddy, my pussy feel fucking! Oooh...shit...that feel good yes!" Robin said as she was coming Jay had her legs pinned down on her chest. Then Jay reached over on the bed and grabbed two more Halls and put both of them in his mouth. He told Dream to eat Robin's pussy out while he put the two Halls in Dream's pussy. Jay blew them right up in there. Then he grabbed two more Halls and did the same thing to Valeria. Then Jay made Valeria sit on his face like a bullfrog, she started fucking his face and going crazy. All behind the effect of the Halls and E pills both together. Robin sat right on his dick with her back turned to him. Dream was between Jay legs laying down. Robin started playing with Dream's pussy and riding Jay at the same time. Dream started coming from Robin rubbing her pussy, "Oooh shit ummm yes...ooooh shit what the fuck oooowww...ooooow damn! Shit Robin, I'm coming girl fuck!" Dream started playing with her breasts with sweat pouring from her head. Spade was on the other bed doing him. He also ate their pussy's out with the Halls. Spade had Eve in the back shot, making her eat Laura's pussy out while Raquel was sitting on Lauren's face. Lauren started fucking the fuck out of Raquel's face. All three of them started comming at the same time. "Damn baby! You know what the fuck your doing...shit...fuck. Ooooow, ooow yes daddy," said Eve as she was biting on her lips with sweat running down her face. "Bitch! Don't stop, I'm about to cum again!" Laura said to Eve as she was pushing her head into her pussy. She started to sweat all over the place. "Get back on my face Bitch!! I'm not done yet with you bitch!" Lauren said to Raquel. Lauren was grabbing her by the hips while pushing Raquel's vagina in her face. Sticking her tongue in Raquel's vagina, Raquel started screaming grabbing the bed's headboard while shaking and cumming out of control. "Ooooh, oooh...shit ummm!. Yes eat that shit bitch!! Eat that. Ummm!...right there!" Raquel said as sweat dripped down her back to the crack of her phat ass.

Back on the other bed, Jay was now fucking Dream. He had Dream laying on her back with both of her legs on his shoulders. Robin and Valeria were doing the 69, eating each other out. "Damn! Jay this dick feels so good boo! Ooooh hit...I--t boo...right there!!" Dream said grabbing Jay by his shoulders while sweat was running down his face and dripping on Dream's face as he had Dream's legs on his shoulders. Dream grabbed her breast, and started sucking on her nipple and playing with the other one at the same time. It was turning Jay on, so he started fucking her harder, making her breast bounce back and forth. Then Jay got up and sat between Dream's breast. Dream started pushing her breast together on Jay's dick. Holding his dick between her breast, as Jay titty fucked her. Then Dream sucks her tongue out sweating hard as shit catching the head of Jay dick in her mouth. As Jay's dick was going through Dream's 36DD breast, he grabbed her breast firmly, rubbing her nipples they were the size of a quarter piece. Dream's nipples was hard as a motherfucker. Dream had her head sitting up, catching all of Jay's dick in her mouth. "Ummmm, ummm damn Jay give...it to me...ummmm," said Dream as she was sucking on Jay's dick.

Spade was over on the other bed fucking Lauren sexy Jamaican phat ass. Lauren was phat in all the right places; 36CC-26-44, 5'9", a dark skinned stallion. Lauren sat over Spade like a bullfrog with her hands on his chest as she was bouncing up and down and side to side. Grinding on his dick like a true Jamaican. Sweat was dropping down Lauren silky dark nice nipples from her face on down to her stomach. "Damn girl this shit is good! Damn ma do you damn!" Spade said as he grabbed Lauren's breast, Raquel came and sat over his face on her knees. Spade stuck his tongue in Raquel's pussy, Raquel had her legs wide open. She started eating out Eve's pussy while Spade was eating her out. Lauren was fucking the shit out of Spade. Then Eve started pushing Raquel's face into her vagina. Eve was starting to cum real hard. So Raquel stuck her tongue inside Eve's pussy and playing with her clit at the same time. Making her top lip rub on Eve's clit and using her finger too at the same time. "Raquel, what the fuck! Your trying to do to me bitch! Shit...yes! Oooh, oooh...shit hhhhh...yes!" Eve asked her as she sweating, and comming real hard all in Raquel's mouth. Raquel was eating it, and shaking it like a pitbull out of control.

Jay was finished fucking Dream for now. Jay now had Valeria laying on her side with one of her legs pushed up to her chest and the other one laying straight down. He was right between her legs and started fucking her brains out. Holding on to Valeria's hip and breast at the same time.

Valeria's mouth was wide open moaning real loud. Her face was full of sweat. Valeria started playing with Dream's pussy while Dream was eating out Robin's pussy. Then Jay stuck two of his fingers into Valeria's mouth for her to suck on. Valeria had two fingers up in Dream with her thumb rubbing on Dream's clit at the same time. Dream had three fingers up in Robin; two in Robin's pussy, and one in Robin's asshole. "Damn bitch! I feel like I got to shit bitch! Shit!" Robin said to Dream while Dream was finger fucking the shit out of her. Jay grabbed Valeria by her hair and then he started smacking her on her yellow phat ass. Valeria was an Italian Stallion; 32DD-26-40 with an apple bottom phat ass with the prettiest pink nipples. While Jay was fucking the shit out of Valeria, he took his dick out, and stuck it in her asshole. As soon as Valeria felt Jay's dick go up in her asshole, she grabbed Dream's inner thighs and started biting on her lips. She was sweating so hard. Valeria's asshole was so tight Jay had to hold her down. "Shit baby!...ooooh, oooo, oooo...shit Jay!!! I feel like I'm going to shit on myself!!! Boo...ooooh..shit!! Ummmm, ummmm, damn boo shit oooh ssssshit!!" Valeria said. Then Dream put her face by Valeria's pussy and started playing with it. Dream opened up her mouth, and stuck her tongue out so Jay could cum on it. As soon as he pulled out of Valeria's asshole, Dream started sucking his dick. Jay busted off right in Dream's mouth and her face. Valeria turned around and started sucking his dick with Dream, and they started kissing each other in the mouth. Jay was now lying on his back on the bed. Robin got between his legs, and started sucking his balls while Valeria and Dream was licking his dick.

Spade had Raquel laying flat on her stomach. Raquel was licking and eating Lauren's pussy out. Eve was sitting on Raquel's back facing Spade holding Raquel's booty cheeks open real wide. Raquel was phat as a motherfucker. An all American Black Stallion, 34CC-26-40. Spade jammed his dick in Raquel's asshole and she started screaming for her life grabbing the bed; she felt like a virgin all over again. Spade was loving it, a nice and tight wet asshole, and her wet pussy too. Lauren started pushing Raquel's face into her pussy. Lauren started coming in Raquel's mouth and loving it. "Yes bitch eat, eat this pussy girl!!" Lauren said pushing Raquel's face into her pussy. Lauren started sweating all over her body. "Shit Spade, take it easy baby please. I never got fucked in my asshole before!! Shit...I really feel like I got to shit," Raquel said as her legs started to give out on her. She was getting weak as shit, and started shaking. Spade had his whole dick in her asshole, and Spade was loving it. Then Spade took his dick out, and turned Raquel on her back. He put both of her legs on his shoulders, and started fucking her in her ass again. Then Spade got on his back, and made Raquel sit on his dick with her back facing him. He stuck his dick right in her asshole again. Raquel fell back on Spade's chest. Eve and Lauren both started eating her out together, and finger fucking her in her pussy too and sucking on his balls. Spade started holding Raquel by her breast playing with her nipples as he was fucking her in her asshole. She was holding him by his head kissing him. She started coming real hard. All of them were sweating. Lauren was still sucking and licking on Raquel's clit, and Eve was sucking on Spade balls with her finger in Raquel's pussy. "Shit!! Shit!!! I'm coming shit!! Wool!!!" Spade said as Lauren pulled Spade's dick out of Raquel's asshole. And then catching all his cum in her mouth, then passing his dick to Eve so she can get some too. While Lauren started sucking on Spade balls, Raquel was holding Spade's head kissing on him. All four of them was sweating and just laying back chilling.

After both of them were done, Spade and Jay decided to switch up. Spade got on the bed with Robin, Dream, and Valeria and as for Jay, he got on the other bed with Raquel, Lauren, and Eve. The party started all over again. By the time they we're done fucking. It was seven in the morning. They we're all exhausted from the Ecstasy and the long night of fucking. Everybody was in slow motion getting dress and getting in the shower. It was now check out time. The girl's got into their hummer, and were on their way home.

Jay and Spade were on their way to the stash house where Wesley was at chilling. As Jay and Spade were coming in, Wesley was just getting up making his way to the shower. Jay and Spade both sat down on the couch in the living room. "What's cracking cuz!" Jay said happy as a motherfucker as he peaces Wesley. "What the fuck y'all two so happy about cuz?" Wesley said as he was walking into the bathroom so he can get into the shower. "Cuz we fucked all six of them bitches last night," said Spade laughing with Jay. "Oh yeah? That's what's cracking cuz," said Wesley as Jay and Spade was telling him all the details. As they were talking Wesley's phone started ringing. But by the time he got to it, he had already missed the call. He thought it was probably Suzie calling him, so he looked at his caller ID. It was calls from Joey all night long. Wesley phone started ringing again this time it was Tasha, his little sis calling him real early. Tasha was a beautiful young lady, she was Black and Hawaiian and born in America. Her complexion was Honey brown, 5'5" with gray eyes, and short curly black and blue hair,36D-27-40, she had pretty small lips, and pretty white teeth. She worked in the D.E.A. offices, so she knew almost everything that went down on the streets, and in the building. "Nigga come see me A.S.A.P. cuz. I got some shit to tell you and show you too," said Tasha to Wesley. "You can't tell me now?" Wesley asked trying to get dress real quickly. "Nah nig, just come one," said Tasha and got off the phone with Wesley. Wesley told Jay and Spade he'll be right back in a few. Wesley told both of them that he going to see Tasha, and for them to take care of everything. "Yo cuz, you sure you don't want us to go with you?" Jay asked as Wesley was walking out the door. "Nah Loc, just take care of shit while I'm gone. I'll be back by four o'clock, I'm hood nigga," said Wesley as Jay and Spade both peaces him. "C-safe cuz," "C-up," both of them said to Wesley as he walked out the door. Wesley jumped into his midnight blue Benz to go meet up with Tasha. His phone started ringing again. This time it was James' lawyer calling him to give him heads-up on the case. "Good morning Wesley, how are you doing today?" James' lawyer Mr. White said to him. "I'm good, what's up with my brothers? Any good news yet?" Wesley asked. "Yes, yes some good news, and some bad news too. Let me give you the bad news first. The bad news is you have a rat in your family. We don't know who it is yet. The good news is the bail review is tomorrow morning at 9:30. I spoke to the girl's lawyer and the DA on the case. The girls are definitely getting bail," said Mr. White to Wesley. "Okay that's good, but what about my brother's, what's up with them?" Wesley asked Mr. White while he was driving. "We will find out about them tomorrow on James, Mike, Ty, Kevin, and Simeon okay? Now as for you, please stay out of trouble. Keep your ass out of jail okay?" White said to Wesley. "No doubt, sure will, I'll see you tomorrow," said Wesley just before he was about to hung up with White. White said to him, "I think you should stay away from the courthouse. I'll call you, and I we'll let you know what's up okay?" Mr. White said. "Okay that's what's cracking," said Wesley. They both got off the phone and Wesley called Tasha to let her know he's right down the street from her. Tasha told him she is right out front of the building. Wesley saw her as soon as he pulled up on the block. He pulled over so she can get in. Tasha jumped in and they drove off down the block to Burger King. As they were pulling in the parking lot of Burger King Tasha said, "What's cracking big brother, Look at this nigga right here Joey." Tasha pulled out Joey's picture to show Wesley. "This motherfucker's a rat cuz!" Tasha said as she was showing Wesley all the picture's of him with the D.E.A. agent. "Oh yeah! That's what's cracking, good looking cuz," said Wesley as he looked at the picture over and over again. "He's a fucking CI, no bullshit. He's the one the feds is going to use to testify against James in his case cuz. He's the eyewitness, the main one at that. And some girl from the club too; she really didn't see anything at all. Well, at least on y'all, for sure. But as for Doggy and them, I don't know. Here is her information anyway," said Tasha as she handed Wesley everything that she had on both of them. "Damn sis, good looking cuzing, and I must say you look fucking beautiful girl," said Wesley making Tasha smile at him. "Stop that shit boy, I love you nigga, take me back to where you got me at," said Tasha. So, Wesley took Tasha back to where he got her from. After that he started making his way back to the crib. He knew something wasn't right with Joey's ass from the beginning. Then

Wesley started to think to himself about Joey asking him for some shit when the nigga have just as much shit as they do. Wesley had something planed for his ass real nice on ice. On his way back from seeing Tasha. He stopped at a store for something to eat and drink. He called Spade and Jay to see what they were doing. Spade was letting him know that they're out doing what they suppose to be doing; picking up money and dropping shit off. Wesley tells him that so they don't go anywhere. And after they do what they got to do, meet him back at the crib, because they got some work to go do tonight A.S.A.P.

Wesley got off the phone and paid for his stuff. He got back in his whip, and drove off. He started driving toward his crib, and his phone started ringing. It was James' lawyer again. Wesley was hoping it was some good news this time around. "What's cracking, tell me something good?" Wesley said to him as he was driving. "I wish I could, really tell you something good. But right now, I don't have none right now. If this eyewitness makes it to court, it does not look good at all. I just got word they're going to use their CI against the girls too to try and stop them from getting bail. I'm just giving you a head's up on what going on," said White to Wesley. "Okay, okay don't worry about it. They will be home, this I know for sure. Call me back tomorrow. Let me do what I got to do, you just let me know something tomorrow okay?" Wesley said with a look in his eyes like he knows what got to be done. "Okay like I said the first time, stay out of trouble okay?" White said. "I got ya," said Wesley as he got off the phone. Wesley already knows he got to go do this tonight A.S.A.P. He made his way back to the crib. Spade and Jay were already there waiting for him. Wesley parked and went straight into the crib.

CHAPTER 13

SHAKE HIM BOYS

Spade and Jay were sitting in the living room getting some more shit together. "What's cracking cuz, what's hood nigga?" Jay asked as Wesley walked over to Spade and Jay at the table. "Yo cuz what's hood," said Spade. "Look cuz, I know who the fucking rat is now. It's that bitch ass nigga Joey. I knew something wasn't right with his ass. You know my little sis works for the D.E.A., so she put me on point about Joey's bitch ass and some bitch from the club too. But she's not the one we really have to worry about at all. Plus, I just got off the phone with James' lawyer. He told me they're going to bring in a government eyewitness in tomorrow at their bail review," said Wesley. "So what's cracking cuz! We going to get this fucking rat or what?" Spade asked mad as a motherfucker at what he heard Wesley saying to them. "You already know that cuz," said Jay. "We going to get that bitch tonight. I'm about to call that bitch now, and tell him I need to see him," said Wesley as he was about to call Joey. "Cuz I think we should just go over there, don't call him at all. More than likely his phone is tap, and if it is and he ends up dead, you will be the main one that the Feds will look at, feel me?" Spade said as he was smoking on some weed. Then he passed it to Wesley. "I feel you cuz, we going to kidnap that bitch tonight, take his ass to the Bronx, and feed his ass to the dogs," said Spade as they all started laughing as they were smoking on the weed getting ready for the big night. "Damn cuz, that sounds good to me. You know them motherfucker's are going to eat his ass to the bones right?" Spade said as he started laughing again. "His fat ass will be at his bar uptown in Manhattan, on third and fifteen Street. Every night around ten his fat ass comes there at night. He runs the place, he picked up his money every night just like clockwork, all the time," said Wesley as he grabbed something to drink. "Okay! Cuz let do this shit for the family," said Jay as he grabbed his glass for a toast. "Y'all go make some runs tonight. At ten we leave to go uptown, he'll be at his bar by then. He leaves every night around two am in the morning. We going to grab his ass then," said Wesley as they toasted to it.

Spade and Jay left back out to go take care of something. Wesley stayed in the apartment pacing back and forth thinking about the plan for tonight. He was making sure everything goes down according to their plan. Wesley's phone started ringing, so he walks over to the table and grabs his phone and answers it. "Hello," said Wesley. Then he heard the recording with Suzie voice on it, so Wesley quickly pressed one to except the call. "What's up baby, I go to bail review tomorrow morning. My lawyer told me that me and Pinkey should get bail. So I should be there tomorrow, so you can lick me, and I can lick you. I got some good news to baby to tell you," said Suzie. "Please tell me some good news. I need some right now," said Wesley while pacing back forth in the living room. "Man your killing the surprise baby. Okay, okay guess what? I'm pregnant baby!!" Suzie said to Wesley. As soon as he heard Suzie say that, he sat his ass right down. At first, Wesley couldn't get a word out at all. He just sat there with his mouth open looking in space for like six seconds. "Baby!! Did you hear me?!! Let me try this again, one more time. I'm pregnant nigga!! Crack, crack motherfucker, say something shit!!" Suzie said as she was holding on to the phone waiting for Wesley to say something back. "Na, na ma I'm sorry, I heard you boo. I'm happy as shit girl. You know I really want a family. I really do, it just so much going on right now. That's all baby," said Wesley as he came back to reality. "Ya! Nigga, you was about to make me come home and crack you on your head, shit!!" Suzie said as they both started laughing at each other. "Na girl, come on now. You know I love you ma. You just don't know how much. Now your ass is going to get fat on me?" Wesley said "And you better love it or I'm going to crack your ass nigga. Damn boo, my time is up, I'll see you tomorrow, I love you," said Suzie as she got off the phone with Wesley. Wesley was just standing by the window looking out of it in a daze. He really felt good about the news. But he knew it had to go down tonight, back to work. And he knows he got to get them home A.S.A.P.

Wesley walked over to the bedroom to lie back for a minute so he could get some sleep. Wesley set the clock for eight o'clock so he can wake up in time and have two hours to get ready.

As for Spade and Jay, they were out on the block in Crown Heights in Brooklyn doing what they do best. Chilling, making sure everything is getting done, what needs to get done.

As it started to get dark, Spade looked at his watch to check the time. It was now going on eight o'clock. Spade called Jay from in front of the building. He told Jay it was time to go. Just as Spade said that his phone started ringing. "What's cracking cuz, we're on our way as I speak," said Spade as he and Jay jumped into their midnight blue Range Rover HSC. "Yo cuz bring the van tonight cuz and some duck tape. And make sure you cover the inside of the van with plastic," Wesley told Spade. "Say no more cuz, keep it cracking Claaaat!! For the team," said Spade to Wesley as he was getting real pumped up as he was driving to get the van. "I'll be here waiting for y'all, C-safe," said Wesley as he got off the phone.

Spade and Jay didn't have far to go to get the van. They were renting out a garage three blocks from the spot they were at. They pulled up in front of the garage and Jay jumped out to get the van out of the garage. While Spade just parked the Range Rover on the block as Spade went to the garage to meet up with Jay. He grabbed a roll of duck tape, and a painter roll of plastic. Everything they needed was right there in the garage. They also grabbed three 9mm Beretta with three 16 shot clips a piece, and three silencers for all the Beretta's. They got dress really quick and were on their way to go get Wesley; he was in the downtown area of Brooklyn.

As soon as they got out front they called Wesley to come outside. As they were out front waiting for Wesley, he called them to let them know he was on his way. He was almost dressed, and was heading his way out the door making his way to the passenger side of the van. They were now on their way uptown. Wesley jumped in the back with Jay to put the plastic all over the back of the van. They reached uptown in good timing; it was going on 9:45. Joey was already there, Wesley could see his car as they were pulling up on the block.

Wesley told Spade to pull over. Wesley loved were Joey was park at; it was a nice dark spot on the block. There were no street lights over Joey's car at all.

They just sat there patiently waiting. All of them turned off their phones. All they can think about is this faggot ass rat bitch Joey. And how their pits and rocks are going to have fun with him. Wesley started up a conversation, because they were sitting there so long. Somebody had to say something to make the time go by faster. "Suzie called me today. She was looking forward to coming home tomorrow," said Wesley as they were sitting there patiently waiting. "You didn't tell her what's up about this shit. Not about this rat did you?" Spade asked. "Fuck!! No, no need to, this shit is as good as done cuz. We got this rat bitch right where we want him. In a fucking rat trap just for rats," said Wesley as he started laughing with Spade and Jay. "So what's up with sis, how is she doing?" Spade asked. "Man she's fucking pregnant cuz!" Wesley said to both of them. "Damn cuz your fucking ass is going to be a father. Damn!! That's fucked- up cuz," said Jay real serious to Wesley. "What the fuck you mean cuzing, that's fucked up," said Wesley as he look at Jay for an answer. "Man I'm just saying cuz, no more fucking around for you at all. That's all I'm saying my nig," said Jay to Wesley real cool. "Shit that's just more pussy for me and you cuz. Don't get it fucked up cuz, I love the kids too now," said Spade as they all started laughing at Spade. "Man cuz it's going to be all about my family, that's within my family. Plus, I'm really thinking about getting married to Suzie. Man fuck all this fucking with all these bitches. You're just waiting to get aids cuz," said Wesley to Spade and Jay. "Yo cuz! No offense my nigga, smile pussy whipped, you suppose to whip that pussy cuz. Not the pussy whipping you," said Spade as he and Jay started laughing really hard. Wesley started laughing with them, and as they were laughing...look who was coming out the bar closing up. Joey's fat, rat ass and the women that was with him. A yellow cab pulled up in front, it was for the young lady. Wesley, Jay, and Spade got ready. All of them put on their ski masks.

The young lady kissed Joey and jumped in the cab and drove off. Joey was all alone now. Joey started walking to his car, as he was walking Spade started up the van, and Jay jumped out the side door to walk down on Joey. Then Wesley told Spade to drive right up beside him. As Joey was getting into his B.M.W. 745; Joey was already in the driver's seat about to start the car. As soon as the van pulled right up beside him the back door to the van was already open. Joey started watching the van. But by this time, it was too late. Jay was getting in the passenger side of Joey 745 already with his gun to Joey's head. Joey turned to look at Jay and his window came shattering in on his lap. Joey jumped back from the glass hitting him in his face. Jay snatched the keys out of the ignition. Joey didn't know what was going on at first and then Jay shot him right in the leg one time to let him know they were not playing. "Get your fat ass in the van bitch now!!" Jay yelled at Joey. Then he pushed Joey out the driver's door and at the same time Wesley was holding him by his shirt pulling him in the van. Joey was so scared he started pissing on himself. "Look, look please don't hurt me. I have money if you need money. Please I have fifty thousand dollars in my bar. You can have it all. Please just don't kill me," said Joey as he started crying like a bitch. Jay yelled, "Man shut your fat bitch ass the fuck up bitch!!" Then he got in the van while hitting Joey over the head with the butt of his gun. Wesley closed the side door and then Spade took off and they were on their way uptown to the Bronx. Wesley started duck taping Joey's hands and his feet together. Then Wesley and Jay started beaten the shit out of him. Wesley kicked Joey down to his back. Then he started punching Joey in his face with his fist. Blood was flying everywhere. Jay started kicking him in his stomach, over and over again.

Spade was just doing the speed limit all the way to the Bronx. They had the music up high so no one could hear Joey cry out. Off to the dog house they go, Joey was as good as dog food. They finally got there, it was a nice size building. James' family owns it and no one was living in it. James and his homey's were raising their Pitbulls, and Rottweiler's in there. They had various kinds of dogs from American Bullmastiff, red nose pits, blue pits from big ones to small ones. All you heard were dogs barking as they were pulling up in the lot. Jay put a pillowcase over Joey's head, so he couldn't see at all. It don't even matter because he's not going to live to tell it as they were getting out. Jay put his Beretta to Joey's back and they took him into the building, and started walking him downstairs to the basement. It stinks of straight dog shit, and the smell of them too. As they were walking down the stairs, Spade turned on the light to the basement. Jay cut the duck tape off of Joey's hands and took the pillowcase off of his face. Then he pushed Joey into a pile of dog shit. He fell right on his face into the pile of dog shit. Joey struggled to get himself up off of the pile of shit. Plus, he was still bleeding from the gunshot wound from his leg. He started begging Jay and Spade for his life. Wesley was just starting to walk down the basement steps. "Please! I beg you don't kill me! If its money you want, just tell me. Please, I have a family that needs me," said Joey as he grabbed Spade by the arm. Spade just punched Joey in the face and he hit the floor on his stomach.

By this time, Wesley was now downstairs right beside Spade and Jay. Wesley walked right up to Joey and bent down right in Joey's face. All

Joey could see at the time was Wesley's eyes. He was trying to figure out who it was. That's when Wesley took off his ski mask, and Jay and Spade did the same too. Joey was so shocked to see it was Wesley and his boys. Wesley had a bucket of pigs blood to put on Joey, because the dogs love pigs blood. That was how they trained their dogs off of the smell of blood. Wesley grabbed the bucket of pig blood, and poured it all over Joey's body. Once he did that, the dogs started barking real loud as they smelled the blood. Joey started crying and reaching his hand out to Wesley. Jay grabbed a baseball bat and walked over to Joey, and broke Joey's hand. "Wesley please wait! I thought we were friends. What is the meaning of this?" Joey asked as he was crying, trying to get up off of the floor. "You fucking rat bitch!! You was trying to testify on my family tomorrow wasn't you!! You rat bitch! You were trying to bring down my whole family establishment. You were providing the Feds with information on my organization wasn't you?" Wesley asked Joey as Joey sat there crying and trying to explain. Wesley just walked over to one of the basement doors where they had 10 different types of pitbulls in the room. "Wesley please, I can explain to you…please wait! Just one minute! Look! Yes I am a CI and if you kill me! They will get you and take you down!! Do you hear me, but let me live and I'll go fifty, fifty with you. Fuck James! Listen to me! Listen!! Please! Just listen…you're smarter than James. I told him a long time ago not to fuck with me!! He fucked up and look at him now. Look you're the man now, don't you do the same thing too!" Joey said to Wesley while breathing really hard trying to keep himself together. Wesley just looked at Joey and then he looked at Jay and Spade while smiling at Joey. And then he started laughing at Joey, looking at

Joey like he was crazy. Wesley held out to him and said, "C up!!! Claaaat!" Then he opened up the door where the dogs were at. All ten of the pitbulls came running out at full speed. As they were coming at Joey, he tried to put his hand up to block his face. But it wasn't doing him any good. You had American Bullmastiffs, two red nose pits, and short pits all on him and hungry as a motherfucker. "If you can convince my dogs!! You can live bitch!! Get him boys!!! Sick him!! Sickem!!" Wesley said. Then the pack of pits ran up on Joey attacking him from every direction and tearing into Joey's flesh like it was paper. "No, no, no!! You motherfucking nigga no!!" That was Joey last words as one of the bullmastiffs grabbed Joey's throat and started shaking onto his neck. He was locked on his neck. It was sounding as if it was about to pop off. Two of the red noses were on Joey's left leg, ripping it apart. Some of the blue noses were gnawing away at Joey's hands and arms. One of the smaller pits was between Joey nuts gnawing them. Joey's lifeless body was being ripped into pieces. Some of the pits took off some of his fingers, toes, intestines, and some of Joey's spine from his back. They were running off in corner of the basement, and started fighting for the spine. They all were eating it like they had got a snack. And when one of them would try to go to the next one, they would start fighting all over again over it. Wesley, Jay and Spade just stood there, they felt no way at all. This is what they do, this is how they live; this was how they survive. "Well, there goes the Feds eyewitness," said Spade as he lit up a blunt of purple. Then Spade went and opened up two more rooms of pits and rocks. They all started fighting for the remains of Joey body parts. Blood and the smell of human flash was everywhere. Now it was time for them to clean up the mess.

Spade took all the dogs and put them back into the rooms and started washing them off one by one. Wesley and Jay started getting all of Joey remains together with a shovel that they put in 3 thick plastic bags. They got some ammonia and bleach and washed down everything. They picked up all the bones and flesh that was left and put it all in the bags. Joey skull was one of them. They put Joey's remains in the back of the van, and they drove to the Staten Island Ferry. When they got into the middle of the ocean they threw the bags over board. That was the last of Joey.

They put ammonia and bleach everywhere there was blood and everywhere it wasn't just to be on the safe side.

CHAPTER 14

COURT WAS NOW IN SESSION

They made sure to put some weights into the plastic bags, so whatever was left of Joey's body wouldn't float back to the top. They stayed on the ferry and took it back to NY. They went back to the stash house to lay back and while they were chilling, they started rolling up some weed to smoke. It was now going on four in the morning and after they smoked all of the weed, all three of them (Wesley, Jay, and Spade) fell asleep. As Wesley was falling asleep, he was hoping everything was going to work out. One thing's for sure, he knew the girl's were going to make out okay.

It was now 10 am and they were all still asleep. Meanwhile, while they were sleeping, court was now in session for James, Mike, Ty, Simeon, Kevin, Pinkey, Suzie, and the rest of the team. Their case was about to be called on. The Court Clerk of the Courts said, "Case number 7222BC7 is now being called upon in front of Judge Brown for bail hearing!!!" "Are all the lawyers here?" Judge Brown asked. That's when White spoke in the behalf of James, "Good morning Your Honor! I'm here on the behave of my client James Campbell. I'm also representing the rest of the clients that are to my right, and the females to my left have their own consul here as well. Let me just start telling the court that my client is not a flight risk at all. My client has too much to lose by leaving the state. My client is an American citizen!! Born here in NY!! He doesn't have a criminal back ground at all. Therefore, we are asking that a bail is to be set Your Honor somewhere in the range of three hundred thousand to five hundred thousand dollars," said White to Judge Brown and then he sat down. "Okay Ms. Jones what do you have to say about this case here before me?" Judge Brown asked. That's when Ms. Jones got up ready to fight. "Your Honor!! It's real easy why Mr. Campell shouldn't get bail. Not just because he's a flight risk! Because he's an animal!!!" Ms. Jones said, while she was turning red and talking real loud. Then Ms. Jones continued saying, "He kills people for a living!! He's a gang banger and the leader of the Crips in N.Y.C.!!! Him and his friends are a menus to our society. They need to be locked away for good. That is the only way the killing is going to stop!! Is by keeping these animals in jail!! It will stop some of the killing that is going on in our city. We lost a police officer behind these animals, Your Honor. I rest my case right there...Your Honor, somebodies family is without a father sir. Please keep them in custody thank you.", Then Ms. Jones, and The State Attorney took a seat while Judge Brown made his decision about the case. "I hereby the court say all defendants are to be held without bail. Due to the fact they are a danger to themselves and to our society," said Judge Brown. The DA looked over to James and Doggy and the rest of them and smiled.

The next case was being called, it was all the girls going up now. The DA really didn't have anything on them and due to the fact the CI was missing and nowhere to be found. The courts called their case number, "Case number 2577BA7 is now being called, is the defendants in custody?" The court clerk Ms. Itaily said, "Yes Your Honor to my left is Suzie Campell and Pinkey Keys. I'm here on their behalf." "And Your Honor, I'm here on the behalf of Tanya Simeon and Amber Aiken a.k.a. Shitty and Meka Fisher," Ms. Lowes said to the court. "Okay who would like to start first about this case?" Judge Brown asked as he was flipping through some papers. "Good morning Your Honor, this is a very simple case. The states eyewitness is not here to testify, so there is no proof that my clients or Ms. Itaily clients has any involvement with either parties the Bloods or the Crips as far as gang affiliation. Suzie Campbell can't help what her brother does or Ms. Pinkey Keys. Yes, they have a relationship with James, but not with his criminal activity. All of the young ladies are in school and none of them have a criminal record. We both think they should get out on their own recognizance," said Ms. Lowes to the court. "I feel the same way Your Honor," said Ms. Itaily to the court as she sat down. "I don't have too much to say at this time Your Honor. But I do recommend a high bail. If any bail is going to be giving at all," the DA said as she sat down holding her head down looking at some papers. The Judge sat there for one minute looking at all of them. Then he said to them, "I'm going to give these young ladies bail. Bail will be set at three hundred and fifty thousand dollars for each of them. I hope they stay out of trouble, because if they don't, I will take their bail from them, understand that please. Court is adjourned." Then Judge Brown walked out of the chamber doors.

All the girls made bail, so they should be out tonight. James' lawyer already knew that James and them were not going to make bail, but at least the girls were able to. He had to tell Wesley the good and the bad news. It put a smile on Wesley's face to hear some good news. "Okay good looking...that's what's hood White, thanks for letting me know what's hood," said Wesley to White as he started C-walking back and forth. "Okay whatever that means," said White as he was getting off the phone with Wesley.

After Wesley got off the phone he turned to Jay and Spade to let them know the good and the bad news, that James and the rest of the Loc's didn't get bail. Wesley also told them that Doggy and his boys didn't get no bail either, but the good news was Suzie and Pinkey will be coming home tonight. Wesley told Jay and Spade to go to James' family house to give Mrs. Campbell and Mr. Campell the money for Suzie's and Pinkey's bail. Then for them to make sure everything was running smooth. Spade and Jay both left out A.S.A.P. on their way to Mr. and Mrs. Campbell's house.

After they left out, Wesley just sat back and started smoking on some purple feeling real good about the girls coming home so he can see his babygirl, some time tonight. So he called Tasha to let her know the good news, "Tasha!! What's up cuz I got some good news to tell you. Suzie and Pinkey are coming home!!!" Then he took a pull off of his blunt. "That's what's cracking my nigga!!! Now just make sure they stay out of trouble, and call me as soon as you get them," said Tasha. "I sure will sis, you okay?" Wesley asked as he was sitting back smoking on his blunt of purple. "Yeah, yeah I'm fine, I'm just working. You know, it's hard out here boy, a sister got to do what she got to do," said Tasha to Wesley. "I feel you C-love, 306 I'll call you later on tonight," said Wesley. "Okay baby C-up Claaat!!" Tasha said as she was getting off the phone. "You already fucking know Claaaat!!! C-up," said Wesley.

Wesley got up and went into the bathroom to get in the shower. He really didn't know what to do with himself until they got out. So he made plans to go to see a movie. He decided to take his niece and nephew out to the movies with him, and get something to eat as well. So he called his aunt to let her know he was on his way to come get them, so she could have them ready for him.

Meanwhile, back up in the Bronx on 187 stand (The Grand Concourse), Tommy Gun just got off the phone with Tanya's and Shitty's lawyer. She was just letting Tommy Gun know that the both of them just got bail. Tommy Gun was one of the Bloods that didn't get caught up that night at the club. By the time they even thought he was there, he was long gone. He just been laying low waiting to hear from the rest of them.

As for the game room in Brooklyn, it was closed down where Jimmy got killed at. Tommy Gun have been uptown in the Bronx just chilling trying to keep their set together from up there in the Bronx. He's the only one left from the original crew. Tommy Gun called a bail bondsman that he knew to post their bail. "Boy bail bondsman. What's up? Where's the bail?" Slick asked the bail bondsman. "Yo what's popping it's me, Tommy Gun. I need a favor for tomorrow?" Tommy Gun asked him as he was walking back and forth in the apartment. "Yo! Tommy Gun what's up...what can I do for you my friend?" Slick said to him. He was happy to hear from Tommy Gun because he knew that he was going to make some money. "I need you to post them three bails that I called you about early today. But only the three females, that's it," Tommy Gun said as he was drinking on a Heineken about to light up a blunt. "Okay, okay I got you. I'm on it, I have their names and date of birth," Slick said as he was smoking a cigarette sitting in his chair.

As Tommy Gun got off the phone with Slick, he had one more phone call to make. Tommy Gun was the one who would always go out and meet the new connect. His name was Poblow, and Tommy Gun met him uptown Manhattan on 127 and Broadway. You would of never knew that Poblow was the man on the downlow. You see Tommy Gun was Dominican and he spoke Spanish very well, so it was easy for him to get Poblow to fuck with him. And Tommy Gun was loyal to his set as a Blood. At first when he first met Poblow he couldn't believe the shit he was hearing. It was just to unbelievable to him that he had to see it for himself. So he met up with Poblow to see what he was talking about. "What's up my man! Let me show you what I'm talking about. I knew your affiliation with the Bloods. It don't matter to me at all just as long as you can do good business, okay my friend?" Poblow said as he patted Tommy Gun on his back as they were going in Poblow's building to check the shit out. "I can feed your whole establishment and the Crips as well, but I'm going to fuck with you my friend. I will provide you with all you need Tommy Gun, believe me when I say that to you," said Poblow as he took Tommy Gun on to the elevator to go downstairs to the basement.

As soon as they got off of the elevator there were three men with AK-47, and they had two Rottweiler's. As they were walking down the long hallway, the basement started turning into an apartment. It was starting to look real luxuriously, and it was well furnished out. As they were walking, there were three more men with Thompson machine guns with drums on them. And that's not counting the four men upstairs as soon as you walk in the building to get on the elevator. As they were walking Tommy Gun was mapping out the building, he was counting how many men he had in and out the entire building. He knew it was a way out of the basement, he just didn't see it yet. As they were walking through the luxuriously basement apartment there was a room with three Spanish women in it just chilling. Then Poblow walked Tommy Gun to a big open area where there were barrels just sitting there with one more man back there with an AK-47. Poblow had a nice small army of men, but you have to remember this is Tommy Gun's profession, this is what he does for a living. "Okay baby!!! This is it right here, you ready to get big money, big money?" Poblow asked him as he took Tommy Gun over to one of the fifteen barrels. As Poblow opened up one of the barrels, Tommy Gun couldn't believe his eyes of what he saw in front of him. It was pure cocaine from the bottom to the top of the barrel. "What you thought I was bullshitting you? This right here my friend is more than two hundred key lows just in this one barrel alone my friend. I don't play no game, I'm the shit and so shall you be. Now do you believe me my friend?" Poblow asked as he looked Tommy Gun in the eyes. "Yeah, yeah no bullshit. I'll be back tonight, and I'm going to bring you three bitches too. You can do whatever you want with them. Just don't kill them, my friend. And I'm going to bring two million dollars with me to start with okay?" Tommy Gun said to Poblow. "Ha, ha, ha, don't kill them, that I liked my friend. That's what's up, come around like two in the morning. Just you and the three bitches, that it." Poblow said to him. "Yeah, I need two of my boys to watch my back. I hope that's okay with you?" Tommy Gun asked him. "That would be fine. No problem with me at all. I'll see you then, my friend." Poblow said.

After all was said and done, Poblow let Tommy Gun out from a side door in that room. The door led them out into the alley right by his car. That's was all Tommy Gun needed to see right there. Poblow walked Tommy Gun to his car and went back in the building. All Tommy Gun had on his mind was to go get Tanya and Shitty now so they can get all this shit in Poblow's building from him. As for Pablow, all he had on his mind was fucking pussy. But little did Pablow know it was going to be his last time getting some pussy, and the last night of his life if everything goes down right as planned. As for Tommy Gun it was on and popping. That's what he thought, but he also knew that anything can happen, and anything can go wrong if it's not done right.

So Tommy Gun stopped at the Bronx to get some homey's that he's going to need besides Tanya and Shitty for tonight. As soon as he got there in the Bronx, he called the bail bondsmen to see what was going on with their bail. "Yo Slick, it's me again homey, what's popping homey with my ruby's?" Tommy Gun asked. "Don't worry it's done my man, all three of them are on their way home. They should be out by twelve o'clock, if all goes well," Slick said as he was sitting in his chair rocking back and forth. "What the fuck do you mean if all goes well, homey!!?" Tommy Gun asked while yelling as he grabbed a Heineken out of the refrigerator. "It's not me man, take it easy...it's the damn system...they move real slow. I did what I had to do already," Slick said. "Okay, I get it, thanks...call me if you hear anything," Tommy Gun said to him. Then both of them hung up the phones with each other.

Tommy Gun started thinking how else can he get to go on the jobs with him. He started thinking of some homey's he knew in Brooklyn that was down for whatever and played no games at all. He gave them a call and told them to be on standby, and that he'll be there to pick them up around ten, and for them to be ready. Also, to eat less and have seven homey's there. He told them he will have everything they need to get the job done tonight. After that Tommy Gun got off the phone with the little homey, and just sat back and lit up a blunt of purple and finished his Heineken off.

He was getting his mind right for tonight because he knows he cannot make any mistakes at all. He cannot afford none, because they need this to put them back where they belong, and this time it will be better than before. Better than ever!

Back at the jail, Pinkey was getting herself together. She was getting ready to leave out of there, and at the same time getting her new friend Nadia's information. She was also letting her know that she was leaving out tonight. "Girl I'm out of here, give me all your information. Here's mine, don't lose it, use it okay?" Pinkey said to Nadia and gave her the information. "Damn girl! That's what's up, I'll call you. As soon as I get out," said Nadia to Pinkey as she gave Pinkey a hug as if she was leaving herself. "Now girl make sure you call me tomorrow, I'll make sure I'll help you get out," said Pinkey to Nadia as she was holding Nadia's hand. "I'll call you, you just make sure you stay out of trouble," Nadia said. Then both of them went and sat down for a while and started talking.

Some time had passed by and the CO came to get Pinkey, telling her it was time to go. Pinkey got up and turned to Nadia and gave her a hug one more time and told her to call her. Then she walked out with the CO to a bullpen where she meets up with Suzie. They were so happy to see each other. Suzie said to Pinkey, "Girl what's up! You ready to get the fuck up out of here or what?". Then she gave her a big hug. "Hell yeah, I'm ready to get the fuck out of this motherfucker," said Pinkey back to Suzie as both of them started walking back and forth waiting for their names to be called.

As soon as their names where called they were on their way out the building. Wesley, Jay and Spade was out there waiting for them. All of them jumped in Jay's truck with Wesley and Spade. "What's up baby I miss you boo boo," said Suzie as she gave Wesley a big kiss for like three minutes straight. "Yo I'm hungry as a motherfucker, let's get some food please?" Pinkey asked. "Me too, let's go get some food," said Suzie while hugging on Wesley. "What would y'all like to eat?" Wesley asked. "Something fast like McDonalds," said Suzie as she put her head on Wesley's shoulder.

Jay drove to the first McDonalds that he knew of to get some food and then take them all home so they can get into the shower and a bath. Both of them started telling them about their jailhouse stories. They all started laughing at them, because some of the shit they were saying was funny as a motherfucker to them.

While Wesley, Jay, Spade, Suzie, and Pinkey where chilling in Brooklyn. Tommy Gun was outside by the jail waiting for Tanya, Shitty, and Meka. He sat there for one hour before they came out. "What's popping homey's! Blaaaat!!! Blaaaaat!!!," Tanya, Shitty, and Meka all said to Tommy Gun. "You already fucking know that five homey. All day...every day," Tommy Gun said while piecing all three of them as they jumped in his candy apple red Escalade, Banging Styles P. "

As they were driving Tommy Gun turned down the radio. He started talking putting them on about tonight and said to all three of them, "Look homey's, I got something lined up for us tonight. I met this nigga the other day. This motherfucker got crazy weight homey's. I mean crazy weight homey's!" They just sat there listening to him to hear what he had to say to them. "Damn nigga a bitch just got out of that motherfucker. That's what's popping, that's what the fuck I'm talking about," said Tanya happy as a motherfucker. "Look homey's, his name is Pablow, at first I thought the nigga was on some bullshit right. Then this dumb ass nigga took me to his stash in the Bronx. This dummy got a building full of coke homey's. So he takes me in the building right? Then we get in the elevator to go downstairs right? Four niggas was out in front of the building. And as soon as we get off the elevator, two niggas with rocks was downstairs, right there. Then he took me down a long hallway in the basement. It started looking real fly as shit. Then it was three more niggas and three bitches in there. Then he took me into another room with one more nigga in it with fifteen barrels of cocaine homey's, big fucking barrels!!! I saw this with my own eyes, it was about fifteen of them all together."

Tommy Gun told all three of them this and all of them was starting to get pumped up. "What kind of guns did they have homey?" Shitty asked Tommy Gun. "AK-47 that's what I mostly saw downstairs, and some Thompson submachine guns. The niggas outside had hand guns, but we can hit this shit. I know we can, and then we'll be right back on our feet," Tommy Gun said. All the girls was in for it. So Tommy Gun started telling them the plan on the way to Tommy Gun's crib, so they can get ready to go. Tommy Gun let them know that he already got clothes for all of them at the crib waiting for them, and this was not a game. He told them they're going to have to play it off as if they're going to fuck him. You should already know they don't have any problem with that at all. It was on and popping tonight. "Man my poor baby, damn I wish he was home with me," said Pinkey while she was eating her food. "Don't worry Pinkey he'll be fine, all of them will be. They all got the best lawyer in N.Y.C. that money can buy," said Suzie to Pinkey trying to make her feel better. "Don't worry sis it's going to be alright. Just keep your head up okay. We're all family," said Spade trying to reassure Pinkey. "Pinkey I know it's hard for you right now, but it will be okay...it's going to get better. Believe me when I tell you that," said Wesley to her as he went over to try to make her feel better. "I know, I know it's just that I miss my baby," said Pinkey Only one good thing came from that whole jail shit. I met a girl in there, her name is Nadia. I'm going to try and help her out," said Pinkey to Suzie and the rest of them.

Wesley's phone started ringing it was Tasha seeing if he got them yet. "What's cracking big brother, please tell me, they are with you already? Tasha said as she was driving down the street. "Yes they are cuz, they're right here with me, Suzie!" Wesley called out to her and then he passed her the phone. "What's up! Tasha how are you doing babygirl?" Suzie said real happy to hear from Tasha. "I'm okay, how are you doing and how is Pinkey doing, is she okay?" Tasha asked. "Yes I'm fine, it's good to know you care. Thank you for asking. When are we going to see you Tasha?" Pinkey asked her, as she took the phone from Suzie. "Girl I'm on my way now, I can't stay to long. just for little while. I'll be there in ten minute or so," said Tasha to both of them. "Okay we will be here, just call when you're right out front," said Pinkey. Then they got off the phone, and started talking about their jail experience again. Spade and Jay was laughing at them. Wesley was too, but he really had a lot of shit on his mind. He had a lot of shit to take care of. He had to make sure that their hoods stay their hoods, because it was an ongoing war for years with them and the Bloods. And sometimes they got into it with the Latin Kings too, but not as bad as they got into it with the Bloods. Plus, the street was real hot right now. As for business it was not the same as usually.

CHAPTER 15

ON TOP OF THE WORLD

Back uptown in the Bronx, Tommy Gun, Shitty, Tanya, Meka, and the rest of the Bloods was getting ready for tonight, they didn't have to much longer to go at all. "Okay homey's, I got the tools we need, all the guns we need, and most of all the rides we need to do this with. Yo if you can only see all that shit!!" Tommy Gun said as he started telling them again. "We will see homey, just calm down. We're going to get this bitch. I decided we will fuck his bitch ass first, and then kill his bitch ass when he's real weak. Meka you're going to take care of the nigger in the back where all the shit is at, you already know what to do to him. Suck him off until he can't take no more. Please tell me you got some silences to homey?" Tanya asked Tommy Gun. "Homey's, I got what the fuck you need. This is not a game at all," Tommy Gun said as he pulled out a big wooded boxes full of guns and knives, all type of shit. "Homey's, I got Glock 40, H&K mp5 with drum, Ms. 9mm, 45 Cal. Whatever the fuck you want homey's," Tommy Gun said as he started passing the guns around. Tanya grabbed two 38's the ones that don't have a hammer on them. "Meka boo we're going to do what we got to do boo. You feel me homey? Shitty you fuck the nigga, me and Meka got your back homey," said Tanya to Meka since Shitty going to fuck him. Tanya decided that her and Meka going to put the guns up in their pussy because they're not suppose to be gangsters, they're suppose to be prostitutes. So they're doing what they got to do to get this money for their homey's. All three of them grabbed knives because that is something a prostitute is more likely to have. Tanya put both of the 38's in plastic bags, and put KY Jelly all over them first. Tanya laid down on the bed with her legs wide opened and she started putting the 38 up in her pussy. "Yooo aahh shit...that shit felt good...damn," said Tanya and then started laughing. Meka did the same thing then they got dress.

They were already to go now, and this was not a game at all to them. They do what they got to do to make it happen. "Homey what's up, we're ready let's go!" Shitty said to Tommy Gun. "Chill it's not time yet, I got you," Tommy Gun said. "Homey's, when this shit is over with we're running N.Y. for sure homey's," said Tanya. "Fuck yeah we will have enough shit to take James and them down for sure," One of the little homey's said that was going with them tonight. "Don't get it fucked up homey's that crab ass nigga got long money for years. He been getting money for a long time now. The only good thing is the Feds got his ass right now," Tommy Gun said to the young homey.

It was time for Tommy Gun and the rest of the homey's to make their move on Pablow. They have three vans to hall the shit in and his candy apply red Escalade truck. Tommy Gun and four of his homey's was in it loaded and ready to go. Tanya, Shitty, and Meka were in a black Dodge Caliber with the money, two million dollars in cash that Poblow was not getting. Tommy Gun went over the plan with his young homey's one more time as they were on their way to Poblow's building to see him.

As soon as they got there Tommy Gun rode through the alley to show his two homey's where the back door was at. Then he parked on the side of the street. Tommy Gun told two of them to stay inside the truck until he two-wayed them on the Nextel. Then to come to this door on the side and it will be open for them to come in. There are three vans parked down the alley from the door. Tanya, Shitty, and Meka are parked right in front of Tommy Gun in front of the building.

Poblow met them in the hallway of his building. "Yes, yes my friend damn!! They look good yes!!" Poblow said as he smacked Tanya on her phat ass. As she was getting on the elevator all she did was smile at him. It is very hard for anyone to refuse these three sexy ladies at all. When they got off the elevator they saw everything just like Tommy Gun said. It was two men with rocks there. Then they started walking down the long hallway, and they got into the luxuriously part of the basement, where it was three more men, and three Spanish women there. "I must say real nice Tommy, all three of them I like. Would y'all ladies like something to drink?" Pablow asked. Tommy Gun didn't like for no one to call him Tommy, without the Gun. "Absolutely do you have some Jacques Cardin VSOP?" Tanya asked as she took a seat on the couch. "Yes that would be real nice please," All three girls said to Pablow. "Yes...yes you have good taste ladies," Pablow said. Then he started speaking in Spanish to one of the men to get the drink. "Do you have something for me?" Pablow asked Tommy Gun. "Yeah homey right there," Tommy Gun said pointing to Tanya to give him the briefcase with the money in it. "Do you have something for me?" Tommy Gun said right before Poblow was about to open up the briefcase. "What my friend?" Pablow asked. "Where my bitches at my friend?" Tommy Gun asked Pablow started laughing real hard. Then he started speaking in Spanish again to the three ladies. They took Tommy Gun into the room so they can fuck him. That is when

Pablow got up to take Tanya, Shitty, and Meka with him. "Ladies please follow me, we have our own party to do," said Pablow as they walked through to the back and through two more doors. They were right next to the shit where the one man was at chilling that is when Tanya tapped Shitty on the shoulder. All three of them knew where they were. "Popp what's up with your friend over there? He looks like he needs some pussy?" Meka said to Pablow. "I'm not good enough for you baby?" Pablow asked with his hands up in the air. "No baby she didn't mean it like that at all," said Shitty. Grabbing Pablow's dick, his dick got hard immediately. That is when he told all three of them to come out of their clothes. Pablow could not resist what he saw all three of them was in Victoria Secret see-through red bra and panties set. Tanya 36D-27-44, Meka 36DD-25-44, and last but not least Shitty 36DD-26-44. Pablow went to grab Tanya first. "No baby she's going to suck your dick. But you're going to fuck the shit out of me first daddy," said Shitty to him as she laid back on the bed taking off her panties. Revealing her pink and red pussy, she was wet as a motherfucker. Tanya got down on her knees and started sucking Pablow off while Pablow started playing with Tanya's nipples, while she was putting Pablow's eight-inch dick deep down her The one man that was in the back came in to watch Pablow's back. Pablow said something in Spanish to him for the man to leave back out. Pablow started watching Meka eat Shitty out. That when Shitty started acting like it was making her go crazy and Pablow was loving it all. "Ammmm, ummmm shit yes...lick it...ummmm ahaahh...sss hit yes," said Shitty to Meka, as Shitty watched Pablow real hard. Pablow immediately moved Tanya told Meka to eat Tanya right beside him while he got between Shitty legs and put them on his shoulder. As soon as he put his dick up in Shitty, she started playing the role. "Yes pop...ummm ahhh yes...umm...oooooh! Damn your dick is big as shit daddy...yes!!" Shitty said. The man in the back with the barrels looked in one more time. Him and Meka locked eyes for five seconds and then he left back out. Pablow thought he was doing something real big to Shitty, only if he knew she was faking him out. She started moaning real loud, the sound of Shitty moaning was making Pablow about to cum. Shitty knew it too because she could feel it. "You about to cum poppa?" Shitty asked as she was fucking him. "Yes baby yes!" Pablow said. "I want you to put it all on my stomach, my titties, and my face," said Shitty to him. She started to stick her tongue out to catch it. Tanya already had her knife out in her hand. He wasn't even watching them two anymore. His full focus was on Shitty. As soon as he pulled out, Shitty grabbed his dick. Shitty started jerking him off. The first shot of cum that came out, hit her on the stomach. By this time Tanya was right behind him, slicing his throat. Tanya had her hands over his mouth as well, so nobody could hear him if he tried to yell out. Blood shot out all over Shitty from his throat. Shitty was still jerking him off. After Tanya sliced his throat, she stab him in the heart one time. Pablow was out of here.

Meanwhile, Meka was already out the door going into the room were the one soldier was at with all the coke. "Hey baby he told me to come in here and take care of you," said Meka as she walked over to him making him put his gun down. She dropped his pants down to his knees. Then Meka dropped to her knees, and then she started giving him head. The head was so good he started coming in one minute all in Meka's mouth, she can feel him getting weak. As he closed his eyes Meka jumped up to her feet, sliced his throat, and stabbed him in his heart too. He was out of here. Meka quickly let Tanya and them know it's done.

Tanya ran to the back and opened up the back door. That is when Tanya two-wayed everybody so they could move in fast through the back door. And it also put Tommy Gun on point, because once he heard his two-way go off. He knew what time it was. The four men that were out front got hit up real quick. The rest of the Bloods started moving in, making their way through the back door where Meka was at. Meka bent down like a bullfrog and got out her 38 by putting her hand up in her pussy.

By this time Tommy Gun and the rest of the homey's up front was putting in work. They shot up the three men that was in there. They had the three Spanish ladies in the room with two homey's. One lady grabbed a knife and ran and stabbed one of the homey's in his chest. The next one grabbed a gun and started shooting the other homey up. Tommy Gun kicked in the door and shot all three of the Spanish women up, but both of the homey's were dead.

As the two soldiers was by the elevator with the two rocks. They seen them running toward them, so they let the dogs loose so they could attack. Two of the homey's shot them up, and the two soldiers as well. They now had the entire building.

At that time Tommy Gun two-wayed the driver of the vans on his Nextel to pull the three vans up. They pulled up around back in the alley by the back door. Tanya, Shitty, and Meka came out back just to watch the shit get put on the vans while the rest of the homey's put the shit in the vans. Tanya goes into one of the vans, she takes out two big gas cans full of gasoline and kerosene. Tommy Gun was inside making sure they didn't forget any shit at all. Once all the barrels where on the vans. Tanya, Shitty, and Meka went back inside and Tommy Gun went to get his truck. He parked in the alley by the door. Meanwhile, Tanya and Shitty was putting gasoline and kerosene all over the bodies. Meka went over to Pablow and lit him on fire first. Then they started making their way to Tommy Gun in the truck. They got into the truck with Tommy Gun and got out of there while the building was burning down and though to themselves *"Burn Baby Burn"* as the whole building was in flames.

They got back to Tommy Gun's place and unloaded the cocaine into his basement. Shitty still had Pablow's blood all over her from head to toe. The first thing she did was get into the shower and washed all of his blood off of her. Meka and Tanya got into the shower right with her. "Man that motherfucker put his dick up in my asshole girl! No bullshit, that motherfucking shit hurt like shit girl," said Shitty and all three of them started laughing at each other as they started washing each other up getting all the blood up off of them. "I believe you girl, I heard a scream that sounded real as shit, oooh!" Tanya said. They all started laughing again. "Bitch fuck you, one thing's for sure we're on and popping now," Shitty said to them. "No bullshit dummy, our homey's, Doggy, and 007 should be here right now," said Meka to both of them. "Not just them homey's, Baby Gangster and Jimmy should be here too," said Shitty. "Yeah I feel you sis, it's all good. But they are looking down on us," said Tanya to them. "Or there looking up one or the other homey," said Shitty and all three of them started laughing. "No bullshit homey's, we love you and miss you," said Meka. Tommy Gun walked in the bathroom looking smiling at them. "What's up baby you okay homey?" Shitty asked him. "Yeah homey! We did it. We running NY Blaaat!! Blaaaat!!!" he yelled.

On the other side of the city where the society ran normal. Back at headquarters, Frank got some information on the whereabouts on the Bloods and the Crips stash house that is in the city. Frank called everybody for a meeting. Frank knew he had to act fast because he knew they always change locations. The information that Frank received was that they had their whereabouts on Doggy and James' main stash houses. James' stash house had artillery in it, and as for Doggy it was all drugs. And word on the street was James have enough artillery for a small guerrilla operation. The only problem Frank had was getting someone on the inside to work for them and they had no luck at all. But they do have the location and that is good enough to go on. As Frank goes over the plan with the rest of the team, he sits and waits for the search warrant from the Judge. The Judge has to sign it first and then they can move in. Frank started going over all the details about both stash houses, everybody is there Cox, Thomas, Paris, Det. John, Stg. Green, and George from S.W.A.T Team. They had to go over everything real carefully because one thing's for sure they know they would shoot a cop without a doubt. Both parties were famous for that shooting at cops. So this time S.W.A.T was involved to make sure no cops get killed this time around. "Okay ladies and gentlemen this is the situation that we got going on here, the drug house where going to hit first belongs to Doggy, he's the ring leader of the Bloods. We believe it's more than three hundred keys of cocaine in there," said Frank as he was passing the picture around of the place. "It's up in

Manhattan around 14th Street in a warehouse. There are men that has socially graded the place, and they are not reasonable people at all. Remember these two organizations like to shoot cops first. That is why today the S.W.A.T Team is providing us with their help. So I must say, it is important to give them everything we got on these animals. And plus gentlemen, this must stay top secret, because believe it or not people we do have a rat around us. That is why who you see here, this is it," said Frank walking back and forth and around the table where everyone was sitting at. "So ladies and gentlemen in other words, this don't leave the room at all," said Cox out loud backing up his long time friend Frank.

CHAPTER 16

CRACK THEM DOWN

Okay men you definitely have my teams help. I have a team of 50 men ready to go sir whenever you are ready," George said. George was the leader of the S.W.A.T Team and they were ready to go to work. "It's good to know that sir, and welcome aboard Operation C and B Cartel Take Down," said Frank while sticking has hand out to George to shake his hand. "Thank you sir! Happy to be onboard sir," said George while grabbing Frank's hand. "I just hope everything go down successfully when we get out there," said Frank. Because Frank knows one mistake and that is somebodies funeral. "Sir! No need to worry yourself sir! I was a General in the U.S. Army. Head of Ground Guerrilla Operation, my men are well trained sir!" George said very confident of his people. "It's very good to know that sir, okay gentlemen!! That is all...let's go to work. Let's get everybody in position and move in," said Frank. All of them walked out of the office to go gear up and then get on their way to where the rest of the team was waiting for them.

Everyone left out except for Frank and Cox. They sat back just this one time so they can go check on their last eyewitness Ms. Candy to see if she can identify one of them out of the five girls that are in the pictures. It was Tanya, Shitty, Meka, Pinkey, and Suzie. They both know it wasn't Suzie or Pinkey that killed Trigger because he was a Crip not a Blood. Plus, he knew that Tanya, Shitty, and Meka were animals. But all it takes is for something to happen to them two girls Suzie and Pinkey. And they can be just as bad or worst. That's something he didn't want to happen to them because he sees that they have gangster potential. He tells Cox he sees it in them. He puts his mind back on Wesley and his two boys Spade and Jay. He knows they are animals that need to be taking off the streets.

As soon as they got over to Ms. Candy's house, she wastes no time at all. She identifies Meka off the brake as the girl that was at the bar with Trigger. Now Frank and Cox are on their way to the warehouse on 14th Street in Manhattan. The raid was about to begin. Everybody was in position, and ready to move in.

By the time Frank and Cox arrived on the scene. Tommy Gun, Shitty, Tanya, and Meka they were just walking in the warehouse. Frank grabbed a radio, and Cox grabbed a bulletproof vest. Frank was now ready to make the call for them to move in. They had the whole warehouse surrounded. The only way out was for them to gun their way out. "All units on my call, moving only on my call. George is everyone in position?" Frank asked him while he was standing in a door of a police car. "Yes sir! The building is well surrounded, snipers are ready," George said while he was looking out a window with a 30.r6 rifle ready to fire. "Okay men!! Move in now!! Move in move in go, go, go, go all units!!!" Everybody started moving in at once, the S.W.A.T Team was the first ones at the steel door taking it down. As the door was coming down, everyone on the inside was running around with guns in their hands trying to find an exit, but every door they ran to the police were there trying to come in. "The whole fucking building is surround! Let's get to the roof," Tommy Gun said. Grabbing his 45 caliber Thompson submachine gun with a hundred round drums to it. Tanya had two sixteen shot buretta, Shitty had a 9mm ozzie pistol.

Meka had two Glock 9mm's and four 16 shot clips. As the door came down the S.W.A.T Team was moving in. "Get down!! Everybody down on the ground now!!!" yelled out one of the S.W.A.T Team police. Gun fire started to be exchange Shitty fired the first shot. "Fuck you pigs hold that homey," said Shitty as she squeeze off at the police. All of them opened fire upon the S.W.A.T Team as they were coming in. Tanya jumped to the ground. Right behind some crates as the S.W.A.T Team took fire at her. Meka pushed Shitty to the side so she wouldn't get hit. Tommy Gun started banging on them with his Thompson. Taking one of the S.W.A.T Team men down. "Yeah homey! Take that keep it popping," Tommy Gun said running and sliding across the floor while shooting at the same time to get to Tanya as she was reloading her two Berettas. Then she started shooting back at them so Shitty and Meka can make a run for it to them. "The only way out of here homey!! Is the basement back door. We got to make a run for it now," Tommy Gun said as he covered them with three more homey's as Tanya, Shitty, and Meka was making a run for it. As soon as all three of the ladies got to the door. Shitty and Meka returned fire covering Tommy Gun and the two homey's that was with him so they could make a run for it over to the door where they were at. The S.W.A.T Team was closing in on them. Stg. Green, Det. John, Thomas, and Paris where in the middle of the S.W.A.T Team. As they were moving in on them, Paris shot one of the homey's in the head, and his brain hit the floor like it was cool whip. It was everywhere on the ground.

Tommy Gun saw his little homey hit the ground before he ran down the stairs, he quickly turned around and busted off at Paris hitting her twice in the vest. "Paris!!!" Thomas yelled out. He started running after Tommy Gun while banging his Glock 40 at the door as it was closing. Then John ran over to Paris to make sure she was okay. "She's fine...go get that son of a bitch now!!" John yelled to Thomas. Thomas turned back around and shot the lock off the door, and flew down the stairs after them. Thomas started running down the steps only to run right into Tommy Gun. Tommy Gun was hiding right behind the stairs. Tommy Gun was waiting for Thomas. Tommy Gun walked right behind him and put his gun right to the back of Thomas' head. "Don't even think about it. Tell your men to back the fuck up now!!" Tommy Gun yelled. Turning Thomas around facing the rest of the police. "Hold up men don't do nothing crazy!!" Thomas said to the rest of the police as they were coming down the stairs. "You fucking heard him!! All of you, back the fuck up now!! Or this fucking pig gets it in the head!!" Tommy Gun said as he was holding the gun to the side of Thomas' head. Tommy Gun was sweating real, real hard. Meka was right beside him. Pointing her Glock 40 at the rest of the police. "You fucking pigs!! You fucking heard him!! Back the fuck up!!" Meka said ready to shoot. "Y'all will never get away with this shit," said Thomas with his hands up in the air, and Tommy Gun was right behind him with the gun to his head. "It looks like to me, I already did motherfucker!!" Tommy Gun said with spit flying from out of his mouth hitting Thomas in the face. Frank and everybody were on the outside but heard everything that is going on inside over the radio. The two homey's Shitty, and Tanya, got to the back door first. There was nobody around back by their truck. They got in and yelled for Meka and Tommy Gun to come on so they can get out of there. The police backed up so Tommy

Gun and Meka could make their way to the back door. Meka comes out first and jumped in the truck. Tommy Gun come out with Thomas with his hands still up. "Good night you fucking pig," Tommy Gun said. He was now ready to pull the trigger, Thomas closed his eyes. One shot goes off, but Thomas is still standing and still breathing. He opens his eyes thinking that he is in Heaven. But instead, Tommy Gun's blood and brain is all over his face. Tommy Gun was on the floor, his legs and arms was twitching. Thomas couldn't believe his eyes that he was still alive. Some more shots started to ring out. That's when Thomas made a run for it back in the building. Shitty was trying to take his head off as he was running. As they were pulling off, the truck was getting shot up. It was George on top of the roof, it was his one shot that saved Thomas' life.

"Drive nigga drive!!" yelled out Tanya to the little homey. Shitty was crying shooting at the S.W.A.T Team as they were driving off. All of them started shooting at the S.W.A.T Team as they were trying to get out of there. The back windshield of the truck shattered as gun fire was being exchanged. "Fuck! fuck! Fucking pigs, one killed Tommy Gun fuck!!" Tanya yelled out as she started crying. "Motherfucker I hate cops! Fucking pigs," said Shitty as she was reloading her ozzie pistols. Hearing the siren coming up behind them. "We got pigs!" Meka said as she took aim at one of the police car tires to take them out. Making them crash into each other and flipping one of the police cars over.

Back at the warehouse the agents was finishing up what they started. Some of the Bloods surrendered, and the ones that didn't were killed. As S.W.A.T and F.B.I. secures the building they found over one hundred key loads of cocaine, some guns, and some money, but it was nothing compared to what they still had left. But to Frank and them, it was a nice bus.

A small fire had started but they had managed to put it out. "Okay bag this shit up and take it all in for evidence. And whatever animals that were left alive, take them in for questioning," said Frank as he walked over to Thomas; he was still shook up from what had happened to him. "You okay Thomas?" Frank asked. "Yes, I'll be fine thanks," said Thomas to George. "All in a day's work...any time," said George to Thomas and Paris as they came over by him. She sat down beside him helping him get himself together. "You okay baby?" Paris asked wiping the blood from off of his head. "No, are you okay boo?" Thomas asked touching her vest wear the bullet hit at. "I'm fine, thank God for this bulletproof vest," said Paris as she was showing him were she got hit at.

Back at headquarters, everyone was starting to celebrate except for Frank, Cox, Thomas, Paris, and George from S.W.A.T "I would like to know what the big celebration is for people!" Frank said angry as a motherfucker. As he looked at all of them like if they were crazy or something. "Sir we just took down the Bloods stash house sir," said one of the cops out loud to Frank. "Yeah! What about the cops that died today, and yesterday, and the day before that! Are they celebrating right now?!! No!! They're dead. Are their families celebrating? No!! Because their father or love one is dead!! The job isn't over yet, suit the fuck back up now!! Where going back out A.S.A.P. We didn't even put a dent in their shit yet!!" Frank said as he walked off to his office, and slammed his door behind him. "Okay you heard him party over, let's go back to work. People we're rolling out in 30 minutes, let's go!" Cox said as he yelled at everybody so they can get back on the streets. This time they were going after the Crips.

Paris went and knocked on Frank's door and let herself in. "Sir sorry for disturbing you, can I please come in for a minute sir?" Paris asked as she entered the room. "Yes, yes Paris please come in, what's up?" Frank asked her as he turned around in his chair to face her. "Sir I would like to let you know we're here for you, you're not alone. As far as me, Thomas, Cox, George, John, and Green sir," said Paris to Frank standing in the door. "Paris, you and Thomas don't have to come back. If you don't want to...it's okay. After what happened today," said Frank to Paris as he was getting up to move out," Sir we wouldn't have it no other way, we are here to the end," said Paris to Frank as they were walking out the door to go meet up with everybody else; they were ready to go. They were on their way to James' warehouse. As Frank was about to walk out of his office, he got a phone call that Pinkey just went to pay bail on a young lady by the name of Nadia. Frank immediately looked up everything he could find on her. He noticed her boyfriend was still locked up. That was what Frank was going to work on A.S.A.P. "We have to get to the jail A.S.A.P. It seems like one of our girls made a friend when she was inside the jail," said Frank to Cox as they were on the way to the jail to see if they can crack her boyfriend. His name was David Crown.

The S.W.A.T Team and the rest of the police are in position at James' stash house in Brooklyn where Wesley, Jay, and Spade are at. The police was watching their every movement, it was about to go down. They were just waiting for Frank's word, so they can move in on them. None of the girl's was there with them.

Frank and Cox were just reaching the jail where Nadia's boyfriend was at. Frank was really hoping that David would be their breakthrough in the case. Plus, Frank knew that he was locked up for two keys of coke. It would be a while before he saw the streets again. "Hi my name is Agent Frank Anderson, and this is Agent Cox. We are here to see a David Crown please," said Frank to one of the CO's in the building while showing his badge and paperwork to another one that was sitting there as well. "Okay sir...give me a minute please," The CO said as she got on the phone. Then she told Frank to follow her. She took Frank and Cox to a small room with three chairs and one table. "Please wait here someone will bring him down in a minute," she said as she walk off leaving Frank and Cox in the room.

As they were sitting there, Cox whipped out a pack of cigarettes and started smoking one of them as him and Frank was waiting for David. "You know one day them things is going to kill you," said Frank to Cox as he was smoking. "Not if these streets don't kill me first," said Cox as he was taking a pull off of his cigarette. Just then the door opened with two CO's and David with them in handcuffs. "You can take them handcuffs off of him," said Frank to one of the CO's. The CO took the handcuffs off of David then walked out of the room. Frank told David to sit down; David took a seat rubbing his wrist while trying to figure out what was going on and why is he here. "Okay David I'm going to get straight to the point. Do you want to get out of here?" Cox asked him as he was smoking his cigarette. "Yeah I do, but what is the catch twenty two?" David asked. Then he asked Cox for a cigarette. "We're here to help you. Do you know that your girlfriend made bail on you?" Cox asked him as he gave David a light for his cigarette.

"No! When she made bail?" David asked taking a nice long pull off of his cigarette. "Sometime yesterday, some girlfriend she is to you," said Frank to David, David had a dumb look on his face.

CHAPTER 17

THE RAT FOR FREEDOM

Okay so what do I have to do with this whole picture?" David asked Frank and Cox as he was sitting there looking at both of them. "We need you to help us crack this case for us. And if you do, you and your girlfriends case will be dropped. But you do have to testify, you know that right?" Cox said as he walked over to David. David without thinking twice is down to do whatever to get a get out of jail card from the F.B.I. "Yes I'm in whatever it takes to get my life back. Who the hell are these people that bailed out my girl?" David asked not knowing everything that's going on. Frank opened up a big yellow folder with everybody's picture in it and he looks over the pictures with him one by one. "So whose these people in these pictures?" David asked looking through them. "They are members of the Bloods and the Crips. The one girl that bailed out your girl is a member of the Crips," said Cox to David. "Hold on Cox she's not a member yet, she affiliate yes. But she not a Crip yet," said Frank to both of them. "So when I'm I getting out of here?" David asked as he pulled on his cigarette one more time before putting it out on the floor. "You will be released from here within an hour from now to us. If you try to run, I'll shoot you myself. If you try to tell them anything, I'll shoot you. Do I make myself clear?" Cox said as he was talking to David. Letting him know what's up. If he evens think about doing anything wrong at all. He's dead or back in jail. "I get the picture, I'm trying to get the fuck out of here. Please can we hurry up?" David asked. Frank told him they will see him on the outside at that time both of them got up and walked out of the room.

The Co came and got David to take him back to get his things from his housing unit. Cox and Frank both had two big smiles on their face as they were leaving because this was one of the biggest crack in the case yet for them if everything goes down right. Frank and Cox calls someone at headquarters to come get David.

Frank and Cox was on their way to James' stash house in Brooklyn were Spade, Jay, and Wesley was at under twenty four hour watch.

As soon as Cox and Frank get there the S.W.A.T Team was already in position to move in. John, Green, Paris, and Thomas were already to move in on Frank's command. "Is everybody in position to move in?" Frank asked over the radio. "Yes sir, at your command sir," George said ready with his 30r6 rifle in his hand. "Okay moving, moving, go, go, go, go!!" Frank yelled out. As all units moved in at once, on the inside Wesley, Jay and Spade started to hear a siren, and a car door opening and slamming. They even heard a helicopter flying back and forth over the roof. "Yo! Cuz cops are everywhere fuck! We got to get the fuck out of here," said Spade as he backed up from the window as he seen the police trying to run their building. Gun fire was starting to be exchanged as the police was making their way inside. Jay grabbed his AK47 and was standing at the stairwell banging at the police as they were trying to make their way in. Spade quickly ran for his two twins 45 Colt to back him up; Wesley did the same with his H&K MP5 with a hundred and twenty round drum banging out through the window. George took a shot at one of the Loc's on the roof top killing him instantly. His body fell down to the ground.

Wesley saw his young Loc and started going crazy yelling, "C-up motherfucker! We clap back bitch!!" Wesley said as he was gunning them down, the police and their police cars outside. As Wesley was moving from the window, he got shot in the leg by George with the 30r6 sniper rifle. Wesley yelled out, "I'm hit! I'm hit!!" Then he fell to the ground. Spade quickly ran to his aid to help him up. They started making their way through a back window to the back alley. Wesley car wasn't that far away from them, Jay stood by the window just to make sure the police wouldn't follow them. "Go get the car cuz! I'll be here go!" Jay said to Spade and Wesley. Wesley gave Spade the car keys and stood there with Jay gunning anything that came out that window. "Get in! get in!" yelled out Spade as he pulled up on Jay and Wesley. As both of them was backing up into the car banging off at the police. Spade smashed on the gas as hard as he could making the tires spin out getting them out of there. The police started shooting at them as they were getting out of there. As they were pulling off one of the police shot out the back windshield, as they were turning the corner full speed. The police was right on their ass. Wesley is banging out through the window at them. The helicopter was in the air on them as well. Wesley's leg was still bleeding, so Jay takes his flag off and wraps it around Wesley's leg to try and stop the bleeding. "It's not much, but it should hold you cuz," said Jay to Wesley. Wesley knows deep down inside there was no way of losing the helicopter like this at all. "Look cuz we going to have to split up," said Wesley as he was still shooting at the police car that was still behind them. "Yo cuz you can't even run homey what the fuck you're talking about?" Jay said as he was sitting beside him in the back seat. "Look this is what I want y'all to do cuz," said Wesley to them. Just as he said that a police car shot out two of their tires making their car flip right by a supermarket. Spade was the first one out of the car. Spade helped Jay out first, then Jay helped Wesley out. While Spade was watching their backs. the police was right on their ass. Jay started banging that AK-47 flipping the police car as they were coming down the street. "Look every man try and get a car and we meet up at Mike's house," said Wesley as he told Jay to go while he stands there and covers him and Spade. "Cuz you better be there too," said Jay to Wesley as he was shooting at the helicopter in the sky. Making it move out of his range before he take it down. Spade grabbed a car that was park in front of the supermarket. It was just sitting there running with the keys in it. Wesley and Jay jacked two people that was laying down on the ground right by their cars in the parking lot. All three of them had cars now. So all three of them got out of there. They went in different directions and the helicopter couldn't chase all of them. So it stays with Wesley, not letting him out of his sight. After like six minutes behind him, some police cars started to pick up on the chase. Wesley knew it was a matter of time before they catch him, Therefore, he gave them a run for their money.

So as he was driving he shot out the back windshield as he was shooting at the police cars that were behind him as he was doing 100 miles per hour. He got on the Linden Highway running red lights, taking them for a long ride. They had a road block set up on the street. Wesley started praying while he was driving fall speed to the road block. "C-up! Motherfucker!" Wesley yelled out the window as he was driving right into the road block. Not knowing they put down a spike chain. As soon as he ran over the spike chain. He started to lose control of the car. Because he was going to fast the car started spinning out of control. It hit into a pole causing the car to flip over two time. Landing on its back smashing the top down on Wesley. The chase was all over. The police was pulling up jumping out of their cars with their guns out. "Let me see your hands now!!" yelled out one of the police officers. But Wesley was not moving at all.

As for Jay he hit the highway and got out of there his phone started ringing. "Yo what's cracking cuz, you hood?" Jay asked Spade as he was driving. "Almost cuz, I won't see hood until I'm at Mike crib cuz," said Spade to Jay as he was driving. That is when Jay told Spade he's going to try and call Wesley to see what's cracking with him. As he dials Wesley's phone and got no answer. He knew something was wrong, so he threw his phone to the floor. He started zapping out while he was behind the wheel. "Fuck, motherfucking bullshit!!" Jay said as he started banging on the dashboard.

He finally got to Mike's house and Spade was there waiting for him with his two Colt 45s in his hands. They knew where Mike kept a spare key at all the time. Just for times like this so they could let themselves in. They knew they had to get rid of the hot cars A.S.A.P., so Jay quickly called Pinkey and Suzie to come over and get the hot cars, so they can get rid of them for them. They took the cars two miles to where they could drive them straight into the water and as they did that they would jump right into the car with Suzie, Pinkey and Nadia. On the way back to the house they were letting them know what was going on. Suzie just broke down and started crying because she had been trying to call Wesley all day, and she got no answer from him.

Back at headquarters Frank, Cox, and the rest of the police. They were getting David ready to take down Pinkey Suzie, Jay, and Spade. They had Wesley in custody at the hospital. He had a slight concussion. David was there best possibility yet in the case. By getting David in on the inside one of the officers was showing David. How to put on the wire so he can tape all conversations. "Okay I'm ready, so me and my girl get off free right. That's what you said right?" David asked to Cox as he was putting on his shirt. "Yes David just do what you got to do. We'll be there the whole time watching your back. So if anything go wrong we'll be there," said Cox as they were getting ready to call his girl Nadia on a tap phone to see if she will meet him. "Look kid, once you get the evidence...we need you to testify and then your home free okay?" Frank said as he passed him the phone to call Nadia. "Okay let's do this shit, fuck it; what do I got to lose?" David asked himself as he dialed Nadia cell phone number.

Meanwhile back at Mike's house everybody was still upset at what had happen earlier that day. Nadia phone was ringing so she got up from Suzie and Pinkey to get her phone. She looked at the caller ID. It was a number that she never saw before. "Hello," said Nadia. "What's up ma...I'm home," David said to her as he was trying to play real cool. "What's up baby where you're at?" Nadia said real happy to hear her baby's voice. "I'm in Manhattan ma can you come and get me please?" David asked her trying to bate her in. "How did you get out baby? I was going to get you soon. I just had to get my money right," said Nadia as she walked into the bathroom to piss. "Yeah...how the hell were you going to do that ma?" David asked her as he was smoking a cigarette real hard to calm his nerves down. "I'll talk to you when I see you, but how did you get out baby?" Nadia asked him again as she flushed the toilet. "My uncle from Washington DC got me out," David said as he was sitting in front of Cox and the rest of the agents. "Okay I'm on my way to get you," said Nadia as she walked back into the living room where everybody was. "Boo meet me at our old place, I still have it," David said. "Okay I'll be right there," said Nadia as she was getting off the phone happy to hear from her baby. Nadia started to tell Pinkey, Suzie, Jay, and Spade what was going on. "Yo! Guess what y'all? My baby is home. His uncle got him home. He wants me to meet him at our old place," said Nadia happy as a motherfucker. "Didn't we go there the other day and you had to get your stuff from the landlord?" Pinkey asked. Nadia thought about it and said while looking at them, "Yeah we did didn't we?" She remembered the landlord saying she was going to rent out the apartment. Just to be on the safe side of things, she decided to call his uncle in DC to see if he had heard from him like he said. "Hello Mr. Jackson have you heard from David lately?" Nadia asked almost sure that David was telling the truth. "No not at all baby and he better not call here. And you need to stay away from him. He is no good for you, you're too good, beautiful and smart for him," said Mr. Jackson to Nadia. "Thank you Mr. Jackson I'll keep that in mind. Have a good day," said Nadia as she hung up the phone. "So what's up Nadia what you want to do?" Pinkey said to her as they were getting ready to walk out the door. "Can find out any information for me on him?" Nadia ask Suzie and Pinkey. "Yeah we can; what's up girl?" Suzie asked as they jumped in Suzie's Benz truck to go meet Nadia's boyfriend David. "Man he told me his uncle bailed him out right. But something told me to call his uncle just to make sure so I did that right. His uncle said he haven't heard from him. Something is just not adding up...my gut feeling is telling me this," said Nadia as they were on their way to see him.

Suzie got on the phone and called Tasha giving her David's information. Tasha tells them she'll call back later on with the 411 on him. Meanwhile they're still on their way to Nadia's old place so she can see him face to face. "Look just to be on the safe side, just drop me off at my old place. Let me see what's up first," said Nadia as she was smoking on some purple haze. "Look if you're not sure. We will stay with you there, fuck that shit?" Suzie said as she grabbed the blunt from Nadia. "Na a bitch got to do this on her own. You feel me?" Nadia said to them. "Na let us come with you because a real nigga would want you to stay and give him some pussy. Let's just see if it true or not let's wait until Tasha calls us back with his information. Do you feel me?" Pinkey said as she grabbed the blunt from Suzie. "Okay that's what's up. How would your man say that? That's what's cracking cuz," said Nadia as all three of them started laughing at each other.

They made their way over there by the house. As soon as they pulled up Suzie started to blow the horn. She saw him looking out of the window. Then David made his way to the door and then he comes outside to the truck. Nadia get out to give him a hug and a kiss. The police was already there taking pictures of their every move. "What's up baby I'm home," David said with a big smile on his face. Suzie and Pinkey stepped out of Suzie's truck, David was looking like damn. "What damn!! Baby you got some pretty friends. What's their names?" David asked as he was standing there looking at them. She introduced him to Pinkey and Suzie. Just then Tasha called back telling Pinkey everything so far looks good on him.

Pinkey got off the phone calling Nadia over to the side. Pinkey start telling Nadia the good news. It put a smile on Nadia face. She runs over to him telling Pinkey and Suzie they can leave now. "Na let's all go out baby show me what you've been doing baby," David said as he walked over to the truck. "Damn it looks like your man getting it damn!!" David said as he was checking out the truck. "We doing okay...why don't y'all do your thing. We'll come back later and get y'all," said Pinkey to both of them. "Yeah do that Pinkey please, I'll call y'all when we're ready," said Nadia grabbing David's hand to go inside the crib. "Na man we got all night, let's hang out first and get to know each other," David said jumping in the truck.

At that time Nadia didn't know what to say at all so she just looked at Pinkey. Then Pinkey looked at Suzie, and Suzie just shrugged her shoulders at both of them as if none of them was feeling him at all. "Baby what's up...you don't want me?" Nadia asked him as she went over to him and rubbed him on his chest. David quickly stopped her from rubbing him on his chest like if something was wrong or something. So that is when Suzie turned to everybody and said to them, "Let's go get something to eat." Then she turned to Pinkey and just looked at her.

All four of them jumped in the truck, Nadia was in the back with her David as she was trying to rub him on his chest. He just kept telling her to stop. Plus, all he wanted to do was talk about drugs. Nobody else was talking just him. He was telling them how much weight he can move for them. "Baby what make you think they're into drugs boo?" Nadia asked him with a look on her face like shut the fuck up. "Come on now baby, I wasn't born yesterday...just look at y'all, it shows," David said as he started calling out the name brand clothes that they had on. One by one what they were wearing. And he started talking about the truck Suzie was driving.

As they finally got to the restaurant in Brooklyn called Junior, they walked in and got a table. Nadia asked Pinkey to come with her to the bathroom. David grabbed her ass as she walked pass him, Nadia just looked and smiled at him. "Girl something not right with him at all. He's not acting the same way. Do me one more favor, call back your girl and ask her to look again please?" Nadia asked as she was washing her hands. "If she said he's clean, he's clean, but I'll call her back for you," said Pinkey. So Pinkey got on the phone, but she got no answer. So she just left a message on her voicemail to call her back. "Look Nadia, me and Suzie fuck with you for real girl. Because you don't trust no one at all. We don't have to take him with us at all," said Pinkey to Nadia as they were getting ready to leave out the bathroom. "No it's not that I just don't trust him no more," said Nadia as they were walking out of the bathroom door. When they got back to the table David and Suzie were laughing and sipping on their drinks. "Yo this nigga is funny as shit, your man is funny as shit girl," said Suzie as she was laughing real hard with him. "What's so funny? Fill me in on the joke," Nadia asked as she and Pinkey was taking a sit. "He was just telling me about the highway chase. That y'all was in and how the police was acting and shit, that's all," said Suzie as they were sitting there waiting for their food.

Pinkey phone started to ring again and David was still telling his jokes. So Pinkey got up from the table. it was Tasha again with more information. "Yo that nigga was bailed out by the US Marshall. Girl he is working for the F.B.I. at first, I didn't see nothing in his paper work. Something told me to look at his bail just one more time. Plus, I got your massage too. But that is who bailed him out," said Tasha. Pinkey told her good looking then got off-the phone with her. Then she walked back over to the table. David was still running his mouth about his police encounter. That is when Pinkey stop the conversation and turn to Nadia as a joke and said to her. "It seems like your boys a hot boy Nadia and that is what Tasha just told me. That outfit is a no go...a not to wear, you feel me?" Pinkey said. Hoping she'll pick up on it. And she sure did right away they just played it off like it was nothing. But deep down inside she already knew he was a rat. David not knowing what was going on, just kept on running his mouth thinking everything was all good.

Nadia just couldn't take it no longer she stop him in the middle of his conversation to ask him some questions she did not feel bad about at all. And once she discovered he was a rat working for the Feds that really did it. "Baby stop for one minute please. Let me ask you some questions boo. How did you really get out of jail?" Nadia asked him as she was looking him dead in his eyes waiting for a response from him. All three of the girls were waiting for a response too from David. "Baby! What do you mean! I already told you what's going on. My uncle got me out," David said as he looked at all three of them as if they were crazy or something. "No nigga I called him, he didn't get you out. Nigga!! you're a fucking rat!! working for the Feds bitch!!" Nadia said real loud the whole restaurant got real silent for a minute. Then Nadia got up and threw her drink in his face. "Bitch!! Is you fucking crazy or something. I fucking love you," David said as he was holding her hand. Nadia snatched her hand from him, and ripped off his shirt revealing the wire that he was wearing. "What the fuck is this? You fucking rat bitch!! Fuck you!!" Nadia said as she spit into his face right in his eyes and mouth from the back of her throat.

He was just about to hit her and that is when Suzie and Pinkey jumped up in between both of them. Suzie and Pinkey both was four months pregnant. All three of them started fucking him up. That is when the F.B.I moved in to stop the fight. "Okay okay! Break it up now the fight is over come on people. Before all of you go to jail," said Cox to all of them as he tried to break up the fight. "I hate you, you fucking bitch!!" Nadia said as the police was breaking it up. She scratched David in the face and spit on him again. "Bitch! I did this for you, for us so we can be free!" David was yelling out at her. "You know at one time I would do anything for you. My mother was right I regret not listening to her at all. You fucking rat bitch!!" Nadia said as she was ready to explode again. Cox let her know if she hit him again she will be going downtown for a assault on a CI and that is a serious offense. Cox decided to take them in so she can cool down. And at the same time question them all about the shooting in Brooklyn where some cops had got shot. Plus, Jay and Spade was still out on the run and they had no leads on them at all. They were hoping that they could get one of the girls to talk. But none of them was giving up any information at all. "Look Cox this is not working at all. What we need to do is let them back on the streets. And hopefully they will lead us to the other people involved in this shooting case," said Frank as he was talking with Cox in his office. "Your right Frank. That's what I'm going to do because we really didn't establish nothing with the information at all. He fucked up for real...if he only had a brain," said Cox to Frank about David.

"Why don't you try this Cox. Take Nadia out of the room with them two ladies. She might talk if she's around him, her boyfriend. Give it a shot," said Frank.

Both of them walked out of Frank's office to the interrogation room to get Nadia to take her to were David was at so they could talk. "Look Nadia I'm going to take these handcuffs up off of you. Please don't do nothing okay?" Cox said as he took off the handcuffs off of her. She grabbed a chair and moved it from David. She sat in the chair rubbing her wrist from the handcuffs. She just look at him with tears running down her eyes. "How could you do this to me David?!! After all we been through?" Nadia said as tears was running down her eyes as she looked at him. "My plan was not to hurt you baby. Just them I don't know them bitches out there at all. I love you baby, me and you was going to be free. After all of this was over baby," All she did was look at him shaking her head, crying real hard. He reached out to her. Nadia just jumped back started spiting and kicking at him. Calling him all kind of bitches. David grabbed her trying to hug her, she bit him in his face so hard that he smack the shit out of her, down to the grown. "Hey, hey! What the fuck is wrong with you. Are you fucking crazy or something? Don't you ever hit a lady ever again," said Cox as he pushed David up against the wall, putting his finger up in his face. "Miss if you want to press charges you can?" Cox said as he help her up off the floor to her feet. "Man fuck that bitch! I was looking out for you bitch!" David said as he pulls out a cigarette so he can smoke. "You know what David...fuck you. You're not a fucking man at all. You're a bitch ass nigga! You wasn't looking out for me. You was looking out for your bitch ass self nigga!! You're a bitch ass rat. No I don't want to press charges on him. Fuck his rat bitch ass!!" Nadia said as she spit at him again and punching him in the mouth. Then she kicked him in the nuts he went down to the grown. Then she kicked him again. This time in his face and he was down crying like a bitch. That is when Cox stepped in and breaks it up. "I want to press charge on that fucking bitch fuck that bitch!!" David said as he was holding his nut still on the ground. "Bitch ass nigga, man up for once in your life. Didn't you smack her down to the ground man up," said Cox as he got all up in his face then he took Nadia out of the room, and got her some ice for her face. Then he took her back to the room where Pinkey and Suzie were at.

Both of them was looking at her like what happened to her as she walked in the room. "Girl what the fuck happened to you? What the fuck did they do to you?" Pinkey asked her as she looked at her face, Suzie did the same thing too as well. "If y'all hit her it's on and cracking in this motherfucker," said Suzie mad as a motherfucker. "Hold on we didn't do shit, take it easy okay," said Cox, letting them know they didn't do that to her at all. "Them motherfucker's didn't do shit to me. It's that bitch of a boyfriend that did this to my face...that bitch!! Ooh! I can kill him!" Nadia yelled. "What the fuck? Oh no we're going to kick his ass. Where the fuck is he at?" Suzie asked as she was getting up ready to fight. "Down the hall on the ground holding his nuts and face," said Nadia. "I know that's right girl," said Pinkey as she gave Nadia a high five. As soon as she gave Nadia a high five Frank was walking pass with David and all three of the girls tried to get at him. None of them gave a fuck, all they knew is that he tried to fight one of them so now he has to fight all three of them. "You faggot motherfucker. That is why she fucked-you up bitch!" Pinkey said mad as she spit at him while trying to get through Cox and Thomas. "That why your balls in your stomach, you faggot bitch!!" Suzie yelled as she was trying to kick though Thomas and Cox. "Okay girls okay that's enough! This is what going on unfortunately at this time. Y'all are free to go at this time, but we both know it will be a next time," said Frank to all three of them. He told Cox's to let them go. So Cox's just took all three of them downstairs to their SUV and gave Pinkey the keys to the truck. They all got in, and Pinkey put the key in the ignition and then they took off. "Yo what the fuck they think we were some weak ass or something?" Suzie asked them while sitting in the passenger seat. "Let's go straight to Mike's house and see if Spade and Jay is okay first," said Pinkey. "Look I think for real we need to get rid of this truck A.S.A.P. and get something else because you never know what might be in this motherfucker, a fucking wire or something. I don't know about y'all but a bitch be watching CSI and shit," said Nadia as she looked all around the truck. They all started laughing but they took her very serious at the same time. They knew she just might be right so they decided to go to a car shop where James use to go to let his man look at it for them. Suzie called him to let him know she was on her way to see him. As soon as they got there they just gave them the truck keys and told them they will see them tomorrow. So they just went to Pinkey's place in Brooklyn where Top Gun was killed at so they can take a shower, get some clothes, and lay back for the night. They didn't want to make Spade and Jay hot, so they stayed out for the night.

CHAPTER 18

NEWS FLASH TRAIL TIME

Back at Mike's house in New Jersey, Spade and Jay was just chilling watching the eight o'clock news. So far so good, they didn't know who they were. Plus, they got rid of both the cars already. The only thing they were thinking about was their man Wesley. They both had a gut feeling that he got caught up. "Damn cuz, I knew this bullshit was going to happen to cuz I felt it coming," said Spade as he was rolling up a blunt with some purple haze. Jay went and got a six pack of Heineken out of the refrigerator for them. Jay cracked two of them, and gave one of them to Spade, and then he sat back on the couch with Spade. "Man we should of stayed together cuz, but it was a OG call. I hope cuz is okay, I wonder what's going on with Pinkey and Suzie cuz?" Jay said as a news flash came on about Wesley's car crash. Both of them couldn't believe their eyes at what they saw on the news. "Damn cuz what the fuck! I knew we should of stayed together," said Spade as he lit up one of their blunt to smoke. "Man what's up with the girls, cuz the last time we heard from them they were on their way to get Nadia boyfriend," said Jay to Spade as he grabbed the blunt from him. "If something was wrong someone would of called by now," said Spade as he laid back on the couch. That's all they can do for right now until someone calls them to let them know something.

Meanwhile Tanya, Shitty, Meka, and the two young Bloods that was with them were hiding out at the Doc house. They had been there for a few hours, they were trying to make it back to the Bronx but the street was to hot right now. All five of them are mad as a motherfucker, one of their big homey's is dead. "Fucking pussy! I hate cops Doggy going to be mad as a motherfucker," said Tanya with tears running down her eyes. "Fuck it homey! I'm ready to run up in headquarters for my homey. What's popping Blood in Blood out?" Shitty said. She had tears coming down her face as well while grabbing her guns, ready to walk out the door. Meka and Tanya stopped her from leaving out the room. "That not going to bring Tommy Gun back homey or help Doggy, 007, and the rest of the homey's out. You're going to get killed homey!" Meka said holding Shitty back from leaving. "What Bitch!" Shitty said to Meka as she smacks the shit out of Meka and started fucking her up. Tanya jumped in the middle of Shitty and Meka smacking the shit out of Shitty. So she can cool down because Tanya already knew Shitty was a zap out. "Shitty, what's the fuck is wrong with you? That your motherfucking homey is not the enemy bitch!! You need to get it together Meka right, that's not going to help none of us at all. And it's not going to bring Tommy Gun back from the dead," said Tanya as she was all in Shitty face. "Man homey!! fuck her! Shit okay homey you are right, you'll right. I'm going to lay back," said Shitty as she gave Meka a hug and peaces her too. "That's what it is homey, roll this shit up. What the fuck is your name anyway homey?" Shitty asked one of the young Bloods. "My name is Donovan a.k.a. Killer Machine a.k.a. Bloody Mess. That's who I be, now pass that motherfucking weed homey," Donovan said while looking at Shitty real crazy like what nigga. "Yo Donovan yo a.k.a. Killer Machine, Bloody Mess here you go homey, roll up. So who gave you that name homey?"

Shitty asked passing the weed to him. "Motherfucking Tommy Gun gave me that name, that's who. That's my uncle, blood uncle at that. I want to get even just like you homey, but that shit you talking is crazy homey. I definitely want to get them back myself homey. I fuck with you for that Shitty, but we can think about it first, something else for big homey, you feel me?" Donovan said as he lit up the blunt looking at her. "Man shut the fuck up and pass that blunt little nigga. I like you but don't push it," said Shitty as she took the blunt from him. "I'm just saying big sis we're all family right? So we suppose to act like one B-up homey," Donovan said as he threw their set up high. Showing his loyalty over everything Shitty just smiled at him. "I like you little homey, your little ass can drive too homey," said Tanya. "I use to steal cars for a living at one time, and I was always bumming through the hood. I use to see y'all with my uncle and shit. Doggy, 007, and Pit they all know me. Y'all bitch's was always into something," said Donovan as he rolled up another blunt. "I'm not going to lie I like him say bitch again little nigga. You make my pussy wet...say it?" Shitty asked him as she was holding her pussy like if it turned her on. "Like I said y'all bitches was always into something," said Donovan again to them they just started laughing; Shitty's pussy got wet too. Tanya lit up the next blunt that Donovan rolled up and she passed it to Meka. Donovan passed his to Shitty and let the other little homey hit it.

Back at headquarters Frank, Cox, N.Y.P.D., S.W.A.T, and the DA were having a meeting making sure they had enough evidence and eyewitnesses for the trial because the trial date was a few months away. "I thought I'll never live to see this day come true. The Cartel Gangster's going down," said Frank to all of them that was in the meeting. It was a day that he had been waiting for a long time. "Unfortunately we didn't get all of them at one time. But at least we got some of the big players. Their organization is going downhill, most of their main streets are locked down. Right now, NY and B-more are still running. New York is almost done, it's just a matter of time before we get them out there in B-more too," said Frank to everybody in the room. "It was real difficult but we did it. We fucking did it," said Frank with a smile on his face. "I don't know about y'all but I'm going on a vacation. I'm going to take off for a while," Detective John said as he kicked his feet up laying back in his chair. "I'm still on the street because as long as one of them bastards are still on the streets I can't rest at all," Stg. Green said as he looked at everybody in the room. "He's right, he made a very good point there because it's still a lot of them left," said Frank as he looked at Stg. Green then looked at everybody else. "Frank, I must say we did it, both sides are down and out of the game right now," said Cox. They just didn't know about the robbery in the Bronx yet. Because if they knew about the Dominican's that were killed. They wouldn't be sleeping at all.

A few months gone by it was now time for trail to start. Pinkey and Suzie was nine month pregnant ready to have their baby's. It was nine thirty in the morning the courtroom was packed. All of the agents were there, all lawyers were there, and all of their clients as well; all of them was looking real professional ready for court. Everybody was in Sean John three piece suits or Rocawear suits and they were all in their colors.

Suzie, Pinkey, and Nadia were there; Spade and Jay stayed at Mike's house just to be on the safe side of things. As for Tanya, Shitty, and Meka, they were not there yet. It looks like they might be running not coming at all. "Where are your clients Ms. Lowes? I don't see them anywhere in the courtroom, and they're about to call this case," said Ms. Jones the DA for the case. "Look I spoke to them last night they said they will be here this morning," Ms. Lowes said as she looks around the courtroom. "Ms. Jones I need to speak to you for a minute," said Frank walking with her over to the side of the courtroom where no one could hear them talk. "What's up Frank?" Ms. Jones said. "We might have a problem we can't find some of our witnesses. None of them at all Ms., Candy the girls from club Jacks. It looks like there nowhere in the city," said Frank with a look on his face like he fucked up big time. "Look we need them witnesses so we can get life out of these punks. Paris or Thomas can't identify none of them in the shooting at the club at all," Ms. Jones said holding her head as they talk.

Three minutes later Meka came walking in the courtroom. Ms. Lows walks over to her asking her if she has seen Tanya and Shitty. "They said to let you know they're not coming. Fuck the court just like that," said Meka to Ms. Lows as she was walking over to have a seat because Shitty and Tanya look at it like this. Who to say they don't know who it was in Manhattan and as soon as they walk in through the door. They don't try and lock them up. "Did y'all take care of what I gave y'all last night?" Ms. Lows asked Meka real low so nobody can hear her talk. "Fuck yeah! Them motherfucker's not coming at all. Not in this life time here," said Meka, letting her know they did what they had to do.

The Judge made his way into the courtroom. Everybody stood up in the courtroom. The Judge told everybody to be seated, so everyone took a seat. The court clerk started calling out their court case. Everyone was standing by their lawyer as their name was being called out. CO was standing in between them to make sure it wouldn't be any fights at all in the courtroom being that the case isn't going Federal. It's being held at Supreme Court in Brooklyn. "How do the defendants plea?" The court clerk asked but little did Frank know all of their lawyers already had something in mind. Plus, it made their case better that their witnesses wasn't there to testify at all. So all three lawyers approached the Judge, with the State's Attorney so they can work something out in this case. "Your Honor we would like to work out a deal in this matter. No longer than ten to fifteen years of jail time with parole sir?" James' lawyer asked for all of them only if they can work like this together; they might rule the world. "Yes your Honor there is no eyewitnesses in this case. Yes they do have some evidence, that is why we want to take a deal sir," Doggy's lawyer said to the Judge. The DA was going along with it, there wasn't much she could do about it without her witnesses to testify in the case. As for Judge Brown he absolutely didn't like the idea, but he went along with it because their case was starting to fall apart at the last minute. Because without no witnesses it was going to be hard to get a conviction. So they made a deal; all five of the girls got unsupervised probation. Tanya and Shitty got off even though they were not there.

Ms. Jones had to tell Frank and the rest of the police what was going on. Cox was pissed off about the whole situation. "I don't fucking believe this, they made a deal for ten years!! That's fucking it!!" Cox said mad as a motherfucker and then he started sweating. "Look at it this way, ten years and we don't have to worry about them at all. Now we just have to work on the rest of them," said Frank as he was trying to calm Cox down in the courtroom. All the lawyers and the State's Attorneys went back to their seat. The lawyers told their clients that they all agreed with what was going on. The clerk called the case again while Judge Brown was looking over their plea agreement before he said anything to anybody. "Being there is no eyewitnesses in both of these cases. I'm going to except this plea today. Ten to fifteen years, ten mandatory and no less than five on parole. This sentence is to be done in Upstate NY Maximum Society Prison. Now as for the young ladies, I was going to give y'all five years, but I see that it is really no evidence in this case. So I'm going to give y'all unsupervised probation for all of y'all. And I also see that two of y'all are about to be mother right?" Judge Brown asked as he looked at Pinkey and Suzie as they were standing beside their lawyers. Then both of them said at the same time, "Yes Your Honor we are." "I also see that two of y'all that is here before me is also in college at L.I.U. in downtown Brooklyn?" Judge Brown asked as he looked at both of them. "Yes, both of them are Your Honor," Ms. Itaily said. "Look I'm going to let y'all ladies go today. Do not let me see you in my courthouse ever again. Do I make myself clear ladies? I'm talking to all three of you," Judge Brown said while looking at them. All three of them said yes to Judge Brown and sat down. "Now do all of you wish to take this plea agreement today?" Judge Brown asked to all of them. All of them one by one agreed. The Judge hit his mallet on the table and that was that. "All parties have a good day this court is over," Judge Brown said as he got up and walked into his Chambers. One group at a time said their goodbyes. Pinkey and Suzie said theirs to James and them as they were leaving the courtroom. Everybody made out today money talks and bullshit walks. That is what it is all about in the world today, that we live in.

As for James, Doggy and the rest of the Bloods and the Crips, they were now on their way to Upstate New York. It was more Bloods than Crips upstate, but one thing's for sure, the Crips that are there go real hard. And one thing's for sure, it's a long ride upstate another thing they will be socially graded. They're going to make sure that nothing goes down. The Feds are riding along and the D.E.A. to make sure nothing happens. "Will this is it cuz and guess what cuz, Wesley on his way down here too cuz damn. We need cuz on the outside to hold shit down on the streets. I don't think Spade and Jay is ready for that kind of shit cuz?" James said to Ty and Mike as they were riding on the bus to their new home. "Man them niggas better be ready, we all know one day this might happen. You feel me cuz?" Ty said as he was talking to Mike and James. "Yeah, yeah I feel you Loc...what the fuck you think might happen to cuz?" James said to both of them. "Man we just got to hope for the best and look out for the worse feel me Loc?" Mike said to James. "Yeah cuz I feel you," said James looking out the window as he watches the road as they drove on the highway. "Fuck it Loc, it is what it is," Kevin said to everybody. "Cuz just know this when we get there it's on and cracking. Full blaze with them slobs, I'm going to drink me some cuz," said Simeon while looking at Doggy and them on their bus right beside them. "Man you already know what it is six cracking, five slacking all day every day. Blue light up across the sky to my casket drop Claaaat!!" James said as he threw up his set up high. "Once we get to where we are going, cuz I got some Loc's in the Bronx. I can call for some help with Jay and Spade," said Ty to James. "Yeah that might work," said James thinking about Pinkey and Suzie. Both of them were pregnant about to drop any day now.

Back in Brooklyn at the supreme court when the girls was leaving out both of them were crying and Nadia was right there for the both of them. As soon as they got in the truck Pinkey put Alicia Keys CD *"As I Am"* on to track four to the song *"No One"*, and put it on repeat to hear it over and over as they were driving. They were on their way to Mike's place, and they already called Jay and Spade to let them know what had happened in court.

On Doggy's bus, all of the Bloods were getting ready for war. It's always the younger ones trying to put in work, so they can move up in rank and get respect for the big homey's.

"Yo homey, when we reach y'all already know it's on and popping homey. We going to get them Crab ass niggas," said Doggy to all of his homey's, its look like it's going to be an all out war. "And you know we got a lot of homey's up there already too. Rock Face been up there for a while now. He got it on and popping right now," said 007 to Doggy. "Man it's on homey's as soon as we touchdown," said Pit to some of the little homey's that was on the bus. "Pit you not saying nothing we don't know; plus, we made out big time homey's," Mad Max said to Pit as they were all getting ready for war. "Damn I wish we hurry the fuck up I need something to smoke homey's," said Sam. Looking out the window as he was watching a man in his truck smoking a cigarette. "Nigga lay your ass back homey, we're almost there damn," said Doggy to Sam watching him go crazy for a cigarette. "Yo homey's, Blood Face and his homey's soon come home. So I gave him Tanya and Shitty number. So he can hook up with them when he get uptown," said 007 to Doggy. Doggy thought that was a good idea to do so. "Yeah homey, we definitely got to give them a call and see what's up with Tommy Gun," said Doggy. "For real homey, I know homey is holding it down uptown," said Pit to all of them on the bus. They just don't know yet if their homey is dead. That he died in a gun fight with the police because Frank made sure that they didn't put his face on TV news. And as for Tanya, Shitty, and Meka had been laying low for a while. They were just reaching the prison in Upstate NY sing, sing. One of the notorious prisons in NY. They were on their way through the big steel door. Cox, Frank, and Thomas went along for the ride just to see that everything goes as plan. It was two loads of gangsters going to prison. One bus had the Crips on it and the other one had the Bloods on it.

As they were unloading the buses they were side by side each other. Some CO's was in the middle of both buses with K9 barking at all of them coming off of the buses. "Welcome ladies to home sweet home for the rest of your stay here. Some of y'all have ten...some of y'all have life. Now!! Move it ladies!!" yelled one of the CO's there with a dog by his side barking at everybody. They had the Bloods going to the right and the Crips was going to the left. This is their final stop and no one leaves from here unless they're going to the hospital, home, dead, or alive. You're a prisoner of N.Y.C. and because of their affiliation it just makes things worse for them. "Damn cuz I guess this is it for the next six years," said James Looking around as they were walking through. "Man fuck it cuz. Pinkey and Suzie is going to have the baby real soon right?" White Mike asked as they were walking through the door to where they got to strip at. Coming out of all their clothes and get searched before going anywhere else. "Yeah Loc and cuz just got locked the fuck up," said James to Mike and Ty. "Yo Jay and Spade we'll be okay, both of them will keep it cracking...you already know," said Ty as they were stripping out of their clothes getting ready to get searched. "Damn my nigga, I know you would like to be there too?" Kevin said as he was asking James as they were standing waiting to get in the shower. "You already fucking know Loc. My first one and it's a boy too," said James to all of them. "Man I just hope when a nigga gets out. They go around the way and keep it cracking too cuz," said Mike to James. "Not like us but they will at least keep the hood Loc out, you feel me?" James said to Mike as they were getting out, and putting on their DOC clothes. "I feel you that is all I ask of cuz and them to do," said Ty as they were going to their cell.

On the other side of the jail Doggy, 007, Sam, Pit, and Mad Max was making their way through the jail. As they were making their way through the jail, a whole bunch of little homey's saw them as they were coming down the hall and started throwing it up to them as they were walking through. As they were almost to their cells they ran right into their homey Rock Face. Also, a lot of the little homey's saw them on TV, so they knew who they were already. And one thing's for sure, Doggy and 007 always looked out for Rock Face while he was locked up doing time. "Blaaaat!! What's popping homey, long time know see," Rock Face said as he peaces Doggy, 007, and the rest of the homey's as they were coming in. "Nigga! You already know homey that five do or die. Doggy a.k.a. Bloody Dog Blaaat!! Blaaaaat!! I see you got shit the way I like it homey," said Doggy to him, smiling at Rock Face happy to see him for real. "Man you should already know big homey, Bloods run everything out here. Homey, them Crabs don't fuck with us like that," Rock Face said showing everything to Doggy. As all of them made themselves at home, their new home that is.

"Man fuck them niggas, it's a Bloods world we're living in homey. Bloods in Bloods out," said 007 laughing as he said it feeling good as he took a look around. "Tell me homey you got some bitches homey that is on the team?" Doggy asked as he was about to light up a cigarette to smoke. "You already fucking know homey. I got a house full of fucking Ruby's homey. And they do whatever the fuck I tell them to do too," Rock Face said to Doggy letting him know it's their world, and the Crips are just living in it. "Now that's what's the fuck is popping homey. That's what the fuck I'm talking about some motherfucking pussy for real," said Doggy to Rock Face as he peaces him and they break the Crab. "Ruby's we're the fuck they at homey? Don't forget me homey when they come," said 007 to both of them as he walked over to them. Rock Face, Doggy, and 007 just started laughing at each other. They haven't seen Rock Face in five years. Every since he got caught up for a body, he got twenty five years for it. He gave back fifteen of it and got five more on the ten to do. He did a good job of locking shit down.

Back on the other side of the prison, James and the rest of the Loc's make their way through to where they got to go. It was a lot of Loc's there, but not like the Bloods on the other side of the jail. Loc's was showing them mad love and some of them started C-walking and throwing up their hood were they're from. One of James Loc's was there at the top of the tear as they came in. "James, Mike, Ty what's cracking big cuz, cuz what the fuck y'all doing on TV cuz? And now up in here at that. What it is cuz?" Black Dice asked. He was one of Ty Loc's that had got caught up in some drug spots so he's now doing some time for. "Man cuz we got caught up in some shit fucking with them fucking Mutts," said Mike to him and peaces him at the same time. Throwing C-up and breaking the five. "No bullshit cuz we heard about that shit that was going on uptown. What's up with that shit Loc?" Black Dice asked as he started piecing everybody one by one. "Man we was out to drink all them niggas. They got some of us too cuz. Top Gun and Trigger gone cuz to the blue sky," said Mike as he was piecing some of the Loc's. "Neap cuz!! Trigger can't be dead, fuck no cuz!" said one of the little Loc's. He was mad as a motherfucker about what had happened. "Yeah little homey it true what had happened. But we got the motherfucking Mutts that did it," said James to the little homey, because both of them was under Trigger. "Man what bitch was that... that set cuz up?" Ace asked a.k.a Baby Cuz. "Word on the street it was that Mutt bitch Meka cuz. She set it up to get cuz killed," said James to all of Trigger little homey's. "Man I'm going to get that bitch if it's the last thing I do big homey," Ace said mad as a motherfucker. They couldn't believe their big homey was gone just like that. "Yo cuz, how many Loc's we got here in this building all together?" Ty asked as he looked around the whole housing unit. "About seventy five in all cuz, why what's cracking?" Black Dice said to Ty waiting for a response back. "Yeah I was just saying because all I saw on my way in was Mutts everywhere," said Ty. "Yeah them bitches is everywhere cuz. It's five of them to one of us, you feel me? Fuck it cuz it was what it was cuz," Ace said letting Ty and them know that the Mutts already knows what it was. "Man fuck them Mutts, slob as bitches they jump out there if they want to. It would be chitty, chitty, bang, bang! You already fucking know," said James as he throws it up breaking the five stacking on their shit. "That's what the fuck I'm talking about cuz, but for real though. It like over 200 of them Mutts on that one side alone cuz. Them bitches are deep as shit. But they know what it was already," Ace said letting James and the rest of the Loc's know because they put in a lot of work already. "Damn cuz! Y'all niggas was doing it big uptown for real cuz. Yo cuz I heard you're married James. What's up with that? I heard shorty was a stallion too?" Black Dice said laughing because the James he knew wasn't out that mob at all. "Na, not yet, but I will be real soon cuz. I'm damn sure about to have a baby cuz," said James as he started Crip walking throwing it up. "That's what's cracking, I'm happy for you. But what's up with Wesley cuz? I heard cuz got shot the fuck up and shit. Then I saw cuz on the news in a big police chase, what's up with that?" Ace asked James, but just before he was about to say something Simeon did. "Ya cuz my brother's locked up, he'll soon be over here with us. Sad to say, but at least he's still here with us you know homey," said Simeon to Ace. "Yeah I feel you cuz, so who's out there holding it down in the hood cuz?" Ace asked. "Right now Spade and Jay is out there holding it down for a nigga with my girl and sister," said James to all of the Loc's. "Damn cuz that's it...were the fuck is everybody at cuz?" Black Dice said to James. "Cuz the rest of them is to young, but one thing I can say they go hard," said Mike as he was rolling up a jailhouse cigarette. "Well, let me put you on to what's cracking around here cuz. See that CO over there cuz, she's a Loc. And the one in the property room she's a Loc too cuz. We do have a few on our team. But it more Mutts than anything here for real," said Black Dice as he was filling them in. "Cuz no bullshit you did good for yourself here. But we still got a lot of work to do," said James. Because James was the type of person if something was done good it can always be done better and everybody knows that about him. "Cuz we been doing good as far as them not jumping out there. But now that big slob is here. They might try and jump out there," Ace said to everybody as they were smoking. "Man fuck them niggas, chitty, chitty, bang, bang nothing but a Crip thing," said Mike as he was C-walking throwing up their set.

Black Dice took them in front of one of their little Loc's cell, took James inside the cell to show him all their knives. Ty walked right in there with Mike because both of them love knifes. James was also checking out the drugs and the cell phones that they had. Black Dice had a nice set up going on there, but you know James he can always make it better. "Yo cuz I like what you got going on here you just need a little bit more shit, and it would be all good cuz," said James to make it better the shit that Black Dice already had. "Well, now that you're here cuz, do your magic. I have no problem learning from you big homey. Do what you do Loc," Black Dice said. Because he knew James knew what he was talking about. "No bullshit Black Dice you did good for the Loc's in here cuz," said Mike playing with the knives. "Man cuz I heard about you make it fucking happen cuz flat out!" Ace said to all of them. The CO came on the unit to let them know it was lunch time. "Do we eat with them Mutts or what?" Ty asked putting a knife in his dip as they were getting ready to go to lunch. "You fucking know it cuz. So we got to be on point today, it might crack off," Ace said as they were getting ready to go to lunch.

CHAPTER 19

CRIPS & BLOODS AT WAR

"Man fuck them Mutts cuz. If it wasn't for them bitches we wouldn't be in here right now," said James as he stepped up getting ready for whatever. "Cuz I swear to God I just want to kidnap Doggy's bitch ass and skin his ass alive like a fucking deer. But the only difference is he'll still be alive cuz," said Ty as he stepped up, as well; all of them was ready for whatever. "That sounds like a good plan to me cuz," said James as they were walking to lunch to eat. One thing's for sure, the jail was socially graded by the CO's everywhere. So whatever they did, they had to do it quickly and look for blind spot. As they were walking down the hall all they could see are some Bloods in front of them. And all the Bloods already knew that James and his Loc's are already there. You could feel the tension in the air as they were walking down the long dark hallway. If it was going to go down, this is where it would go down at. Even the CO knows something is about to happen. It was just a matter of time before somebody strikes from either side. "Yo homey, see the pussy right there, fucking Crab ass bitches, there right in back of us. Him and his fucking Crab ass crew, man you already know it on and popping homey. Rock Face get one of these little homey's to put in some work cuz?" Doggy said talking to Rock Face as they got to the dinner hall. "Say no more homey it's already done. I got the right homey for it. Yo! Daze come here for a minute," Rock Face said. Daze walked over to him and Doggy to sit down beside them in the dining hall. "What's popping homey? I already know, just say the word homey and it's done," Daze said as he was looking at James as they walked in the dining hall. Daze was trying to earn his rank today because he knew if he can hit James. He definitely would get it today for sure. "Yeah handle that homey on the way back. That nigga James and let all the little homey's know it on and popping too," Rock Face said to Daze. Daze walked over to the rest of the little homey's and passed the word around while they were standing in line getting the food. "Say no more, full blast on and popping homey. I'm going to do him real nice," Daze said as he was passed the word down the line. "It's done big homey my little homey's on it A.S.A.P. as soon as we leave from out of here," Daze said as they got their food and sat down to eat. "I hope them Crab ass niggas don't think they're going to be safe in this motherfucker," said Doggy to all of his homey's. They were sitting on the right side of the dining hall; as for James and the rest of the Loc's they were sitting on the left side.

Everybody in the dining hall can feel the tension in the air, and one thing's for sure James knows Doggy is up to something, and the Loc's are definitely ready for it today. Most of the CO's knows what was going on. "Yo cuz let everybody know stay on point," said James to Mike, Ty, and Black Dice as they were sitting in the dining hall eating. "Everybody on point cuz. It's going to crack off when we get out of here," said Ty as they were eating at the table. Every last one of them is strap with joins. And ready to go all out. "I say cuz we make the first move on them niggas, flat out," said Mike as the CO was calling table by table, one by one leaving out. "Yo cuz my little Loc's can get at him flat out. That is what they are there for to put in work cuz," Black Dice said. It was almost time for them to go. They were two tables away from them. "That's what it is cuz it on and cracking. Say know more chitty, chitty, bang, bang!!" James said to Ty, Mike, and Black Dice.

They were almost at their table as for Doggy and them, they were walking out real slow. Some of his little homey's was trying to hide in the dark spot in the hallway so they can jump out on James and hit him up. As James and them was walking out the dining hall, some of the Loc's was walking in front. Ty, Mike, Black Face, and Simeon was around James and the rest of the Loc's was in the back of them and everybody was on point. As they were walking down the long hallway. The Bloods that fell back can see James and them coming down the hallway. The Loc's that was in front got their eyes out ready for whatever. The Loc's had their hands in their dip with their hands on their joints just as they were walking pass them. The Bloods jumped out of nowhere trying to run down on James. The Loc's that was in front turned around and started running at the Bloods full blast ready to crack off. James, Ty, Mike, and the rest of the Loc's already got their joints out, but the Bloods never had a chance to hit James at all. It was on and cracking, Doggy and them ran down with the rest of the Bloods trying to hit up the Crips that was in front. Doggy was making his way through the crowd like an animal. The young Loc's did have enough experience to handle Doggy. James was running toward everything that was coming at him playing the art of war to the end. They were laying it down on the Bloods; him, Ty, Mike, Black Dice, and the rest of the Loc's. It was a all out back to back blow for blow war. Mike and Ty were flipping Bloods left to right putting in work. Kevin and Simeon was doing the same getting work done. After they ran through the young puppy's. It was now time to face off with Pit and Sam. CO's was now trying to make their way through them. Shooting mace at them into the crowd to calm them down and throwing tear gas in between them.

James and Doggy was now face off with each other. They started hitting each other up; back and forth, blood was everywhere. The CO's released the dogs on them, and some more tear gas on them at the same time. so hopefully they would stop killing each other. One dog is on James, and one dog is on Doggy. The dogs was taking them down. The CO's moved in on them to put handcuffs on all of them. They took most of them to the hospital. As for James and Doggy was hit up so badly and Sam, Pit, Kevin, and Simeon. All of them went to the hospital beside Mike, Ty, and Black Dice. The situation is now under control, but it didn't look to good for James and Doggy. They had to go to a outside hospital to get work done. They almost killed each other Doggy and James. And as soon as they leave from the hospital they are going straight to lock up. Both of them hit each other up pretty badly. Both of them was hooked up to an IV they lost a lot of blood and they had to stay in the hospital for a while. And both of them was socially graded at the same time too. Making sure nothing happened while they were at the hospital, both of them are going to be on lock up for a long time, nine days and nine nights. As for Sam, Pit, Simeon, and Kevin they are already there. As for Ty, Mike, Black Face, and the rest of the Loc's was good. 007 and the rest of the Bloods were good too because none of them got hit in the fight, but the jail was on lock down until further notice. This was the words from the Warden herself.

Some time had passed, a few weeks and the prison was still on lock down. "Damn cuz got hit up real bad, man when we come off lock down. It's on and cracking all over again. I'm going to kill that Mutt Doggy," said Ty as he was talking to Mike, X-man, and Black Dice from out his cell. "Man...all them bitch ass niggas is going to get it, that bitch 007 still here cuz. I'm going to hit that bitch when we come off cuz," said Mike as he was lighting up a cigarette. Mad as a motherfucker playing with his knife. Looking forward to stabbing up a Blood. "One thing's for sure cuz didn't go out like a bitch. That nigga was doing him as always cuz," X-man said standing at the cell bars with his hands through the bars talking to all the Loc's. "Damn cuz big cuz in the fucking hospital. Cuz just got here fuck!!" Ace said mad as a motherfucker. "Man it's going down cuz, but for right now. The Warden not going to let us eat together no more. We going to have to get at this slob on the low cuz," Black Dice said as he was doing some push up in the cell. "Yeah cuz I'm feeling that, that's what it was," said Ty as he was doing his pushups. "What's up with school we can get with them there feel me?" Mike said as he was playing with his knife. "Yeah, I feel you that's what it is cuz for sure," Ace said while he was doing his sit ups. But for right now the jail was on lock down until further notice because they have to do a full investigation. And it can be weeks or months before school starts back.

Back uptown some time had went pass, Pinkey and Suzie had their baby a few month ago. Spade and Jay were trying to hold down the hood. As for Pinkey and Suzie their mother, and Nadia helped out a lot with the two boys, she's the godmother too. Also, Ms. Campbell, helps out time to time when she's not running the store. So this way they can still get shit done on the streets. But it not easy at all one they still have the Feds on their backs. The Feds took damn near everything from James. James was down to his last two cars, one bike and some of their houses was seize from him by the government. It was not looking to good for him right now, but the girls are keeping their head above water.

CHAPTER 20

PINKEY, SUZIE & NADIA GO TO LA TO SEE PAUL

"Suzie and Nadia this shit isn't easy at all, we're down to our last two hundred thousand. We need to do something real fast, because it's not looking to good right now. How would my man say it, this shit is not cracking at all," said Pinkey to Nadia and Suzie as they were driving downtown Brooklyn. "No bullshit we need some money fast, and shit needs to get back to how it was," said Suzie as she lit up a blunt for the first time in a while. She and Pinkey stopped for a while due to the fact they were both pregnant. "Man...what's with Paul in LA. I think we should go to him. So he can put us on that is my baby man right?" Pinkey said as they were parking in the garage so they can go shopping for a few things. "Yeah I feel you, but I don't really know him like that. Plus, all this shit going on with the Feds. He probably don't want to fuck with us right now no way," said Suzie as they were walking in the mall. All eyes was on them as usually all three of them. "You're probably right, but you'll never know until you try. So let's do it me and you. So let's fly out to LA and see his ass. What do we got to lose? The Feds not even fucking with us right now at all," said Pinkey as they walked into a baby store looking at the Baby Phat Farm outfits. "You right fuck it what do we got to lose, I'll talk to my mom and see if she'll watch the kids so we can fly out to LA to see him," said Suzie as the three of them were checking out some Phat Farm outfits. "My baby owes him some cash, something like three hundred thousand. Not much compared to what he was making for him. So let's give him one hundred thousand out of two hundred thousand we got. And tell him will pay the rest when we make it?" Pinkey said as they were walking to the cash register to pay for their stuff. After they finish paying for their shit. They started getting ready to go see Paul. First they called him to let him know they were coming out there. Then they called the airport to see if they had a flight available for them. Paul knew Suzie real good, he met Pinkey a few times before too, but he never talked to her. He knew everything that was going on with the Feds and all. He still was going to see them. He just didn't want the heat that came with it, but he still going to see them out of love for his man. Plus, he fucked with Mike and Ty real hard as well. "Girl...we definitely got to get it together because them bitches is running the street right now in Brooklyn. Spade and Jay was keeping the hood together. But they need some shit to flip on the street because all this money being spent and nobody bringing nothing to the table...is never no good," said Pinkey while she was booking her flight to LA. "I definitely feel you on that for sure, because my man is locked up too and shit is real fucking hard for me as well," said Suzie making some bottles for the babies. "Look all I can tell you is, don't worry we still have each other forever. We will be okay, we will make it through this bullshit together because a bitch got to eat," said Nadia as she was playing with both of the babies. "Yes Nadia we feel you, so let's make it happen," said Pinkey and Suzie. "Now that's what the fuck I'm talking about. I told you Pinkey when I met you. I'm with you until the end for sure," said Nadia to both of them. "Man let's just do this together flat out. I love you'll forever," said Pinkey to both of them. They all sat together as one. The three of them sat back hugging each other. Then they prayed on it, and went out to eat and have some drinks. There flight was two days from now before they go to LA to see Paul. So they spent some time with their kids. Suzie's mother agreed to watch their kids until they came back from LA.   Sometime had went pass, It was now time to go to LA. They reach LA around 6pm at night. They got to their five star hotel around 7pm that was in Beverly Hills, it was called the Avalon Hotel. The entire hotel was made out of glass and it had a bar by the pool. And to stay in this hotel you had to pay at least 500 hundred dollars a night. So they checked into their room and started taking a shower. Then they called Paul to let him know they are in town and that they will be out to see him real soon. Thirty minutes had went pass Right after they got off the phone with Paul, the phone ring it was the front desk telling them that their limo was out front waiting for them. All of them was surprised that Paul sent a limo over for them. Plus, the limo driver told the front desk to tell them to take their time. "Damn now, that's what the fuck I'm talking about girl. Paul sent us a fucking limo. It's outside waiting for us," said Suzie as she was getting dress putting on her Victoria Secret panties and bra set. "I'm glad I came girl, this is the good life. But I'm not ready yet, shit you know a bitch got to look good," said Nadia as she was putting the coco butter on her honey brown skin. "He told the front desk to let us know to take our time," said Suzie as she was putting on her midnight blue Gucci outfit from head to toe looking real good. "I know that's right Paul...first class all the way. So let us take our time," said Pinkey as she jumped out the shower drying off. grabbing the coco butter to put on her beautiful light skin ass. As for Nadia, she was in an Apple Bottom jeans suit with some pole shoes on with her Louis Vuitton bag to match. Pinkey was wearing a

Prada jean suit with Channel frames and a Fendi purse to match. It took them 45 minutes to get ready.

As they were leaving the hotel jumping in their limo looking like divas all eyes on them, the limo driver got out and opened up the door. You would think they were stars from Hollywood somewhere. They look so good and the smell through the air as they walked was just unbelievable. They just got into the limo one by one. The driver told them he was told to take them to this real nice restaurant in Beverly Hills. That is where Paul will be at waiting for them at. They got there in about thirty minutes. As soon as they got there, the limo driver got out and opened up the door to let them out. All three of them was looking like true stars. People stopped and looked and some even took pictures of them. As soon as they walked in the lady at the front desk asked them their names. Pinkey told her all three of their names and who she was here to see. The young lady immediately took them to their table to where Paul was sitting and waiting for them to eat. Two ladies was sitting with Paul as well. Pinkey and Suzie knew one of the ladies there with Paul. They didn't know the other one, plus, this was Paul's first time meeting Nadia too. She was new all the way around to Paul. As soon as Paul saw them he helped them to their seats. Nadia just sat there playing it real cool, not saying much of anything. She was more listening to what was being said then anything else. "Ladies how was your flight to LA. I hope it was a good one. I see you brought a friend along with you. What is your name pretty lady?" Paul asked her as he stretched his hand out to her to shake her hand. "My name is Nadia I heard a lot about you. Nice to meet you," said Nadia to Paul as she gave her hand to him. "It is nice to meet you and very nice to see y'all too. How are my boys doing? I heard they have ten years with the state. That not bad at all," said Paul as the waiter was bringing more wine over to their table. "Yes, we know they're doing fine keeping their head up. It was a big fight in there. You know my baby was in the hospital for a while too you know. Bloods and the Crips shit, but it's okay now, because the jail is on lock down," said Pinkey to Paul as they sat there drinking some wine. "How was the wine would you like anything else to drink? Are y'all ready to order y'all food? Please feel at home," said Paul to all three of them. "Paul it's always good to see you, you know me and Pinkey had babies you know, both of us had boys," said Suzie to Paul as they were making their order. "You must let me see them one day. Do you have any pictures of them with you?" Paul asked to both of them. "We sure do and, they are just for you. This is my baby right here, and this is Suzie's baby right here. And this is our family picture of all of us together," said Pinkey as she showed him the picture and giving them to him. "Yes, yes I see they are very beautiful, you must raise them up right," said Paul while he was looking over the pictures before he put them in his pocket. "You already know we're not having that shit Paul. Not with these two boys, we're going to make sure of that. They damn sure have it better than we do," said Suzie to Paul as they were eating their food. "How is everything is everything fine over here sir...ladies?" the waiter said checking up on them making sure everything is okay. Everyone just stopped talking and started eating all different types of seafood; salmon with honey with yellow rice, fried shrimp's with crab cakes, some fried cat fish, red snapper, and all types of seafood dishes. Everyone was just eating and drinking doing them having a good time. A little comedy going on it a real nice restaurant. Everybody is done eating by now and they're just having a few drinks. They're having more laughter than anything right now. Paul pays for the food and drinks. He tells the girls about a real nice club going on tonight, and asked them if they would like to go with him. All three of them said yes, so their limo followed his limo to the club. They got there in about thirty minutes and walked right through the long line. Everybody knew Paul because it was his city. So it was no problem at all, they walked straight to the V.I.P. part. The music was really jumping off in the club Sean Paul and Beanie man was playing. They were all having fun, but Pinkey wanted to talk about business. So Pinkey decided to walk over to the table where Paul was still sitting at because she needed what she really came for. It's all good...all the fun, but she want to get shit right back home. "I see you're the man out here. Thank you Paul for a real good time. We really needed this, we haven't been out in a long time, thank you Paul for everything," said Pinkey while she was chilling at the table with Paul. "No problem baby, you and Suzie is like family to me. Please don't every forget that we are family. And I know you have a lot on your mind. Please wait until tomorrow to talk to me about business. Right now let's just have some fun, okay," said Paul. He already knew what she was going to say. So Paul just grabbed a bottle of Moet and gave Pinkey some, and he gave a toast to their friendship. "Okay, that's what's cracking Paul. That is how my man would want me to say it. Tonight let's have fun and tomorrow we'll talk, a toast to us," said Pinkey as she called Suzie and Nadia over to the table so they could all toast together. "What going on over here Pinkey? You and Paul was trying to leave me and Nadia out?" Suzie asked as they all took a toast. "Not at all let me call my girl over too.

We all toast together," Paul said. They all stood together and made a toast together. They sat back and was just kicking it for a while, then they got back on the dance floor with Paul and the two girls that he had with him. All of them are having fun. Suzie and Pinkey sat with Paul, Paul just sat back smoking on a cigar playing real cool doing him. So Pinkey and Suzie decided to go on the dance floor by their table where Paul was at. It was now going on 3:30 in the morning and the club was about to close. Nadia was chilling with the two lady that came with Paul. They were all getting ready to leave now. They all go out through the back of the club where both of their limos are waiting for them. The two ladies jumped in the limo with Paul. As for Suzie, Pinkey and Nadia they all jumped into their limo together. They told Paul they will see him tomorrow. They went into their room and went straight to sleep.

The next day Pinkey got up real early in the morning. She jumped straight into the shower as if she was going somewhere or something. Nadia heard the shower water running, so she looked to see who was in the shower, she only saw Suzie in the bed. So she got up and turned on the TV and sat on the end of the bed and started watching TV waiting for Pinkey to get out of the shower. Fifteen minutes went pass and Pinkey was coming out of the shower. "What's up Nadia you up real early can't sleep or something?" Pinkey asked while she was drying herself off. "What you doing so early is the question and in the shower? That's what woke me up," said Nadia while lighting up a blunt that they had from last night. "I got a lot on my mind today. I don't know if Paul is going to help us right now. Because shit is still real hot on the streets for us. Even though the case is over, but if you know Paul, then you would understand what I'm talking about. You see Nadia Paul is in the Columbian Cartel. They are very careful with who they deal with, to be real with you. If we wasn't like family we wouldn't be here at all," said Pinkey as she was putting on some cocoa butter. "Look Pinkey stop worrying so much. All I can tell you is I'm here to the end. And I'm not going nowhere no matter what happens...I'm right here," said Nadia as she passed the blunt to Pinkey giving her a hug. "I know girl you don't have to keep telling me that, but we do need to make this happen for us. Once we leave from here I'm going to see my dad," said Pinkey to Nadia as they were sitting there smoking their blunt together. "Pinkey I'm not trying to be funny or nothing. I though your father was dead, and that your mother lived in Buffalo. What's up with that I'm right, right?" Nadia asked looking at Pinkey like if she was confused or something. "Yeah girl I'm going to visit his grave. Plus, I want you and Suzie to come with me too. It not that far from my mom house," said Pinkey to Nadia sitting on the end of the bed. "What's up? What y'all two doing up so early in the morning?" Suzie asked. She was just getting up to what was going on. "Just chilling talking about shit, you can go back to sleep, sleepy head," said Pinkey to Suzie playing around with her. "Fuck it I'm up now I can't go back to sleep, what time is it?" Suzie asked, but at the same time look right at the clock radio. "Seven thirty in the morning, fuck it roll up another blunt I got some purple over there. Then let's get some food to eat...room service," said Nadia as she was getting the weed to roll up. So they can smoke some more. "That's what's cracking, I got to pee first. I got to go bad as shit," said Suzie making her way to the bathroom. "Yeah and brush that dragon too, that shit is off the hook girl," said Pinkey laughing with Nadia talking to Suzie. "Bitch fuck you just because you got up early as a motherfucker, and brush your dragon first. Big fucking deal," said Suzie as she was sitting on the toilet taking a piss. After Suzie took a piss, she brushed her teeth and Nadia did too. While Pinkey rolled up the blunt, Nadia and Suzie sat with Pinkey, they ordered some food and got high as shit. After they ate Suzie and Nadia got in the shower. They called the limo that Paul let them use to come take them shopping in Beverly Hills. They we're out all day long, it was now going on two o'clock in the afternoon.

As soon as they got back to the hotel Pinkey called Paul and let him know she'll see him around six o'clock tonight. He told her that will be cool with him. After she got off the phone with Paul, they all went down by the pool and had some drinks. Nadia and Suzie got into the pool. Pinkey just sat by the pool watching them have fun. Pinkey was just chilling, because she had her mind on business more than any one of them did. It was all about James because things had to go right their whole survival depended on it.

It was now going on 4:45 pm; Pinkey told them to come on for it was now time for them to get ready to go see Paul. Suzie and Nadia got out of the pool, got into the elevator to go to the 3rd floor to their room. Suzie and Nadia jumped in the shower to get ready. Pinkey was already dress, Nadia and Suzie got dress. Then they called the limo back to come get them.

As soon as he got there, the front desk called their room to let them know their ride was out front waiting for them. "Okay, okay, thank you...will be down in one minute, thanks again," said Pinkey hanging up the phone getting ready to walk out the door. "Who was that Pinkey, was it Paul?" Suzie asked her as they were putting on their clothes. "No it was the front desk letting us know are ride is out front. Are y'all almost ready?" Pinkey asked Nadia and Suzie, because she was ready to go. "Yeah, yeah I'm ready to go Nadia! What's up? Come on, are you ready? Because our ride is here," said Suzie as she was getting ready to go out the door. "I'm right behind you give me one more minute, I'm almost done," said Nadia as she was hurrying up to get ready. "Hurry up girl, it's 5:20. I don't like to be late," said Pinkey walking out to the elevator. "Okay okay! Here I come right now!" Nadia said running out right behind them. The three of them got on the elevator and went downstairs to the lobby. Walked out to the limo the driver was already out waiting for them with the door open so they can get in one by one. The first thing Nadia did was put in Jay-Z's CD to get them in the mood to meet with Paul. It's about a ten minute ride to Paul's house. They pulled up front of Paul's driveway and went through the front gate up to the house. They stopped the car and the driver got out to let them out and they get out one by one. Pinkey, Suzie, and Nadia couldn't believe their eyes on Paul's house. It was the biggest house on the block. Paul had men everywhere in suits with machine guns. You would of thought it was a war about to go on, but that was just how Paul lived. They walked up to the front door and as the door opened up it was one of the young ladies from the club. She told them to walk with her, she took them through the back where there was a Olympic size pool out back with six young ladies swimming in it. Paul was sitting by the pool at a table under some shade with the two girls from the club with him with a few of his men out back. The girl walked over to their table and sat down with Paul. Paul asked them what would they like to drink, and told one of his men in Spanish to get it for them. You would think Paul doing big pimping or something like that. Pinkey got straight to business. "Damn Paul your crib is phat as shit, you doing it real big for yourself," said Pinkey as she sat at the table across from him. "Yes no doubt, you suppose to...you know. All them bricks your man helped move for me!" Paul said as he was smoking on his Cuban cigar drinking his Remy. "Yes you're very right, but as you know the Feds took a lot from us. We still have shit, but not like we use to," said Pinkey to Paul as she sat there at the table. "Yes and I'm so sorry for what they done to y'all. But they are still watching y'all, and that's the only thing that worries me," said Paul as he was smoking on his cigar. "Yes Paul you are right, but the Feds haven't been fucking with us for a while now. And whatever comes are way we can handle. And I know my man still owes you three hundred thousand right? I have with me right now one hundred thousand with me today. And I'll give you the other two hundred thousand, as soon as we make it right off the top. The only reason we don't have it right now, is because of the Feds, but it's not that bad right now. I will make sure you get your money off the top," said Pinkey as she put the briefcase on the table with the one hundred thousand in it. Paul just looked at the money for a few seconds then started talking to her. "Pinkey, Suzie y'all two know me for a while now. Please know I would love to help you right now. But I can't, my hands are tied right now. Because the police can be still watching you right now as we speak. So please don't take it no way. I want you to know I'm all for y'all. But this is bigger so thanks, but please keep your money, and if you need anything please feel free to ask me or call me. The money your man owes me, he owes no more. Please understand this is bigger than me right now. Plus, them Bloods are bad business on the streets. They robbed one of our shipments the other day in the Bronx. They make the streets hot and something has to get done about it. So please understand me its bigger than me," said Paul as he gave them back their money. He also told them to stay in touch with him. Pinkey just sat there with a feeling like the world was over. That made her hate the Bloods even more than before. Nadia just grabbed her hand to let her know she was right there for her. Suzie just really didn't know what to say, because there was no one else for them to turn to. Paul really wanted to help but he knew if he did his people would come down on him right now. So he had to stop for right now until things die down in NY. "Please understand me it is not my call on this. It's out of my hands for now. But if you need anything call me, okay?" Paul said to all of them as they were walking to the door. "Paul take care of yourself, and thank you," said Suzie giving him a hug on the way out. "It was nice to meet you, I hope to see you real soon take care," said Nadia as she was leaving out the door. "Yes, yes do y'all need anything right now. My house is always open and my money is too. If you need anything just tell me," said Paul walking behind them. They got in the limo and took it to their hotel. Pinkey got in and jumped straight in the shower and started to cry. It was like the world was coming down on her. She cried for about 10 to 15 minutes straight and then she grabbed the washrag and soap and started getting herself together. She knew she had to be strong for all of them. Nadia was at the bathroom door and said, "Pinkey do you want to hit this blunt? Hurry up if you want some of this girl!!!" "I'll be out in two minute a bitch got to wash her ass," said Pinkey trying to be strong but really can't stop crying.

"Bitch you're not even getting no dick right now. So hurry up in there," said Nadia laughing at her smoking while she was smoking with Suzie. "It don't mean a bitch don't wash her pussy and shit. Dick or no dick, I still wash this motherfucker. Tell Suzie to call the airport and see what time is the last three flights to NY," said Pinkey as she let the water run down her head through her hair. "I hear you I'm on it A.S.A.P., it was fun but it time to go home," said Suzie as she picked up the phone to call the airlines. Pinkey got out of the shower and started to dry of in the bathroom getting herself together so she can face them in the room, she walked out grabbing the blunt from Nadia and Suzie. They called room service one more time for some food, and smoked the last of their purple that they had. Room service came with their food and wine. All three of them was hungry as hell from all that weed they were smoking all day. Their flight wasn't until 11:00 pm it was only 8:00 pm. They had to eat and drink, so they did that. Then they called the limo back to come get them to go home.

The limo came in 30 minutes, they checked out at the front desk. They jumped the limo and off they drove to the airport to go back home. They drove down Beverly Hills by the shopping part one more time. All Pinkey could think about was what the hell is she going to do. And what was she going to tell Jay and Spade when they got back to New York from LA, everybody was looking forward to this move because Tanya, Shitty, and Meka was running the city right now. They were making all the moves back home in New York, and that was not good right now because Suzie and Nadia looked at Pinkey like a big sister for real. They got to the airport around 10 pm and they got their bags to baggage. They went straight to their airline terminal to check inn and then they boarded their plane and off to New York they went.

The flight was a long flight at least six hours long. All three of them fell asleep on the plane. After about three hours had went pass, Pinkey got up to use the bathroom. She had so much shit on her mind, she had to get herself together. As soon as she got to the bathroom she started to cry again. It was just so much running through her mind at the time. But she knew she had to get it together before she left back out the bathroom so she washed her face off with soap and water. She took a look in the mirror, opened up the bathroom door and went back to her seat. By now Nadia was up having a drink. She ordered three drinks and when Pinkey got back she just sat down like everything was all good. So they started to talk about what they need to do when they get back. Pinkey started talking to Nadia about how they need to go upstate for a while so that she can get her mind right. And that they can get themselves together up there too because that is her hometown where she from, and she has family out there. A uncle and some cousins that would help them out and help them get back on their feet. Suzie's up by now trying to keep up on what was going on. So Pinkey and Nadia feels her in on what going on. They need to start making money fast. It almost time for the plane to land, the Stewardess told everyone to buckle up their seatbelts. Everybody buckled up and the plane landed safely. The girls got off the plane and made their way through the airport to the airport car garage where they parked and the three of them jumped in the truck and off they went to Brooklyn to Suzie mother's house to check on their sons. It like six in the morning and it was morning rush hour traffic on the F.D.R. to Brooklyn.

As they were driving across the Brooklyn Bridge all three of them was back on point with guns out in their hands, because they can't take no chances at all. As they were driving through traffic Pinkey yelled out, "Home sweet home we're back!" As soon as they got to Suzie's mom house, they parked the truck, got out and walked to the front door. Suzie took out her keys and opened up the door. They all walked inside and everybody was still asleep. It was like clockwork, they were just in time to feed their kids. Nadia runs upstairs first to them while Suzie and Pinkey went to make the bottles.

By this time, Ms. Campbell was just getting up, coming right behind Nadia to help her out with both of them. After Suzie and Pinkey made the bottles, they went straight to Suzie's room to check Suzie's answering machine to see if Wesley called and James. Suzie sat at the end of the bed with her head down as if she was about to cry or something. Pinkey just sat down right beside her and hugged her to let her know that everything is going to be alright. Ms. Campbell and Nadia walked in with the babies. Suzie took her son and Pinkey did the same. Ms. Campbell and Nadia went down to get the bottles from downstairs. Both of them came back upstairs with them so the babies can eat. Ms. Campbell goes back to bed now that they are there.

Back on the other side of Brooklyn, Tanya, Shitty, and Meka are running shit; hitting all there little homey's off with cocaine. All of the Bloods from Brooklyn to the Bronx is doing it. Their numbers are growing day by day because they are what's happening right now. They have the weight, they have the manpower and they got the money too. They're moving so much weight on the streets. The four of them is what's hot right now with the help of Donovan with them. Donovan have good street credit, also to top it off, Tanya, Shitty, and Meka are running around town in a candy apple red may back looking real good right now. Platinum and rose gold down, also they still have twelve barrels of cocaine left. The Loc's wasn't doing too much at all, but holding down their hood keeping it together, that's it. As for the Bloods they been making money through party's locking shit down. But one thing's for sure, they would not fuck with the Crips hood right now. Plus, all the crack heads are coming to them, so why should they start a war right now. Life is real good for them and it just wouldn't make no since at all to start a war when they're making all the money., Plus, the Feds isn't on their back right now. So it would be real foolish for them to start a war. So they were just sitting back enjoying the ride, also they were starting to make back moves with the Bloods out Baltimore. So you can say life is real good for them right now. They got Brooklyn, Manhattan, Bronx, and some of Queens on lock now. And who every don't want to get down lay down. There not playing no games with no one at all. It's all about the Bloods right now. The Crips aren't doing much of anything beside keeping the hood alive, and keeping the Bloods out of their hoods because on the outside its a Bloods world.

As for Tanya and Shitty they're driving around town in a red Bentley GT coup. And as for Donovan and Meka there in a red MB CL550, and both of them is riding back to back doing what they do making their way through their hood. As they pull up on their block, Blood Face, Mack, Tek, and Bloody Pimp all of them is out on the block, they were all locked up with 007. Now there all home helping hold the hood down. They have the hood on lock, Tanya and Shitty got out the car and walked over to them. "What's popping homey? Blaaaat!!! I see y'all niggas doing alright," said Tanya as she peaces them one by one, as she got out of the car. "Shit... is good in the hood. I see my big sister doing it real big in the hood. You are you going to let a homey push that pretty red motherfuckers?" Blood Face asked as he walked around the GT coup. "Chill homey, what you don't like your Grand Cherokee homey?" Shitty asked him looking at him a little crazy. "Yeah, I just won't to drive that motherfucker or at least let me drive with y'all one day," said Blood Face while sitting in the driver's seat. "That's what's popping homey, you already know. We got nothing but love for you homey," said Shitty while just looking and laughing at him. They were all looking real good in their hood from Bentley GT to MB CL550 to Cherokee to motorcycle. They are doing it real big. Some people that are just walking by just stopped and looked. It something like a car show in Brooklyn. Crack heads all up and down the street and money was flowing through real good. You couldn't tell them nothing at all. As for right now they were on top of the world, rolling up blunts, drinking, and partying day and night. But little did they know Frank, Cox, and the rest of the team was always on their job they were sitting down the block in a van watching their every move. Taking pictures of everything they do. It's a Friday night and all of them are going out to jack tonight and to do their thing and represent for their homey's locked up and the ones that are dead. They're planning to do it real big tonight. Bloody Pimp is taking five of his bitches. Mack and Blood Face are riding together. And as for Tanya and Shitty you should already know. Donovan and Meka doing them, but for right now they're on the block, locking shit down. Their block is jamming, they got three buildings on lock. In every building they have camera watching every floor. The apartment that they use to sell the drugs out of the door never opening up at all. All the crack heads do is put the money through a hole in the door, and then he gives them the drugs. You never see who's giving you the drugs at all. As soon as the money come into the apartment. It leaves right back out, they have a hole in the floor a small one, and it drops right down straight to the next apartment. so if they ever run into the apartment they don't find no money at all. They make about thirty to fifty thousand a day. On a bad day fifteen thousand still a good day. Police come through once in a while to make sure they get their cut, business is real good for the Bloods right now. Tanya walked into the building to pick up the money for the day. "What's popping homey? I got thirty five thousand for you today. The night is still young," said Blood Face as he was giving her the money. "That's what's popping homey. You coming with us tonight to the club?" Tanya asked him as she takes the money and puts it in her Gucci bag. "Fuck yeah, you already know the whole team is going," said Blood Face to Tanya. "I'll call you at 11:00, be ready and keep it popping homey," said Tanya as she peaces him as she was leaving.

Tanya and Shitty headed home so they can get ready for the party. Donovan and Meka were on their way to their new crib to get ready. It wasn't too far from Tanya's and Shitty's house. They moved out to White Plains, NY; not too far from the Bronx. They were out to do the damn thing tonight.

Tanya had on the latest fashion in Gucci from head to toe. She had on platinum earrings which were iced the fuck out with a platinum watch that was also iced out, and a platinum and rose gold chain iced the fuck out. As for Shitty she was out to do the damn thing and she was out to be real different tonight. She had on rose gold and white gold earrings iced out, and a rose gold and white gold chains iced out. And as for her rings on her fingers they had 5 carat of ice in each one. Her watch was rose gold and white gold mixed with 10 carat of ice in it. And Shitty chain was down to her stomach with her set written in ice on it. She was wearing the latest in Chanel with Gucci shoes. And as for her body fragrance it was out of this world, mixed with the perfume that she was wearing Versace for women will drive any man crazy for her. Even on her bad day she still looks good. All three of them are stallions, and was for her and Tanya drove in tonight in a candy apple red Lexus Ls 460 with custom painted finishes active red and black zz inc rims. On the inside a custom wooded red dashboard with red and black leather seats with the windows tinted with a booming system in it. One TV on the dashboard, two TV's in the headrest's, and one on the back dashboard. And they're watching every gangster favorite movie from Scarface and right behind it King of NY and then Belly. They were doing it real big tonight and all eyes' were on them, they were the shit tonight. They were just getting ready to roll out. It's on and popping for them tonight. They were rolling up their blunts of purple. Shitty was playing shot gun Tanya is behind the wheel, and you should already know what playing dip set. They called Donovan and Meka to see if they're ready to go. It's now 11:00 o'clock and nobody ever tries to be there early. The best time to get to a club in NY is at least around 12:00 or 1:00 o'clock. Meka answered the phone, "What's popping homey, we about to step out the door. Right now as we speak." Meka said as she was walking to the car with Donovan getting in. "Okay homey, meet us in the Bronx not in Brooklyn," said Shitty smoking on a blunt while talking to Meka.

"Homey, you forget we live not too far from you. We'll be your house no later than twenty minutes," said Meka as she lit up her blunt as Donovan started the car. "Okay, hit your right, hurry up so we can bounce," said Shitty hanging up the phone. "Call Blood Face and see if the nigga is ready yet," said Tanya as Shitty passed her the blunt. Shitty picked up the phone again and dialed Blood Faces' number, he answered the phone.

CHAPTER 21

SOMEBODY WANTS THEIR MONEY BACK

"Yo what's popping you ready to go or what nigga?" Shitty said as she was bopping her head to Dipset as it was playing. "Yeah, yeah homey, where do you want us to meet you at on the block?" Blood Face said as he was putting his gun in his dip. "Na homey, in the Bronx on 183 and Grandcourse, how long homey?" Shitty said as she was looking at herself in the mirror putting on some red lip stick and eye liner. "We'll be there in 30 minutes homey. It's me, Mack, Bloody Pimp, and his bitches," said Blood Face as he put on his Gucci shoes on. "What the fuck are y'all niggas driving in homey?" Shitty said as she was still bopping her head to the music. "Mack is with me in my Cherokee, and Bloody Pimp in his Hummer with his bitches," said Blood Face as he was putting his jewelry on him. "Okay homey, see y'all player then B-up nigga," said Shitty still bopping her head to Dipset. "All day see you soon homey," said Blood Face as he hung up the phone.

As soon as Shitty got off the phone with Blood Face. Donavan and Meka were pulling up in front of their driveway in a candy apple red Range Rover with Zen 26" rim on it with a booming system. Plus, it had the Asanti Luxury grille on it. As soon as Meka opened up the door, a big cloud of smoke came out right behind her. All of the young ladies looked like dive tonight. As for Meka she is doing it real big tonight, everybody in Gucci. Her and Donovan are in Gucci from head to toe both of them had on platinum earrings with 5-carat in it, and platinum and rose gold chains with 10 carats of ice in them. Donovan had on a platinum pinky ring on one hand with 5 carat in it. As for Meka she had on her finger a platinum and rose gold rings on every finger with ice in them. She was definitely a work of art, a try stallion.

It was definitely their night tonight, both of them pulled off to go meet the rest of them in the Bronx. As they were driving they were flying, in and out of traffic, back to back and side by side. As for Blood Face, Mack, Bloody Pimp, and his bitches, all of them left out together and they were almost there. They were just getting to the F.D.R. to the Bronx. Blood Face and Mack were in the Cherokee and as for Bloody Pimp was in his Hummer with his bitches. All of them were smoking and flying in and out of traffic with their system up loud listening to game in Blood Face truck. In Bloody Pimp's truck they were listening to Jay-Z.

Tanya and the rest of them was already on the block waiting for Blood Face and the rest of them to get there. They were in one of their hoods that they had on lock with a lot of their young homey's around them chilling. Like if they were superstars it was Tommy Gun's old hood. They were still in control of Tommy Gun's hood, as they pulled up on the block all eyes were on them as they jumped out smoking purple. As their little homey's was throwing up their set for them while chilling in front of one of the buildings. All of their little homey's was happy to see them. They were doing real big tonight. Their system in their truck was playing real loud so some of their little homey's were dancing in the street. Blood Face and the rest of them were just pulling up on the block. As they were pulling up, they started throwing it up as well. They pulled up right beside them. They all got out for a few minutes giving dap to their little homey's as they jumped out. Then they all jumped back in their whips, and they were out of there to the club. Jack was doing it like they never done it before.

As they are riding on the highway flying, Tanya and Shitty in front in their LS460, Meka and Donovan in the Range Rover, Blood Face, and Mack in the Cherokee, and Bloody Pimp and his bitches are in his Hummer. You should see the expressions on people faces as they drove through traffic, all eyes were on them. They were being treated like stars as they got off the highway. They were a few blocks away from the club so they lined up one by one behind each other.

As they got in front of the club everybody stopped and looked at them. All eyes on them as they pulled inside the parking lot. One by one they got out and walked straight into the club with no problems at all while people was still standing in line. They already had two tables waiting in the V.I.P. spot for them. They ordered a few bottles of Crystal, Moet, and Don Perignon. As they were getting their drink on the DJ was giving them shout outs on the mic. They are well known in there; plus, what had happen that night in the club before with Doggy and James both of them are well known for what they do to people that fuck with them. That will be a night that nobody will ever forget. Tanya and Shitty doing it up in the V.I.P. spot as they were dancing on the floor with Blood Face and Mack. As for Bloody Pimp, you should already know he's chilling with his bitches. Doing what he does best, straight pimping baby. Meka and Donovan were dancing on the dance floor. Sean Paul was playing and the both of them were kissing on each other. The club was off the hook, the night was theirs. Some girl was trying to get in the V.I.P. spot just to get next to them. As all of this was going on, some more men were walking in the club going straight to the V.I.P. spot. They sat down and ordered some drinks. They were all Spanish men. I believe it was the Columbian Cartel. It might be going down tonight. It's all about that shit they took in the Bronx and the men that's in the club is here for it. It was the people Pablow works for. Word had got back to them about some big high roller in NY that has a lot of weight on whatever you need. And one thing's for sure, if you're doing it real big it's only a few people in NY that you're fucking with and the Columbian Cartel is the main one in NY. And they want it back A.S.A.P., or their money, or their life. It is four of them in the club with ten men. Tanya and Shitty were both at their table looking over at them. As they were sitting there a waiter came over to their table with a bottle of Crystal with a card beside it for Tanya and Shitty to read. Tanya opened up the card to read it *(We would like to talk to you, you have something that belong to us. Please come over to our table to talk with us. It would be in your best interest to talk with us)*. That was all the card said, Tanya looked at Shitty with a look of death on her face. So Shitty asked do she know these motherfuckers over there. That is when Shitty turned to her and told her no. Then she looked over at the four men that was sitting a few seats from them. That is when Tanya put Shitty on point with what was going on. Shitty passed the word to Blood Face so he can watch their backs as they went over to their table to see what they wanted from them. Both of them didn't really want to take a seat, but they did. They sat in front of them facing them, and all around the table was the four men bodyguards. Every last one of them was armed up to the tee. You should already know what Shitty and Tanya was already doing. It would look like they had their hands on their pussy, but their hands was on their guns that was strap to their inner thigh. They were ready to do or die, that is when Tanya asked the man in the middle what's popping. She was thinking he was the one to talk to, his name was Manny. "Hello Tanya my name is Manny. This is Fee, Dingo, and Lil D. The reason we invited you over to are table is because you have something that belongs to us, and we would like for you to return it back to us please," Manny said as he looked at both of them as he took a drink of his double shot of Remy. Fee was looking at them the entire time. "And what the hell is that that we have for you. Please let me know?" Tanya asked with her hand on her gun ready to go. Shitty was just as ready as she was. This will be the first time and the last time that Fee will say anything to them at all. Fee stopped Manny in his tracks before he was able to get out one word. "I'm going to get straight to the point young ladies. The cocaine, heroin and the weed you have belong to us. We would like for you to give it back, that's all," Fee said as he was looking Tanya dead into her eyes as he was waiting for her to respond. "Are you fucking crazy or something!! You want it back!! Right? And I guess you thought that we were going to give it right back to you, right? Man get the fuck out of here. As matter of fact get the fuck out of my face nigger!!" Tanya said. And by this time both of them had their guns out underneath the table ready to pop off at Fee, Manny, Dingo, and Lil D. Fee said something to Manny in Spanish and walked away from the table. That is when Tanya started looking at Manny real crazy. She started telling him y'all isn't getting shit back. She also told him to take it how you want to take it. By this time the rest of the Bloods were around the table. All of Manny and Fee men were ready to roll too. It looked like it was about to go down. Fee walked back over to the table beside Manny. He said something to Manny in Spanish again. At this time all three of the men got up from the table. So they can follow Fee out the club. But it was far from over, Manny's men are still in the club. They're sitting and waiting, ready to get down. Just waiting until the club was over for some reason.

Meanwhile Tanya, Shitty, and the rest of them is still getting their drink on. But in the back of Tanya's and Shitty's mind they both knew it was on and popping. It's now was going on three thirty in the morning and Manny's men have already left out. It was now time for Tanya, Shitty, and the rest of their homey's to leave out. Every last one of them walked out on point. Blood Face, Mack, and Donovan in front of Tanya and Shitty. Meka, Bloody Pimp, and his bitches are right behind them. They all walked over to the parking lot as Tanya and Shitty walked over to their cars. Shitty noticed a note on their car front windshield, so she read it. *(This is your last chance, call me Fee boss of bosses and just maybe we can do some business together homey)* the letter said. Shitty just turned to Tanya and started laughing real hard and gave Tanya the letter to read. Tanya got in the car and threw the letter in the back seat. And they all took off with the rest of their crew behind them. They're being very careful as they were driving out and as they were getting on the highway. Tanya and Shitty got home first, Donovan and Meka got home second.

Blood Face and Bloody Pimp went straight to Brooklyn. On their way to Brooklyn a black van was following them. They both stopped at a red light, and as the light turned green Blood Face and Mack both threw it up to Bloody Pimp as they were driving off. They both went their own directions. Blood Face went one way, Bloody Pimp went straight, and the van went right behind him. It was the Columbia Cartel, but it wasn't the one's that was at the table with Tanya and Shitty. These guys were straight gangsters, dress in all black. They had plastic set up all over their van. Bloody Pimp wasn't paying no mind to the van behind him. He was too busy getting some head, so they were able to follow him with ease. It was four of them in the van strapped with machine guns. As soon as Bloody Pimp pulled up in front of his place. The van pulled up right beside them, blocking them in with the van. Three men jumped out running down on the driver and passenger side with their machine guns out. Pulling Bloody Pimp and the three ladies out of the back seat of the Hummer while the driver of the van had his machine gun out on the girl in the passenger seat sitting right in her face. The Columbian's had the drop on them. Bloody Pimp and the first girl in the back seat was taken by one of the men to the van but they killed the two girls in the back and got into the van. They left the passenger alive so she can tell the story to the rest of the Bloods. And then they drove off to a location in the Bronx where Fee, Manny, Lil D, and Dingo was at waiting for them.

As soon as they got there they took Bloody Pimp out of the van at gun point and left the girl inside the van tied up. One of them stayed back to watch her. They took Bloody Pimp into a building on the second floor. No one was up there, but Fee, Manny, Lil D, Dingo, and two big ass Spanish speaking men waiting to get the order from one of them to tell them something to do. Fee spoke in Spanish to one of them and he left right out. Then Fee spoke to Bloody Pimp. "My name is Fee and you have something that belong to me. I would like to get it back!!!" Fee said as he was walking back and forth with his hands behind his back the entire time. That is when Bloody Pimp just looked at him like if he was crazy or something. "What the fuck do y'all motherfuckers want. I don't have shit for y'all. And your fucking men killed my nigga. What the fuck is popping with that shit? Nigga do you know who the fuck you're fucking with motherfuckers. Bloody Pimp bitch!! It's on and popping nigga!" yelled Bloody Pimp As he was yelling at Fee he was trying to spit at him, but he was tied up in a chair, also his hands were tied behind his back and his legs was handcuff to the chair too. Fee just looked at Bloody Pimp and smiled at him. Then Fee said something in Spanish to the other man that was there to go get the other one. As the man ran off to go get the next one, Fee just looked into Bloody Pimp eyes and smiled at him, both of the men came back with a big green trash can. One of them had a video camera on him. Then the one with the green trash can stood next to Bloody Pimp and the other one set up the video camera. That is when Fee said something in Spanish to the man with the green trash can. That is when the man turned the trash can upside down right over Bloody Pimp body parts and blood started to fall out. A head fell right on Bloody Pimp's lap and rolled right off right in front of his face. Bloody Pimp jumped back in shock; not wanting to look at his girl's mutilated body. He started to throw up all over the place. He looked at her bloody face one more time just to be sure it was her. Then he looked at Fee, Manny, Lil D, and Dingo and asked them, "What the fuck is this all about homey? What the fuck did we do to you nigga?" By now they had his full attention now.

That is when Fee looked over his shoulder and asked him. "Where is my fucking shit at now homey!!" Fee said as he laughed at him and then

Fee kicked the girls head; around like if it was a soccer ball across the room floor to Dingo. Then Dingy, kicked it to Lil D. Lil D kicked it to Manny, Manny kicked it right through Bloody Pimp's legs. "It good! It good!!! Yes!" said Manny, like they were playing soccer for real. That is when Bloody Pimp knew they were not right in the head at all. He never saw no shit like this before. Fee started talking in Spanish again. The two men uncuffed his feet. Grabbed him like a piece of meat and hooked him on a meat rack. The hook went up in his back and then he started yelling and screaming. Blood started coming out of his mouth and tears started running down his face. As the two men grabbed their machetes with the camera on, they started cutting him up into little pieces to do him the same way like his girl. They started cutting off his legs arms one by one. As his limbs were falling off they started twitching, as they were hitting the ground. It was pure torture they were doing to Bloody Pimp. But they saved the best part for last. They started to cut out his intestine out of his stomach. Then they cut off his hands, and cut up his body into small little pieces. And once they started cutting into his stomach that is when he died. They made sure he could feel the pain, he was screaming like a bitch.

No one heard him, no one to help him. This motherfucker was not playing no games at all. They meant business, they were not playing around. Then Fee ordered one of the men in Spanish to take the video camera to Brooklyn where the Bloods be at. Then Fee told the other one, to put both of their bodies inside the trash can. He'll tell them what to do with the bodies later on.

As they were pulling up on the block in Brooklyn, they saw a few

Bloods by a building. They called one of them over to the van, and then handed him the camera, and drove off. At first the young homey was shock. First he thought he was trying to sell him the video camera, but he gave it to him and drove off. As he was looking at the camera, he saw a note attach to it. So he read it, it said, *(Play me please and give it to your boss Tanya).*

So the young homey gave it to Tek. Tek read the note and then he played the tape. He couldn't believe his eyes at what he saw at first. First he saw one of Bloody Pimp girls getting fuck by a pit bull. She was crying the whole time, and he knew something wasn't right at all. And right after that, that is when the horror would begone. He started seeing her body being mutilated into little pieces. That is when he started throwing up all over the place. He couldn't believe his eyes at what he was seeing at all. He dropped the camera on the floor and the next little homey picked it up to see Bloody Pimp being cut up into little pieces. His eyes were about to pop out of his head. He dropped the camera on to the ground throwing up everywhere. Then one of their ruby's went to pick it up. She saw Bloody Pimp being cut up like deer meat. She started crying and screaming running to one of the little homey's. None of them couldn't believe what they saw. Tek immediately called Blood Face to tell him what he had just seen. Blood Face was still asleep he couldn't believe what Tek was saying to him. So him and Mack both got up and headed out the door to see one of the worse killings they had ever seen in their life. They almost broke down and started crying.

It was now early in the morning the sun was up. Blood Face and Mack got themselves together to call Tanya and Shitty to let them know the bad news. Mack called Meka and Donovan, but got no answer at all. The phone just kept ringing out. Blood Face was able to get Tanya on the phone she was still asleep. Tanya kept asking Blood Face to slow down. He finally got his words together and started telling her what he saw. That is when she woke up immediately and got dress. Both of them did. Tanya and Shitty went straight to Donovan and Meka to make sure everything was okay with them. Their truck was there so they knocked on the door and rang the bell at the same time. You would think that Tanya and Shitty was police or something by the way they were knocking at the door and ringing the bell. Five minutes had gone pass, then Donovan finally came to the door with his gun in his hand and let both of them in. They started telling him what was going on. By this time, Meka was on her way downstairs. They all whet into the living room. Then Meka and Donovan got dress they all lift out together. All four of them jump in Donovan truck. They drove straight to Brooklyn to see what was going on. They got on the F.D.R. drive then they got on the Brooklyn Bridge. As they got to the block, no one was outside. They were either on the roof or in the hallway. Donovan parked, and they all jumped out went into the building. Tek was the first one they saw, and then he handed them the camera with the note on it. Tanya and Shitty saw tears in his eyes. Tanya turned on the camera, and all four of them were watching it. The first part with Bloody Pimp's girl, getting fuck by the dog looked real, real crazy to them. They started cutting up her body into little pieces. They were cutting her up like meat. That is when Meka moved away and started to throw up. But she came back to look at the rest of the tape. Then it showed them putting her into a bag into a green trashcan. Then it showed them taking her to Bloody

Pimp right beside him. Then they turned the can upside down on him. Bloody Pimp started zapping out on whomever were doing this to him. Then it showed Bloody Pimp getting mutilated and murdered. Gutting him up into little pieces, crying for his life. That is when Tanya stopped the tape. She just couldn't see her homey going through that no more. Her and Shitty just sat there looking at each other, with tears running down their eyes for their homey. They could only imagine the pain he went through before he died. It would seem like an all out war was about to happen. They went into one of the apartment that they had in the building. So they can get their minds right. Shitty put on the CD player *"Mob Deep"* was playing. She turned it up real loud, as high as it can go. Started rolling up some purple and just let it go. Smoking all day long. It was now around three in the afternoon. All of them was sitting back thinking what to do. The only thing that they had on their mind at the time was the four men at the club yesterday night. The name Fee kept coming up and his face was in Tanya's head over and over again. Tanya told them to find out where these motherfucker lived at and get straight to work. Tek got on it A.S.A.P. It was 7 at night, and Shitty got up and went into the next room so he could watch the tape over and over again. She started laughing to herself. So Tanya stopped and looked in on her just to make sure she wasn't losing her mind. But for real in Shitty own sick way, she was just getting ready for them. The best way she knew how to getting ready to die to go all out like the soldier she is. She turned to Tanya and said to her, "If they ever try to get me. I'll kill myself first." She said this because none of them ever tortured anybody like that before. They all felt the same way but Shitty was the only one to say something. While all four of them sat back watching the tape over and over again.

Meanwhile Blood Face, Mack, and Tek was talking in the other room trying to figure who are they first and where can they find them at. They were all thinking about their homey and his girls; also Bloody Pimp just came home. And just like that he's gone forever. None of them every saw this man name Fee before that night in the club or heard anything about them before. But believe it or not must real big time men. You never seen or heard of unless you're on the top yourself. That is just how the game goes. Now we all know why these Columbia are coming around for. They have something that belongs to them. That was the only reason why they're in the United States in the first place. And one thing's for sure they mean business, and this is just the beginning of what is waiting to happen. Blood Face walked into the room with Tanya, Shitty, Donovan, and Meka to see if they have an idea who did this to their homey that they met last night. Shitty kept popping in to tell Tek so he could know what was now going on. "What's popping homey, did y'all come up with anything yet homey?" Blood Face asked as he was walking over to where Tanya and Shitty while they were still watching the tape. "Not yet homey, I never saw or heard anyone of these niggas until yesterday night in the club," said Tanya to Blood Face as they sat there watching their homey Bloody Pimp get cut up into small pieces. "Don't worry homey, we will get even for homey. That my word on everything," said Shitty looking at the tape but she was talking to Blood Face. "I knew you well, it's just a matter of time. I hope homey can rest in peace, for real," said Blood Face with tears running down his face from seeing his homey die over and over again. "He will homey, he will right now let's just do what we got to do for him," said Tanya looking at Blood Face with tears coming down her eyes as well. "The same shit they did to homey; will be the same shit we'll do to them," said Shitty as she was watching the tape over and over again.

Some time had pass it was now going on eleven o'clock pm at night. The word was on the street everybody that they knew was looking for them Columbians. The only thing that they knew about the four men from the club was their names. Fee, Manny, Lil D, and Dingo, and that they were Columbians. No one in the city ever seen or heard of them before that night to Tanya, Shitty, and the rest of the Bloods it would seem like they we're new faces in the city. But nothing about these men was new at all. They had been here for years. Unseen unknown its a few people in the city that knew these men capability. And how they get down old school, play no games at all. They are out for blood, they want their shit back. And they were out to make sure that more people was going to die. Tanya and Blood Face went outside to talk. Shitty just stayed inside watching the tape over, and over and over again.

She already had her mind made up, she refuse to let this happened to her. She will not be taking alive. Tanya and Blood Face walked to the store to get some blunts and beer, it was a long day for them. And now it was going to be a long night. They had no word on anything yet. As they were walking back up the block a car pulled up right in front of them. It was one of Bloody Pimp's girls. She was by herself all shook up. She was trying to talk but her words wouldn't come out at all. Tanya and Blood Face took her inside, sat her down, and tried to get herself together. All she was doing was crying trying to talk. That is when Shitty came out of the room. After hearing all of the commotion going on in the other room.

The only thing the girl could say at first was, "Roll up a blunt please." Shitty already had one rolled up ready to smoke. Shitty passed it to her, she lit it and took three long pulls off of it. Before she can say a word then she started to talk to them. She started telling them what had happen from the time they were parking in front of their house. And out of nowhere a black van pulled up right beside them right as they were going to get out they all had guns to their face. Some of the other men ran to the other side of the truck with machine guns telling Bloody Pimp and one of the girls to get out. Then they shot up the two girl that was in the back seat with her. And said to her the only reason they are leaving her alive is to tell the story. Then they drove off with Bloody Pimp and her sister. The only thing she could remember was it was four Speaking Spanish men with guns. They were in all black in a black van, but one of them spoke English. That was the only thing she can remember. That is when the one that speak English told her the only reason she alive is to go tell her people. And that they want their shit back A.S.A.P. They made themselves very clear to her. And if they don't get what they want. That they will be back again and again until all of them are dead. Then she said as soon as they pulled off she ran for her life. Plus, she started to hear sirens coming down the street. So she just ran into a ally and sat there and cried for a while. She never seen anybody get killed right in front of her before. After she was done talking to Tanya and telling them what had happen to her that is when she asked about Bloody Pimp and her sister. "Did anyone hear anything about them at all yet?" she asked. Tanya just looked at her and told her flat out that, "They are dead. And someone came around early this morning with a video camera of Bloody Pimp and your sister being killed." Then she just started to break back down again crying. None stopped and Shitty just sat there trying to calm her down. So much had happened to her within the last 24 hours.

Tanya, Mack, and Blood Face were sitting at the round table thinking about what they are going to do about everything that had happened so they can make sure that it don't happen again; to none of them for sure.

CHAPTER 22

IT WAS TIME TO LEAVE THE CITY

Meanwhile on the other side of Brooklyn, Pinkey, Suzie, and Nadia were getting themselves together to go to Buffalo to visit Pinkey's mother who lived out there. And her Father who was bereaved out there as well. The plan was to stay out there for a while until they can get back on their feet, and then return to NY to set up shop. Plus, they all heard about what happened to Bloody Pimp, and they wanted to stay as far away from all of the drama that was going on. They are mothers now, so they have to think like one.

Spade and Jay were staying behind to hold it down. They packed up everything and said their good-byes to Suzie's parents, got a U-haul truck, and off they went to Buffalo.

It was a long drive to Buffalo, and by the time they get there, it will be her Father's B-day. Pinkey's mother always goes and visits him on his B-day. Her mother loved her father still after all the years that have passed, and she never forgot him. Every year, she is there like clockwork to see her husband, and then she goes and sees her son. Pinkey's brother who is locked up, doing life in prison. Pinkey was the type of daughter who always helped out her mother with whatever she needs. So they jumped on the highway, and off they went to Buffalo. Pinkey and Suzie were in one truck with the kids. Nadia was in the other one, right behind them. Spade and Jay were driving the U-haul truck right behind Nadia. After they get there, Spade and Jay are going back to Brooklyn.

Meanwhile, they stopped at a rest stop, so they can get some food, gas, and use the bathroom, and then they jumped right back on the highway. Making sure they do the speed limit, because Nadia has the guns in the truck with her. Also, they have the kids, and money with them as well. So they are doing sixty five all the way.

They finally get there, and Pinkey's mom was waiting for them. It was around two in the afternoon. As soon as they got off the highway, Pinkey called her mom to let her know she was in town, and that she is on her way to the house. She hasn't seen her mother in two years, but she always called her to let her know what was going on with her. She was also calling her to see if she needed anything from the store as well.

They stopped by a store on the way to Pinkey's mom house. The owner of the store remembers Pinkey when she was a little girl. Pinkey always use to come up there with her brother and buy all the candy that they could carry out the store. "Hi babygirl! How have you been doing? You're so grown now. Let me take a look at you," said Ms. Dutch as she put on her glasses to get a better look at Pinkey. "Are these your friends from the city baby? It's very nice to meet all of you. Are you going to stay for a while baby?" Ms. Dutch asked as she walked up on them with a big smile on her face. "Yes Ms. Dutch, we will be staying out here for a while since school is out now. Plus, I decided to come home for a while, and I really miss my mom a lot too. And it feels good to be back home, and it is good to see you too," said Pinkey as she gave her a hug and a kiss while grabbing what she needed. "Baby it's so good to see you! It was nice to meet y'all all. Have fun...come see me anytime, feel free, okay?" Ms. Dutch said while hugging all of them one by one. They all said good-bye as they were leaving out of the store.

They jumped back into the trucks, drove down the street, made a right turn, went down one more street, and there was Pinkey's mom house. She was outside waiting for them when Pinkey pulled right up in the driveway. Her cousin ran up to her and Suzie. She hugged Pinkey through the window, and kissed her too. Then she opened up the back door of the truck, and started playing with the baby.

Pinkey and Suzie started taking everything out of the truck. Pinkey's mother came out and help them out. Nadia, Jay, and Spade grabbed the rest of the stuff out of the truck. All of them went into the house for a while. The rest of Pinkey's family was there too. It was more like a party going on. More like a welcome home party, everybody was there. Some of her cousin's girlfriends were there, her brother friends, her brother baby moms, and his two kids. Everybody was happy to see Pinkey.

All of them went to where Pinkey's father was bereaved at to pay their respects to him. They all had flowers with them to put on his tombstone, and they all sat there, and prayed for him. After it was over, they all went back to the house to party like it was 1999. They partied like rock stars until three in the morning.

After the party was over some of them went home, and some of them stayed the night. Most of them lived right down the street. The rest of them was falling asleep, and it was now going on six in the morning. As for Pinkey and Suzie, they got up real early, because of the babies yelling for some food; it was time for them to eat. Pinkey's phone started ringing, when she went to go answer it, she saw that it was James calling. Pinkey was so happy to hear from her baby James. "Hello baby!! What's up?

How is everything in there with y'all guys in there?" Pinkey said as she was cheesing from ear to ear, happy to hear from her man. "We're okay. Me, Mike, Ty, and the rest of them are doing okay. What's up with my two boys? How are they doing baby and my big head sister? How is she doing?" James asked as he was talking to her on his cell phone in his cell with his bed sheet up so no one could see him. "She okay, she's right here baby, would you like to talk to her?" Pinkey asked him as she was getting the baby bottle's ready for them. "Let me let you talk to your sister, and after that, I have to talk to you about something okay baby?" Pinkey said as she passed Suzie the phone to talk to James. "Hello what's up nigga! How is everything going on with y'all in there?" Suzie asked as she was helping Pinkey make the bottles. "Everybody's okay doing fine, straight soldier in this motherfucker," said James to Suzie while smoking some weed at the same time as he was on the phone with her. "Look I love you, plus, I know Pinkey would like to tell you a few things. So I'm going to go, okay? I'm going to let y'all two talk. I love you," said Suzie to James. "I love you too," said James. "What's up baby guess what?" Pinkey said, happy to just hear his voice. "What's up ma... what's on your mind?" James asked. "Okay look, we're at my mom house in Buffalo and we've decided to stay out here baby. Just for a while, at least until things cool down in NY," said Pinkey hoping that James will understand. "That's what's cracking baby!! And tell your mom I said hi too boo. I would love to meet her one day, but unfortunately I can't," said James to Pinkey. "Don't worry, she understands baby, she knows what's going on. She down with shit, I miss you...I love you," said Pinkey smiling while she was on the phone. "What going on in Brooklyn that made you want to leave boo?" James asked her as he was still smoking his blunt. "We're going to try to make something happen out here. Plus, Brooklyn is not where it's at right now," said Pinkey as she was feeding the baby milk. "Like what ma... what's wrong? Where is Jay and Spade at? Everything is okay, right?" James asked as if he was worried or something. "Yes baby, everything is fine, Jay and Spade was out here, but they both left, they went back to NY in the U-haul truck," said Pinkey as she was feeding the baby. "So what had happened with Paul when y'all went out there ma?" James asked thinking his man helped him out. "Okay, this is what happened with Paul. Okay me, Suzie, and my girl Nadia that I was telling you about, all three of us went out to LA to see Paul. We had fun out there, we also tried to get some work too. I tried to give him the one hundred thousand out of the money you left for us, but he wouldn't take it from me. Plus, he was like shit was too hot right now. But he'll help us out if we need it, but not in that way. So, I brought the money back home with me. And the shit that was left, I gave half to Jay and Spade, and I kept the rest for me and Suzie to push out here," said Pinkey to James. He was a little bit upset about her and Suzie going out to LA. "First of all, you shouldn't of never gone out to LA in the first place. You should of knew that the Feds are still on us ma. And second of all, how long are y'all planning on staying out there in Buffalo?" James asked her waiting for Pinkey to say something back. "Just until things got better in Brooklyn baby, that's all," said Pinkey to James. "Why? What's going on in Brooklyn?" James asked again. "Baby it's like this, every since you been gone, right? Shit have not been the same, okay. Them fucking slob took over. They got the city on lock, right now. And so much shit is going on with them at the same time too. Plus boo, I just had our baby. I'm not trying to take any more chances than I have to. At lease this way, I will be able to get our money right? And our children will be safe out here baby. Please understand me boo. It's for the best baby," said Pinkey with tears coming down her eyes as she held her head. "Okay, okay, well, I'm not out there ma, but please be careful, okay?" James said to her. "Yes baby, I will, and always remember I love you James," said Pinkey as she was crying on the phone to him. "I love you too ma, let me speak back to my sister boo," said James as he was holding his head ready to light up another blunt. "Hold on baby, Suzie phone!!" Pinkey yelled to her.

Suzie walked into the room where Pinkey was at and got the phone from her. "What's up bro?" Suzie said to him looking at Pinkey face as she held her hand. "Look, I'm not out there, so I really can't tell y'all what to do out there. But I do know one thing, I don't really like y'all playing the streets at all...for real," said James while still holding his head. "Okay James, we know we'll be easy out here. I love you," said Suzie as she was smiling at Pinkey. "I love you to Suzie, and by the way Wesley is on his way out here. He'll be out here soon," said James to Suzie. "And make sure when he get there you tell him to call me, okay?" Suzie said. Happy to hear her man was about to be by her brother's side. "Let me let you speak back to your baby Pinkey, here okay?" Suzie said as she gave Pinkey back the phone. "Baby I love you," said Pinkey crying into the phone. " I love you to baby, let me go get myself together. I'll call you back later on, okay?" James said. Pinkey said bye and got off the phone.

Pinkey's mother walked into the room to have a sit down with them about them staying out there with her. That she would like to see them get back into school, get a job, to make a life for themselves, and to stay away from the wrong people. Like her cousin Lisa, because Lisa's up to no good. She works at a strip club. Pinkey's mother don't want that for her and Suzie at all. She lets them know it's nothing but trouble is down there for them, and to stay away from there. Pinkey told her mother she's going too.

Pinkey, Suzie, and Nadia decided to go see Pinkey's father again. This is going to be a new start for them out here, for the five of them. Therefore, they better make the best of it.

To be continued...

In Queen Cartel Gangster Blooded.

ABOUT THE AUTHOR

Simmeon Anderson a.k.a. Fence was born in New York City, and was raised in Brooklyn. He noticed at a young age he was an visionary, but he was using his vision in the wrong way until he came to prison. He took the time to look up to find himself from his worst, which became his best. He transformed his old self into something more powerful. A power that he always had, just never took the time out to use it.

Some of his biggest inspirational people are Stanley Tookie Williams III who wrote a children's book, and was nominated for the Novel Peace Prize. George Jackson who wrote Blood In My Eye. Huey P. Newton who wrote a book on the Black Panther Party. Don King that got his vision while mopping a cell block floor. Steven King, who kids use to laugh at him in college because he couldn't get it right, but stuck with it, and look at him now. Tyler Perry, for his movies of comedy, plays, and who was living in his car. J. K. Rowling (Joanne Kathleen Rowling), that wrote Harry Potter, and who was also living in her car. Donald Trump, who took a fall, but got back up. Donal Gooing that was the first one to open the door way for urban novels. Curtis James Jackson III aka 50 cent, that came from the hood and made it. Last and not least, OPRAH.

You would think that it's all of them I'm giving acknowledgments too, but it goes deeper than that, because of them sharing their stories about their trials and tribulations. I was able to relate with their pains, and said to myself; if they made it, I know I can too. Therefore, I say to everyone don't be afraid to share your life experiences of what you had to go through to get to where you are now. Because someone may need to know, just so they will know that they are not alone. I've been through Hell and back several times, but I never gave up on me! The harder it got, the tougher I became. I walked the street from the young age of nine until the age of thirty-two, and when I became incarcerated I had to become my best from my worst.

If you are free, don't wait until you're like me, doing time. Just know you can make it for yourself.

I will continue to write until I die. I would like to make a movie to show the world my mind is on a definite level. Hopefully, I will someday...JUST DO IT!!!

If you would like contact me here is my address below:

Simmeon Anderson 344-051

18701 Roxbury Rd

Hagerstown, MD 21746